BEING ALPHA

AILEEN ERIN

INK MONSTER
LOS ANGELES, CA

INK MONSTER

First Published by Ink Monster, LLC in 2018
Ink Monster, LLC
4470 W Sunset Blvd
Suite 145
Los Angeles, CA 90027
www.inkmonster.net

ISBN 9781943858453

Cover by Ana Cruz Arts

ALSO BY AILEEN ERIN

The Alpha Girls Series

Becoming Alpha

Avoiding Alpha

Alpha Divided

Bruja

Alpha Unleashed

Shattered Pack

Being Alpha

Lunar Court

Alpha Erased - forthcoming

The Shadow Ravens Series

Cipher

The Aunare Chronicles

Off Planet

Off Balance - forthcoming

For my girl, Isabella.
You are Alpha.

CHAPTER ONE

THE SUN BURNED hot on my back, spreading warmth through my body as I lay on the sand. Waves crashed into the beach and water licked at my toes. The tide was coming in, and even though Dastien and I should move, I couldn't make myself get up. Maybe I would've moved if the ocean weren't so warm, but the water was perfect, cooling me off just enough to temper the heat of the sun.

We can move if you want, Dastien said through our bond.

Shhh, I sent back to my mate. The weather was so amazing, but I'd been trying to force a vision of what was going on at St. Ailbe's for the last hour. I hadn't *seen* anything in weeks—not since we left Ireland—and it was starting to freak me out. *Don't distract me.*

You're stressing about it, but maybe you're not getting a vision because everything is okay, Dastien said.

I let out a long sigh. Maybe, but my gut told me that wasn't right.

Do you want to check your phone?

Dastien had wanted a zero distractions rule for the beach portion of our honeymoon. We'd already travelled to Dastien's

1

house in France, which was more castle than a house. Been clubbing in Paris. Gone to Meredith's Full Moon Ceremony in Ireland. But when we got here, it was just us, and we liked it that way. So, we'd decided to ban our phones. That meant no texting. No checking email or social media. No internet use of any kind—well, except streaming Netflix at night, but that was it.

St. Ailbe's—a now not-so-secret boarding school for were-wolves—was closed and the public's interest in werewolves had slowed down enough that we could fully check out for a bit. With that evil witch Luciana dead, Mr. Dawson (the Alpha of the St. Ailbe's pack), the Council of the Seven (the Alphas that governed the werewolves), and the Cazadores (the werewolves' version of soldiers) were all way more than capable of dealing with supernatural mayhem than we were. Which meant that Dastien and I were more than able to take time for ourselves. Our honeymoon had started out a couple of weeks long, but we'd been having so much fun, we ended up extending it.

I shouldn't check my phone, but I wanted to. "If I can't see anything by this afternoon, then yes. We should probably check-in." Forcing a vision was a little like cheating the no distractions rule anyway, but it felt different. Honestly, it'd been nice not having my phone the last couple of weeks. Mr. Dawson had the number to the landline—we were borrowing his beach house—so if he needed us, he'd call. I trusted him. Which meant I should assume everything was fine.

A niggle of anxiety started to build, and it took me a second to realize that it wasn't my own, but Dastien's. That stank. I didn't want him to worry about my worrying, but ever since we completed our mate bond, our emotions and thoughts had gotten a little tangled. We could read each other completely, and sometimes, I felt like I was in two places at once. It wasn't a bad thing exactly, but it was an adjustment.

Over the past six weeks, I'd learned to filter out most of it. Only Dastien's strongest thoughts and feelings came through now, which was totally manageable. He chose not to filter out as many of my thoughts, but I didn't mind him listening in. I didn't have anything to hide.

"I like knowing what you're thinking," Dastien said.

I sat up so I could see him. Werewolves healed too fast to tan, but Dastien's skin naturally had a hint of gold in it, unlike my own pasty white. He was wearing a blue swimsuit and no shirt, which I appreciated. His abs and chest and shoulder and arms... I was biased, but he was perfect. He grinned as the last thought crossed my mind.

I pushed a curl of still-drying dark brown hair from his forehead. "Doesn't knowing what I'm thinking all the time take away some of the mystery?"

His eyebrows rose above the frame of his golden aviator sunglasses. "No. Do you think it takes away the mystery from me?"

"No. I don't think so?" I wasn't sure how to answer that. Dastien was pretty much my first everything. Before he bit me, I had zero control over my visions. Every time I touched anyone or anything, I'd see things—emotions, thoughts, most recent events tied to the person or object. All things I had no business seeing. My visions made it next to impossible to have friends, let alone date. So, I'd never really known what a relationship was before we became true mates, and I liked us. Knowing what Dastien was thinking and feeling made things easier. There were no misunderstandings, and I'd found that we were usually on the same page, or as close to it as two people could get.

"I like us, too." He sat up. "And our life has plenty of mystery. There's a lot we can't control. All the supernaturals have been outed, and all but a few of the fey have gone into hiding. I'm not sure what the backlash is going to be from all this

3

change. Knowing where you are and how you're feeling? That you're alive and well and safe? It makes me feel secure."

"Secure?" I laughed. That wasn't what I'd expected him to say. I guessed I shouldn't worry about the whole mystery thing anymore.

"Exactly. So, don't worry about filtering if you don't want to. Go ahead and poke around in my head at your leisure." He gave me a big grin, dimples pressing deep into his cheeks.

"At my leisure?" I said, unable to stop grinning back at him. I couldn't see his eyes through his sunglasses, but I knew their amber color would be glowing just the tiniest bit—which meant he was happy. His dark hair was still a little too long, the curls falling into his face. He was planning on having it cut as soon as we got back, but I liked him no matter what.

The man was beautiful, and just looking at him made my heart sing. And the fact that he knew me—every weird part of me—and he still wanted to be with me? That was always a bit of a shock.

So even with how crazy things were within the supernatural world, I was happy. I truly was. But there was just one thing wrong, and I couldn't stop poking at it.

You have to let yourself relax, Dastien said as he settled back onto our beach towel. *Everything is fine. If it wasn't, Michael would call.*

I hoped he was right.

I am right. *Come down here.* Dastien pulled me until I was resting against him.

I had the beach and Dastien and plenty of quiet. We were so far away from everyone and everything, on a private island off of Costa Rica—a long boat ride away from anything—and it was perfect. It was paradise. The only thing that would've made it better was if his stomach had a bit more padding.

Should I apologize?

Your stomach is about as comfortable as a hunk of granite. I rolled over enough so that I could bite Dastien's side.

"Ouch! Watch it."

I laughed softly. "It was barely a nip, you baby."

"Barely a nip? You nearly drew blood. Is this payback for biting you? Or are you going vamp on me?"

I rolled my eyes. "Like that's even possible."

"Well, you were bitten..." His contained laughter was so overwhelming that it became my own for a second before I stifled it.

"You're such a dork."

Dastien rolled, and I was pinned under two-hundred and twenty pounds of handsome. All joking was gone, instantly replaced with hunger.

He ran the tip of his nose along my neck, sending goose-bumps across my skin, before pressing a feather-light kiss just below my ear. I melted into the sand.

Are you more comfortable now?

"Mmmm," was all I could manage. I wrapped my arms around him, pulling his body flush against mine. He moaned against my neck, and suddenly I was on fire. Every place his body touched me was too much and not enough. *This is the best.*

What is?

You. This beach. No people.

He rose and lifted off his glasses so that I could focus on his amber eyes. "I'm glad you're happy."

"I wish we could stay here forever..." But I knew we'd have to go home. Maybe soon. Something was coming—

Stop, Dastien's voice interrupted my thoughts. *Everything is fine. There's nothing—*

You don't know that.

And you don't know everything isn't okay. Dastien had said that about a million times today, and I knew it was true. I just couldn't let this go. *Nothing is going to happen.*

I wanted to believe Dastien, but the what-ifs were driving me bonkers, and the lack of visions was adding to my nerves.

It might not be as bad as you think. It could be something as simple as your subconscious cutting off your visions so you can deal with how powerful our bond has gotten.

I definitely liked his theory better than my own. *I guess that's possible.* There had been a lot of changes in my life in the last few months, but my gut was telling me it was more than that. I couldn't ignore my instincts anymore.

Before I grabbed my cell from my beach bag, I was going to give my visions one more go. I tightened my grip around Dastien and closed my eyes.

I pictured St. Ailbe's in my mind. The quad and five buildings surrounding it. *I want to see St. Ailbe's,* I thought as I relaxed my mental barrier, willing myself to see what was going on back in Texas.

I felt the familiar tingling along my skin as the vision started, but the mental image of St. Ailbe's disappeared.

Everything went dark.

My heartbeat thumped in my ears, and I tried to picture anything, but all I saw was black. All I got were feelings. Despair so strong I wanted to curl up in a ball and sob. Pain. It was like my heart was ripping from my chest. Fear. So much fear. Enough fear to cool my sun-heated skin. My breath whooshed out of me.

Dastien's weight was suddenly gone as he jerked me up to sit, pulling me from the vision. I blinked at him. The sudden brightness was blinding, but it wasn't enough to shake me free of the vision. A trickle of dread tiptoed up my spine, and I wanted it gone. "What was that?" I asked when I had enough air to talk.

"Your heart. It skipped a beat." His voice was barely more than a whisper.

"What?" How was that possible? I'd never had anything like that happen before.

My eyes burned, and I blinked to keep my tears from falling. I tried to tell myself that the feelings from the vision didn't mean anything—that it wasn't some future fate of my friends at St. Ailbe's—but that was too close to a lie. I'd felt that fear and despair for a reason.

Dastien wiped a hand down his face, not really hiding his fear. "You have your phone here?"

I nodded. I'd been using it for music while reading.

"Are you calling Chris or Claudia?"

I'd been planning on calling Chris, but now that he said Claudia's name, I wanted to call her, too. She'd have a little more insight on my visions. "Both. But Chris first." If there wasn't anything immediately wrong in Texas, then Claudia would be my next call.

"I'm going to get us some food. If Chris says they need our help, grab the stuff and come back to the house. It'll take some doing, but we'll get travel booked and head back."

"Thank you." I'd been hoping it wouldn't come to this. "I wish our honeymoon didn't have to end so soon."

"You don't know that it will yet. And if it has to, then we'll have plenty of time to come back. This is just the beginning for us. Okay?"

I nodded. "Okay."

He pulled me against him, squeezing tight. His fear was lingering, making him anxious. He was thinking about how scared he was to leave me alone on the beach.

I'm okay, I said.

No more weird heart things while I'm gone, okay?

I laughed. *I'll do my best.* But it wasn't like I had any control over it.

When he pulled away, I laid back down, focusing on him as he walked back to the beach house. I could feel the sand under his feet. The brush of leaves against his arm as he pushed a shrub out of the way. Hunger was growing in him. My thoughts filled with images of sandwiches, piled high with turkey and avocado.

The water splashed on my toes—drawing me back to my body—so I got up and scooted our stuff out of reach from the rising tide.

I sat back down on our bright red and blue striped beach towel and dug my phone out of my bag. It took me a few minutes to turn on the data and accept the ten-dollars-per-day fee for international usage, which was basically highway robbery. Even with the fee, data on the beach was slower than anything. Before I called Chris, I figured I should check my email and see if anyone had been trying to reach us.

When my email finally loaded, I groaned. I must've gotten over a hundred messages for every day we'd been gone, all of them useless junk—coupons and sales and newsletters from places I didn't care about. Except for the Above and Beyond newsletter. That one was legit.

I started deleting emails, but then gave up and switched to skimming through to see if there were any from actual people I knew. Eighty-ish emails down, there was an email that caught my eye. The subject was *Demon Attacks* from cmatthews@ntxwwp.com.

C Matthews.

Chris.

The chain had five emails in it already. The most recent one dated yesterday.

My thumb shook as I pressed the screen and read his first

email.

Tessa! Mr. D said that you were gonna be MIA for a bit. Just in case you're checking this or see anything, we had a small demon attack last night. No big. Didn't want you to worry. Talk soon.

That didn't sound so bad, and there was nothing for a couple of days. But then Chris emailed again.

Hey, Tessa.

Adrian and I decided to stay at St. Ailbe's. There've been a few more attacks. Figured Mr. D could use a hand. The reporters have mostly gone, but the Cazadores have more work than they thought now with all the patrolling and whatnot. We'll let you know if anything changes. No worries!

I was glad they were able to stay, but I wasn't liking where this was heading. A couple days after that, there was another email.

Getting a little crazy here. We're trying to keep up, but there's got to be a reason why all these fuckers keep showing up. Do you think there's like a portal or something that Luciana left open? The Cazadores burned the witch's compound to the ground almost two months ago, so I'm guessing not, but we're all scratching our heads over here. This has got to stop. If you check this and have any ideas, could you call me or Adrian or Mr. D?

Tried getting through to Claudia, but she's hiking the Inca trail with Lucas and MIA, too. Won't be back for a few more days. If you can even point us in the right direction, we'll get it done.

Just call me. Okay?

I licked my lips as I kept reading on to the next email, dated a few days later.

Do you think Luciana could come back from the dead? Because we're ass deep in demons and if she's back, I'm going to lose my mind. We killed her, right? She's dead. And no witch can come back from that. Right?

Just call me. We're handling it—Mr. D has some backup on the way—but serious stuff is going on here. Hoping Keeney's coming and bringing more of his Cazadores with him. But no one's getting that we have to figure out WHY this is happening. We can slay 'em all night, but until we figure out why, we're SOL.

If you get this, call me. Doesn't matter what time. Thanks.

Then there was nothing, until last night. My heart started to race.

Keep reading, Dastien said. *I'm back at the house, but I can come back if you need me.*

Let's see what the next one says.

I clicked on the next email.

I'm throwing in the towel here. I hate it. But I'm doing it. I tried to be chill and go with what Mr. D said, but that's bullshit. We need you here.

I know I said in my last email that we were handling it, but we're not. Keeney's guys got here. That helped take the load off for a bit, but everyone's exhausted now, and it's making us sloppy. Adrian was slow enough to let a freaking demon bite him!

"Shit. I knew something was wrong," I said to myself.

I'm sorry, Dastien said through the bond. *I should've listened to you, I—*

It's not your fault, but we need to go home. I went back to reading the email.

Doc says he'll be fine in a day or two, but we haven't had a night off since we got back from Meredith's wedding. But it's been two weeks since the first demon attack, and they're getting worse. Last night's group was no less than ten. It took everyone we had to get them taken care of, and I don't know what's coming tomorrow. If they keep increasing in numbers, we're going to be in the shitter soon.

I've been begging Michael to give me your number, but he keeps saying that if we reach the point where we need more help, he'll call you. But he never ordered me not to contact you, so I am. I know he's my Alpha and I should trust him, but why am I the only one that sees that

HE'S FUCKING WRONG! WE CAN'T TAKE ANOTHER NIGHT OF THIS SHIT. If we could handle the demons, then the attacks would be OVER, and I wouldn't be emailing again. There's something bigger going on here, and whatever it is, Mr. D seems to be ignoring it. And no one here is alpha enough to get through to him. You are.

> *Get your fucking asses back here. TONIGHT.*
> *Check your goddamned email already!*
> *Call me as soon as you get this. Thanks.*

I wanted to scream and cry and punch myself. Why hadn't I trusted my gut sooner?

And holy shit. Could Luciana be back? That seemed impossible, but what the hell did I know? In the world of the supernatural, anything was possible.

She's not back. I don't know what's going on, but there's another explanation.

I hoped Dastien was right. *And if there's not another explanation?*

Then we'll deal with her. I'm calling Michael, and then I'll start getting our travel figured out. He tried to send me calm energy, but I didn't want it. I wanted to get home. Now.

Okay. Thanks. Find out why Mr. Dawson didn't call us when all of this started. It was total bullshit that I was only now hearing about the demon attacks. *I'm calling Chris now.* It took me three tries to get the call to connect and then it went straight to voicemail. If he'd been up fighting demons all night, he was probably asleep. I shot off a text apologizing and told him we were on our way as soon as possible.

Shit. What had happened?

For a while after the fight with Luciana, a bunch of baddies had come out of their hiding holes. Vampires. A few goblins. Some lower-level demons here and there, but nothing as bad as what we'd seen when Luciana opened her hell portal. A handful of pissed-off fey who'd stuck around when the courts disappeared. The worst of which Meredith dealt with in Ireland. A will-o'-the-wisp had even popped up at the Grand Canyon and started guiding unsuspecting people off a cliff. It'd been a little more than the Cazadores were used to, but manageable. At least that was what everyone told us. Which was why we'd felt okay disconnecting.

I threw my phone down on the towel and walked to the edge of the water. Everything had been fine, but two weeks ago, clearly something had changed. Chris was right. There had to be a reason for the sudden spike in demon attacks in Texas.

What had changed? And why *after* Meredith's wedding? Was that just a coincidence?

There were no other messages about demons attacking the rest of the world. Why were the demons only in Texas? And maybe scariest of all—why were they only in our specific area of Texas?

My imagination came up with a number of scenarios, but maybe Chris wasn't crazy. Maybe what Luciana had done wasn't over. Maybe we were in for another fight.

That thought sent a zing through my body, urging me to run and hide.

But I wasn't about to hide.

Maybe some of the outbreaks could be well-timed flukes, but this was too much. I didn't believe in coincidences. Everything happened for a reason. I didn't know what was going on yet, but I'd find out.

Left a message for Michael and I'm going to start working on travel now. Want to come back to the house and eat?

I'm not hungry anymore. The swirling pit of anxiety in my

stomach made it impossible to think of eating right now.

Then why don't you go for a swim? Clear your head. When you get back, I'll have our travel figured out.

Are you sure? Shouldn't I be helping?

We only have one reliable phone line, and I need the WiFi to book the airfare once I have the boat and ferry lined up. Go for a swim. If nothing else, it'll kick your appetite back into gear.

I took a breath. The water did look nice. I took a few steps back to the beach towel to grab my fins, mask, and snorkel. *Tell me if you need my help. I'll come back.*

Of course. Go. You'll feel better after a swim.

I walked into the clear water, watching tiny electric blue and green fish swimming around my ankles. The water was waist-deep but clear as crystal. My toes disappeared under the sand as I tried to balance while pulling on my fins. Part of me still felt guilty. Like I should've been helping Dastien and Chris and everyone else right now, but there was nothing I could do yet except worry. That wasn't going to help anyone.

The mask tugged on my hair, but I got the straps in place and dove in.

The warm water was like a balm on my soul. Until we got to the island, I hadn't been swimming since becoming a werewolf. The change had made me a stronger swimmer, but too much muscle wasn't a good thing when it came to floating. I couldn't lay in the water without sinking at least a little bit anymore.

I used my legs, flicking the fins just enough to keep my head above the surface as I watched the colorful fish dart around the coral.

After a few minutes of tuning out, I felt better. Anxiety wasn't making it quite so hard to breathe anymore, and I started to swim farther out. A mile or so away was a tiny island that we hadn't explored yet. We'd talked about kayaking over, but if we were leaving tomorrow, then this was probably my last chance.

We can come back, Dastien said.

That's a given. Now that I knew this place existed, I was addicted.

I froze as a nurse shark swam under my feet. They were harmless, but they still made me nervous. I pulled my legs up, and it ignored me. As I floated there, waiting for the shark to pass, I wondered if I should go ahead and call Claudia. I didn't want to bother her before I had to, especially since she was in Peru on her honeymoon, but I was pretty sure that my messed-up visions had something to do with the demons in Texas. Even if she didn't have any answers for me, I was sure she'd appreciate knowing that there was some stuff brewing. As soon as I was done with my swim, I was going to try texting her.

The water grew rougher the farther from shore I swam. I'd passed the drop-off and couldn't tell how far down the bottom was anymore, even with my enhanced werewolf sight. Maybe if I'd brought a light with me, but I was only snorkeling. I couldn't swim down that far unless I had SCUBA gear, even as a werewolf.

I looked around to make sure the current hadn't knocked me off course. The island seemed a little too far to the right. I spotted the strip of white sand beach that I'd come from behind me. The tree line nearly gobbled up the beach, forming a horseshoe. I'd made it all the way out of the inlet but had drifted too far to the right.

I corrected my direction and started kicking my feet. I'd gone another fifty feet when pain sliced through my knuckles, one by one in rapid succession.

I screamed out bubbles as I sank under the water. Kicking hard, my head broke the surface. Air filled my lungs in one big gasp.

For a split second, I thought the shark had come back, but my hands looked fine even though I couldn't feel my fingers.

What's happening? Dastien asked. His worry beat against my mind. *Are you okay?*

I don't know. I shook my hands, trying to get rid of the pain, but it lingered. I kept kicking, keeping my head out of the water. I didn't know what was happening, but I suddenly didn't feel much like swimming anymore. Whatever had happened to my hands was freaking me out.

Coming back, I said to him. *I don't know what the hell—*

My arms locked in place as pain slashed through my wrists. Through my elbows. My shoulders.

I couldn't move through the searing pain. I started to sink into the ocean.

I kicked harder, my legs burning as I struggled to keep my head above water. *Dastien! What's happening?*

I'm coming! Swim back toward the beach.

I tried to look around, but the pain left me gasping for air. I couldn't focus enough to see the beach. It was like someone had chopped off my arms, bit by bit. But they were there. Intact. I could see them under the water, but all I could feel was the searing pain in my shoulders.

Whatever I was feeling, it wasn't real. It had to be witch-craft. A curse. Something.

Think, Tessa. Think. I had to stop whatever this was. I needed a protection spell. Something to break—

I screamed as the pain multiplied. This time it started with my toes.

Then my knees.

And then I couldn't move my legs.

No. No. No.

I wiggled my body around, but it was no use. I sank like dead weight.

Screams ripped from my throat until my lungs were burning.

Which way was the surface? The light was getting farther away.

Pressure started to build in my head, and my ears felt like they were going to explode.

Oh fuck.

I held my breath, trying not to suck in water. I didn't have any air left in my lungs.

I needed to reach the surface or I was going to die before Dastien got here.

My heartbeat thumped in my ears as I tried to swim with just my torso. With my arms and legs locked in place, I couldn't work up any momentum.

I was still sinking.

I flailed around, tossing and turning as I fell. *Dastien! I can't see the surface!* The water had gotten almost as dark as the night sky, rolling me until I'd lost all sense of direction. *What do I do?*

Why couldn't I find the surface? What magic was doing this to me?

Just hold on! I'm coming! He hit the beach at a sprint and dove into the water, cutting through the waves with all the power he could.

Magic. I needed to break the spell.

Stop. Stop. Stop. I pushed all my will into the words, picturing whatever spell had me shattering.

Suddenly I could move my arms. My legs still weren't working, but I could use my arms.

Hope blossomed. *Thank God.*

I waved my arms through the water like I was digging to the surface. I wasn't sure if I was heading the right way, but I had to keep moving. I had to keep fighting.

The more I moved, the more confused I got. My head was getting fuzzy, making it hard to think. *Which way is up?*

Had to keep swimming. Had to keep grasping for the surface.

I swam wildly as my panic grew.

I needed to breathe.

I needed air.

I slapped a hand over my mouth. I was going to breathe in.

My body was burning for me to breathe. I was fighting it, but I couldn't. Not for long. *No!* I had to find the surface.

Dastien! I can't! I reached along our bond, grabbing for his strength to give me a boost. I felt it flow into me, but without direction, it wasn't a help. He could feed me power, but not oxygen.

Dastien was coming. He'd reach me soon, but not soon enough.

He was going to be too late. He was saying something, but I couldn't hear him. My mind was getting fuzzy.

The last few months flashed through my mind. The cave of vampires.

When I killed Mr. Hoel.

Luciana stealing my powers.

When I killed her.

Closing the portal.

I hadn't fought this hard to give up now, but I couldn't hold my breath any longer.

I'm sorry. My body took in a lung-full of water, and I choked. Unable to swim, I sank farther and farther into the darkness.

Dastien yelled something I couldn't understand.

My heartbeat seemed to slow.

Thump-thump.

Thump-thump.

Thump-thump.

Thump—

CHAPTER TWO

"BREATHE!" Dastien screamed, but his voice sounded a million miles away.

The world shook, but I didn't know where I was or what was happening.

Something hit my chest over and over. Each slam rocked me.

I wanted the pain to stop. I needed to breathe. But I couldn't.

Why couldn't I breathe?

There was cursing in French. It sounded louder than his words before.

It felt like bricks were being thrown into my chest. I tried to yell for it to stop, but then I was coughing.

The world tilted and spun.

Water gushed out of my mouth.

"That's it. That's it. Get it out." Dastien's voice shook as he rubbed a hand up and down my back.

My whole body heaved until nothing else could possibly be left in me.

When I finished, I collapsed back into the sand exhausted as if I'd run back-to-back marathons. Every muscle ached and throbbed. My throat was on fire, and I wasn't sure how I was still alive.

"Hang on." Dastien disappeared for a fraction of a second and then helped me sit up. "Just a sip," he said as he tipped a water bottle to my lips.

One sip was enough. I'd had enough water for the next year. My heart was pounding, and I couldn't believe what had just happened. "Did I drown?"

"Yes, but you're a werewolf. You're hard to kill."

Thank God for that.

I grabbed the water bottle. My hands were shaking so much that more water splashed on me than got in my mouth. The pain had left my limbs, but the terror lingered. The waves still lapped at my toes, and I wanted to move back but couldn't.

I wasn't sure if I should be crying right now, but I felt disconnected. Like I was floating above my body.

"You're in shock."

I licked my lips. "I don't understand..." My hands still shook as I drank from the water bottle again, this time taking little sips. The fact that I'd almost died was so crazy and felt surreal. "What happened?" I asked Dastien, who was kneeling beside me. And then I realized something scarier.

I grabbed his wrist, needing a connection to him. "Why can't I hear you in my head? Why can't I feel—" For a heartbeat, I could feel his paralyzing fear so strong it was as if I was drowning all over again. I couldn't breathe as his confusion swamped me. His anger raged through my veins. And guilt. Guilt so strong I—

He tightened the bond, and all his emotions dulled just enough to make it bearable. "I didn't mean to scare you." He paused his forehead to mine, and I knew he needed the touch just as much as I did. "I don't know what happened. All I could tell was that you were in pain and disoriented. If you never go swimming again—"

"It wasn't the swimming—"

"Being a wolf and sw—"

"It was different." I drew up my knees, creating space between us.

Swimming might be harder as a Were, but I was fine out there. Whatever had happened to me, it was a magical attack. I knew that much. "We've been here for nearly two weeks. Have I had any problems in the water?"

He was quiet because we both knew the answer.

I laid back on the sand, throwing an arm over my eyes to block the sun. My senses were on overload, and I felt raw and empty. What had happened?

"I was trying to get to the island. I was fine. But then there was so much pain. My arms felt like they were being sliced apart and they locked. I couldn't make them move. Then the same thing happened with my legs, and my buoyancy is all shit now, so I started to sink. When I could move again, I was so deep...I couldn't make my way up."

Where had those pains come from? Why did I lose control of my limbs? I had to focus on anything but the fact that I'd died. Not almost died. For a second there, I was gone.

Goosebumps ran up my body, and I met Dastien's glowing amber gaze as he leaned over me. "What happened?" I asked him again.

"I don't know." His wolf was close to the surface, itching to get free. "I took too long to get to you. I'm so sorry. I was distracted. Around the time you started freaking out, one of the Seven died and—"

"Wait. What? Who died?" I grabbed Dastien's arm. My heart raced, and I prayed that Mr. Dawson was okay.

"Other than knowing that it's not Michael? I don't know."

I quietly thanked God for that. When Dastien's parents died, Mr. Dawson had taken Dastien in. Raised him like his own son. Losing Mr. Dawson would destroy my mate.

"I know. For a second, I thought it was Michael, and I..." He rubbed his forehead as grief and fear warred inside him. "I should've been faster. I'm—"

"Stop. I'm fine." But the fact that I felt pain right as one of the Seven died was seriously weird. "If it wasn't Michael, who died?"

"My guess is Muraco. He was fading, but I know what you're thinking, and I don't know why you felt what you did. He would've died peacefully. So, it must've been a poorly timed coincidence. But we both feel the same about those."

I pushed my long, wet hair out of my face. "Is it usually painful when one of the Seven dies?"

"I've only been alive for one other death in the Seven, so I can't say for certain, but both times were painless for me. I didn't feel any pain except yours." He paused. "Don't you remember when Ferdinand died?"

"Honestly, no. I don't." I tried to think back. The last thing I remembered about Ferdinand was Donovan saying that he was sending some guy named Mal to find him, but I hadn't followed up with it. I'd been so focused on dealing with Luciana that I'd forgotten all about Ferdinand, which was probably a bad thing. "Ferdinand died?"

"Yeah. A few days after the chapel in Santa Fe there was a little ripple along the pack lines, and I knew that one of the Seven had died. That's when Michael joined the Council." He sat back on his heels as he thought for a second. "Today, it was the same thing. I only felt a ripple along the pack bonds. And when Donovan left a couple of weeks ago, it was barely noticeable."

"I didn't notice that either." I knew he'd left, but I hadn't felt the exact moment when he broke the bond. I guessed I needed to pay better attention.

"Honestly, I only noticed because I was waiting for Donovan to leave, and I would've blown it off as something else, but Michael texted me about it." He paused for a second, and I could feel him reading my confusion. "The Seven are linked to all the pack Alphas, which means they're linked to every werewolf in every pack, but unless you're the Alpha of a pack—which you're not—the bond is pretty thin. I have no idea why you were in pain today, but I don't think it means anything good."

I licked my lips. "You honestly didn't feel any pain? Not even a little twinge?"

"No. I promise. The only thing I felt was through our bond."

This made no sense. "So, what the hell happened? Why did I almost die?"

"I don't know. We have to call Michael." His jaw ticked as he stared off into the distance.

Anger burned hot. It was eating him up, but I couldn't figure out what he was so pissed off about without digging into his head more, and he was still holding back. "Why are you so mad?"

The glow in his amber colored eyes faded a bit as he cupped my cheek. "I'm mad for a lot of reasons. At Michael. Why didn't he call and let us know that there was a problem? But mostly I'm mad at myself. Why the fuck didn't I check in? Disconnecting was my idea, and it nearly got you killed."

No. He couldn't take the blame for this. I wouldn't let him. "This wasn't your fault. I wanted time alone together as much as you did, but now we have to figure out what's going on. And I really, *really* want to know which member of the Seven died today."

"Me, too." Dastien's sorrow made tears well in my eyes.

I stood to brush sand off my leg but gave up. Sand caked the whole back of my body. Only a shower was going to fix it. "Come on. Let's go back to the house." I grabbed up my bag and towel and started off toward the house.

I couldn't believe I'd drowned. I couldn't believe one of the Seven was dead. And if I was right and I'd been feeling their death, then whoever had died was murdered. Brutally.

Which meant the Seven were down two members. What did that mean for the werewolves?

Three, Dastien chimed in, correcting me. *They're down three members.*

"Three? Donovan and whoever just died. Who am I missing?"

"When Ferdinand was killed after his attempted coup, Michael was chosen to take his place. There's a ceremony involved to become a full member, which he hasn't done yet. Until he does that, he's just a stand-in, and his bond to the Seven is weaker than the rest."

"Wow. I had no idea." I thought for a second. "And then Donovan broke his bonds with the Seven the day after his and Meredith's Full Moon Ceremony." My heart started beating too fast. *Oh shit.* I wasn't sure how Donovan leaving the Seven was connected to the demon attacks at St. Ailbe's, but they had to be related somehow.

Now a third member had been murdered.

I'd had no idea that the Seven was in shambles.

Once I added in the fact that my visions were off?

I was wrong. Something wasn't coming. It was already here.

A SHOWER HELPED CLEAR my head, but I needed a nap. Near

death must've killed a royal fuckload of calories because I was seriously dragging. I threw on a pair of pajama shorts and a tank top and managed to clip my hair up before calling it done. The fact that I was alive was good. Better was the knowledge that Dastien was arranging our travel home to Texas. I'd had an amazing time on our honeymoon, but we couldn't stay when our friends were in trouble. It was time to get back to reality. Something bad was happening, and we had to get home.

Dastien smiled at me as he paced around the house, talking to the water taxi people. *I left a snack for you on the coffee table. Please try to eat.*

Thanks. The polished concrete floors were cold against my feet as I ambled through the living room and settled down on the faded, navy couch. It was covered in a million fluffy pillows. Every time I laid on the couch, it was like getting swallowed by a cloud. The air conditioning was blasting, so I grabbed a cozy, plaid blanket and cuddled into it. A massive flat screen took up most of the wall in front of me and a pack of Bimbo pound cakes —literally the best thing ever—sat on the coffee table with a glass of milk and my phone.

I stared at the cakes. Just the idea of reaching over to grab them seemed like a lot of work.

The shower had helped calm me down a little, but the terror was still lingering, hovering underneath my skin. My body felt like it was filled with Jell-O, and emotionally, I was hanging on by a thread. I couldn't believe I'd had such a close call. My hands were still trembling as I finally reached for the cakes. Food wouldn't solve all my problems, but it would give me back some of my strength.

I usually loved the little pound cakes, but today they might as well have been filled with sawdust. I forced myself to chew and swallow small bites as fast as I could. I tried to think of what my next step was, but besides wanting to get home, all I had were questions. I needed to call Claudia.

My phone started vibrating. I jumped, knocking a sea of pillows to the ground. Claudia's picture and name popped up on the screen.

I froze, watching the answer button blink. I dropped the cake on the floor as I fumbled for the phone, swiping my thumb across the screen. "Claudia? Are you okay?"

"I'm fine, but I'm worried about you."

I spun to Dastien. *When did you call her?*

I didn't.

"One sec." I stepped outside and closed the glass door behind me. Somehow Dastien could pay attention to multiple conversations at once and still converse coherently. I couldn't. Listening to Dastien make travel plans while trying to give Claudia my attention wasn't going to go well.

I walked past the patio table and chairs, a few loungers, and an infinity pool to the railing overlooking the water. The ocean was still peaceful, even though I'd died for a second out there. Whatever had happened out there was magic-based, and I wasn't about to let it ruin paradise. The sun was getting lower, and we'd have to cook dinner soon, but I was glad Claudia had called.

Through our bond, Dastien's voice was now just a faint hum. Good enough. "Hey. You still there?"

"Of course."

"Are you really okay?" Dastien felt pretty confident that whatever happened to me was an isolated incident, but it seemed pretty convenient that she was calling me this evening when I hadn't heard from her in weeks.

"I've been off lately, but..." She sighed. "It's not important. Not after what happened to Muraco. That's why I'm calling."

I froze. "What happened to Muraco?"

"I'm sure you felt him pass. I hear all wolves should've, but...
it was bad."

I swallowed the lump in my throat. "He didn't just fade?" I
knew the answer, but I wanted to hear it from her.

"No. He didn't. Someone *murdered* him."

I was pretty sure I already knew the answer to this, but I
had to ask. "Earlier today I was out swimming, and I got this
searing pain in my hands. It felt like someone was slicing
through my knuckles, very quickly one by one. It was weird.
And then the pain was in my wrists. And my elbows and
then—"

Her high-pitched gasp came through the line. "Your shoulders. Toes. Ankles. Knees. Hips."

I swallowed. "Yes."

"You felt his murder."

"If that's how he died, then I think so?" The question came
out as a high-pitched squeak.

"No. I wasn't asking. That's how he died. No one knows but
a few of the wolves from Lucas' pack. It was a ritual killing. He
was placed in a circle of his own blood. There were candles.
And each joint was severed—from his knuckles to his knees and
toes—in one clean cut."

I sat on the balcony floor, threading my legs through the
rungs of the railing, and stared at the waves crashing on the
shore. "Did Lucas feel his death?" If anyone else had, the Alpha
of Muraco's pack had to have felt it. *Please, don't let it just
be me.*

"No."

Shit. "Then why the hell did I feel it?" And what did it
mean?

"I don't know." Her words were a whisper, like she didn't
want to say it too loud or else it'd be true. "But I'm pretty sure
the spell and the cuts drained him of his power."

It felt as if all the air had been sucked out of me. I couldn't breathe. "Does it look like—"

"No. It wasn't the same magic that Luciana used to take your power, but it's similar. Too similar."

Chris' email came to mind. I couldn't fathom it, but I still had to ask. "Do you think Luciana's back? That she's somehow still alive?"

"No! How could you even think that?"

"I got an email from Chris about the demon activity around St. Ailbe's. He asked me if I thought it was possible, and—"

"Wait a second. What did you say?" Claudia's voice grew cold.

"Yeah. I felt the same way when I heard," I said. "We're heading back in the morning. Apparently, after Meredith's ceremony, demon attacks started amping up at St. Ailbe's and no one told us."

"I know that every Alpha handles their pack, but if there was demonic activity in the area, someone should've told me. I might not be ready to take up the coven, but that's my land. My responsibility." Her tone was deeper than normal with outrage, and I was glad I wasn't the only one a little pissed at being kept in the dark. "It can't be a coincidence that demons are showing up where Luciana did her magic."

"My thoughts exactly." I was glad we were on the same page. It made me feel more confident.

Claudia was quiet for a second. "When I went back to the compound after the Weres burned it down, the land felt evil. I did some clearing magic, but it wasn't working. I tried everything I knew. Eventually, I gave up. I assumed the land would be tainted forever and it didn't seem worth the trouble to cleanse it. The land is in my name now, and I'm not going to let anyone build there again. So I didn't think it mattered if evil lingered on that land, but what if I missed something? What if

Luciana left some magic brewing somewhere that didn't burn? I didn't—" A hiss came through the line as she sighed. "I couldn't force myself to step into the rubble of her house to make sure it fully burned."

"But Luciana herself can't come back, right? The idea of zombie-demon Luciana coming after us is the stuff nightmares are made of."

Claudia laughed for the first time. "No. That's not happening, but I love your imagination, *prima*. You can let that particular worry go. Luciana's dead. She was dead before we saw her in Santa Fe. The demon had full control of her by then."

"So you're saying you're sure it's not Luciana." I barely killed her the first time, and if I had to do it over, I wasn't sure what I'd do differently. Dead was dead, as far as I knew.

"*Sí. Por seguro.* Where she went, there's no coming back from."

"That's excellent news." But it left a huge question. If Luciana didn't murder Muraco, then who did? Or maybe the better question was—what killed him? "Do you think it's the demon that was possessing Luciana? Could it have come fully through to our realm somehow?"

"Possibly. Or she could've let other demons out. Or maybe even another witch that she'd been teaching? And I haven't found the black mages in Peru yet. The ones who taught Luciana. That's another very real possibility."

"Well, that's fan-fucking-tastic news." I chewed on my lip as I thought about whether or not to bring up my visions, but I had to tell her. Everything was connected. I wasn't sure how yet, but Claudia might be able to help figure it out. "There's one more thing."

"What?"

"My visions have been off. Until today, I hadn't been able to see anything at all for a couple of weeks. And then earlier today, all I saw was black. Like there was nothing. And I felt fear and despair and pretty much every other horrible emotion." I paused for a second. "What do you think that means?" It couldn't be the future, could it? Did I see the end of everything?

The Bimbo cakes I'd eaten were threatening to make a reappearance, and I swallowed hard.

"I don't know what it means," Claudia said. "But it can't be good. I just…"

I pressed my forehead against one of the balcony rails and waited for her to finish. She was quiet for a while, and I checked the phone to make sure the call hadn't dropped, but she was still there. I could barely hear her footsteps as she paced around the room.

"I should never have left without fully clearing the compound," she said finally. "I'm such an idiot."

"No. If that's true, then I shouldn't have left either. I never even thought about going back there to check on it." The place burned, Luciana was dead, and I never wanted to step foot back on that land. Both of us had earned a honeymoon, damn it. "You said yourself that you tried everything you could think of. You couldn't know that this would happen."

Dastien slipped out of the house. He sat behind me, threading his legs through the rungs next to mine. He rested his chin on my head, and I relaxed back into him, taking comfort in his closeness. "If it'll make you feel better, I'll go by the compound and try clearing it when I get back. I can find anything left in the ruins of Luciana's house just as well as you could." I couldn't believe I was offering this up, but if she was that worried, then I had to check it out.

"I don't know. I think anyone digging in there is a bad idea, especially you." She sighed. "This is a mess. And I still can't believe that someone got to Muraco…"

"Yeah, but Muraco was old," I said. "He couldn't have been that hard to kill. Don't you think—"

Dastien stiffened at my words at the same time Claudia cut me off. "Muraco wasn't an easy target."

"He wasn't?" He'd always looked frail to me.

No! Dastien said.

"No," Lucas' voice came through the line. "He was old, yes. But when he wanted to fight, he could fight. He was choosing to fade because his mate died, but he could've stopped that at any time. Whatever killed him was powerful."

A powerful alpha getting killed by something mysterious. This wasn't the first time I'd heard something similar. "Are you sure it wasn't that fey beast?" I asked just in case we were tying things together that weren't related. "The one that was attacking the Irish pack? Because I heard that guy ripped his victims apart and—"

"No," Lucas said, and my hope for an easy solution dwindled. "From what I heard, the fey beast didn't leave remains to identify a body. Muraco was in a circle formed of blood. He was laid on the ground, arms and legs stretched wide. Precisely one centimeter spacing between each severed joint." The more he talked, the rougher his voice got. Lucas was one pissed off Were.

"It was a ritual killing. So, it has to be another witch gone bad," I said.

"Or a demon that she released," Claudia said.

I winced. "That sounds a lot worse." I couldn't believe I was at a point where I was crossing my fingers that the bad guy was an evil, possibly demon-possessed witch.

"That's because a demon strong enough to do this would have to be extremely powerful. And now—who or whatever killed Muraco—has an even bigger power boost," Claudia said.

"Motherfucker," I muttered.

"Exactly." She was quiet for a second. "We have to go

31

prepare Muraco for burial, but I'll give you a call tomorrow. *Buena suerte, prima.*"

"You, too." I ended the call. "I wish we had some better answers." I also wished my visions were working.

Wishing wasn't going to make anything happen. "What time do we leave in the morning?"

"Took agreeing to double their regular fare, but the water taxi will pick us up at four a.m. We'll meet a car on the mainland that will take us to the airport, but it's a seven-hour drive, even with cutting across the bay. As long as we catch the right ferry, we should make our flight tomorrow evening."

I groaned. Four in the morning? That was going to be brutal. "It's been nice. Being in your home in France. Paris. Meredith's wedding—"

"Ceremony."

"Whatever." I elbowed him. "But I think my favorite has been this beach."

"Yeah?"

"Yeah."

"I thought maybe you liked the club in Paris the best," he said.

Even with all the gloom and doom hanging over our heads, I couldn't help but grin at the memory. "That was fun, but this has been better. I definitely want to come back."

"We can do that. Michael doesn't use this house much, and he won't mind if we visit again."

I slid out from between the balcony rungs so that I could fully face Dastien. If I couldn't feel the worry in him, I wouldn't have known it was there. His small smile wasn't big enough to reveal his dimples, and I needed to change that. "We can't do anything until we get home, so let's enjoy tonight."

He pressed his forehead against mine, and I leaned into him.

"I don't want what happened today to taint our honeymoon," I said.

He pulled back. "That will never happen. This trip has been everything. Nothing could ever taint it." He brushed a feather-light kiss against my lips. "Nothing." One more kiss. "Not ever."

When he brushed a third kiss against my lips, I couldn't stand the teasing. I wrapped my arms around his neck and sank deep into him.

Tomorrow would come. Then I'd have to face the demon, or evil witch, or whatever was coming for us.

For now, I had Dastien and the quiet, and I was going to savor every second I had left.

CHAPTER THREE

ALMOST DYING TOOK ITS TOLL, which meant it was time to make food, and not just a little food—sandwiches and Cheetos weren't going to cut it—but a ton of food, including lots of meat. Dastien grilled some massive steaks that had to have been at least half a cow, but he said it wasn't even nearly that much. Still, a family of ten could live for a few days on the food I chowed through. I'd made four boxes of wild rice and a large salad.

It'd taken no time at all for us to devour the entire feast, and now we were sharing a half-gallon of coconut chocolate chip ice cream while we watched *The Princess Bride*. I couldn't believe that Dastien had never seen it. For whatever reason, my family watched it every Christmas Eve. Watching it with him was like seeing it for the first time again. All the jokes were a surprise for him, and I got to feel that zing of surprise, too.

But as the credits rolled on the movie, the anxiety started churning again.

Everything is going to be okay.

I hate waiting. I wish we could've left tonight.

I tried. Soonest the boat could come was in the morning.

I squeezed his hand . *I know you did. I'm not complaining. Just anxious. A fight's brewing and we're a million miles away.*

He put down the carton and tucked me in closer to his side. "We'll be home soon enough. For now, relax."

"Doing my best, but if this thing killed Muraco, then are any of us safe?"

"No."

I winced. "You didn't have to be so honest." I grabbed the ice cream and groaned when I saw it was empty. Only more of the creamy coconutty awesomeness with those little crunchy chips could help me now. It was heaven in a carton.

"We have another one. Want me to get it for you?"

"Kind of. I mean, eating more ice cream won't fix anything exactly, but it definitely won't hurt."

"As you wish." He tapped my nose as he got up.

A laugh slipped free, and I realized it wasn't just the ice cream that was helping me feel better. Still, when Dastien came back, I snatched the carton from him. "What should we watch next?"

"Whatever you want?"

I flipped through Netflix for a while before settling on a movie I'd never heard of. "What about this?"

"As you wish."

I snorted. "Dork," I said, but I was glad he'd enjoyed it so much. I hit play, and as the movie started, I realized I'd never said thank you to him.

He raised a brow. "For the ice cream? *De rien.*"

"No. For saving my life," I said with a mouth full of coconut perfection.

"Just don't make it a habit, okay?" His tone was teasing, but he was still freaked out. I didn't need the bond to see that. The white-knuckle grip he had on the spoon was making it bend a bit. I tapped his fingers, and he sighed. He bent the spoon back to normal-ish.

I snuggled into my blanket and scooped out a giant bite of ice cream. It was going to take time for both of us to recover, but this was helping. "I'll do my best to make sure I don't almost die again."

"Good."

I jammed the ice cream into my mouth and pain hit my head so hard that I closed my eyes and dropped my spoon. It clattered to the cement floor, but the sound was far away. I slapped my forehead. "Shit. Brainfreeze." The pain eased a bit, and I was able to open my eyes. Black spots filled my vision. "What the..." Time slowed. It took too long to turn to Dastien, and the black dots expanded.

Dastien was gone.

Everything was gone. I was in a black abyss just like my vision on the beach.

Panic made my lungs grow tight and my heart race, but when magic pricked my skin, fear crashed over me.

What the hell was happening? I tried to blink, but nothing changed. I was sitting in the dark. Either I was about to have the most fucked up vision ever, or someone was messing with me.

I said a prayer for the vision to kick in. For the black abyss to become something else. For anything to happen that would make this into something that I could understand.

When the vision didn't immediately start, I knew something was wrong. Really fucking wrong.

Magic spread along my body, and it felt like slime. Disgusting. Evil. Very possibly deadly.

So what was this? A spell? From who? A witch? Had some fey captured me? Questions raced through my mind at a million miles an hour, and I didn't have any answers.

I couldn't smell any sulfur. Which was good, but when I

thought about it, I couldn't smell anything at all. So, ruling out a demon wasn't smart. At least not yet.

I reached for my bond to Dastien, and suddenly the air grew too thick for me to breath as my panic amped up.

No. This was bad. Really fucking bad.

If I couldn't reach Dastien...

I could still feel the bond, but it was usually like a thick rope, bigger than my thigh, that tied us together. Here it felt like dental floss—so thin and fragile. So far away I could barely reach it. The only other time this had happened was when I went to live with Claudia on *la Aquelarre*'s compound. The boundary of the coven's land had been warded to keep anything from crossing. It'd cut Dastien and me off from each other, nearly driving Dastien mad.

This wasn't as bad, but it sure as shit wasn't good either. The bond was too thin for me to tell if he was freaking out or losing his mind or...

My mouth grew dry, and I tried to control my panic spiral. I had to find a way out. I had to get back to Dastien.

I got off my ass and walked, holding my hands in front of me. If I was in some kind of room or chamber, I'd hit a wall eventually. If there was a wall, then there had to be a door. If there was a door, I could try to break it down either physically or magically.

That was a lot of if's, but it was a theory. My best one so far.

I walked and walked and kept walking for what felt like hours. After a while, I started counting my steps. When I passed ten thousand, I growled. Fur rippled along my arms, and I closed my eyes as I fought for control.

I gritted my teeth as I tried to think through my frustration. Losing control to my wolf wasn't going to help. What I needed was a plan. If I had that, then I had a goal, and I could figure this out. I was smart. I wasn't going to be stuck here forever.

I let out a breath, and the wolf settled down.

I needed to get out of here—wherever here was—but walking wasn't working. I was stubborn enough to keep trying to reach a wall, but if I hadn't reached one yet, I had to assume that this place didn't have them. And if there weren't any walls, then there probably weren't doors either. It had to be a magical holding pen of some sort.

I had to try some magic to counter it. But what spell? What did I need most?

To see. I needed to see.

If I could see, then I'd have at least some sort of an answer as to where I was.

Since something had put me here, chances were good I wasn't alone. But I had to be able to see who to kill.

Just thinking that made me feel a little better. Not as good as I'd feel when I physically got back to Dastien, but I had a plan. I was thinking it through. Step by step.

First, I needed a light spell.

I tried to remember that it didn't matter what I said exactly, just my intention and force of will. I had to believe in my spell.

I held a hand out in front of me and pictured a ball of light forming. "Bring me light. Bring me light. Bring me light."

Light flared for a split-second, but it only made me see spots. Damn it. I hadn't believed in my spell enough.

I blew out a slow breath as I tried to center myself. *I can do this. This spell is easy. Just say the words, and it'll work. No problem.*

I lifted my hand again. "Bring me light. Bring me light! *Bring me light!*"

The light flared brighter this time. I did a little happy dance and started to glance around, but beyond a little halo of light around me, there was nothing to see. The floor somehow absorbed the light, making it look like I was floating in an

39

endless pool of black even though I could feel the firm ground under me.

I froze as a draft rustled strands of my hair against my face.

A greasy blob of magic plopped against my hand. The light flickered, and then it was gone.

"You asshole!" I rubbed my hand on my pants, trying to rid my skin of the feel.

Oh, hell no. This guy wasn't getting the best of me.

Ignoring the sickening feeling of its magic, I held my hand in front of me one more time. "Bring me light. Light! *Light!*" I yelled the spell, putting my willpower in it.

The light bloomed brighter—floating on top of my hand—but blipped out faster. This time the greasy magic spread all the way up to my elbow.

No. No way. I wasn't going to let this asshole win.

I threw all the will and determination I had into the words. This spell would light the world up. I screamed the words. "*Light! Light! Light!*"

The light burned so brightly I had to squint. Aside from the ring of light around me, everything was black. There was no horizon. No ceiling or walls. Just the black endless pool around me.

Maybe if I ran—

The light was slapped from my hand. The magical blow knocked me on my ass, and I was bathed in darkness. Again.

Someone was messing with me.

I jumped up from the ground. "You piece of shit!" I stomped around in a circle. "You're so fucking scared of me you won't show yourself and you won't even let me have any light? You're pathetic!" Spit flew out of my mouth as I shouted. My breath heaved. Fur rippled on my arms again, but I wasn't ready to be a wolf. She couldn't help me here. Not yet.

By the time the last echoing remnants of "pathetic" hit my ears, my wolf was under control.

I needed to know who or what I was up against and why it'd dragged me here. If it's ultimate goal was to piss me off, then it was doing a fan-fucking-tastic job. But there had to be a better reason. And I had to figure it out. Fast.

I couldn't walk my way out of here. Taunting hadn't worked. It could snuff out my magic like it was nothing. So what was left?

Wait? I hated that, but I wasn't sure what else to do. So, I sat cross-legged with my hands on my knees. As freaked out as I was, I had to find a way to calm down. There had to be a way out of this. I just hadn't thought of it yet.

I closed my eyes, and then I heard a noise.

It was faint and so far away that I held my breath until my lungs burned, straining to hear it again.

My heart picked up its pace. The sound was like a whisper on the wind.

My jaw cracked as I clenched my teeth.

At least I didn't have to wait long. Whoever—whatever—had taken me was going to show itself very soon.

I stood and balanced on the balls of my feet, hands loose at my sides. I was either going to run or fight. I wasn't sure yet. But I was going to be ready.

I licked my dry lips as I listened, focusing all my energy on hearing whatever was approaching. At first, the noise was nothing more than a soft hiss, but as it grew louder, I realized the noise wasn't a hiss at all. It was a voice. Not just that. The tiny gap of silence between the sounds meant that the demon was saying two words.

But I couldn't decipher them.

The voice grew louder, becoming a dark rumble that made the hair on my arms stand on end, but I still couldn't make out the words. It was more of a rumbling growl than anything else. I wasn't sure if it was the dark or the tone of the growl or the magic under it that made me want to run.

I clenched my fists as I waited in the dark for whatever this was to show itself. I couldn't run. I wouldn't give it the satisfaction of knowing that I was getting scared. I was going to face whatever was messing with me. I was going to get the hell out of here. I was—

"You're mine!" The voice suddenly yelled so loud my ears rang. Evil magic hit my skin. It was like I was dropped into a pool of ice-cold slime. It coated my body—my soul. Dread tip-toed up my spine, and I knew I was majorly screwed.

I didn't care about not having a direction to run anymore. I didn't care about not showing my fear. And screw fighting.

I moved—hauling ass as far and as fast as I could.

Everything in me screamed to keeping running until I couldn't run anymore. And then I was going to have to run some more. I didn't want to see this thing's face. I never wanted to see whatever that was. I only wanted to get out. Away. Now.

My breath came in pants as the panic that I'd been holding back ripped free. I hadn't reached for Dastien yet because I wasn't sure the fragile connection would hold, but I reached now. I grasped the tiny little thread of our bond and screamed, *Dastien! Get me out of here!* I shoved the words through the bond, hoping that by some miracle he'd hear me and be able to do something about it.

Then there was light. Too much light. I skidded to a stop, closing my eyes, but it burned through my eyelids.

I covered my eyes. "Stop! Stop this!" My legs gave out, and I fell to my hands and knees. *Dastien!* I called out, and a faint scent of pine and dirt and home hit me. I hadn't gotten any power, but his scent was there. I breathed it deep into my lungs and remembered who I was. Where I was.

I'd forgotten that. In my panicked run, I'd forgotten who I was.

Witch. Werewolf. Alpha. Mate.

Strong.

I was stronger than this. I didn't need to let myself be trapped. I could find a way out. If I could smell Dastien, then he was near, even if our bond made it feel like we were far away. Which meant I was in my mind, under mental and spiritual attack. But it wasn't physical.

If I was in my mind, then I just had to kick whoever this was out of my head.

That switch in perspective was enough to shake me free from the panic.

First things first. I kept my eyes squeezed shut against the burning light and started building up my mental barriers one by one. I pictured a brick wall, but that wasn't enough. I could still feel this thing's magic slithering up my arms like a thousand oil-slicked snakes.

I built a second barrier outside the wall, forming an igloo made of concrete bricks laid three thick. I made sure to keep my tie to Dastien present in my mind so that I wouldn't accidentally cut off my lifeline to him.

Slowly, the light started to fade to a reasonable level. I blinked my eyes open, revealing Dastien standing in front of me.

"You okay?" Dastien was wearing a pair of green scrubs that I'd never seen before. A little worry line appeared between his brows, but I couldn't feel his worry. "Need help with that?"

I looked down to find myself on one knee tying the laces of my white canvas shoes. The laminate floor glistened like it'd just been cleaned, but I couldn't smell any disinfectant.

Couldn't sense Dastien's feelings? No smells? White canvas shoes?

This was all kinds of wrong.

Dastien squatted in front of me. "Everything okay?" One of his dark curls fell across his forehead, and he brushed it back. A move I was so familiar with that I questioned my gut for a second.

This was my Dastien, but the rest of it... "I don't know." I looked around as I stood, but I didn't recognize the place.

We were in the entryway of a large building. Behind me was a desk with a security guard. Three hallways branched off from where we stood, but everything was white. There were no signs to give me a clue. "Where are we?" The best I could come up with was some kind of office building, but that didn't explain why Dastien was wearing scrubs.

"You don't know?"

I licked my lips. "No." If I was still in my head, then maybe I'd switched into a vision. Was I seeing a future possibility? No. That didn't quite fit. I didn't think Dastien had any desire to be a doctor. Did he?

What the hell was this?

"Are you having one of your episodes?" His condescending tone made my hackles rise.

"Episodes?" What the hell was he talking about?

"Maybe it's time to get you back to your room."

My room? Was I supposed to be a patient in a hospital? I didn't feel sick.

And then I almost laughed. I stood and pushed past Dastien into the courtyard outside. The sun hit my face, but it didn't have any heat.

Dastien and I once had a conversation about this exact fear. I'd woken up one morning in Dastien's house in France, and despite everything that had happened, I was so thankful with how my life had turned out. Even if I'd almost died multiple times, I'd survived and was on the perfect honeymoon. I'd wondered offhandedly if my life was just a dream. If maybe I was Freaky Tessa and was having a mental break in a psychiatric facility.

If the thing that was attacking me had bothered to look a little deeper in my mind, they'd know this wasn't a valid fear of mine. If anything, it was more like a joke Dastien and I had shared than a fear that I spent any real time worrying about.

"Nice try, fucker!" I screamed at the too perfectly blue sky. "Show me something scary, you miserable piece of—"

Everything went black again. The only sound was my breath rushing in and out too fast. "Shit." I wasn't in control yet. I was in my head, but somehow this asshole had the upper hand. I needed to gain it back.

In the quiet dark, I reached for my bond to Dastien. This wasn't one of my normal visions, but it was still *my* mind. And if I could use some of Dastien's power, then maybe I'd have enough juice to get control and kick this motherfucker out of my head.

I started pulling power through the paper-thin bond and—

"You're mine," it said right by my ear. Its magic plopped onto my shoulder and wormed its way down my back like tiny maggots.

I twitched, trying to shake the little magical worms off of me.

When I blinked, the scene changed again. I stood in front of the hostess stand in a diner.

What the hell was this? A diner? I understood the metal institution reference, but a diner seemed lame in comparison.

"Table for one?" A girl, not much younger than me, in poorly fitting khaki pants and a polo shirt, stood holding a menu.

I glanced over my shoulder to be sure, but no one was behind me. Only a dusty claw crane machine was there. "Me?" I asked, pointing to myself.

45

"Yes." She scrunched up her face as if she'd sucked on a lemon. "You're the only one standing here."

The diner wasn't packed, but there were a few people scattered around. A family with two kids sat at one table. Two senior men played chess while sipping their coffees at another. There was a salad bar in the back, and a few people were picking through the food. One guy used his fingers to grab a shrimp. He dipped it in a red sauce and made an approving sound before dropping the tail on the floor and reaching for another.

I barely contained a gag.

"You need a table for one or is someone meeting you?" The hostess asked, bringing my focus back to her.

I thought about saying just one. I'd rather get one million shots than meet whoever was messing with me. But there was no point in putting it off. "Two, please."

"Do you want to wait for them here or be seated at the table?"

I shook my head. "No." I was done waiting. "I'll sit."

The hostess led me to a booth and waved me in. The green vinyl was ripped and covered in spots with duct tape. I put my hand down as I scooted in and touched something sticky. I grabbed a bunch of napkins from the chrome dispenser on the table and tried to wipe my hands off to no avail.

"Server will be with you in a bit."

"Cool," I said without looking up. It was rude of me, but she wasn't real. None of this was real.

It didn't make sense. Why a diner? What was the jerk trying to accomplish?

I grabbed for Dastien again, but nothing came. No thoughts. No feelings. And no power.

Damn it.

I tried to shake off my frustration. This thing wanted to play games, and for now, there was nothing to do but go along with them. At least until I could reach Dastien.

I grabbed the menu from the table and scanned the contents. Pizza with shrimp and cream sauce. Hotdog hash with chopped beets. What kind of menu was this? Everything seemed to have either shrimp, beets, chicharrones or a combination of all three.

I closed the menu with a sigh. Of course. Everything I hated. "Nice touch, douchebag."

I closed my eyes, trying to focus on my bond to Dastien. Even just a little extra power might be enough to get me out of this mess.

Tingles ran up my spine, raising goosebumps in their wake, but they weren't from Dastien.

Someone was staring at me.

I twisted in the booth. The family was leaving. The little girl was yammering on and on about some toy that she wanted, and the parents were ignoring her as they each grabbed a mint from the bowl on the hostess' stand. The little boy—maybe about four years old—stood quietly behind them. He was wearing a blue, puffy ski jacket with the hood pulled up over his head. He was the one staring.

I thought it was odd that he was wearing a jacket, but it was winter, even if it didn't feel like it was almost winter in the Caribbean.

What the hell was I even thinking about? This place was fake. Not real. Neither was the family. Who cared what kind of jacket the kid was wearing?

I turned back to the menu. Was I supposed to order something? I hadn't seen any waitstaff, so I was assuming not, but who the hell knew? What was the point of this? Was this some insane, stalker witch who wanted a date? I understood what it was trying to do with the mental hospital, but I was having trouble figuring out what the diner had to do with anything.

But maybe that was the point. Maybe it was just supposed to frustrate me. I looked at the menu again. And gross me out.

I closed my eyes and tried to reach for Dastien again. *Dastien. Dastien. Dastien.* I put my magic behind his name as I reached along our bond, but he was too far away.

I growled as I picked up the napkin dispenser and hurled it across the stupid fucking diner.

My breath heaved in and out of me, but no one had even flinched at the sound of the dispenser crashing through the window.

Shit. This was so dumb. "Come on. Show your face."

"Y'all have a nice day," the hostess told the family behind me.

The dad murmured something, and the door chimed as it opened and closed.

The family was gone, but I still felt like someone was staring at me. I glanced a little to the side, but the hostess was wiping down menus. So, it wasn't her.

To the right of me, a clock hung on the wall. I watched the seconds tick by. My knee bounced under the table as I glanced out the windows. In the distance, I could see a city. I knew it wasn't actually there, but I couldn't just keep sitting here waiting for whoever—whatever—this was to show up.

Nope.

I started to get up but froze.

The tingling was back. Stronger this time. An evil twinge of magic was stronger, making my skin crawl.

I didn't want to look. I didn't want to turn around. It was here.

But I had to look. I geared myself up for it.

Three.

Two.

One.

I spun, but no one was behind me except the little boy. He didn't look too concerned that his family had left. He just stood there and stared at me. The mom, dad, and little girl were walking through the parking lot outside.

I glanced back to the menu to buy myself some time. Something wasn't right with this boy. My gut was screaming demon. It lined up with the greasy magic and ability to sneakily take over my mind and the creepy child. This wasn't the first time I'd seen a demon take the shape of a kid, but seeing something so evil shoved into an innocent body was more than unsettling.

Was that it? The demon wanted to creep me out? Was this whole diner thing just for that?

I turned around, and for the first time, really looked at the boy.

There was nothing out of the ordinary about him. His shoes were dirty and one lace untied. His jacket had a few stains but looked warm enough.

Why was I thinking about his jacket when I should've been meeting his gaze? But no matter how I tried to look at his face, I couldn't seem to meet his eyes.

I stopped breathing.

An alpha werewolf could meet any gaze, especially one as powerful as me. Unless this thing was more—

I swallowed down the lump in my throat.

The demon was more dominant—more powerful—than me.

My heart hammered in my chest. Other Weres had talked about not being able to meet Mr. Dawson's or Donovan's gazes, but I'd never experienced that. Not until now.

What was I going to do?

I could try to fight it, but if I couldn't even meet its gaze, I was screwed. And I was alone.

I rested my forehead on the damp, sticky table. *Think, Tessa. Think.*

A wave of reassurance came through the bond, and I sat back up. It was faint, but it was there.

I wasn't alone. I had help.

I didn't know what he'd done to get through to me and I didn't care. I grabbed Dastien's power, pulling as much as I could and hoping I didn't damage the barely-there rope.

A surge of Dastien's power hit me like I'd just downed a million Diet Cokes, and with it came a buttload of confidence.

I twisted in my seat, finally able to meet the little boy's gaze.

His eyes were a standard brown—not red like other demons —but they were vacant. As sick as it was to think about since he —it—was in the shape of a little boy, looking into its eyes was almost like staring at the glass eyes of a taxidermied animal. They glinted a little too much in the light and were devoid of any emotion.

Then it grinned, and a chill went down my spine.

Its mouth opened, lips thinning until they were just lines. The mouth was too big and too wide for its face. More like a jack-o'-lantern than anything human. As it smiled, the black hole of its mouth grew bigger as if it was going to suck me in.

Its laugh boomed in the small diner. Power pressed against my skin, making it feel like I'd been rolled in a layer of its black slime.

I started to slide out of the booth, but I hadn't consciously moved.

I gripped the table, and my fingers squeaked as they slipped down the linoleum.

No. No. No. This was bad. This was really bad. It was drawing me toward it. The demon was done messing with me, and I had zero illusions that I could fight it and win.

My gut screamed that I couldn't let it reach me. If I touched the demon, then it would have me. Forever. There was no coming back from that black pit. I knew what was on the other side. I'd seen it that day in the chapel in Santa Fe.

Inside the pit, a giant demon clawed its way to the top. It looked like it was made of molten lava, scarring the rock with fire as it climbed. It spotted me and roared, moving faster.

"You're mine." The words sent terror through my soul. The same words he'd said in Santa Fe.

"No! Never!"

It was like gravity changed. I was sucked out of the booth, falling horizontally toward the boy—the demon.

My fingers were slowly slipping down the table, no matter how hard I tried to hold on. I needed a better grip.

In a split-second, my wolf rose to the surface, my fingers stretched, and my nails lengthened, turning into claws. I punched them through the table. It shook and cracks formed around my hands, spreading toward the edges.

This wouldn't last. The table would break in half before long, and I'd be sucked toward the demon.

I needed a way out.

I hung parallel to the floor. The demon was still in the same spot, waiting for me. He was enjoying my panic. I was sure it could smell the sickly-sweet stench of it as well as I could.

He was waiting for me. He didn't need to move. I was trapped.

As I hung there, floating in the air, trying not to be sucked into his evil vortex, I looked back. I stared him in the eyes. And I knew. All I had to do was look at him, and I *knew*.

I'd felt his evil magic before.

It was his power that had allowed Luciana to strip me of my magic and shove it into two jars.

As the realization hit me, he laughed.

That's why. That's why I was here in this stupid place. In

this diner. Waiting. Because the demon wanted me to know who he was. He wanted me to feel how strong he was. How he could own me again because he'd never let me go. Not since that day in Luciana's craft room.

There was only one thing left I could do.

I pulled more power from Dastien. As he gave me more power, I started to feel the magic that was holding me hostage.

My physical body wasn't here. That was true. But I was trapped. And this place didn't exist in my head.

The dark abyss that I'd been walking in was more than just an abyss. It was something far worse. And as I realized where my mind had gone—where the demon had taken my soul—my chest wound so tight, my heart raced, my palms sweated, and I knew that if I didn't get out of here soon, I was going to be worse than dead.

I was going to be a demon's slave in Hell.

"Let me go. Let me go. Let me go!" My magic and power mixed as I threw my will and everything Dastien had sent to me at the demon.

His laugh came again.

I didn't look back. I knew what I was up against and I needed more power than Dastien could give. That he and I together weren't enough to beat the demon scared the shit out of me. But the thing about being a werewolf was that you always had the pack.

I pushed away any doubt. I closed my eyes, shutting out the sound of his laughter and air rushing past my ears as he tried to suck me deeper into Hell.

All I needed to do was hold on while I found the pack.

I reached out mentally, but couldn't find them.

I tried not to panic and reached out again.

Nothing.

They were there. I just had to try harder.

I let my wolf rise a little more. *Pack, please!* I finally felt them like little tendrils against my inner wolf. The spiderweb of power that tied every Were to each other. There were weaker links between the packs—tied from alpha to alpha. From one bond, I could reach every single werewolf alive if I needed them.

For now, I used the St. Ailbe's ties. I'd thought my bond with Dastien was thin, but the ones to my pack were impossibly thinner. But as I called, power came through. It was just a little trickle at first, and then a huge rush hit me. My arms grew fur, and I was barely able to hold onto my shape. I let the power build for a second longer before screaming. "Let me go!" My voice was thick with my rising wolf. "Now!" I backed the word with all the power from the pack.

"No." The single word sent a chill down my spine. "You're mine."

"No! No one owns me!"

He just laughed, and the air grew too thick to breathe.

No. The demon was wrong. He had to be. I swallowed down the panic that was choking me.

He started to grow taller, morphing until his head touched the ceiling. "You can fight me, or you can give in, but you're mine either way. You're the key. I tasted your magic in that circle, and I knew you were the one I'd been waiting for. There's no breaking free of me now."

"The key?" I wasn't sure I wanted to know, but I had to ask.

"The seal is gone. The portals are locked, but your magic is the key. You're already tied to me. It's over. Just let go."

Fuck that. I didn't know what seal he was talking about or what portals he meant, but I wasn't tied to the demon. And if I was, I was breaking it as soon as I got out of here.

But one thing was certain. I was never giving up. Not while I was still alive.

I started saying the Hail, Mary, but his magic only grew stronger, skittering over my skin like a swarm of cockroaches.

Shit.

The demon didn't seem to be weakening, but my arms ached, and the tie to Dastien was on fire. It was too much power for the little thread. I was going to burn it to ashes if I pulled much harder.

The pack bonds weren't doing much better. They were glowing, but I could feel them weakening. It was only a matter of time, and I wasn't getting any closer to breaking free from the demon's hold.

Which meant I was losing and I was out of ideas. I was out of time. The splinters in the table dug into my fingertips, and it moaned. The whole thing was about to shatter. There was going to be nothing left to hold on to.

I gathered all the power the pack had sent me. It was time to use it. The demon might've been strong, but he'd made one mistake. He'd told me that there was a tie between us, and if there was a tie, then all I had to do was break it.

"Find the tie. Break it. Kill it dead. Find the tie. Break it. Kill it dead. Find the tie..." I said it over and over until I was hoarse and out of breath. The pack's powers were waning, and I hadn't found it.

Why hadn't I found it?

"Because it's a part of you. You'll never be rid of our tie, Teresa." He drew out my name, spending to much time on the s. I never knew the sound of my name could terrify me so much, but as he spoke, I realized a few things.

He was right.

This was hopeless.

And by using the pack's power, I was going to drag them down with me.

A sob finally broke free. I'd fought so hard for so long, and I was happy. It'd been an insane few months, but with Dastien, I'd found true happiness. Never in a million years would I have thought that I'd find happiness and a home in a school for werewolves, but I had. I'd found friends. Power. And love. So much love. I thought I could hold on to that forever, but I couldn't.

My heart felt like it'd turned to stone and then pulverized until all that was left were tiny grains of sand slipping out of me.

I didn't want to let go. I didn't want to die. I wanted a lifetime with Dastien. That house on our land. Travel and adventure and dancing and laughing and everything else that came our way.

Please, God. If you can hear me, help. I said a prayer, but there was no answer.

Only the demon's taunting laugh.

I started to let go, giving the pack back what was theirs, but a wave of reassurance crashed through the bond. Not just the bond to Dastien, but to the pack. More power surged through.

Stop! I yelled through the lines of the pack bonds. I wasn't sure if they'd hear me, but I had to try. *I can't beat him. I don't want to drain you, too.* I rested my head on the table. *I love you,* I sent through my bond to Dastien. I started to relax my grip.

No!

I raised my head. *Dastien?* I clamped down on the table. The splinters cut into my hands, but I wasn't letting go. Not now.

Claudia is working on something to help.

A seed of hope sprouted. If Claudia was helping, then I had a shot. I grabbed what the pack was offering. The power grew, and I realized it was more than just my pack now.

The table groaned. It was going to shatter any second. *Tell Claudia to hurry! I can't hold on much longer!*

Then it was like there was too much of everything. Too much air. Too much pressure. Hot liquid dripped down my face. The copper scent of blood filled the air, with undertones of pine and something so familiar I—

Dastien's blood.

On the count of three, let go of the table. Crash into the demon. Dastien's voice echoed in my head. I didn't know how he knew what was happening here, but I wasn't going to think about it too hard.

But his plan was crazy. *No! I can't let go. There's a vortex around him. If I touch him, I'm worse than dead.* They had to have another plan. One that didn't involve me going to Hell and having the demon use my magic.

Trust us. Claudia says you need to touch him to break his hold on you. But it has to be timed.

Timed? I wasn't sure what he meant, but it didn't matter. *No. There has to be another way. If you're wrong—*

He was quiet, and I could almost hear him thinking again. *Claudia says she's not wrong. You're my other half, and I wouldn't tell you to do something unless I knew it would work. Please, trust me. When I say, let go.*

One of my claws broke, and I screamed.

Don't let go! Not until I say three.

Hurry!

We're moving fast!

"You're not getting away. I own you." The words slid down my spine like ice.

"Never!" Maybe it thought it owned me. But no one did. No one but me.

One.

Two.

Three! Now, chérie. Let go!

But I couldn't make my fingers move.

Let go! I promise. You'll be okay.

If anyone else had said those words, I would've told them to fuck off, but I trusted Dastien with every fiber of my being. He wouldn't tell me to let go if he didn't know for sure that I'd survive.

I closed my eyes and let go of the table.

"Shit!" I screamed as I fell through the air toward the demon.

And then I slammed into him.

I thought that would be it. That hitting the demon would somehow shatter his hold, but that didn't happen.

He wrapped his hands around my neck, squeezing. I choked as I clawed at his hands, trying to break his hold. This close up he couldn't hide what he was. His red eyes flickered like fire and heat radiated off him. His fingers were rough, scaly, and impossibly strong. No matter how hard I pulled, I couldn't get them to budge.

He squeezed harder, and I gasped for air.

I kicked my feet into his stomach as hard and as fast as I could, but he didn't even flinch.

Calm, chérie. Claudia said you had to be touching him. Now tell him to let you go.

I already tried that.

Do it again. Do it now!

Dastien shoved more power into me until I was swimming in it. I looked straight into the demon's fire-filled gaze. "Leeett. Meeee. Go." The words were soft and raspy, but slowly I squeaked them out.

Power and magic mixed. Everything turned to darker than night.

But no hands tightened around my neck. No more spinning. No more falling. No more evil magic.

I was frozen.

"BREATHE FOR ME. Come on, *chérie*. Take a breath." Something brushed my face. "I can hear your heart beating. I know you're there."

I gasped, and my eyes flew open.

"Shit." Dastien pressed his forehead against mine.

I licked my lips and tasted blood. "What the hell just happened and why is your blood on my face?"

He started laughing, except it kind of sounded like sobs.

"Dastien?"

He rolled off to lie next to me.

I tried to sit up to look at him, but the room swam. "Are you okay?"

"No." His fingers brushed mine, and my hand felt numb as I tried to grab hold of them. "Not even a little bit."

We laid there for a while, just breathing. I wasn't sure how to process what had happened, but I knew that a demon had attached itself to me. A very powerful demon. Even if we'd broken his hold on me tonight, the demon wasn't gone. I could feel the evil magic like a tick that had burrowed under my skin, and I had no idea how to get rid of it.

It'd taken the power of hundreds of werewolves to escape whatever nightmare I'd been sucked into. If I had to go head to head with this thing, I'd lose. Big time.

What were we going to do?

CHAPTER FOUR

WE STAYED LAYING on the floor together, catching our breath. My teeth were chattering loud enough to annoy me. "I can't stop shaking."

"The adrenaline's wearing off. It'll pass." Dastien's voice was a weak rumble, and from what he was feeling, it was with good reason. I'd never seen him so exhausted before. "I'll be fine. Just give me some time." Dastien said as he squeezed my hand.

I tried to squeeze back, but even my fingers felt weak. Dastien wasn't the only one exhausted.

This was so messed up. I never wanted to go back to that place again, and since that place was kind of in my head, I wasn't sure how to stop the demon from taking over again until I broke the tie he had on me.

I swallowed the lump in my throat. I was scared.

No, scared was too tame a word. Terrified fit better. "How long was I out?"

"Four hours."

"What? What time is it?" I tried to sit up, but couldn't gather the energy.

"Just after midnight."

"Shit." I'd been in that abyss for hours. "Where's my phone?" I needed to talk to Claudia. Maybe she'd know more about demon ties and what I should do.

"On the coffee table, but I can't get it for you. I'm not sure I can move yet." He was a blob on the floor, eyes only half-open.

I wasn't much better off. It was probably better to wait anyway. I wouldn't be able to hold the phone until my shaking stopped. I gripped my hands into fists, hoping that would help, but it only used up precious energy.

I licked my lips and winced as I tasted the coppery-yuck of dried blood. "Why do I have your blood all over my face?"

I couldn't reach you with my bond, so I called Claudia. She told me that my blood would renew and strengthen our bond. I grabbed the first knife I found in the kitchen.

I felt flashes of his panic through the bond. He'd been frantic as he sliced his arm, way too deep. If he'd have been human...

I reached over, grabbing his arm. "It's healed." I couldn't tell what exactly was under the dried blood, but I didn't feel any cut.

Yes. I knew I'd be fine. But... He sighed. *You're a mess. Worth it though.*

"Agreed." Once I had some energy, I'd see about washing my face. The floor felt wet with blood, too. But I was less worried about cleaning that up. "Any chance she's still on the phone?"

No. The call failed right as Claudia was finishing her spell.

Right. Because that would've been too easy.

After a few minutes of laying there, trying to get ahold of myself, I realized I was having zero luck because I wasn't feeling just my fear. I'd thought the terror I was feeling was all mine, but it wasn't.

I've given you CPR twice in one day. It's going to take me some time... Dastien said through the bond. *So, no. It's not just your fear.*

Wait, what? *Twice?*

The last couple of minutes, you weren't breathing. And the phone was dead. I wasn't sure if the spell worked and if you'd... His fear blossomed again. The shaking stopped all at once as it hit me. If I hadn't been breathing, then that meant I'd almost died. Or kind of actually died. Again.

My teeth chattered again, and the shakes returned full-force. "What are we going to do?"

I don't know.

That was enough sitting around. I couldn't stay here swamped by fear.

I groaned as I sat up. Every muscle throbbed. It took everything I had to reach for my phone on the coffee table. When I relaxed with my back against the couch, a sheen of sweat covered my body. It took me three tries to unlock my phone, and then a few more to call Claudia.

The ringtone filled the living room before her voicemail picked up. "Hi! You've reached Claudia. Leave a message, and I'll get back to you when I can." I waited for the beep and started talking.

"Freaking out over here. Thank you so much for helping. Are you okay? Also, I need to know how to break a demon tie. Call me back." The phone slid out of my grip and clattered to the ground. "Shit." I wasn't sure if I'd hung up, but I was leaving it.

"Claudia's fine."

He felt pretty confident, but why? "How do you know?"

"Because Lucas' bond is still among the pack."

That was excellent news. If Lucas was okay, then Claudia was okay. Or at least alive. She was probably doing the same thing we were—recovering. That had to be why she hadn't answered.

I wasn't sure what kind of demon he was, but I knew for sure he was stronger than me. When would he come back again? I had to pray that if I were this drained from the whole experience, he had to be at least a little exhausted from it. Maybe that meant that it'd take a while before he showed up.

Taking me over like that had to have been a massive power drain. I wasn't sure why the demon had so much power at his—

Damn it.

Do you really think so? Dastien asked.

The timing... Muraco had been drained by something with Luciana-esque magic, and then not a few hours later, the demon who helped Luciana drain me of my magic and power took over my mind. *It can't be a coincidence.*

Merde.

No. This could be good news, actually.

How could this possibly be good news?

Because it means that he doesn't have that much power at his disposal. So theoretically, we should have time to regroup. Unless he drained someone else of power, we should be okay. For now. If I was right.

I was under no illusion that he wasn't coming back. It was only a matter of time. And when he did, we had to be ready.

For now, that meant we needed food. I'd burned a lot of calories pulling all that power. At this point, the shaking in my limbs wasn't exclusively fear-based.

"You pulled enough power from me that I'm useless, too." His voice was a little slurred. "But you're right. We're going to need food."

"Know any djinn that can magic us some?"

Dastien huffed. "That would be handy, but even if I did, you wouldn't want to mess with a djinn. They're tricksters."

I filed "djinn" away as something to ask about when we weren't so weak. "I guess I'd better get my ass up."

He gripped my hand harder. "You don't have to. I'll get up in a second. I swear."

Dastien's skin usually had a golden tan to it. Now it was ghostly pale. He was covering his eyes with one of his arms. He hadn't even turned his head to look at me.

He was wrong. I definitely had to get up. My legs were wobbly, threatening to give out, so I stood still, holding onto the edge of the couch in case they did.

He moved his arm just enough to see me, his gaze still a glowing amber. "How are you moving?"

"Sheer stubbornness. Plus, I still have a bit of energy left from everyone else." That was the only explanation for why I was only eighty-five percent useless, and he was one hundred percent zonked.

He grunted and closed his eyes. I figured since my legs hadn't given out yet, it was safe enough to drag myself to the kitchen.

Even if I was better off than Dastien, it wasn't by much. Being this weak made me nervous. I couldn't protect myself. But feeling Dastien so weak was even more unsettling.

I tried to funnel him some power, but he shut it down. "Stop. One of us needs to be strong enough to get food. If you give me your energy now, we're both going to be blobs on the floor. You don't have enough to spare right now."

"But—"

"I'll be okay. Just work on food."

I licked my lips and winced. They still had the coppery tang of Dastien's blood on them. I stumbled to the sink and turned the water on hot. I couldn't do anything else before washing my face. The scent of dried blood wasn't exactly appetizing. It was in my hair a little too, but that would take a shower. I didn't have the energy for that yet.

I splashed my face until the water was clear and then rubbed some more. I could still smell the blood. Trying not to cringe too much, I squirted a tiny dot of dish soap in my hand and lathered my face. After I was done, I smelled like fake lemon, but that was better than old blood, so I was calling it a win. I dried my face with a dishtowel and threw it on the counter. That little bit of effort had me out of breath.

Time for food.

I leaned against the counter, trying to figure out what we should have. The fridge was fully stocked, but I didn't have the energy to make anything. Before I became a werewolf, a large part of my diet had been taken up by yogurt and Zone bars or avocado toast and eggs. Now I had to eat so much more. Learning to cook was part of surviving. Over the course of our honeymoon, I'd upped my chef skills, but everything I could come up with was going to take too much time and require too much effort. And we needed so much...

The room swam as I stepped toward the fridge. I grabbed a chocolate bar from the door and ate a few bites to get some instant energy. Even eating my favorite thing, I had to force myself to chew. This was so messed up.

I followed the chocolate with a swig of OJ straight from the carton and then dug through the freezer until I found a few meat-lovers pizzas. Minimal effort with a decent amount of calories.

I took another swig of the OJ and tried to think of what I should do next, but all I could picture was the demon's face. The smile that sent fear rushing through every fiber of my being. Everything in me was urging to run but what good would that do if he could get inside of my head and take control. I couldn't—

Stop. Dastien's voice cut through my panicked thoughts. *We need food first. Then we can figure out what's happening.*

Right. I'm on it.

I slid the pizzas onto the baking trays and put them in the oven, skipping that whole pre-heating nonsense. Then I grabbed a few mini-cakes and fed them to Dastien.

"You okay?"

He gave me the tiniest of nods. "More food, though."

"I'll be back." I went back to the kitchen and started grabbing everything out of the fridge and dropping it on the couch. It took me a few trips, and I made a mess. Cheese and deli meats and mini-cakes and pickles and fruit and anything else we had in there were strewn all over the couch and the floor beside it.

My last trip was the hardest. I grabbed a two liter of Coke and two cups. The bottle might as well have weighed a million pounds. It took me a second, but I managed to get some liquid in the cups.

I held the one out to Dastien, and he just looked at me. He was thinking about how much effort sitting up would take and was the soda really worth it.

"Shit." He was seriously weak. I had to fix that.

I set the sodas on the coffee table and then bent down next to him. I grabbed his forearms and jerked, but he didn't move at all. "Come on. Help a little." I tried again and managed to get him sitting up, resting against the bottom of the couch. My breathing was a little too labored. The guy was heavy, but I was a werewolf. I should've been able to bench press him without much effort.

"Here. Drink." Water probably would've been better, but it also didn't have calories. I handed him the glass.

The soda sloshed around as his hands shook. I looked at the sea of food on the couch as I slid to the floor next to Dastien. "Here," I said grabbing a package of cold cuts. "Eat this." When he was chewing, I figured I should find something myself. I grabbed a pound block of cheddar and tore the wrapper open with my teeth.

Then it was a bag of potato chips. A pile of Bimbo cakes. More cold cuts. A jar of pickles. I made a few more trips to the kitchen to empty out the pantry.

By the time the oven dinged, we'd gone through basically everything except the condiments. I dragged myself up and went back to the kitchen.

I didn't mess around with plates. We'd inhale the food too fast to need them. I grabbed the mitts and pulled the pizzas from the oven. They smelled so good that my stomach growled.

"How am I still hungry? I just ate an entire jar of Nutella with a spoon."

"Do you want me to answer that?"

"Shut up." I thought about cutting the pieces but decided against it. We were going to eat the entire thing anyway. It would be easier to fold them like a taco and dig in. I headed back to the couch, where we continued our eat-a-thon.

I didn't usually care for meat lover's, but I couldn't stifle a moan of happiness as I ate the first hot bite. "This is much better than I thought it'd be."

No, it's not. You're just starving. He swallowed. "I'm feeling a lot better already. Thanks."

"Least I could do." I looked around at the mess we'd made—wrappers and crumbs littered the floor. "But you know, it's a good thing we're leaving in three-ish hours because we're pretty much out of food and it's not like we can walk to a store from here. We'd need a boat and a car."

Dastien laughed, and the sound warmed my soul. For the first time since I'd woken up, I took a full breath. "Why did you let me take so much of your power?"

"It's what you needed," he said without hesitation.

He was right. If he hadn't given so much, I probably wouldn't have survived, but I still didn't like it. I'd drained him so much, and that made me wonder how the rest of the pack was fairing.

"I'm fine. The pack is fine. We know the drill. We'll eat everything in sight, and by morning, we'll all be okay. But trust me, it's better for the pack to get drained one time than for them to try fighting this demon by themselves. They won't even think twice about it. By helping you now, the pack ensures that you're around to protect them. That's why we have packs. That's why there are leaders. Like it or not, you're an alpha. *The* Alpha."

"I'm not *The* Alpha. I'm *an* alpha at best. I don't have a pack to rule over." And I was pretty sure I never wanted one.

"I know, but you're too strong and—"

That was bull. "You're stronger than me."

"No. I'm really not." For a second I thought he was being nice, but his tone wasn't nice. It was dead serious. "I'm not being polite, *chérie*. I'm a better fighter than you, but I've had my whole life to train, and you've only just turned. In a few years, you'll be able to beat me." He squeezed my hand. "And one day you'll have a pack. You won't be able to help it. Alphas draw betas to them. It's just in their nature."

I could believe that was the case for other Alphas, but I wasn't sure that applied to me. I knew I was a strong werewolf, but that didn't mean that I *had* to be a pack Alpha. That was a lot of responsibility. Would I ever want to tie myself down like that?

For now, all I really wanted was to get away from the demon.

"You got away."

"No, I didn't. Not for long." I shook my head slowly. "I think I just mostly pissed it off." *What are we going to do?*

We're going to take it one step at a time like we always do.

67

That was a good plan, but the first step was figuring out who the demon was, what exactly its powers were, and how to break a demonic tie. I wasn't sure what seal the demon had been talking about, but if the portal was to Hell and I was somehow the key, then there was *much* more on the line than just my soul.

CHAPTER FIVE

THE LINE RANG AND RANG. If there was a more annoying sound, I hadn't heard it. My knee bounced. It was fully dark, we were minutes away from St. Ailbe's, and I still hadn't been able to get ahold of Claudia.

"She's fine, *chérie*."

I wanted to snap at him. Dastien didn't know that Claudia was okay, but he was trying to stay positive, while I was imagining that the demon was torturing her.

I sighed as voicemail picked up for the millionth time today. "Hi! You've reached Claudia. I'm sorr—" I cut off the recording and threw my phone in the cup holder of Dastien's black SUV. We'd only been planning on being gone for a couple of weeks, so we'd left it at the airport. I wasn't sure how much that had cost, but I was glad to be alone for the first time today.

"Maybe she doesn't have it on her. She only recently got the cell, right?"

He had a point. "I guess that could be true." But it didn't make me any less anxious.

We'd had a long day of travel. I'd nodded off a few times

during the car ride to the airport, but the sleep had been in little spurts and didn't add up to anything nearly sufficient.

If I was being honest, I couldn't blame the fact that I hadn't slept on the travel. Every second that passed felt like a second closer to the demon coming for me again. I'd closed my eyes, willing myself to sleep, but it was too much like the black nothingness I'd wandered through yesterday.

I spent time googling how to break a demon's tie, but there wasn't a ton of information out there about them. Until I had a specific demon to research, I was SOL. Plus, I wasn't sure I could trust anything I found on the internet. Too much was on the line to put all my hope in something I found from an unverified source.

I'd texted with Meredith what was going on before we got on the plane. She said she was down to do some research in the Irish pack's library, but she couldn't leave. The pack there was still coming back from all their drama. Which was a bummer, but I got it. I'd managed to talk to my mom for a second to tell her we were coming home. She was worried but said she'd be there to help if she could.

What I really needed first was to get ahold of Claudia.

She'd managed to help me snap the demon's control once, and if I knew the specifics of the spell, then maybe I could do it myself to prevent him from doing it again. Maybe she'd know some way to break a demonic tie. At the very least, if she could just overnight some of those crystals she found in Peru that saved Raphael, then maybe I could use them to fight the demon.

I grabbed the cell phone and dialed Claudia again.

"*Chérie*. She'll call you when she can."

My knee bounced faster as I held my breath, waiting—hoping—that this time would be the time Claudia answered. "This is bad. With what happened, she should've called us by now." I chewed on a fingernail.

"Maybe she's been traveling, too? For all we know, she could be on her way here."

That would explain it, but we didn't know that for sure. "Or maybe saving me hurt her."

"We'd know if something was wrong."

"Would we?" Because I wasn't so sure that we'd know anything unless she died. There was a whole spectrum of not okay between being alive and being dead.

While I usually loved Dastien's cup-half-full attitude, I was feeling more like the fucking cup was empty.

I'd been calling Claudia all day—well, at least every time I had service—and I still couldn't get ahold of her. Last night I'd been able to brush it off, but I couldn't do that anymore. My stomach was churning with the thought that she might need my help, especially after she'd saved my ass. Until I heard word from her or someone in Peru, I just had to wait. But waiting around was *not* my strong suit.

Dastien flicked on the blinker. "We're here."

I looked up from my phone to see the break in the brick walls that separated St. Ailbe's from the outside world. As we pulled up, the massive black wrought iron gates opened, letting us into the parking lot. It was odd not to see any reporters at the entrance, but it'd been six weeks since we'd been here. Hopefully, the constant stream of reporters had died down for good. The ten Cazadores guarding the gates might have finally become a deterrent. Or maybe it was the demon attacks.

Either way, that was one thing I wasn't sorry to see go.

Dastien waved to them as he passed and then pulled into a spot right by the path to campus. As soon as he stopped, I swung open the door and breathed in. Pine. Cedar. Dirt. Home.

The last took me by surprise. I wasn't sure when St. Ailbe's had become my home. I'd lived in Los Angeles most of my life. We'd only moved here at the beginning of the school year, and it was almost Thanksgiving now. But oddly enough, St. Ailbe's was the only place I'd ever felt free to be myself, even if this version of me turned furry every once in a while.

"I thought you'd never get here," a familiar voice said, and I spun in time to see Chris coming around the bend in the path. The sight of my friend made my anxiety ease a bit. I could focus on something a little more trivial—Chris and his need for a haircut. His dirty blonde hair looked like it might almost be long enough to pull back into a small ponytail and he had a full beard. He'd said he was tired in his email, but his easy grin was in place as he opened his arms, pulling me in for a hug.

"Hey," I said. "After nineteen hours of travel, it's really nice not to be moving."

"I bet." After one last squeeze, he stepped away from me.

Chris' blue eyes were the color of the clear summer sky. Like just about every other werewolf I'd met, he was well over six feet tall and thick with muscle. The beard made him look older and a bit more rugged. He was wearing a faded navy polo under a gray hoodie and a pair of dark jeans. Which was good. That meant he still wasn't into being a Cazador, even if he'd stuck around to fight demons. He was too chill and calm to join their numbers, but he'd stuck around to do what was right. That was one of the many reasons why he was amazing.

He narrowed his gaze, apparently noticing my too long once-over. "What?" He asked.

"Nothing. Can't I be happy to see you?"

"You sure can," he said with his slight Texas drawl. He gave me a big grin that made his eyes shine. The guy was a flirt. He just couldn't help himself. "I missed you, too."

"Quit flirting with my mate." Dastien teased him as he stepped beside me.

Chris pulled him in for one of those manly hug-back patting combos.

"What's going on?" Dastien asked. "Anything we need to worry about tonight?"

Chris looked over at the Cazadores. "Still nothing, right?"

One of them nodded. "Quiet as far as I know."

"Good," I said. "Because I'd like to get settled." I reached into the car for my backpack.

Dastien was getting the bags out of the back. "Go on ahead. I'm going to chat with them and then catch up."

Chris started walking down the path, and I followed. "So, important things first," I said.

"What's up?"

"Your hair. A beard? What's the deal?" I poked his beard, and he swatted my hand away. It suited him, but as a friend, I couldn't let it by with at least asking.

He rubbed a hand over his stubble. "Been too busy running around to shave. After a while, it seemed like a bother. Same with the hair." He shrugged. "I've been spending so much time as a wolf that it doesn't matter."

"How are you holding up? Your emails sounded pretty crazed toward the end."

He blew out a breath. "I'm tired. You know me. I've trained like the rest of them, but it's not my thing. I enjoy life too much to go around hunting every night." He was quiet for a second. "You know, I never thought I'd see another one of them after Santa Fe, but they keep coming. Sometimes it's just one, but sometimes it's twenty. We—"

"Twenty? Jesus. No wonder you're tired."

"Yeah. We gotta do something to stop it or we're going to die trying to keep up."

"Agreed. How's Adrian?"

"Good. The guy was made to be a Cazador. He's pretty much all but joined them. He loves a good fight. Aside from the demon bite, he's been having fun. The bite is still healing, but he's back on patrols tonight."

"Already? Any chance that it could lead to demon possession?" I hoped not, but we couldn't be too sure.

"Nah. He's good. We did the usual holy water and potion routine. I'm sure he'd like a little downtime, but we need every Were we have."

That didn't seem smart to me. If we didn't have time for injured Weres to heal fully, then things were much worse than I'd thought.

"We'll figure out why they keep coming." I just wasn't sure how we'd find the answer exactly, but I needed to make sure that Luciana didn't have any leftover magic brewing somewhere on the old witch's compound. But there wasn't a chance I was stepping foot on that place until sunrise.

"All I know is I'm not the only one getting tired. We don't have enough wolves to keep this pace for much longer. We're all exhausted...which reminds me."

I thought I knew what he was getting at, but I wasn't sure. "Go ahead. Ask."

"You going to tell me what you were up against last night? Felt you pulling as if your life depended on it."

"It was depending on it. I, uh..." I wasn't sure how to say it, but I finally decided just to spit it out. "A demon took control of my mind and was trying to drag me to Hell," I said so quickly that my words ran into each other.

"What the fuck, Tessa!" His mouth dropped open, and even under the beard, I could see his skin had paled.

I winced. "That sounded bad."

"Hell, yes. It sounds pretty much like the worst. And with these demon attacks, I don't like it one bit."

"Me, neither." I blew out a breath. "Me, neither," I said again, softer this time.

I checked my phone for the millionth time, just in case I'd somehow missed it vibrating. Nothing. The screen had zero alerts. I shoved the phone into the back pocket of my jeans, promising myself that once I was in my room, I was going to call her nonstop until she picked up.

"Anyway, I'm sorry if you're exhausted, but thanks for the help. I really—"

"Please. Stop. I only brought it up because I was worried." He nudged me. "You take what you need. That's what the Alpha does."

"I'm not the Alpha," I mumbled.

"You say that, but we all know it's not true. That first gym class, we knew you'd become our alpha."

"I'm no one's alpha." And it bugged me that both he and Dastien thought that.

"Maybe not yet, but you'll get your own pack soon."

I was under the impression that I didn't have to do anything I didn't want to, and I for sure didn't want to rule a pack. But arguing with Chris wasn't going to change his mind. Still, I was curious what he was talking about. "Remind me what happened in gym class. Because I have no clue what you're talking about."

He gave me a raspy laugh. For some reason, Chris always sounded like he had a pack-a-day smoking habit, but he swore he never touched them. "We were running laps in the gym. Mr. Dawson was with us. Remember now?"

"No."

"Really?" With the way his voice pitched up, he sounded genuinely surprised.

Even if there'd been some big moment, I didn't remember it. "Between being bitten and all that crap with Imogene and then Luciana and the demons, I don't remember my first gym class. I remember the first time I tried to spar. Is that what you're talking about?" My cheeks heated with the memory of prac-

75

ticing with Chris and how Dastien reacted. And I still couldn't believe I'd pretty much attacked Meredith.

"No, but that was hilarious," he said, and my cheeks burned hotter. "When we run as a pack, the Alpha sets the pace, so Mr. Dawson set the footfalls. Everyone was in sync except for you. Which should've been impossible."

That did sound vaguely familiar, but I remembered it differently. "I just didn't like being a monkey. Following the lead. You know? It rubbed me the wrong way."

"Which is exactly why *you're* our next Alpha."

I wasn't sure he was right, but Dastien had already said the same thing to me. Maybe that was how it'd worked in the past, but I refused to believe I *had to* lead a pack. Saying that wasn't going to get me anywhere, though. Werewolves were set in their ways.

We hit the end of the path, and I paused, taking in the campus. If I didn't have werewolf eyesight, then I would've been stumbling around in the dark.

There were usually lights in the trees surrounding the quad and the pathways between the buildings. Tonight, the lights in front of the doors to the cafeteria and dorm buildings were the only ones lit. The ones for the admin/med unit and the classrooms were out, as well as the quad and pathways.

"Why are the lights out?"

"Campus is technically closed. We're only here to use it as a base for patrols, and it's better for us if it's dark. Easier on our eyes."

"Right." I knew that campus was closed, but the darkness felt wrong to me. It was usually so well lit, and before curfew started, people were always wandering around. And not only that, the quad was always perfectly mowed which always struck me as such a stark contrast to the forest that threatened to swallow up the school's five squat brick buildings.

Today it was quiet and dark, and it looked like the lawn hadn't been mowed in weeks. The bushes and plants in front of the buildings were overgrown. It felt like I'd walked into the middle of a zombie movie. A team of Cazadores patrolling in wolf form caught my eye. The ten wolves weaved in and out of the trees across the quad as they made their rounds.

Maybe I wasn't that far off from reality. The once-thriving school had turned into a ghost town. Goosebumps rose along my arms, and I rubbed them away.

Don't let it get to you. The school will come back and—

You don't know that. With everything that had happened, I wouldn't be surprised if the temporary closure turned permanent.

Why are you even in the quad? Dastien sent along the bond, changing the subject. Because I was right and we both knew it.

What do you mean? I'm on my way to my— Wow. I was an idiot. *Oh. Right.* "I can't believe I did this, but in my defense, I'm pretty worn out. I need to head that way." I pointed to the now-overgrown path that led around the admin building.

Chris huffed a raspy-laugh as we changed directions. "Sorry. I was on autopilot."

"Me, too." The drama of the day before on top of the day of travel was clearly catching up to me. "So, what else has been going on?"

"Besides demons?" Chris blew out a breath. "Not much."

"Any word from Cosette?"

"Some." He shrugged. "She's doing fine but feeling a little cooped up in the Underhill. I think it'd been a while since she was stuck at home for so long."

We weren't ten feet from the cabin when Dastien came running out of the front door, holding his cellphone. "I'm putting you on speaker. Tessa and Chris just got here."

"Hey!" Adrian's voice came through the line. "I've got a situation on *la Alquelarre's* land."

I looked at Dastien, but he shook his head. Which meant it wasn't the demon that attacked. "What's going on?"

"There's some guy here asking for you," Adrian said.

"A demon?"

"No. Definitely not a demon." He sounded pretty firm about that.

"A witch?" I asked.

"I don't think so." His voice pitched up, which meant it could be a witch.

"Fey?" Chris asked.

"Maybe? Honestly, I'm not sure what he is, but says he's got information for you about the demon that attacked you last night. He says it's urgent."

This could be a trap, but I think we have to go. Any information could be a huge help. Dastien said through the bond.

Agreed. Was I nervous? Sure. Especially after last night, but if this guy had information for me—even if he was only going to spout out a ton of lies—I had to go.

I chucked my backpack in the general direction of our front porch. "You coming with?" I asked Chris.

"Yeah." He rubbed a hand along his beard. "Guess I should, just in case."

"We'll be there in twenty to twenty-five," Dastien said.

"Make it less than that. I don't know how long this guy will wait, and he just saved our asses."

"On it." Dastien hung up the phone and tucked it into his pocket as he leaped off of the porch.

As we sprinted back through the woods to the parking lot, I couldn't believe I was about to willingly go to *la Aquelarre's* land at night. It seemed pretty convenient that this person showed up right when we got home. But I had to trust Adrian to know an enemy when he saw it. If this guy was out to hurt me, none of the Cazadores would have wasted time on a phone call, especially not my friend.

Even knowing that I hoped we weren't racing into some kind of a trap. Because that would seriously suck.

CHAPTER SIX

THE CAR RATTLED as we passed over the cattle guard and onto *la Aquelarre's* land. Now that the compound was abandoned, Claudia had changed the wards. The only ones left in place were specifically set for humans, instead of the old one for all non-coven members. The headlights on the SUV lit the road between houses. Dastien flipped on the brights, and a shiver ran up my spine.

I was wrong. St. Ailbe's wasn't a ghost town. The witches compound was. Grass had sprouted on the dirt road that separated the two rows of burned-down houses. A few support beams had survived the fire, but most of the buildings were just concrete foundations covered in ash and rubble. Only Raphael, Claudia, Shane, and Beth were left from this coven, and I highly doubted they'd want to rebuild here. I knew I wouldn't. Too much evil history had seeped deep into the soil. There wasn't enough sage on the earth to cleanse it.

Dastien had parked by a few other black SUVs, but no one was in sight. "Where's Adrian?" I asked as the three of us got out. I didn't want to be here for one more second than we had to be tonight. I planned to dig around in Luciana's stuff to see if any of her magic had survived and was causing all the demon attacks, but I was waiting to do that under the noonday sun.

"That way." He pointed toward the woods. "He said they were about fifty yards east of the cars."

The scent of sulfur was light at first, but the farther into the woods we went, the stronger it got.

"Anyone else have a bad feeling about this?" Chris said, and I almost laughed.

Bad feeling? I had a *terrible* feeling about it. Whatever we were about to meet knew me by name and Adrian wasn't sure what the hell he was, aside from not being a demon. That left a whole lot of unknowns.

A twig snapped maybe fifteen feet ahead of me. I froze. Someone was walking towards us. They took a few more steps, and the moonlight hit his face.

Adrian.

His short black hair glistened with sweat, even in the cold night. His shoulders were hunched, making him look shorter than his six feet. He was wearing a pair of generic sweats that he must've grabbed them from the Cazadores' stash after shifting back. Whatever Adrian had just been through, it had to have been a tough fight.

"Are you okay?" I said as he strode to me.

"Okay-ish." He pulled me in for a quick, one-armed hug. "I'm sorry to drag you out here the second you got back. We were on our nightly demon sweep, but this time there were a lot more demons. It was going to be a bloodbath, but this guy showed up. Saved our asses and then asked to talk to you. He wanted me to put in a good word for him. I guess he thought you'd blow him off without it. Anyway, the guy saved our butts. So, would you mind talking to him?" The way Adrian was asking, thick with an unspoken apology, made me wonder what the other shoe was and when exactly it was going to drop.

"That's why I'm here."

"The only thing is...he kind of knows things."

I wasn't sure I liked the sound of that. "What do you mean? Like he can read minds."

"Yeah. I think?" He crossed his arms. "He says that he's got a beef with Astaroth, and—"

"Wait. Who's Astaroth?" This conversation was getting frustrating. It felt like Adrian was burying the lead.

Adrian shrugged. "Apparently, a demon none of us ever want to meet, but this guy said you met Astaroth last night. I figured that was why you pulled all that power through the packs?"

"It is." The demon in the black abyss. Astaroth. His name felt right, somewhere deep in my gut.

If we could trust this guy, then I was about to be a step ahead. Or at the very least, not so many steps behind.

Before I could think too hard about what I was doing, I quickly followed the trail of sulfur deeper into the woods. When I saw a group of people standing around, I paused.

The earth was scorched in spots all over the small clearing between the trees. Each spot marked a demon killed. Broken branches and debris littered the dirt. I was almost sorry to have missed the fight. Actually getting to fight an opponent, instead of getting magically and psychically attacked, would've been a nice reprieve.

A few Cazadores were off to the side, talking quietly amongst themselves. They looked like they'd been through it. Blood dripped down one Cazadores' arm. He was going to need some holy water. Fast.

Five more Cazadores were standing around a guy who was leaning against a tree. None of them were saying anything. But the Cazadores—all in their black sweats—were giving the man some serious side-eye.

I stepped forward, and the Cazadores who'd been talking came over to us. Dastien spoke to them, but I tuned them out. My focus was on the guy in a white V-neck, leaning lazily against the tree. His relaxed stance gave off the impression that he wasn't intimidated at all being surrounded by a group of Weres. He looked to be maybe in his mid-twenties, but I couldn't assume anything. Donovan looked about twenty-five, and I knew he was much older than that.

Coming here, I didn't know what to expect. We'd rushed over here so quickly, I hadn't really thought it through, but I didn't expect him. The man was beautiful. Like stepped-out-of-a-magazine beautiful. His long, white-blond hair brushed his shoulders. His brows were dark and furrowed. Deep-set pale blue eyes caught the moonlight, glowing just enough to hint at his supernatural nature, but his face was soft. Sweet. Almost cherubic.

He wore relaxed fit, light washed jeans, and his white shirt didn't have a speck of blood on it. Even after saving Adrian and the others from a horde of demons.

If we were anywhere else, I would've thought he was just a pretty face or a model, but something was seriously off with him. Why was he so freaking handsome? And where the hell were his shoes?

As if he could read that thought, a smirk spread across his face.

I wasn't sure if he was reading my mind like Adrian suggested or just something in my expression, but either way, I built up my mental barrier and tried to school my features into a calm mask. "You wanted to talk to me?"

He stepped toward me, and I could feel Dastien's heat as he came to stand right behind me.

"I'm not going to hurt her." The man's voice sent tingles down my spine.

The Cazadores stepped back, giving us room. Clearly they trusted him, but my mate was having the opposite reaction.

What did he just do to you? Dastien said, but his words barely registered.

I don't know, but there's something magical about his voice. "What are you?" I asked. It came off as rude, but I didn't mean it that way. I had to know what—or who—I was dealing with. Especially if he was using magic on me.

"A friend."

"If we're going to be friends, then I need to know—what are you?"

"You werewolves are always big on scent. Come closer." He held out his arm. "Take a good whiff. Let's see if you can make a guess."

I started to step toward him, but Dastien grabbed my wrist. *No.*

I'll be fine. The words came out before I could overthink it. My wrist slipped from Dastien's hold as I stepped toward him, closed my eyes, and breathed in.

He smelled like earth and sun and the grass on a hot summer day. And jasmine. The scent of jasmine grew and grew until it overpowered all the sulfur that lingered from the earlier demon battle. When I opened my eyes, it was all I could smell. "Are you fey?"

"No." His blue eyes were brighter than the summer sky.

This was going to be a stretch, but I might as well ask. "Angel?"

He grinned as he stuck his hands in his pockets. "Not likely." His voice was like a cooling balm on a hot summer day.

"Are you using magic on me to make your voice sound like that?"

His grin widened. "No. Not magic. That's just how it sounds."

Okay. I was out of ideas. "What are you?"

"I'm an archon."

Dastien was wondering what an archon was, so he was just as clueless as me. I looked back to Chris and Adrian, but both just kept staring at the guy.

Great. None of us knew what that meant. "What's your name?"

"You can call me Eli."

I laughed. "Eli? Really?" It was way too ordinary, too plain for someone who looked like him.

He shrugged. "In the end, it doesn't matter what I am or what you call me. Only that I'm someone you *should trust*."

"Why should I trust you?"

"Because you're going to need my help if you want to stop Astaroth."

My throat tightened at the name. "Who is Astaroth and why does he want me?"

"Astaroth is one of the Great Dukes of Hell and part of the evil Trinity. If you're not very careful, everyone will die."

One of the Great Dukes of Hell? Evil Trinity? Everyone will die?

The air turned heavy, and I struggled to get in a breath. What the hell had Luciana gotten me into? "I don't understand. Why me? What does he want?"

"Your power is unique. You're a powerful witch that has been bitten by a powerful Were. The fact that you straddle different supernatural lines in this plane means that he can use you to merge the planes—ours with the one beyond—and bring the end of times." He paused. "If that happens, this plane will be swallowed by demons."

"The apocalypse?" That's what he meant. I was sure of it, but I needed him to be clear before I fully freaked out. "He wants the apocalypse? That's what you're saying, right?"

"Exactly."

This was worse than I'd thought. So much worse. "How do I stop him?"

He stepped closer, leaning into my personal space. "You have problems, and they're only just beginning." I could feel his breath on my cheek. He spoke so quietly that even with my hearing I had to fight the urge to lean closer to hear him. "What the witch did here tipped things off balance. The Seven is in shambles. Not just because they're missing *three* members, but because fey magic brewed the bond. Without the fey returning, they can't fix what they've broken. Their bond was the seal between the planes. They were the good that balanced the bad. That's gone now, and because of their mistakes, Astaroth has a window to use your power and merge the planes. Do you understand now?"

I was starting to, and he was freaking me out. "This is really bad."

"Worse than bad. This is catastrophic. Unknowingly, the fey and the wolves started a chain of events that could destroy all life."

"Are you sure?"

"Absolutely."

My heart raced, and its throbbing beat in my ears. "Astaroth's stronger than me. I can't beat him, especially if he's somehow tied to me. Can you break the tie?"

"I would if I could, but it's too complicated for that. He's woven himself through your magic. You're going to have to figure out how to break the tie yourself." He stepped back from me, raising his voice. "It's not just the tie that's the problem. You're going to need to renew the seal between planes. And before you ask—no, I can't help with that either. At least not yet. Archons aren't allowed to meddle in the affairs of this plane. At least not much. We wait. We watch. We only step in when the time is right. I'm only here to set you on the path. You're the key. Not just for Astaroth, but for everyone. Once you've found a way to fix what's been broken, call to me. I'll be waiting, but my help will come at a cost. One you might not want to pay."

And with that, he was gone.

It wasn't like how Van disappeared with Cosette. I didn't feel any magic in the air. No spell brushed along my skin, so it wasn't witchcraft. It was like he was never there. Even the scent of jasmine had disappeared, leaving me choking on the sulfur again.

"What the hell was that?" Dastien's anger beat at me. "What did he say to you?"

I stumbled as I stepped back from the tree the guy had been leaning against, bumping into Dastien.

"Tessa!" Dastien spun me to face him. "What's going on?" He held on to my shoulders and gave me a shake, but I couldn't speak. I couldn't think. I felt like I was floating outside of my body as the enormity of what Eli had said hit me.

The apocalypse? Seriously? How was this possible?

What had the Seven done to start off this chain of events? I knew that they needed new members, but the way Eli talked about it, the problem was bigger than that.

If the fey leaving was part of this broken seal, how the hell was I supposed to bring them back? I didn't have that kind of authority. I wasn't sure anyone did.

I didn't know where to start. I wasn't even sure if what he said was true. If the world was falling apart and for some insane reason it was up to me to fix it—

No. This was insane. He had to be lying. Maybe he really was a demon, and he'd faked his scent and killed some of his own to save the werewolves in some sort of ploy to gain my trust. All to mess with my mind. To mess with *all* of our minds.

But what if he wasn't?

Astaroth—one of the Great Dukes of Hell—had somehow tied himself to me. How was I going to break it? What cost would I pay to stop the apocalypse?

The realization that I would do way more than I thought I could made my stomach churn.

Suddenly, the sulfur was too strong. Too real. I turned and ran through the woods. I had to get out of here. I needed off this land before I had a total meltdown.

The next couple of hours went by in a blur. My movements were more rote than anything else as I got in Dastien's car with him and Chris and headed back to campus. I ate with them in the cafeteria, and I know they talked, but I stayed quiet. Overwhelmed didn't seem to cover the spread of emotions I was feeling.

I just wasn't sure how to process everything that'd happened in the last thirty-six hours. Between nearly drowning, Muraco's murder, my visit to the black abyss with one over-possessive demon, and then the hot guy-archon-whatever thing in the woods...

It felt like I was back in the ocean, twisting and turning, trying to find which way was up. I couldn't see the light. There was no end. At least not one that was pretty.

As I got into bed, I was waist deep in my pity-party, but then something else occurred to me.

Everything wasn't lost. Sure, I might have been thrown into the deep end, but I was good at digging my way out of messes. This mess was worse than most, but I could do it. I just had to snap out of it.

I had a name. Astaroth.

I was going to have to do some research to confirm the demon's name and everything Eli said, but it was a start. And if I could get ahold of Claudia and some of those Peruvian crystals, then maybe this wasn't going to be as hopeless as I'd thought.

I also had information that something the Seven had done by not having Seven members had started this off. That was another big clue. And I was super lucky. I knew Donovan and Mr. Dawson. Two excellent resources.

If I could somehow reach Cosette and convince the fey to come back, then I could make this all work out.

The last one was probably going to be next to impossible, so I'd start with the easiest stuff first.

I wasn't sure when or how I'd need Eli's help, but if I did and he wanted to make a bargain? Well, then I'd just have to figure that out.

And with that thought, I snuggled up against Dastien's warm body and was finally able to fall asleep.

CHAPTER SEVEN

THE MORNING WOKE me up six hours later. The light cut through the curtains in Dastien's tiny cabin, and I was still exhausted, but I had to deal with everything. It was time to get up. I needed to grab some food and start digging up everything I could about Astaroth.

Dastien was sleeping soundly next to me. His soft, even breaths told me that he was in deep REM. The cabin was basically a studio apartment. Along the back wall was a kitchen with a breakfast nook. The countertops were wood instead of granite or laminate like the ones in other houses I'd been to, but they worked for the cabin. I could sneak and make breakfast, but that would make too much noise, and I wasn't sure if there was any food stocked. Plus, I didn't want to wake Dastien, and if I was honest, I didn't really feel like cooking again. Not when the cafeteria was a short walk away.

My stomach rumbled as I thought of devouring a mountain of pancakes and bacon. I rolled over, trying to muffle the sound with the mattress. I was debating whether or not to sneak out of the cabin when one of our cells started vibrating.

Claudia.

I jumped out of bed, tossing things around and trying to find where I'd put my damned phone in my panicked haze. "Damn it," I muttered to myself.

"It's mine." Dastien's voice was groggy with sleep. "Hello?"

"Welcome home," Mr. Dawson said.

It wasn't Claudia. I slumped to the floor for a second before starting to gather up the mess I'd made.

"Thanks. What's up?" Without our bond, I wouldn't have even noticed a twinge of annoyance in Dastien's voice, but it was there.

"Can't I just call to say hi?"

I wondered if Mr. Dawson knew that he was annoying Dastien.

"Sure." Dastien paused to answer me through our bond. *He totally knows. Other than you, he's probably the person who knows me best.*

Interesting. Sometimes the bond was extra handy. I not only got to know my mate better, but I also got the benefit of his knowledge about other people and things.

"So, what's going on?"

"We're having a meeting this afternoon."

Who was having a meeting?

"Who is?" Dastien said, echoing my thoughts.

"The Cazadores, what's left of the Seven, and a few others."

Dastien sat up. "A meeting like that would've taken a while to plan." And really well timed. I wondered if they knew at least part of what Eli had told me yesterday.

"It did. I started organizing this meeting three weeks ago and had it set for next week. But with Muraco's death, we moved it up. Flights are getting in this morning. Meeting's at three."

Dastien glanced at me, and I gave him a nod. *Yeah. Of course.* There was no question that we'd be going.

"We'll be there."

"Good. I'm heading to breakfast. Hopefully, I'll see you there."

"Possibly."

Possibly? Was he kidding? *We're totally getting food. I'm starving.*

I know. I can hear your stomach from here.

"Good," Mr. Dawson said.

The line went dead, and Dastien set down his cell.

"How much do you think they know?" I asked as I sat on the edge of the bed.

"I don't know, but I agree with you. It's really well timed. They have to know that the Seven is broken, but they might not be aware of what that means."

"Telling them is going to be fun." My tone dripped with sarcasm. I'd been in a room with the Alphas once before, and to say that it'd been intense was a gross understatement.

"I'll be there with you." He reached for my hand, giving it a reassuring squeeze. "Is the pity party over yet?"

"Yes." I hoped that was true, but Eli's parting words had left me terrified.

"You shut down on me last night, and I didn't like it at all."

"I'm sorry. I didn't mean to." I just needed a second to catch my breath.

"I know. I was there, listening in on your thoughts. What Eli said really did a number on you."

It really did. "I just couldn't stop thinking about what he said, and how this whole thing with the demon seemed so hopeless and..." What cost would I pay to save everyone? I didn't even want to say it through our bonds. I didn't want to think about it at all, but I had to. What was I going to—

"Don't," Dastien said. "Don't go there. Not yet. We just got

93

home. We haven't even started to fight Astaroth. And I'm not about to blindly believe Eli. You shouldn't either."

I knew that. I really did, but the fear was still there, hovering over me and I couldn't shake free of it. "I just keep thinking what if—"

"You can't live your life by what if's. Only what *is*."

I fell back against the bed. "You sound like my brother."

"I like Axel. Smart guy."

It was good that Dastien and my brother got along. I wasn't sure what I'd do if they didn't because Axel wasn't just my brother. For the longest time, he'd been my best and only friend.

He scooted closer to me. "Just don't shut me out again. It wasn't cool."

"I'm sorry. I really didn't do it on purpose." My stomach rumbled again, and I pressed a fist into it. "I hate to say it, but—"

"We have to get up and get you some food."

"Yes, please. Are we okay?"

"Yes." He brushed a kiss against my lips. "We're okay. Just don't do it again, please. It was miserable."

"Okay."

He slid off the bed. "Let's get going. I bet the chef will even make you some Benedict."

If the grumbling stomach wasn't enough, my mouth started watering at the thought of eggs Benedict. Or biscuits and gravy. I could eat the shit out of that. Or even—

A stomach rumbled, and it wasn't mine. "All your thoughts about food are making me hungry," Dastien said. "And I ate dinner."

"I didn't?" I distinctly remembered sitting at the dinner table in the cafeteria with him and Chris. With food. I couldn't say what kind, but there had to have been food.

"Yes. There was food. Pot roast with mashed potatoes and gravy. Fried okra. Biscuits. You didn't take more than a few bites. Chris and I kept trying to get you to eat more, but you mostly just moved the food around on your plate."

Huh. That was weird, but given my state of mind, not at all surprising.

I was wearing one of Dastien's T-shirts and a pair of his boxers, which meant I was going to have to find something else to wear if we were going to the cafeteria. I slid off of the bed to dig through the mess I'd made of our suitcases, looking for a pair of yoga pants. We hadn't had time to unpack, and I'd pretty much taken all of my clothes with me on our honeymoon.

I finally found a pair of pants that didn't smell and grabbed one of the screen-printed T-shirts I'd made myself. "I'll be ready in five," I said to Dastien, but he hadn't gotten up yet. "What are you waiting for?"

"Nothing. I just like watching you rush around."

"What?" Why?

He shrugged. "If you don't get it, I don't think I can explain it to you." As he got up from the bed and started digging through his drawers, I totally started ogling his muscles. He grabbed a shirt, his arms flexing, and suddenly I didn't care so much about getting food.

He looked over his shoulder at me and winked.

Oh, come on. Dastien was messing with me? "Point made." I'd showered before bed, which meant my hair was knotted and looking crazy, but I could skip that whole rigamarole for now. I'd have to come back and get presentable before the meeting, but I had hours to do that. I pulled on the yoga pants, ditched the shirt for a bra and my Rabbit in the Moon shirt, and was ready to roll.

I twisted my hair into a double knot. It was long enough to stay, even without a rubber band or clip. Now, if only I could find my cell phone.

I circled, trying to spot it, but finally gave up. "Can you call my phone? I..."

Dastien had a curious look on his face. "Is that some sort of tribal alien on your shirt?"

I glanced down and laughed. I guessed that's what it looked like, but it was actually a logo of an EDM group I loved. "It's actually a rabbit."

"A rabbit?"

I put my hands on my hips. "You don't know."

He grinned. "No. But I love that you're going to tell me about it."

"Good. Because that's totally what I'm going to do." He threw something at me, and I caught it. My cellphone. A few months ago, this would've been met with great celebration and more than a few pats on my back, but my reflexes had gotten so good, it was almost like cheating. "Thank you. Rabbit in the Moon is a DJ and live performance group. Axel found them when he was searching for info on Chinese folklore about a rabbit who lived on the moon and shared it with me. They don't perform very much anymore, but I really dig Floori.d.a." I grabbed his hand, pulling him out of the cabin. "We'll listen to it during our run."

"Can't wait."

I paused. "Did you really not know about Rabbit in the Moon or are you just trying to cheer me up by making me focus on something that's not about demons sucking my soul to hell?"

He laughed. "You don't have to ask. If you want to know, you have a very easy way to find out."

I rolled my eyes and took a peek in his head. I didn't have to search hard. He was pretty much thinking the answer at me without sending the words. *You didn't know!* This was a first. Even though we had the same taste musically, his knowledge was way more extensive than mine. *But you were trying to distract me.*

Anything to get you to respond. I didn't like how you checked out last night. It was like you weren't even there. I'm trying to keep the mood light this morning, he said as we walked out of the cabin. *That guy really messed with you.*

I didn't mean to check out that much. I just needed to process.

But you forget that you've got me. We're a team. Astaroth doesn't know who he's chosen to mess with.

I grabbed a fistful of his shirt and pulled him down to my face. *Thank you.* I pressed my lips against his and for a second, truly lost myself in the heat of his kiss.

By the time we stopped kissing, I was out of breath. I pressed my head against his chest, and he rubbed my back.

You have a lot of friends. Don't count us out before the fight's even started.

I nodded. *You're right. I just have to get Claudia and Lucas here.*

They're probably already coming.

I hoped so because Claudia hadn't even returned one of my million phone calls.

As we walked, I started doing a basic search on Astaroth on my phone, trying to confirm everything Eli had said. Not that the internet would be entirely accurate, but getting started made me feel a little less anxious.

The first page of the sites all said the same thing. Great Duke of Hell. Evil Trinity. Forty legions. But nothing more about who he was or more importantly—how to get rid of him. Permanently.

A search on demon ties plus Astaroth got me a ton of information about how to summon a demon, but I wanted to do whatever the opposite was of summoning Astaroth. Banish him?

Kill him? I didn't care. I just wanted him gone. "Do you think people actually try this garbage?" Messing around with demons was mega stupid.

"I'm sure they do."

People were dumb. "This is getting me nowhere."

"We'll grab food and then hit the library. I'm sure there's more in there about Astaroth than you can find on the web."

"I hope so." What I really needed was to talk to my cousin.

As we walked through the doors of the cafeteria, I pressed Claudia's contact info. The buzzing ring was endless. Until finally, the buzzing stopped.

I prepared to hear her voicemail message again, but it never started.

"Hello?" Claudia's voice came through the line, but it echoed.

I looked up and nearly jumped out of my skin. "Holy shit." Claudia was standing there in the flesh. Right in front of me. Her long hair was braided as usual. Her typical peasant shirt was hidden by a fleece hoodie, and her flip-flops were gone. Were those hiking boots?

She was really here. My phone slipped through my fingers, clattering to the floor as I jumped at her, attacking her with a hug. "I thought that—"

"I'm okay."

It took a second for her words to sink in, and then I let go of the worry that had been a rotting pit in my stomach. I closed my eyes and breathed in her scent. She'd been burning sage recently, but I could smell at least seven other herbs—probably from whatever spell she'd been working on—covering up the smell that made her Claudia. "I was worried sick."

"I'm sorry. We have a lot to talk about. Like—"

"Like why you didn't answer any of my phone calls?" I stepped back from her.

She winced. "That's not so supernatural of a problem. It took me a while to recover from my spellwork the night you were attacked, and when I did—I noticed there'd been a bit of an electrical fire and my charger was trashed. We were already going to be heading to St. Ailbe's in the morning, so I figured I'd just see you when I got here. I picked up a spare charger at the airport, and only just now turned on my phone. I never thought you'd be so worried about me."

Was she joking? "Why wouldn't I worry about you?"

Her cheeks turned a bright red. "I don't know."

Her mate came up behind her, pulling her into him. "We're working on her confidence." His black fleece hoodie almost matched hers as did his hiking boots.

I tried to hide the smile that was threatening to break free. They were too cute all dressing alike. "I'm going to grab some food. You sit. We have to talk."

"I agree. There are some things I think you need to know before you head into that meeting," Claudia said.

I turned toward the food but stopped as Claudia's words sank in. "What—"

"Get food, and we'll talk."

Claudia and Lucas wove through the empty tables to sit with Chris and Adrian. *Do you think she knows more about what Eli said? About the Seven being in shambles and how Astaroth was going to use that?* I asked Dastien.

I have no idea what she wants to tell you. Dastien grabbed my hand, half dragging me toward the food. *But I wouldn't doubt your cousin. She's reliable, and if she says you'll need the food to keep your wolf in check, then you need to eat. You already admitted that you're starving.*

He was right, but there was so much on the line. I didn't like waiting, even if it was just to load up a tray.

The chef already had out biscuits and sausage gravy, like

he'd read my mind. I hefted more than I thought I could possibly eat—which was a lot—on my plates. Then I grabbed another plate and loaded up some hash browns. For some reason, being back at St. Ailbe's reminded me of my first meal here. More specifically—my first run-in with Imogene.

I still can't believe you dated her. I sent through the bond as I dumped a pile of perfectly cooked scrambled eggs on my plate.

Let's just call Imogene a moment of weakness, he answered back without missing a beat.

I snorted. *Shut it. You thought Imogene was hot, and she wanted you.*

He shrugged. *It was easy. Convenient. But she was already too much drama, and I'd broken up with her before I met you.*

I grabbed a bowl of fruit. *How long before?*

He was quiet so long that I looked up at him. He had sense enough to blush with shame. *It doesn't really matter, does it?*

You're trying to distract me again, and it's totally working.

It's easier now that I'm in your head.

"That's cheating!" I screamed aloud before I could stop myself. "Sorry. Didn't mean to say that aloud." Good thing the cafeteria was mostly empty except for our friends, otherwise, that would've been embarrassing.

As I picked up my tray and headed toward the tables, I realized that whatever Claudia said, I could handle. I had Dastien. Sitting at the table with Claudia, Lucas, and Raphael were Chris and Adrian. I wasn't alone. Adding in my parents, my brother, Tia Rosa, Meredith, and Donovan, then I really had nothing to worry about it. We'd fought a whole chapel full of demons, plus one powerful demon-possessed witch. Astaroth might be more powerful, but we would figure it out together.

Was some super scary demon after me? Yes.

Was the supernatural world coming apart? Also, yes.

Had Eli told me I was going to have to sacrifice something in order to get his help to stop the apocalypse? Again, yes.

But at least I had friends to help figure out how to fix this whole shitshow that my life had turned into.

Christ. Who was I kidding? This was a freaking disaster.

Go back to the part about the friends. I liked that part, Dastien said.

And with that, I started laughing. Even my mind wasn't my own anymore, but I didn't really mind that part.

Would seeing my abs again help? He grinned, and his dimples deepened.

And then he winked.

It was too much. I laughed harder. *You know, it might. Let's see them.*

Oh, I'm not actually undressing here. I was just curious.

Is everyone a tease today?

Nah. Just me and Claudia.

As the laughter faded, I was left feeling a little lighter. I wasn't sure what was going to happen next, but laughing through the crazy was as good a plan as any.

CHAPTER EIGHT

CLAUDIA WAITED while I ate my mountain of food. She insisted that I eat first, and then talk, but the suspense was killing me. Instead, Chris and Adrian peppered her with questions about the pack in Peru while I shoveled everything in as fast as I could. Raphael stayed quiet through the whole barrage. Instead, he tapped his fingers on the table as he stared into space.

Does he seem off to you? I asked Dastien.

I don't know him well enough, but he seems really uncomfortable.

Hmm. I settled in to hear about the pack in Peru. Everyone was curious about them, and Claudia seemed okay to share. Even if Lucas shot her a couple of looks. From what I could tell, he liked to keep an air of mystery around his pack, which I got. Privacy was a thing.

When I couldn't eat another bite, and there was no chance of the wolf breaking free, I put my tray on the table behind ours. I couldn't sit here and have an important conversation with half-eaten plates of food in front of me. "So, what's going on?"

Claudia cleared her throat before starting. "After our talk, I

AILEEN ERIN

did some research and tried out a few spells. It took me all after-noon to find the right one, but once I did...let's just say that it had some unintended results."

I didn't like the sound of that. "What do you mean?"

"I called a minion of a demon named Astaroth into my circle."

"You did what?" Fur rippled along my skin, and I fought to calm it down. "Why would you do that? Why would you mess with—"

"I didn't mean to, but it came. And I think the reason it showed up has to do with what happened with Muraco."

At least we were on the same page. "Astaroth killed Mura-co." She looked around the room, but besides a few Cazadores on the other side of the room, it was empty. There was no reason for her to stay quiet.

"What's really going on?" I asked.

Claudia glanced at Raphael, and they shared a look. The twins were usually on the same page, finishing each other's sentences, but not today. Claudia had a pained look on her face, and Raphael seemed to be getting angrier by the second. For the first time, I really took in Raphael. His hair was a little grown out and standing on end, and dark circles hung under his eyes. He looked terrible.

After a moment, she shook her head and focused back on me. "I had to be sure that I was right. So, after we talked, I did some digging. Muraco was drained of power, just like you were. I know I said it felt familiar but I wasn't sure what that could mean..." She sighed. "It was just *too* familiar to the spell that drained you of your magic. Same setup. Same demon. Deadlier spell, though. Which was good that Luciana didn't use that spell on you, but why the change? Why now? I had too many ques-tions, so—"

"It was my fault Muraco died," Raphael said.

I spun to him. Raphael's face was red, and he kept staring off at nothing.

"How could it be your fault?" It didn't make sense to me. "You don't do magic."

"No," he said, finally looking at me, eyes swimming with guilt. "I don't. I leave that to my sister, but ever since I was bitten by the zombie version of Daniel, I just..." He rubbed his arm where the bite had been. A puckered red scar marked the spot. "I felt a weight on me. I know I was cured. I *know* it logically because I'm alive and talking to you. But something wasn't right. I was..." He trailed off, and pain flickered across his face.

When Raphael came back from Costa Rica, I figured he was okay. I hadn't even given him or what he'd gone through a second thought. He'd seemed fine, and I didn't want to pry.

I was a shit cousin. "I'm sorry. I—"

"Don't apologize. I didn't want to bring it up." His tone was sharp enough to cut, but it wasn't meant for me. It wasn't me he was glaring at. It was Claudia.

I didn't know what had happened between them, but it was bad.

"Muraco saw that something was bothering me and he was trying to help. I felt like I had a shadow of evil and negativity hanging over me that I couldn't shake." He licked his lips, and I knew whatever he was going to say, it wasn't good. The sorrow and guilt were pouring off of him. "When I told him that, Muraco said his mate was a witch, and he could do a spell to make sure that the magic that brought Daniel back from the dead wasn't still affecting me. But the spell went wrong. Astaroth came, and I was thrown from the circle. I tried to get help, but everything happened so quickly and..."

Oh my God. This was making so much more sense.

He squeezed his eyes shut. "It was my fault. I did this. I'm the reason he came after you next, and you almost died. I—"

"Stop it!" Claudia snapped. "No one blames you."

"I do." His tone was knife-sharp, but he didn't mean to hurt anyone, except himself. "I blame myself." He met my gaze. "And you should, too." His chair screeched against the floor as he stood and strode out the door.

"I don't blame him." I'd been shocked at what he said and stayed quiet too long. He was already gone when I'd spoken, but he was wrong. This wasn't his fault.

Claudia started to get up, but Lucas grabbed her hand as the door slammed shut behind Raphael. "Let your brother go. He's angry with himself, and he keeps taking it out on you. He needs time. Just let him be."

"It's just hard to see him suffering, and—"

"I know." Lucas cut Claudia off. "You're kind and caring and generous, so it makes sense that of anyone, you'd want to help your twin through this. But he needs time. He's got to figure this one out on his own."

The room was quiet as Lucas pulled Claudia into him. I figured they were still talking, so I didn't say anything for a bit. I was glad Claudia had someone by her side, making sure she didn't take too much on herself. Lucas was good for her.

"Well, shit," I said after a while, breaking the silence that had spread over us. "That wasn't what I expected."

"Me either." Claudia tugged nervously at her braid before flipping it over her shoulder. "When Dastien called me while you were under Astaroth's hold, I already had one of his minions in my circle. That's how I was able to help you. I used his power and connection to Astaroth along with your bond to Dastien to get you free. But the magic Luciana used on you and me and my brother? It's lingering. We're tied to Astaroth."

"I know we're tied."

"You know?"

"Yeah. You haven't checked your voicemail." It wasn't a

question, because I'd for sure told her about the tie multiple times on there.

Claudia shook her head. "No."

"Okay. So this is what I know." I filled her in on what had happened from my perspective while I was in Astaroth's black abyss and what Eli said about the Seven, the fey, the seal, and Astaroth's plan. "Please tell me you brought some crystals back." I wanted to believe there was an easy fix to this, and that the crystals would be it.

Claudia took a second too long to answer, which meant that she hadn't.

Nope. No. We needed those crystals. "Can you go back and get them? Or have someone overnight them or something?"

"Even if I had any crystals—which I don't—they won't work. Not on a demonic tie. Otherwise, Raphael wouldn't have one."

Right. That made sense. "But they might still come in handy. Maybe we can use them in a potion to—"

"They're gone."

"Gone?" I prayed I'd somehow misunderstood her.

"Yes. I went back, but the crystals were dead. All of them. I think some of those evil monks must've found the mine and—"

"Shit." So that was a bust. I wanted to scream and cry and throw the table across the room, but that wouldn't solve any of our problems. "I can't believe Luciana's magic is still fucking us over. It's unreal."

"I know." Her voice was so quiet, but I could still hear the pain in it. Dealing with the fallout from Luciana's magic had to be just as hard on her as it was on me. If not harder.

I thought back to what I knew and what I didn't know. "A few hours after Muraco was killed, I was pulled into the abyss. I'm assuming that Astaroth needed the power boost from Muraco to take me, and he's going to need another one before trying again. Do you think that's accurate?"

"Abyss? Is that what you're calling it?" Claudia asked.

"Yes." My heart started beating too fast. "Don't say it." I didn't actually go to Hell. I wasn't sure there was any coming back from that, and my body had stayed with Dastien. But my soul had been somewhere close.

Claudia pursed her lips together. "I think you're right. Astaroth will need more power if he's going to make another grab for you or try to enter this realm. But it gets worse..."

I wasn't sure how much worse it could get, and I also wasn't sure I wanted to find out.

I closed my eyes and tried to prepare for what she was going to say next.

Whatever it is, we will handle it, Dastien said. *I don't know how, but we'll figure something out.*

The way he was talking, I wasn't sure who he was trying to convince more—me or him. *I know. I just don't know how it got this messed up so quickly.*

It's been brewing. We just didn't know about it, but we do now. So, we'll deal with it.

We will. We'll deal with it. I blinked my eyes open. "Tell me what you know." I was on the edge of my seat as I waited for her answer. Dastien was trying to be calm on the surface, but I could feel his rising fear. We were both still shaken up, and from how this discussion was going, there wasn't going to be an easy way to get rid of Astaroth.

"I don't think I should call another circle," Claudia said. "I'm pretty sure Astaroth can cross any circle we try to close. And I'm not sure any of my magic can be trusted. And I definitely don't think you should do any either. Especially force a vision."

That was basically tying our wrists behind our backs. "If we can't call a circle or do any magic or use my visions, then how are we going to fight this demon and win?" I laughed, but only because we were so ridiculously outmatched and she was nixing just about every advantage we had. "I know that werewolves are strong and all, but we're talking about one of the *evil mother fucking trinity* here. We're not that strong. Not even together. So what do we do?"

Claudia shook her head slowly. "I don't know. If we somehow could fight and win, that would be the end of it. But I agree. I don't think we'd win. With the Seven down so many members and the fey courts gone and us tied to Astaroth, I'm not sure there's enough magic in the world to stop the demon from getting what he wants."

"No." I refused to believe that. "He can't get to me. If he does, he'll use my power to open a portal and start the apocalypse. Eli said if we found the right solution, that he'd help, but..." If he helped me, I could be trading my tie from Astaroth to him. And maybe that was better, but—

No. I don't want you tied to anyone but me and the pack.

I don't disagree. But it might have to happen.

"Forming a tie with someone isn't a little thing. You should be very, very careful," Lucas said.

"We're in agreement there."

"What do we even know about an archon anyway?" Adrian asked. The guys had been so quiet as Claudia and I talked, I almost forgot they were there. "He seemed to be on our side, but I don't know what we should trust anyone at this point."

"No one knows anything about them," Lucas said.

"What do you mean no one knows?" Chris asked.

"I've only seen one once before. It was a long, long time ago, but he stayed away from the battle. Just watching. I did some research after that. They're mentioned in a few different texts, but there's not any information on them. And I've never personally known anyone who's spoken to one."

He wasn't making me feel any better about my run-in with

Eli. Dastien grabbed my hand and squeezed, letting me know that he was there with me. "Except for me."

"Yes. Except for you."

"What else do you know?" I asked. "Anything could help."

Lucas leaned forward. "They were around during creation according to most sources, but have been quietly in the background since then. They pop up now and then but mostly keep to themselves. There are supposed to be seven good and five evil archons. And I use good and evil liberally. Meaning the good ones will usually, but not always, favor on the side of light, depending on their purposes. The opposite is true of the evil. Iao, Seth, Saklas, David, Yaldabaoth, Eloiein, and Elilaios. Paraplex, Hekate, Ariouth, Typhon, and Iachtanabas. That's where all of my knowledge ends."

"Eli is Elilaois?" I asked.

"I think so, but except for the fact that he's on the lighter side of the gray area, I don't know anything about him."

There had to be more. This couldn't be everything that everyone knew. If there was no more information on archons, then how was I supposed to figure out how to make a deal with one?

I sent a look to Claudia begging for more, but she gave me one solitary shrug. "I don't know anything about them."

Okay. So that was horrible. "So Eli is what? A god?"

"No." Lucas's voice was so firm, I wondered if I'd offended him with the question. "Not God. Not an angel. Not a demon. But something in the middle of all of those things."

"So, how do I get ahold of Eli?"

"He's a watcher. If he's spoken to you, then we—meaning everyone on this plane—are in grave danger. And he'll show up and make a deal with you, but only if you meet his terms."

"Perfect. I guess it's too easy to assume he'll break the tie."

"No. Not if he said you had to do it," Lucas said. "But I'm not an expert. I know next to nothing about archons."

I almost laughed. The way he explained it, he was the only one who knew anything about them. "What do you think?"

Claudia glanced at her cup of tea on the table for a second before meeting my gaze again. "I wish I had an answer."

"There's always an answer," Adrian said. "There has to be a way to break the tie. We're just not thinking of it."

"Yes. Exactly that." Finally, someone besides Dastien was on the same page as me. "We don't have the crystals, and they probably wouldn't work anyway, but there's got to be a way. I'm open to any suggestions, as long as it doesn't involve me dying or selling off the rest of our souls. Once that's done, we can focus on figuring out how to restore the Seven so that this doesn't happen again."

"Random question, y'all." Adrian cleared his throat. "My demon bite is from one of Astaroth's minions. That isn't going to have the same effect—"

"No!" Claudia said. "Raphael was bitten by a zombie that was powered by Luciana's magic—which was actually Astaroth." She reached across the table to pat his hand. "You're fine. There's no tie."

Adrian let out a breath. "Well, that's one thing I don't have to worry about."

"Yes. You're fine," Claudia said. "The only reason I have one is because of the blood oath. Luciana was using me to amp her own power, and I knew she'd added something extra to my oath, but..." She let out a long sigh that was full of regret. "I thought Raphael was fine, but my best guess is that the demon saw a way in he could use later and took it. And Tessa—"

"The tie's been there since I was stripped of my magic," I said, and Dastien squeezed my hand tighter. "I just didn't know it."

"Shit," Chris said. "I'm sorry."

"Not your fault." *What are we going to do?*

I don't know, but Adrian is right. There's always a way. I'm not about to give up.

Me either. "If Claudia and I can't use magic to break it, then what are our options?" I asked, but all I got was silence. "Maybe Cosette could—"

"Nah. Not a good idea," Chris said. For whatever reason, Chris always seemed to connect with Cosette. So, I trusted him when he said that it wasn't a good idea, but from what Eli said, the fey had a big hand in this, too.

"Why not?" Adrian asked.

"Just don't." Chris's voice was as firm as I'd ever heard, so I was taking him at his word.

"Okay." But I might try messaging her on my own. "So what is a good idea? Who has power enough to break a tie to a demon? Do we know any demon experts? A witch. Some sort of Van Helsing person? Lucas, you're old. You've got to have something."

"I wish I did," he said. "We asked everyone we could before we came here, and got a whole lot of speculation, but nothing helpful."

I was starting to think that there was no good way out of this, and I couldn't do that. There had to be a way. I just didn't know what it was yet.

Chris shrugged. "I'm just here for moral support. This demon and magic stuff has always been so far from my area of expertise. But Cosette isn't going to be able to help."

Not the crystals. Not Cosette or any of the fey. Not magic. What else was left? What was I missing?

"There is someone else who maybe could help us," Claudia said, interrupting my thoughts. "The thing is, I don't know if she will. Or even how much she could help. I don't—"

"No. No! Don't backtrack now," I said. If Claudia was bringing it up, then I had to believe it was a plausible solution. "I can convince her. Or I can make Dastien do it. He's got the good abs. Just tell me where to point him. He'll say something in French. Take off his shirt. It'll work."

What are you dragging me into, chérie? He was laughing, but only on the inside.

I'm sure it won't come to that. I'll try to protect your virtue as long as I can. I let go of his hand and leaned across the table. I was desperate not to get sucked into Astaroth's realm again. I had to stop his plan from ever coming to pass. "Who do we need to see?"

"Her name is Samantha Lopez. She's kind of a cousin. Sort of. And she lives in LA, but—"

I shook my head. "A cousin in LA and I never met her? No way." I didn't have any relatives in LA.

"She's from my father's side. A second cousin once removed or something."

Okay. That made more sense. Our mothers were sisters. So, if it was her father's side, then I wasn't related to her, and maybe my mom didn't know about her. "She's a witch?"

"Not exactly."

"So, how can she help?" Adrian asked.

"She's got a unique ability. She deals exclusively in hauntings, but she does have some experience with demons."

"This girl sounds awesome," Chris said. "But we've been ass-deep in demons for a while now. If she has specific knowledge about them, why are we just now hearing about her?"

"Well..." Claudia looked at Lucas, and I knew they were talking, but whatever was said, it needed to be aloud.

"What is it?" This girl—whoever she was—sounded perfect. "You haven't brought her up until now. So, what's her deal?"

Claudia sighed. "She's a couple years younger than me, so

she's your age. Maybe not yet eighteen? Anyway, she visited a couple times before my parents took off, but I hated to drag her into Luciana's evil world. Plus, she's had enough stuff on her plate to deal with. The last time I spoke to her, she'd been looking into ways to bind her abilities. When everything with Luciana started to get worse a few years ago, I stopped emailing her back. She needed a friend, and I turned my back on her."

Claudia wasn't the type to do that kind of thing and not feel one hundred percent guilty about it.

"At first, when everything went wrong with Raphael, I thought about calling her, but it seemed like a long shot. Especially if she'd managed to get rid of her gifts like she wanted. And she wasn't super good with demons last I heard." Claudia glanced at her mate, who gave her a reassuring nod. "Muraco was so sure that Peru was where I needed to go, so I went there. But after everything in Santa Fe, I did some digging. With Luciana gone, I wanted to see how Samantha was doing and explain. I've been emailing her for weeks, but she hasn't answered me. But from what I've found out, I don't think she was able to bind her abilities. In fact, I think she's gone the opposite direction."

I had questions—like what kind of things this girl could do and what she was exactly—but I kept it zipped. None of that mattered. All I needed was help, and at this point, I couldn't afford to be picky.

"I feel bad asking her after all this time, but Samantha's the only other person I can think of," Claudia said finally.

"Let's give it a shot. The worst thing she could do is say no." And if she was open to it and could maybe cut the tie between Astaroth and myself, then it was worth it.

"I second that. Let's call her," Chris said.

"Actually, I think it's best if we go see her," Claudia said. "I haven't gotten her to take my calls or emails. But we're a little harder to ignore if we're on her front porch."

"And if it doesn't work out?" I asked.

"Then we come back here and do more research. We find another way, and we try that. Because I'm not giving up. Are you?" Claudia asked.

"No," I said.

"Neither am I," Dastien said.

"Me, too," Adrian said.

"We're all in. Let's go," Chris said.

"What about the meeting—" Claudia started, but Lucas cut her off.

"I'll talk to Michael. I think we can delay it by a day if necessary."

"Great." I stood up. "How soon can we head out? Do we need to book tickets? What's the—"

"Two hours." Lucas pulled out his phone. "We'll take my plane. We can be in LA by this afternoon."

The chokehold around my chest started to ease. This was good. We had the start of a plan. Something that we could actually do. A demon expert to talk to. It wasn't a ton, but it was a start. "I'm going to shower and grab a bag in case we're there overnight. Then I'm heading to the library. Going to do a quick search and grab anything I can on Astaroth for the plane ride. Meet in the parking lot?"

"Sure," Lucas said. "Everyone be there in an hour."

I let out a long breath. "Great."

"I'll head to the library, too. Get a head start on research," Adrian said.

"Awesome. Thanks." We all got up from the table, heading off to get ready for our sudden trip to Los Angeles.

It was funny how much my life had changed since I'd been

there last. That city wasn't home anymore, yet I felt a sense of comfort and relief about going back.

Yes, what was happening now wasn't good, but a lot of bad things had happened, and we'd come out of them kind of okay. And if this girl couldn't help us, then I'd find another way. Someone else. Something else. But I wasn't going to stop. Not while I had enough air to breathe.

Astaroth hadn't known what he was signing up for when he attached himself to me. That motherfucker was getting sent back where he belonged, and I sure as shit wasn't going to be joining him.

CHAPTER NINE

BY THE TIME we landed at the Los Angeles International Airport, I was ready to get something concrete done. We'd each brought a stack of books with us but found a whole bunch of nothing in them. Sure there was info on who Astaroth was— Great Duke of Hell, blah blah blah. Evil Trinity, blah blah blah. But the overarching theme was if you saw him, run or else you'd *die*. Painfully. Miserably. And him knowing who you were meant death.

It was safe to say that he knew me. I was pretty cool with the running part, but once he had enough power to cross the barrier between hell and earth, I was screwed. And I was still pretty much screwed even if he couldn't cross it. The demon had already managed to suck me into his world. He'd killed Muraco to do that.

The clock was ticking, and I couldn't run forever if he was tied to me.

If Astaroth won, he'd have the power to open a giant portal to Hell and demons would overrun the mortal plane. My death would fuel the end of the world.

Fun times.

As I stepped out of the plane, the sun hit my face. I grabbed my sunglasses from where they were hanging on my shirt collar and slipped them on. "Seventy-two and sunny." I moaned. "There's so much wrong with this city, but man, the weather's awesome. I've missed it."

"The smell is what bothers me the most," Lucas grumbled from behind me as I started down the stairs to the tarmac.

"What is that? I never smelled it before, but I'm assuming it's because my nose is so much better now..." Exhaust and sweat and dirt and garbage—so much garbage—all rolled into one indescribable aroma.

"Eu de big city," Chris said.

"Paris didn't smell this bad." It was bad, but not quite so revolting.

"Paris isn't in a valley," Dastien said.

"Ah. Right." It made sense. The smog was so bad that I usually couldn't even see the mountains, but a good rain or the Santa Ana winds would roll in and clear it out. Those were the days I used to look forward to. I could really see how pretty LA was then.

An SUV was waiting for us with a driver. *Is he Were?* I asked Dastien.

No. This driver will take us to the lobby of the private terminal. But the driver there will be a Were. Lucas wouldn't want to be driven by anyone else.

From the local pack?

Nah. LA is too crowded for a pack. We like space. But there are a few Weres who have made a home here.

I thought everyone had to have a pack?

No. It's better to have a pack, but you can live without one.

That sounded like an excellent option. One that I would be happy to take advantage of—

We're going to have a pack. I don't know why you think of it as a burden. Having a pack is a privilege, and if you stop to look around, you've already started one.

Lucas isn't in our pack. He's the Alpha of his own.

Right, but Chris and Adrian would be in our pack. More and more will come, and soon you'll have a pack full of people that you care enough about that being their Alpha will be an honor.

I don't even know what it takes to be the Alpha of the pack.

You're already being Alpha. You're always rushing to save everyone. Leading the charge. Protecting the werewolves that you care about and the ones that are weaker.

But aren't my friends rushing to save me right now? I mean—Astaroth is after me.

Only because if he takes you down, the rest follow.

Maybe so, but I still didn't feel like I knew what being the Alpha meant. All I knew was I was doing the best I could to keep myself and everyone else alive.

I blew out a breath. I had enough to worry about for now. I'd deal with the pack stuff later. Much, much later.

The private terminal was legit. Blue metal slats wrapped around the small, one-story building, hiding what was beyond it from view. A man in a suit stepped through the door, holding it open as we got out of the car.

"Just this way. We have your baggage already loaded into the car."

Wow. I've been to LAX a bunch, but I'd never flown like this. Please tell me we can come through here on the way back.

I'm pretty sure we can.

Okay. This did it. Being a Were was seriously awesome. Dastien and I had flown first class on our honeymoon, but this was way better. "Do you always fly this way?" I asked Lucas.

"Usually, but there are times when it doesn't work out."

"Like?"

"Like when a fey named Gobble transports you to Costa

Rica, and we're in a rush to get back to Texas," Lucas said with a little grin, and Claudia snorted a laugh.

"That's pretty specific."

"Well, it was a pretty specific kind of an event." His grin faded away. "But yes, I usually travel this way. The flexibility comes in handy when dealing with werewolf business, and I've made considerable investments for many years that have paid off very, very well."

I whistled. "You guys. Lucas is loaded."

He laughed it off, but it was impressive.

I hadn't been too keen on the whole going wolf thing at the beginning, but I enjoyed it now. And the perks? I wasn't sure I would've risked my life by getting bit for this, but it was still nice.

Another giant SUV idled at the curb on the other side of the building. "Where does Samantha live?" I asked as we all piled into it.

"I looked her up, and she's still living in the same apartment in some neighborhood called Los Feliz. Someone should tell them that's grammatically incorrect."

I snorted. "It's pronounced fee-lez, not fah-lease, and I don't think the locals care about grammar much. She's probably pretty close to Griffith Park, which is nice, but it's going to be a haul from here."

We settled into a comfortable silence as we headed into the thick LA traffic. We'd debated too much on the plane. I was all talked out, and until we had new information, I was settling in for a wait. I leaned against the door, resting my head against the window. Being back was weird. I'd spent my whole life here, but I never missed it. Not until now.

We could come visit.

Maybe. I'm sure I'll be tired of it in a few hours, but there's something nice about it.

He grinned at me, dimples denting his cheeks. *It's okay to like where you came from.*

I couldn't help but smile back. It was the dimples. They got me every time.

I poked a finger in one of the dents, and he laughed. *Just relax for now,* he said, and I shifted in the seat to lean against him. He wrapped an arm around my shoulders, drawing me closer to his warmth. *We'll be there soon enough, but being calm and centered will only help. Especially if Samantha's powers are anything like yours. Or how they were before I bit you.*

Fair enough.

At some point during the drive, I nodded off to sleep, waking only as we jerked to a stop.

"This is it," the driver said, pointing out the passenger side window.

I rubbed my eyes as I tried to fully wake up.

You were really out, Dastien said. *I'm glad you got some rest.*

Me, too. I feel like I could sleep for a million more years. I miss anything?

Not really. But we're here. Dastien nodded toward the window.

There was nothing to make this apartment building stand out from the others in the area. The street was filled with similar two-story buildings—tandem parking spaces took up the bottom stories and top stories broken into units. This particular one was painted a fading light pink with mint green accents that had yellowed over the years of sun and pollution.

Claudia checked her watch. "I checked into Holy Ghost's site, and it says—"

"Wait." Chris perked up. "What's Holy Ghost?"

"It's the private Catholic school that Samantha goes to." She shrugged. "As I was saying, the school's site says that it got out thirty minutes ago. It should take about that long for her to walk home. So, we should be here just in time to meet her."

"Does she know we're coming?" I asked.

"No. I was worried if I called or emailed, she'd disappear for the night. So, we're surprising her."

Great. Sounded like Samantha was going to be a *dream* to work with.

I got out of the car to stretch my legs, and the others followed. Adrian and Chris were shoving each other, laughing about something. Claudia and Lucas cuddled together, leaning against the car. Dastien stood off to the side, letting me take everything in. Giving me the space he knew I needed and would never ask for.

As I turned to take in where we were exactly, I spotted a girl coming up the road. She wore a blue, gray, and white plaid skirt. A white button-down was untucked, its long sleeves rolled up to her elbows. Her brown hair—almost the exact shade of mine— was piled up into a messy knot on her head. But it wasn't those things that stood out to me.

It was the silver skull earbuds that glinted in the sun. The way she side-stepped anyone who came close to her and looked like she was stepping over some things I couldn't see. She kept her head down as she walked. Sunglasses shaded her eyes from me but from her hunched stance, she couldn't be staring at anything else but the ground.

I stood in the center of the sidewalk, waiting as she approached.

When she was a few feet away from me, she stumbled back a few steps and froze. Slowly, she pulled the earbuds out and draped the wire behind her neck. "Whatever your question is, the answer is no. I'm not fixing that." She motioned her hand up and down at me as if my whole mojo was in need of fixing.

She was pretty spot on for not even touching me. Whatever power she had, it wasn't small-time.

Claudia's footsteps sounded against the pavement as she moved closer. "*Prima?*"

Samantha pulled her sunglasses off, squinting at Claudia. "Do I know you?"

"It's me, Samantha. Claudia."

Samatha's eyebrows raised. "Wow!" She looked Claudia over and then took in the guys. "Seriously, cuz? Why in the hell would you get mixed up with them?"

"They're good people," Claudia said, and she didn't even mumble. I wanted to give her a big high five for sticking up for herself, but I figured Samantha wouldn't appreciate it.

Samantha's gaze went back to her cousin, and her brows furrowed as if she were seriously considering whether or not that was true. "They're trouble."

Shit. She wasn't going to help us. Whatever happened between Claudia and Samantha back then must've been bad. "I need your help," I said.

Samantha nodded. "Yup. I can see that."

"What can you see exactly?"

"More than I want to." She slid her dark sunglasses over her eyes again. "A lot more."

"Like?"

"Like I know they're all werewolves, but you're not just wolf." Her tone is very matter-of-fact and almost bored, and I get the sense that she doesn't appreciate me testing her. Because that's exactly what I was doing.

"I can see the pack ties all wound around and spreading out like a yarn shop vomited up all over you. I can see the ties that bind you to the hottie back there, and the ones that tie my cousin to that one—" Samantha pointed to Lucas. "But that's all pretty obvious."

She finally looked back at me. "Because I also recognize you, Teresa. I've watched the news. And now that I'm looking at you, I want absolutely nothing to do with any of you. Two of you have ties to a demon, and from the look of the tie, he's a real asshole. So, if you don't mind, I've gotta get started on my homework. Midterms are next week, and my chem teacher thinks we should understand the material regardless of how shitty a teacher he is."

That was a pretty cold brush off, but at least she was honest. And she was right to not want to get messed up with this. If I were her, I wouldn't want to either. But I had to convince her to help us because Samantha Lopez was definitely the person we needed.

"Please, *prima*. We need your help." Claudia's tone was a borderline whine.

"And where were you the last five years?" Her words weren't too hostile, not yet, but I could see it coming from the defensive stance Samantha had taken. "Where were you when I was begging for help? Where were you when I got taken away by those idiots at child services and thrown into an institution?" Her words were dripping in bitterness.

I couldn't stop the hiss from coming out. She was institutionalized for her abilities. That was enough to fuck up even the toughest person.

"Yeah. It was as fun as it sounds," Samantha said. I couldn't see her eyes through the dark sunglasses, but I was sure that part was aimed at me. "You never came to help no matter how many times I wrote to you." She walked toward Claudia. "I begged you—"

Samantha looked off to the side for a long moment, and it was like the anger drained from her. When Samantha finally looked at Claudia again, she was much calmer. "You know what? I'm not doing this. Look, Cloud. I don't blame you for bailing on me after we found out all that stuff about my dad, but don't expect me to help you now."

With that, she stuck her earbuds back in and pushed past me and the rest of the guys. We stared at her in silence as she went around the side of the building to the stairs.

The door slammed behind her, and I sighed. "Well, that went fantastically."

"There's so much I regret, but what I did to her... I couldn't help her. I couldn't even help myself." Claudia tugged on her braid. "I'll go talk to her. I'll make this right. If she can see the tie to Astaroth, she can cut it. I just have to convince her we're worth helping."

I caught Claudia's arm as she started forward. "Actually, let me give it a shot." I didn't have all the history that Samantha and Claudia had, which might make her more agreeable. Or at least less bitter.

Claudia looked at Lucas and then shook her head. "No. It's my—"

"I'm not going to pretend to follow whatever was going on between the two of you, but I can relate to some of what she said." I huffed a laugh as I ran a hand over my forehead. "I mean, it sounds like she pretty much lived through one of my nightmares. My parents worked damned hard to teach me to keep my mouth shut about what I *saw*, especially at school..."

She seems very broken, chérie. That stuff about begging for help? It sounds like she's had as rough of a time as Claudia these last few years. Maybe worse. You want me to go in there with you?

No. As much as I want you there, I don't think it'd help. I can't imagine being locked up like that. And if she was in there long...

He stepped toward me, pulling me against him. *I'm thankful that never happened to you.*

Me, too. Samantha was like an alternate version of myself. If my childhood had gone any differently, I might've been her, instead of mated to Dastien and living a nice life. Granted, we were here because that life was being threatened, big time. But even in the worst of times, I was thankful for who I was, what I was, and for my friends. I had a lot to be thankful for.

Maybe Dastien had a point. Maybe I did have a pack. Maybe I would draw people to me. If there was one thing Samantha needed, it was a pack of her own. People who got her, despite the crazy. Even if she couldn't help me, I had to let her know that I was her friend if she wanted one.

But the fact was, I did need her help. I hoped that I'd find a way to convince her because I wasn't sure how much longer I had before Astaroth used his tie again. I had to break it or be prepared to lose everything.

CHAPTER TEN

THE STAIRS CREAKED a little as I walked up to Samantha's front door. The wood was nearly rotted through. If someone didn't fix them soon, there was going to be a terrible accident. I was a little nervous as I reached up to knock. I'd faced a lot of terrifying things the last few months, but nothing was as scary as Astaroth having a tie to my soul. I wanted it gone more than I wanted air to breathe. This girl was the only person I knew of right now who could help me. I had to change her mind, but I didn't have a clue how I was going to do that.

A whispered conversation filtered through the door. Spanish. Finally something not French. This I could understand.

What are they saying?

Shhh. I whispered back. *I can't listen in when you're talking to me.*

Dastien was quiet for a second, and I heard the mom telling Samantha not to be scared of her gift. To use it for good. It was something I'd heard from my mother time and time again growing up. I almost laughed as the conversation progressed. It was like stepping in a time machine, only not. We clearly had different abilities and were on different paths. But some of it was so familiar...

Then her mom started talking about how she needed friends. How she needed to open up. And Samantha said she had friends—her mom and some priest dude.

Her mom and a priest.

Fuck it. I was siding with her mom on this one. Samantha needed me to help her as much as I needed her help. I knocked three times, and the conversation stopped.

"Claudia," Samantha said as she swung the door open. "I—" She stopped. "Oh. Uh. It's you. I thought you were going to be—"

"Our cousin?" I shrugged. "Nope. It's just me."

"*Our* cousin?"

"Yup. We're kind of related."

Samantha looked back at a woman who had to be her mom. The mom was standing in the kitchen, where she'd been slicing some onions—the scent made my eyes water. The mom shrugged, telling Samantha that she didn't know who I was.

"Well, my mom and Claudia's mom are sisters. And—"

"Oh! You're Gabby's daughter," Samantha's mom said. "We met a long time ago. You were very young, and probably don't remember me. You girls actually played together."

"We did?" I smiled because I didn't know how else to react. "Sorry. I don't remember."

She waved it off. "Of course you don't, but you were having such a tough time with your abilities, and so was Sam and... Well, I lost touch with your mom, but now it seems like you're doing fine."

"I am." I shrugged. "Except for the whole needing your daughter's help if I want to live and stop the apocalypse."

"Oh, come on. Don't you think you're being a little dramatic?" Samantha asked as she leaned against the door jamb.

"I wish I were." I really, truly did. "I need your help. *Please*."

"Of course Sam's going to help you. Come on in, honey," Samantha's mom said.

Samantha shot her mom a look and then stared at me. Right in the eyes. We stood there like that for a while. She wasn't a Were, but she was something supernatural. I'd thought she was a witch, even if Claudia said she wasn't, but my eyes started to burn as I waited to see who would look away first. It was my first clue that I had no idea what Samantha really was. Witches didn't do dominance displays like werewolves, but Samantha wasn't a werewolf.

As the thought crossed my mind, she raised an eyebrow and moved back from the door. I took my gaze away from hers only as I passed through the entrance to the small apartment.

I hadn't been sure what to expect from outside, but it was pretty nice inside. Sure the furniture was a little well loved, but it was beyond tidy. The front door opened into a living room. They had a small dining table off to the right, and beyond that was the kitchen. It was an older apartment, and except for the cream-colored carpeting, it hadn't been redone at all.

Samantha's mom cleared her throat. "I'm going to clean up real quick and get you something to drink. You girls get comfortable on the couch."

I sat, but Samatha kept standing. She looked down at me as if she wasn't sure what to say, and I wasn't sure either, but I knew I had to say something. "A few months ago, I never would've been able to sit on this couch. I'd touch it and see a million things at once—visions of when it was being made. Flashes of anyone who touched it. Glimpses into their lives. If I touched a person, it was worse. I saw what no one is supposed to see or know except for them. I learned the hard way never to talk about what I saw, and until recently, it seemed like there was no happy ending in my future. I'd always be this freak and never get a second's peace."

She stepped closer. "So what happened?"

"Dastien bit me."

She snorted. "A werewolf bite isn't going to fix me."

"I wasn't saying that. I don't even know what your ability is, but life can get better. Sometimes in the weirdest ways."

She sat in an armchair bedside me. "I've already hit my low point, so anywhere I go from here? It's better. But uh... I'm not like you. I'm not a witch."

"So, what are you? Fey?"

She laughed. "No. Not that either. And despite the display outside, I'm not broken."

"I didn't—"

"He didn't have to say it aloud for me to see the look on your guy's face. I know pity when I see it." She leaned forward, keeping my gaze the whole time. "Here's the thing. It's not that I don't want to help you, but I've learned the hard way that messing in the spiritual realm isn't smart. It can do more harm than good, and from what I can see, you don't need anything else going wrong."

She paused as her mom brought over two glasses of lemonade and a tray of sugar cookies. "Thanks, Mom."

"Anything for my angel." She brushed a kiss on Samantha's forehead.

She laughed. "I've got too much of Dad in me to be anyone's angel."

"Nonsense." Her mom winked at me. "I'm going to leave you girls to it, but I'll be in my room if you need anything."

"Thank you."

She left and disappeared down the hallway. A door clicked shut, and I felt like I was missing something. Who was her dad? Or maybe more importantly—what was her dad?

"So what's this about the end of the world?" Samantha asked.

"A demon named Astaroth—"

"Oh shit." She leaned back in the chair. "You're really in it." Her voice was quieter, and her eyes seemed to lose focus as she stared at me.

"You know him?" This was good. I had a feeling she was going to be better than the pile of books we brought on the plane.

She blinked a few times. "No. I've never had the pleasure, and I never want to."

"He says that I'm the key to opening a portal from hell to here. Some sort of seal has been broken, which happened because the fey disappeared and there are a few missing members in the Council of Seven Alphas that rule all the were-wolves. We've been looking into it, and that seems to line up, but I don't think I can fix either of those problems. So, it's up to me to stop him, and I don't think I can do that without breaking the tie."

I tried not to feel disappointed as she closed her eyes for a second. I wasn't sure what else I could say. "Please. You can see the tie, which means you can break it. Right?"

"I don't know that I can. If it was some simple demon, sure. But Astaroth?" She finally opened her eyes. "Damn it. You're really screwed, huh?"

That was pretty accurate. "How can you see the ties? What are you?" From the outside, she looked like an ordinary girl in a private school uniform. The navy polish on her nails was chipping off. She wore a little too much eyeliner, but besides that and the nude gloss, she wasn't wearing any other makeup. Her eyes were as gray as a stormy sky, and as I watched, the storm in them roiled and turned dark.

I didn't smell anything on her besides coconut, rose, and

sage. Nothing flowery like the fey. No spice of a Were. Definitely no sulfur smell. And if she were lying about being a witch, she hadn't brewed any spells lately.

"Don't worry about what I am. Just know that I'm me. The better question would be what can I do?"

"Okay." She was right. It didn't matter what she was, even if I was curious. All I cared about was how she could help me. "What can you do?"

"You know how there are two planes?"

"Two planes?" I thought I knew what she meant, but I wanted to be sure we were on the same page.

"Like the living, mortal one. That's where we are now. And then the other one. Supernatural. That's where the underworld is. Where the demons live. Ghosts. All those fun things."

Ah. That I knew. "Sure. I'm following you."

"I exist on both."

Wait. What? "How is that possible?"

"I was born this way. It's just how I'm wired. I'm part human, part something else, which amounts to something like a medium. Or a medium meets an exorcist?" She shrugged. "I don't know what to call myself. I can't really do magic, but I can see the ties as physical things. If someone is possessed, I can usually separate the demon from the human. If there's a haunting, I can get the spirit to move on to their next life. Usually. Some of them are stubborn as hell."

Fascinating. The more she explained, the more questions I had, but I kept my mouth shut. I was just thankful she was telling me this much.

"Just know that the more you start messing in the other plane, the more stuff is drawn to you. No one needs that kind of drama, especially not me. Helping you means I'm opening myself up to who knows how many attacks, and I just—" She pressed her lips together as if to stop herself from saying more than she wanted to. "Apocalypse. How serious were you about that?"

"Extremely."

"Tell me everything. Start at the beginning."

At the beginning? "Like from when I got bitten? Because it's all sort of snowballed..."

"If that's where you think the story starts, then yes."

"It's going to take a bit."

"You got somewhere else to be?"

You take your time, Dastien said. *We're going to grab some food around the corner, but I can come back in a few if you need me.*

Go. I'll be fine. "I'm good here." Especially if in the end, she was going to help.

"Lay it on me." She grabbed a cookie and a glass of lemonade and sat back in the chair.

By the time I was done, the cookies had all been eaten. We'd slid down to the floor to be closer to the plate and made a few trips to the kitchen for lemonade refills.

Samantha leaned against the bottom of the armchair as she stared at the popcorn ceiling. "Shit." She looked at me. "Shit. This is really bad."

"I know. So, do you think you can help me? I'll owe you big time. Anything you need, any time of day. I'll be there. Although, I'll be there even if you don't help me." I winced. "I probably shouldn't have said that."

"Probably not." She blew out a breath and stared at the ceiling. "My dad is going to be so pissed." She stood up and brushed the crumbs off her skirt. "Okay. I'm going to help you." I started to jump up, but she stopped me. "But I don't know how much I can do for you. I *think* I can fully break the tie from Astaroth to

Claudia. Raphael, too if it's like his sister's. Except he's far away, so that could be an issue. But yours... It's sticky."

"But you'll try."

"Yes. But I can't promise anything."

A zing of triumph ran through me at her words. This was good. I didn't care that she couldn't promise anything. That she could see the tie and try to break it was a huge step forward.

This will work, Dastien said. *We're coming back.*

Good. The sooner we do this the better. I wasn't sure when Astaroth was coming back, but this was our chance to head him off. I wasn't about to wait. "What do we need to do to set up?" I didn't know how she did what she did, but if it was anything like the magic I knew, there were going to be things that had to be done first.

"It's not so much a set up as a timing thing. 3 a.m. is when the veil between realms is the thinnest—"

"So, we do it at 3 a.m."

"*But* that's also when his hold is the strongest."

"So not 3 a.m. Then when?"

"I'd say dusk because it's an in-between time, but my gut says 3 a.m. But it could get ugly. There's really not a great answer here."

I didn't like the sound of ugly. My stomach twisted into a giant knot and I hoped I wasn't about to be sick.

We'll all be there. I won't let him take you again.

I wasn't sure Dastien would have a choice. "Okay. Sounds like a plan." One I hoped would work. Because there was one easy solution that no one wanted to talk about.

If Astaroth was tied to me and that tie couldn't be broken... If him stealing my magic was going to bring on the end of the world... There was one thing I could do: eliminate myself from the equation.

No! Pure, white-hot rage burned through our bond.

Stop. It's just a worst-case scenario. But the fact remained—if it was my life or literally everyone else on the planet, then I couldn't rule it out.

CHAPTER ELEVEN

THE SUV PULLED into the parking lot of a crappy strip mall. Samantha said she needed supplies and a place to do her thing. So, we'd headed out in the wee hours of the night to kill both birds, but this wasn't what I'd pictured when she said shopping. Everything was locked up tight.

A boarded-up laundromat took up the majority of the block-long building. The ever ubiquitous but unique to LA combination Chinese fast food restaurant and donut shop took up the last storefront. From the painted hand and tarot deck on the widow of one of the middle stores, I figured that was where we were heading. It didn't have a name, but it was pretty clear that it was a place to get your fortune read. I used to avoid those places like the plague. I never was sure what someone else with the sight would see when they met me, and I didn't want to find out. But if this was where Samantha was heading, then that's where I'd go.

"Are you sure it's safe here?" Claudia asked, and I couldn't help but laugh.

"Define safe," Samantha said as she squatted down to undo the lock on the security grille that covered the front door. "Here we go." The metal groaned and clanked its way up, but no one would notice. It was nearly three. Cars were moving up and down the road, on their way to who knew what, but not even one person slowed down to check what we were up to.

If someone had told me that I was going to end up in an apartment above a tarot shop in South Central LA having some sort of a séance today, I would've totally called bullshit. But apparently, it was happening.

Samantha swung the door open, and five lawn chairs crashed on the ground. "Come on in," she said as she kicked the chairs out of the way.

"What is this place?" Adrian asked.

It could've been a little mercado with all the racks of goods crammed in here, but instead of groceries there were crystals and herbs and candles and who the hell knew what else.

Chris sneezed. "Sorry. Can't handle the sandalwood. Gets me every time." His eyes were looking red and starting to water. The way my eyes were burning, I was sure mine looked about the same.

"We won't be down here long. Angie set some stuff aside for me. Just gotta grab it and then we'll go on up." Samantha disappeared from view, and I started to check out the shop. A pack of tarot cards caught my eye, but Claudia slapped my hand away.

"You don't want to mess with that, *prima*."

"Why?"

She raised a brow. "While you're tied to a demon? You think that's smart?"

"Point taken." I turned away from them to check out a rack of candles. They were shoved haphazardly on the shelves in a rainbow of colors. Some were loose and looked handmade. Others were religious with saints on them.

From the various types of candles and dried herbs and incense, not to mention all the other junk crammed into the store, it was hard to concentrate. "We couldn't do this at your house?" I shouted toward where Samantha had disappeared.

"No way!" She yelled back. "No one should ever live where they do magic, let alone mess with realms there."

"Why not?" Claudia said. "That's how our whole compound was set up. We all have a craft room in our houses."

"I know. And it was dumb." She came out from the back of the store hauling a large canvas tote bag. "Anything you do between realms thins the veil and makes it so bad things can happen. Like a demon taking over the head of a coven."

Claudia's face went pale. "And you never said anything?"

"I was thirteen." She shrugged. "No one was going to listen to me, and it was already too late to matter for Luciana."

Over dinner, it'd gotten super awkward between Claudia and Samantha. The fiery scent of anger kept wafting off of Samantha, and if we had any chance of this working, they needed to get their drama sorted. So, while we waited for it to get late enough to come here, Dastien, Chris, Adrian, and I had gone for a hike in Griffith Park, while Claudia and Samantha talked it out. When we came back, things between them seemed a lot better.

Now, Claudia was the one smelling fiery, but it didn't seem to bother Samantha. "This way." She motioned for us to follow her to the other side of the store.

Yikes, I said to Dastien. *Still not going well between them.*

Might take more than one conversation, but it seems better to me. Dastien gave me one of his half-shrugs.

I nearly rolled my eyes. Sometimes guys just didn't get it.

What don't I get?

Nothing. I gave Claudia's shoulder a squeeze as I moved past and followed Samantha.

A beaded curtain covered the entrance to a darkened stair-well. I pushed through it and went up the stairs.

Samantha unlocked the door at the top. "It's not much, but I can't afford to rent a space of my own. Angie uses this for clients who want a reading with an audience. She's cool with me using it whenever I need to, and I help her out when I can." She flipped on a floor lamp. "Not a lot of lighting in here. Angie likes to keep the mood, you know?"

Thin wood planks made up the floor with a perfect circle painted in black in the center of the room. Wax remnants of candles long burned out dotted the circle. Some were white, others were red, black, or blue. It didn't have a super welcoming feel, but it didn't feel evil like Luciana's circle. So, I was calling this place a win.

"Is this Angie lady the real deal or fake?" Adrian asked.

"Fake mostly. Every once in a while she has a moment, but the people who come in here want a pat on the back or to hear that everything is going to get better." She snorted. "But that's not accurate. For most people, shit just sucks."

"You really think that?" Chris asked.

"That's what my experience has shown me so far."

"Damn. I hope things get better for you soon. We'll owe you one, so if you need anything, you can call me." Chris ran a hand along his beard as he looked her up and down. "But I won't be going to you for my fortune anytime soon."

"Thanks," she said. "And that's probably for the best, but let me know if you change your mind. Things are looking up for you." She gave him a wink. I didn't want to read anything into it, but I was starting to wonder if there was a connection between them.

"Are you being serious?" Chris said. "Because—"

Samantha laughed, and I looked at Dastien. *Are they flirting?*

When is Chris ever not flirting?

True. But maybe there's chemistry here...

I thought you thought he was going to end up with Cosette.

No. I said I thought they'd be good together, but I have no idea what's going on with Cosette and—

"Oh man. All this constant buzzing." Samantha rubbed her forehead. "I can't hear what you're saying, but the psychic chatter along both mate bonds is out of control."

"Sorry. We'll stop. All conversation will be out loud." I stared down at the circle on the floor. After what Claudia had said, I was a little terrified to even be in the same room as a circle let alone sitting in one. "So, what's the plan?"

"Chris, Dastien, Adrian, and Lucas are going to light the candles while you and Claudia sit in the center with me."

"Are you going to activate it?" Claudia asked.

"Yeesssss." Samantha drew out the word like Claudia was being slow.

Claudia started backing away. "No. I cannot get in another circle, and I don't even want to think what could happen if Tessa entered one."

"Don't worry," Samantha said. "If he comes through, we split. We've got the car out there."

Was she high or just insane? "But he'll chase us. We won't get away," I said.

"This is dangerous, but from what you told me, there isn't another option. Right?"

I gave Claudia a look, and she nodded slowly. "Right."

"Here's what's important to know. Yes, Astaroth can come through an active circle with an anchor like either of you." She looked at Claudia and me. "But without having a host, he can't stay in our plane for long. He doesn't belong here."

This was more info than I'd had before. If we could hold Astaroth off for a while, maybe we wouldn't have to defeat him. Maybe he'd just get sucked back to his plane. "How long can he last here?"

She shrugged. "Hours at the most."

I laughed, but not because it was funny. "That's more than enough time for Astaroth to slaughter us all."

"Not if we run. The farther away we are from the circle, the weaker he'll get until he's forced to come back here and recharge. He probably has a radius of about a mile. Maybe two-ish because he's so strong. And he could hang out here in the circle for a while waiting for us to come back, but a few hours later, he'll have to go back through the portal. Otherwise, he'd be too drained to do what he really wants to do. It takes *work* for him to exist here. He's got power, but it's not endless. And he's not going to sit here and grow weaker and weaker. He likes his power. Once we get away, he's going back through the portal to wait for his next chance. I'll feel him if he's getting close, and we'll run to the car. The driver is out there with the engine on. As long as we don't sit around, we should make it out of here alive."

"Sounds like you know a lot about Astaroth," Adrian said.

"Not personally, no. But I know demons. Honestly, they're pretty much all the same. He's worse—and more powerful—than most, but..." She shrugged. "Look. You gotta trust me. You guys came all this way for my help. I wouldn't suggest anything that would make your situation worse."

She was right. We'd come to her for help, and if we weren't up to taking her advice, then we were wasting everyone's time. I had to trust her. I'd told her the whole story, and she was the expert.

I started forward, but Dastien grabbed my hand. *Are you sure about this?*

She's right. Why would we come here if we weren't going to trust her enough to let her try to help us?

"Cut it out, dude," Samantha said.

"Sorry. It's habit," I said to Samantha but didn't look away from Dastien. I needed a second just in case this went to shit. I trusted what Samantha said, but I was scared. My heart was hammering so hard my chest felt like it was about to explode. This was either going to work, or it was going to be bad. As in totally fucked up.

He pulled me closer, and I brushed a kiss along his lips. A battle waged in him. He wanted to throw me over his shoulder, run, and never look back.

But we couldn't. I let go of my mate and stepped into the circle. "Let's do this." I was proud of how steady my voice sounded.

Samantha gave me a tight smile. "Great. Let me just get everything else ready." She hauled her tote bag into the center of the circle and pulled out four white candles. She went around the room, giving them to the guys, before going back to the bag. "And a match." She pulled the long stick out and handed it to Lucas. "Strike it anywhere."

He took it with a nod.

Claudia looked at her mate and then leaned into him. There was a bit of silence as they talked through their bond and then he gave her a big kiss. I looked away, giving them a bit of privacy.

You're scared. Dastien said.

Nervous, but that's normal. I mean, I can't be any worse off than I already am. Right? So, nothing to lose. I just hoped I was right. Claudia's nerves were making mine worse. A lot worse.

"You guys!" Samantha said. "Again with the silent talking?"

"Sorry. It's a habit. I'll try to remember." I rubbed my sweaty hands on my jeans. "What's next?"

Samantha was digging a few more small items out of her bag. She placed a small cast iron bowl next to her and then started emptying little zippies of dried plants in it. "As soon as Claudia gets in here, the guys will light the candles. I'm going to burn some herbs

—mostly sage, but a few other things, too—just to try and keep things at least neutral, and I have some crystals somewhere in here..." The contents of the bag clanked as she dug around. "Why is it always—Oh. Here we go." She held a crystal out to me. "Celestite for purifying." She showed me a light blue crystal that looked clear as glass. "Amethyst spirit quartz. Really good for detoxifying the spirit, which you need. Like whoa." The last one was a light pink-ish-purple chunk made up of a cluster of tiny little crystals.

She dropped all of them into my hand, and I stared down at them.

They felt warm, but I didn't know anything about crystals. If they worked, I was going to have to look into them.

"And finally, one last one. I just picked this one up down-stairs." Samantha pulled it out of her pocket. "A Herkimer diamond." My eyes grew wide, and she laughed. "Not that kind of diamond. It's a type of quartz. It's especially good with someone like you—who needs more of a psychic cleansing."

"Good call." I took the last one from her. "I could've used something like this for a while."

She turned to Claudia. "And for you, a celestite, amethyst spirit, and moonstone. The moonstone should calm you a bit. You've had a lot on your plate for a while now, so..." She dropped them into Claudia's hands as she stepped into the circle. I thought that something would happen when she crossed the line painted on the floor, but nothing happened.

Everyone was quiet for a second, and I caught Adrian shrug-ging at Chris. I guessed I wasn't alone in thinking that just by us standing in the circle together, Astaroth would come. But the circle wasn't active yet. So, there was still plenty of time for everything to go to wrong.

"What's first?" Samantha snapped her fingers. "Right. Gotta clear those crystals, or they won't do you any good." She squatted back down and grabbed out a match, scratching along the floor, sparking into flame. Then she grabbed out two bunches of sage and lit them.

"You have to do the crystal clearing yourself," she said as she held out the bunches for us.

"Anything in particular I should say?" I asked. I'd gotten much better at magic-y stuff, but I'd never done anything with crystals before. This was too important to mess up.

"Whatever you're feeling. I agree with the witches on that front. The words don't matter, but you have to cleanse the crystals or else they'll have the energy of everyone who touched them before you. Which I'm sure you appreciate the implications of, Tessa."

"For sure." I took the burning sage from her and sat. The scent of the sage overpowered everything in the room, but I didn't mind it. Especially since it was going to help me.

"You just want to make sure what you're saying and feeling is that the crystals are clear of whatever came before and only hold good intentions for you," Samantha said.

Claudia blew out the flame on the sage and started her chant. "Cleanse these crystals, remove the past. I've found my happiness at long last. Fill this space with joy and love. Send blessings from above."

Samantha shrugged. "Or you could say that?"

I laughed and blew out the sage. "Only good vibes here. Only good vibes here. Only good vibes here." I glanced up at Samantha.

"Not as poetic, but it'll do." She sat next to me and patted the floor on the other side. "Come on, Claudia. It'll be fine. You're going to be easier. The tie he has to you looks more distant or maybe superficial? So, you first. And hopefully, since you're linked to your brother, I can try to tweak him."

Claudia gave one last look toward Lucas and then sat. "What should I do?"

"Nothing. Just sit there. Guys? Light the candles."

Dastien sat directly in front of me outside of the circle. I wanted to reach out and hold his hand but knew I shouldn't.

Samantha lit another match and dropped it in the cast iron bowl. "If you're done, I'll take the sage." Claudia and I both handed her our bunches, and she added them to the burning bowl. "No such thing as overkill. Right?"

"I'm with you," Chris said. "Let's not pussyfoot around. I think I can speak for both Adrian and me that we're done with demons. We've been fighting them nonstop for weeks, and we want this over with."

"I'll do my best," Samantha said. "But you're mixed in some seriously bad stuff."

"We know." Lucas rubbed the match between his fingers. Light flared as he pressed the flame to the candle and then passed it to Adrian. "Please tell us if you want us to do anything else."

Samantha shook her head. "You're here for moral support. But not so much yammering along your bond, please. It's distracting and painful."

"Understood," Lucas said.

"Okay, cousin. You first," Samantha said.

"What do I do?" Claudia was clasping the crystals so tight that her hands were turning white.

"Nothing. It'll either work or it won't." She got up on her knees and faced Claudia. "This might hurt. You've got a lot of ties, and I gotta make sure I'm grabbing the right one." She held her hands in front of Claudia and started picking and poking at invisible things.

Lucas growled, and Samantha straightened as she pulled away. "Whoops. Sorry."

I sent Dastien a look. I didn't want to use our bond and distract her, but he gave me a nod. This was going to be okay. It had to be.

I knew I was getting my hopes up, but I couldn't help it. We needed this to work in a big way.

Samantha grunted as she swirled her hand in the air, and Claudia gasped. When I focused, I could see the bonds between the werewolves. Dastien had thought that unusual, but it seemed like Samantha could see exactly what I could. Claudia didn't have as many ties to her. She was only loosely attached to the Peruvian pack because of her tie to Lucas. But I could see the thick, bright line that tied Claudia to her mate.

Samantha pulled on it, and Lucas growled again. "Sorry. The tie ends somewhere behind it. I'm having trouble…" A bead of sweat rolled down Samantha's brow. "Hang on." Claudia gasped, and for a second, I thought Samantha's hand disappeared into Claudia's chest.

I blinked, trying to figure out where Samantha's hand had gone, but in that split second, Claudia gasped again. This time she fell flat on her back.

She laid there, heaving in giant gulps of air. I didn't want to mess with anything, but my cousin was thoroughly freaking me out. "Are you okay?"

Claudia started laughing.

"Dude. Are you okay?" Chris asked. He was on his knees, ready to jump into the circle.

"Everything is fine." Claudia jumped at Samantha, hugging her tightly. "Thank you. Thank you. Thank you."

"No problem." She pulled away and gave Claudia an awkward pat on the back. "Raphael should come see me. He's too far away for me to do much for him. Your twin link is weaker these days."

Claudia nodded. "I'll have him come as soon as he can.

Thank you. I really... I'm so sorry for everything that happened, and I appreciate you helping me more than I can say."

"My pleasure. Glad it worked."

I looked between them. "It really worked?"

Samantha wiped the sweat off of her forehead, and then started digging in her bag again. "Yup. She's good to go." She pulled out a big water bottle and started chugging.

"How? I saw you pulling at her mate bond, but I couldn't see anything else."

She set the bottle down for a second. "I'd say magic, but that's not accurate. Remember what I said before? That because of who and what I am, I can see both our plane and the spiritual."

"Yeah."

"Comes in handy. If a ghost is being a jerk, I can kick it to the next plane. Physically. But stuff gets a little overwhelming at times. I see *everything* that exists on top of each other all the time. Looking at Werewolves is mega annoying. You have all your pack ties and mate bonds and links to this Were and that Were. Claudia's a little easier. She's just a witch, even if she's tied to Lucas. Still took me a second to find the tie to Astaroth. It was hiding under her magic. Just think of it like a little tiny string that was wrapped around her soul. I ripped it off of her. Sucker was strong, but no big deal."

She made it sound like no big deal, but the way she was sweating and drinking water, it wasn't exactly easy.

"So, you ready for me to do the same?" Samantha asked.

"Yes." If it'd worked for Claudia, then I was all about it. Samantha was going to be my savior, and I'd owe her big time. I had a good feeling about this. "Whenever you're ready."

Samantha waved a hand in front of me and then jerked back. "Shit. This is really bad. I can barely see straight. Too many ties. Umm..." She turned to Claudia. "You should leave the circle. I don't want to be distracted."

"Can I come in?" Dastien asked. His anxiety beat down hard on me.

"No. You'll distract me worse than Claudia. Your bond to Tessa is a little overwhelming. If anything I'd have you leave the building, but I doubt you'd go," she mumbled the last.

I wanted to scream for him not to leave me, but I didn't need to. "Never." My mate's voice was firm, with a hint of wolf.

"I figured." She narrowed her gaze at Dastien. "I see your wolf coming closer. Don't go furry on me. Freaks me out."

I laughed. "And messing with the other realm doesn't?" Because I was more than a little freaked out by it.

She shrugged. "It all depends on what's normal to you. For me, this is normal."

I couldn't imagine seeing what she did every day. At least when my visions had been at their worst, I was able to put on gloves, and it was all good for the most part. From what I could tell, Samantha never got that kind of a break from her abilities.

She waved her hands in the air, and a searing pain went through my mate bond like someone was trying to rip it apart. "Not that one." My voice was sharp, but it didn't seem to phase Samantha at all.

"Calm down. Just moving it out of the way." Her gaze seemed to look through me as she tilted her head. "It's like Astaroth hooked into your soul. I'm having trouble separating it out. The tie to Claudia was superficial—like I said before, it was just looped around her—but you? It's in and out and all over the place. I don't know that I can get the tie out. Not without doing some serious damage."

No. No. Just no. "I don't care about the damage. You have to try." I sounded desperate, which was entirely accurate.

She blinked, and it was like her vision cleared. "This could be bad. Like so bad it might be dumb to try. I don't want to damage your soul or mess with all those bonds. And even if I can get a little strand and start pulling this thread out of you, Astaroth will notice. He could be here before I finish. I... You sure you want me to try?"

My stomach sank. I didn't come this far to give up. "There's a chance that you can do it?"

"Maybe."

What do you think? I asked Dastien.

I don't know.

I squeezed my eyes shut. Fuck. This was dumb, but my desperation and hope that she could somehow fix this was stronger than my fear. "Just try. Please."

She let out a slow breath. "Okay. Maybe lie down?"

That was easy enough. Whatever she needed, I was going to make it happen. She leaned over me, both hands resting just above my stomach, and closed her eyes.

She swirled her hands, fingers gesturing above my body. Then she stood up and yanked her hands upward, and I gasped. My whole body tingled like everything had instantly gone to sleep.

She clasped her hands together, knuckles facing away.

The tingling turned to a buzzing so strong, I was worried my teeth might rattle out of their sockets.

Samantha twisted her wrists again, and all the air left me as I flew up in the air.

I glanced down, and my body was two inches below me.

"What the—"

"Shut up," Samantha snapped, her eyes still closed. Her hands moved up my body, towards my heart and then she dropped down, laying flat on her stomach next to my body.

"Here you are, you asshole," she muttered to herself. "This

might hurt," she said a little louder, and then she reached between my body and soul.

Fire ripped through my body, and I screamed.

My soul slammed back into my body, and I writhed on the floor as the pain slowly receded. My ears were still ringing from my own screams in the silence that followed.

I had a second to breathe, and then everyone started yelling at once. A million questions. "What happened?" "Are you okay?" "What the hell was that?" My friends all had questions, but my eyes were glued to Samantha.

Samantha's eyes were wide, and her hands shook as she brought them to her face. "Oh fuck." She glanced around the room. "No. No. This can't—" She leaped for her bag, upended it, and then frantically sorted through the mess. "Where is it? Where is it? Shit! Yes." She grabbed something and spun to me, a knife in her hand.

I sat up. "What's happening? Is he coming?"

"Yes." She let out a whistle, and the sound rippled through my soul.

"What was that?"

"Help on the Otherside."

My heartbeat whooshed-whooshed, whooshed-whooshed in my ears.

I started to get up, but she grabbed my wrist, stopping me. "Astaroth's coming. Fast. And he's super fucking pissed." She was talking so fast, I barely understood her. But with every word she said, my heart rate ramped up another notch. "We maybe have five minutes before he's here. Probably less. Maybe a lot less."

"Then let's go!" Chris said.

"Wait. I should've brought this up before, but I honestly didn't think it'd come to this. And now there's no time, so listen

AILEEN ERIN

really fucking carefully. Like everyone's life in this room depends on it. Because it does."

"I'm listening," I said, trying not to freak out.

"We have two options. One, we run like hell. You get on a plane and leave."

That was a pretty solid option.

"Two, I give you a bit of my blood. You said at dinner that you had visions of the future which has helped you out of some seriously bad situations, but that he was blocking you from having them. Right?"

"Yes."

"Okay. It'd take too long to tell you why, so don't ask. But if I give you my blood, you can have a vision. It's a risk for both of us, but—"

Holy shit. I was so in. "Let's do it."

"No. Wait. We'd be bound for the next forty-eight hours, or until your body processes my blood out of yours, but there's a big con, especially when you have a demon on your ass."

"No. I'll take the vision. I don't care—"

"Wait! You have to hear the con. Are you listening?"

I hadn't always seen my visions as a gift, but they were. They were the reason I was supposed to lead the coven. I couldn't see the future exactly, but I had some foresight that showed me when I was making a wrong decision.

I needed that tonight, more than anything.

If I couldn't get rid of the tie to Astaroth tonight, then I had to have a vision. Not having access to them while trying to take down Astaroth was going to be impossible. He was too powerful. I couldn't afford to make a mistake.

This could be the difference between living and the apocalypse.

Whatever the con was, I didn't think it'd matter. "I'm listening."

"If you take my blood, you cannot let yourself get sucked into Hell again. Because you were alive here on this plane, Astaroth couldn't take you fully there last time. Your living body anchored you. With my blood, you can exist on either plane. If he took you again, your body wouldn't be on this plane anymore. You'd be alive when he took you, and you'd be alive for a while in Hell, but there wouldn't be any way for Claudia or anyone else to do some miracle magic and get you back. You'd go to Hell fully. You'd die there. Your soul would be his. Do you understand?"

What the shit? "That's one massive drawback." Especially knowing what I was up against.

"I know. You have about another ninety seconds before we need to run. Maybe two minutes if we're lucky. I have a friend on the other side trying to trip him up, but it's not going to last long. I can feel Astaroth getting closer. What is a vision worth to you?"

Right now, it was worth a lot. "I'm not going to get sucked into Hell again. I'll die before I let him take me there."

"Are you sure? Because—"

"A vision is worth the risk." We were running out of time. I was forgetting something important. "Will my blood turn you?"

"No." Her voice grew tight. "I am what I am. No amount of werewolf blood or bites is going to change that." Back at her apartment, Samatha had seemed pretty okay with who she was. With how she said that now, I wasn't so sure that was true.

This is scaring me, chérie. I don't know if this is smart.

I took a steadying breath and looked at Dastien. *I have to do this. We need info. We just can't let him take me again.*

Merde.

"Let's do this," I said to Samantha.

"Not much time left," she murmured as she swiped the blade against her hand, then handed it to me. "Grab my hand as soon as you cut yours. You'll have maybe five seconds to force a vision and then we have to run or we're all going to die."

Before I could think too much about it, I sliced my palm open and gripped Samantha's hand.

Everything stilled as her blood seeped into mine, and then the vision slammed into me.

CHAPTER TWELVE

THE FIRST TIME I died in my vision was just outside of the tarot shop, in the parking lot. Astaroth, still in the shape of a child, lifted me up by my neck. There was a crunch. My vision had a flash of black.

I was sucked back to the moment when Samantha and I touched hands.

And then I was speeding forward again. This time we got away fast enough. We floored it to the airport. Got on the first plane. We landed down in Texas. Argued in a room with the Seven about how broken it was.

Astaroth showed up.

Snap.

I was slammed back into the circle in that shitty room in south central LA. Samantha's hand hit mine. This time I tried going back to the compound when I got back to Texas. To see if Luciana had left anything behind. I was dead minutes after stepping on to the ruins of her house.

Snap.

Samantha's hand touched mine, and I was rushing forward again.

AILEEN ERIN

I went back to the circle with Samantha no less than twenty times before it stopped. I was laying on the ground, panting. Unable to process half of what I'd seen or any of the emotions that went with what I'd seen.

Dastien was leaning over me. The only way I knew it was real again was the fact that life wasn't whizzing by. Instead, it was painfully normal.

"Holy shit."

"What'd you see?" Samantha asked.

"How long was I out of it?"

"A minute. Maybe more," Dastien said. "You weren't breathing. I was about to start CPR." *Again. For the third time!* He yelled through the bond.

Everything clicked at once. "Run! Now!" I leaped up. "*Now!*" I screamed as I jumped through the door and down the stairs. I didn't wait to see if they were coming behind me. They would. None of my friends were dumb.

I swung the SUV's door open so hard it bent backward. "Shit."

"What the hell?" The driver yelled.

"Just get in!" Lucas was right behind me with Claudia on his back.

As I threw myself across the row of seats, I saw Dastien carrying Samantha. *Good call.* We could move much faster than she could.

Lucas slid Claudia down and into the car with one smooth move. Chris and Adrian jumped in after her. Next was Dastien and Samantha.

A roar rattled the windows of the tarot shop.

"Now, Lucas!" I screamed, but he was already jumping inside, bending the door as he moved.

As soon as he was in the car, the driver took off. "What the hell is that?"

The ground behind us shook. I couldn't see Astaroth, but I knew he was there.

A truck passed to the right of us, and it lifted into the air, flipping end over end, sandwiching the car next to us.

"Don't look back." I slapped the back of the driver's seat. "Just keep going. Fast."

"You don't gotta tell me twice," the driver said as he swerved across the lanes.

Only the sound of breathing, honking horns, and skidding tires followed us for the next few minutes.

My heart was racing. My body felt hot. And my hands were shaking. Again. I'd almost died—We'd all almost died. If we'd been a second slower...

We weren't. We got away. Dastien ran a hand down my back and then pulled me closer.

This time. But I'd failed. Not once or twice. But over and over. In my visions, I'd died so many times, and nothing we'd done had ever made a difference. The failure and fear hit me, and any last shred of hope I'd managed to hold onto was gone. "Fuck."

I couldn't stop the sobs that followed, even if my friends were in the car and I wanted to seem strong for them.

I wasn't strong. I was trying to be, but there was no way out of this. Not one with a happy ending.

There will be a way. Just because you didn't get all the answers doesn't mean we should stop fighting.

We can't stop, but we're going to lose. You didn't see—

I started crying harder. This was embarrassing. Humiliating. And to make it worse, I was going to die at Astaroth's hands. And if that happened? Everyone was going to die. All of us. No one could live for long if this plane was ruled by demons.

The pressure and weight of trying to find some way to stop

it from happening but knowing that I would fail...it was too much. I couldn't breathe.

Chérie. Stop. You have to stop. His arms were wrapped tight around me and his forehead pressed against mine. Waves of calm and confidence came through the bond, but I couldn't stop crying.

There was some grumbling and rustling as someone climbed over the seats. I felt Dastien's confusion as Samantha plopped over the back of the seat, kicking my shoulder with her knee on the way. I tried to get out of her way, but the driver braked just at the wrong time, and she flew the rest of the way over, hitting the floorboard in front of me with an umph.

I wiped my eyes with the back of my hand, but the tears were still falling. "You okay?" I managed to get out.

"Yeah. One sec." She grabbed my ankle, and then closed her eyes.

A second later, it was like the fog had lifted. I could breathe again. The despair and self-doubt I'd been drowning in a second ago were gone. "How..."

"Astaroth's good at making you feel like shit. A lot of demons can mess with emotion, and he's a strong one. Plus, he's got a hook embedded in your soul and he was just hella close and you have some of my blood in you. So, try to remember that. When I let go, those feelings will still be there. Ignore them. It's not about you. It's *him* making you feel that way. You have to separate yourself from it. Once he's back on the other plane, it should ease up. Okay?"

I nodded, and she slowly let go of my ankle. Her hand hovered over it just in case I freaked out again.

The emotions I'd been feeling weren't gone exactly. They were still there, a bubbling brew of soul-sucking nastiness. But this time, I knew that wasn't how I felt. Astaroth was making me feel this way so that I'd be easier to take down. Giving into the emotions was as good as letting him win. And that so wasn't fucking happening.

Better? Dastien asked.

I think so. Yeah.

I can still feel you—

I know. But that's not me. That's the tie to Astaroth. And I'm stronger than the tie.

Good. Dastien pulled me fully into his lap and rested his chin on my shoulder. "Thank you, Samantha."

"No problem. But I'm assuming we're heading to the airport?"

"Yes," Lucas said. "I think it'd be good if you came back to Texas with us."

"I second that," I said. "We need you."

"No. I can't..."

"Is it because of me?" Claudia asked.

"No. It's because of me. I..." She was quiet for a second. "I come with a whole truckload of baggage. The kind that will make your fight harder."

"Harder? How?" From all I could tell, she was only helping.

She pressed her lips together as she thought. "It's a long story, and none of it's important right now. But just know that wherever I am, demons find me. From the sounds of things, you've got enough of those. So, I'm going to keep my distance." She sighed. "I'm really trying to keep away from demon drama."

"And how's that going for you?" Chris asked.

Samantha settled back against the seat. "Some days are better than others."

"You helped us. We've got a lot of friends with a lot of different skills," Adrian said. "Maybe we can help you? Why don't you come with us and find out?"

She closed her eyes for a second. "Nah. I've tried a bunch of different things, and you know, sometimes you just have to be what you are. I'm cool with it now. But thanks for the offer."

"If there is ever anything we can do to help?" Claudia said.

"You'll be my first call, cuz. For sure."

"Good."

"Not to interrupt," the driver said. "But I heard you say that you were going to the airport?"

"LAX," Lucas said. "Plane should be ready shortly."

The driver didn't say anything or let out a sigh, but his shoulders loosened a little. He was going to be glad when we left, and I couldn't blame him. He'd had a brush with Astaroth, and that was enough to scare even the toughest of Alphas.

I leaned my head against the window. The tie wasn't broken, and I'd had a series of completely messed-up visions. I hadn't gotten what I'd come for, but I wasn't leaving empty-handed either.

It was now clearer than ever that I had to find a way to take Astaroth down or things were about to get a whole lot worse.

CHAPTER THIRTEEN

THE DRIVER GOT out and opened the door for us as we pulled up to the private terminal. This time the door fell off the hinges.

He looked at it like I would look at someone who took my last donut.

"Shit. I'm really sorry." I wasn't sure that helped anything, but I meant it.

"That's alright." His words were a little sharp, so I knew he was at least a little annoyed with me, but he wouldn't meet my gaze. "We all lose control every once in a while."

That was nice of him to say, but I still felt terrible. "We owe you one. Let me know if you ever need anything."

"I'll take you up on that," he finally dared to look at me for a second before glancing away again.

My visions had always made it hard to have normal interactions with people, but the fact that this guy was a little afraid of me and my power? It was odd. I wasn't sure I'd ever get used to the dominance displays. "Please do." I moved past him to wait for everyone else to get out of the car.

Dastien was next. He gave Samantha's shoulder a squeeze as he walked by. "Thank you for the help."

"No problem."

He came to stand next to me, but I waved him past. *Go on inside. I want a second with Samantha.*

You sure?

I nodded. *I just want to make sure she doesn't want to come with us.*

You already asked her, chérie.

I knew I had, but I wanted to ask her again. Just to see. I had a feeling that if she'd come with us, we'd have an easier time taking down Astaroth. I didn't like to ignore my feelings.

I don't like you ignoring them either, but we'll find a way. Even without her. He brushed a kiss on my forehead and went inside.

My attention went back to the car. Claudia was giving Samantha a long hug. "Please call me," Claudia said as she pulled away. "I don't want to go so many years before we see each other again."

Samantha shrugged. "That'd be nice, but I'm going to have to invest in some aspirin before I do. You werewolf couples and your silent talking." She rolled her eyes, and then looked to Lucas. "Be good to my cousin. You wouldn't want me as an enemy."

Lucas' laugh echoed my own. This girl had some real guts to threaten him. "I'm sure I wouldn't want that, but I do want to know more about what you do. We'll be visiting."

"Looking forward to it."

Claudia slid a hand around Lucas' waist as they moved past me into the private terminal.

Chris and Adrian got down from the car next. Samantha whispered something to Chris too quietly for me to hear and he gave one of his raspy laughs. "I don't see that happening," he said loudly. "Not a chance."

Holy shit. What did she say? I was going to have to ask Chris.

"Trust me," Samantha said. "Just be open to the possibility. Okay?"

He ran a hand along his beard. "If you say so."

"I say so."

Adrian punched Chris, and they walked into the terminal, leaving me with her.

I closed the distance between us. "Are you sure you don't want to come with us?"

She nodded. "I'm sure."

"Any way I can convince you to change your mind?"

The corner of her mouth lifted in a smile. "Nah. Honestly, you don't want me there. You'll find a way. I know it, but anything I do is tainted." I started to speak, but she cut me off. "You'll be better off without any more help from me."

I wasn't sure how we'd be better off without her, but at least I'd asked. I couldn't really blame her for not wanting to get even more mixed up with Astaroth than she already was. "Alright. Well, if you change your mind?"

She smiled. "Not a chance in Hell—"

I winced, and Samantha laughed.

"But I'll let you know."

"Okay." I blew out a breath. "Well, thank you. If you need anything…" It was the same thing that I'd said to the Were driver, but I felt like I owed her even more. She'd risked her life for us.

She nodded. "I'll let you know if something comes up."

"Great." I still felt like I was leaving unfinished business with her. I just couldn't look away.

Chérie. She's a big girl. She'll be fine.

He was right, but still. "You sure it's safe for you to go home?"

"Yeah. Astaroth isn't after me. Don't worry about that, but I just want to reiterate the forty-eight hours thing. It's not precise, just a guess. But be careful."

I stepped closer. "Can you tell me what you are?"

"I can, but you have to promise not to hold it against me."

"I won't."

"I'm sort of part demon."

My eyes were open so wide, they nearly fell out of my head. "How is that possible?"

"It's not entirely accurate, but it's the easiest way to explain it. My father was possessed and the whole parentage thing is a little blurry. But my mom totally makes up for how evil my dad is." She shrugged like it was no big deal, but it totally was a huge deal. "Anyway, that's life, right? Kind of intense for people like us." She stared off into the distance for a second.

Jesus. It was worse than I'd thought. I wasn't even sure what to say to that. "I'm sorry."

"No. *I'm* sorry I couldn't do more for you. The thing is, Astaroth really tied into you. Into your soul. The tie is on both planes, and I don't know how to break it, but I was thinking on the way here, and I have a guess."

Yes. This was it. I knew it. "I'll take it." Any guess was better than none.

"You're going to need something to cut the tie that exists on both planes, and before you ask, no. I'm not it."

"Then what?" I needed to know what to look for.

"I don't know. A spell won't do it. It needs to be something more concrete. Maybe a crystal. Or another demon. Or some sort of weapon. Just keep your eyes open to possibilities."

That wasn't as good of a clue as I'd hoped. "Even if I found something like that, how would I even be able to see the tie to cut it?"

"I don't know."

I blew out a hard breath. "Thank you." It was more information than I had ten seconds ago, and she might have been saving my life. "Just. Thank you."

"No worries." She gave me a half-smile. "I gotta get home before my mom loses her shit completely. I'll see you around, okay?"

I sighed. "Okay, but you'll let the driver give you a ride home?"

"Nah. I've got an app for that. He's got a lot to deal with." She motioned to the empty hole in the car where the door had been.

"If you're sure?"

"I'm sure." She reached for me and pulled me into a hug. "I know it doesn't seem like it now, but you'll find a way to get rid of Astaroth."

I swallowed. "You think so?"

"I do. I really do." She smiled as she spun around and walked away. I watched her go, waiting to see if I could think of something that could change her mind, but in the end, I kept my mouth shut.

She pulled a pair of earbuds from her pocket, quickly unwinding them and shoving them into her ears. Her head was down as she walked away while looking at her phone, and I let her go. But seeing her disappear in the distance left me with an empty feeling. Like I was leaving something undone.

All at once, I knew what was bothering me. I'd come here for help, which I'd sort of gotten, but Samantha felt like a kindred sister. I was leaving her here no better off. That felt wrong.

Had I come with the intention of helping her? No. Not at

all. But after meeting her, I felt like I was abandoning her. I was leaving her here alone to fight her own demons—literal and metaphorical—when maybe I could help.

She'll be okay. I could feel him moving towards me.

Will she? Because I wasn't so sure. *Did you hear what she said?*

Yes. And now she knows you have her back if she needs anything. He put an arm around my shoulders, pulling me back toward the private terminal. *Let's get on the plane. We need to start thinking up a new plan.*

He was right. I knew it, but I wasn't sure what kind of new plan we could come up with. In my visions, I'd seen a lot of new plans, and none of them had worked.

I spotted a small mini fridge under the counter in the waiting room. A spread of snacks was artfully placed on top of it. I grabbed a Diet Coke and downed it. Lucas said there was going to be food on the plane, but I needed something now. I grabbed a couple bags of trail mix and started eating.

It took about ten minutes for the personnel at the terminal to check us in and run our bags through metal detectors. We had to walk through them, too, but that was it. No long TSA lines. No fighting for seats at the gate. Before I knew it, we were getting into another SUV to drive us through the busy tarmac. The sun hadn't risen yet, but there must've been plenty of early morning flights today. I watched out the window as the car stopped for planes to pass by us on their way to and from the runways.

I was quiet as we finally got on the plane. My friends moved around, talking amongst themselves as the pilots got ready. The layout of a small plane was much different than a commercial flight. There were only a few seats that were actually close together, and as much as I didn't want to talk to anyone, I wanted Dastien close by. Hopefully, my friends would sense my mood and not take the two chairs facing ours or the couch beside them.

I took the seat against the window and settled in to wait.

Just try to relax. It's going to be okay.

I didn't know what to say to him, so I stayed quiet. My mood was partly Astaroth's influence, and I knew that, but I was also having trouble processing all of the visions and trying to figure out what not to do. They'd flashed by so fast that in the moment, I couldn't absorb them, but they were catching up with me, and it was making my head hurt.

I was a Were. We didn't get headaches. Even if there were a couple extra-strength aspirins tucked away somewhere on board, Weres processed medicine so much faster than humans, I wasn't sure they'd do any good.

I rested my head against the cold glass of the window and watched all the people rushing around on the ground. Everyone had problems. I knew that. But from where I was sitting, I envied them. It seemed nice to just be doing your job, and not have it be so life or death or end of the world.

I closed my eyes as we started to take off. I needed to find a solution before we landed. That gave me a little over three hours. I knew there had to be something that I wasn't thinking of, but all I could come up with were things we should definitely *not* do. So many things. I needed a notepad to write all of them down so I could sort through them all, and start opening my mind up to other options. Other solutions.

What the hell was I going to do?

In my visions, I'd tried everything. Or at least I thought I had. But there was something I was missing. There *had* to be. I knew it. But what?

The pressure to find an answer was suffocating me.

Everyone had gotten quiet as we took off, but once we were

167

in the air, the chattering started again. Louder than before. Until I couldn't concentrate.

I held up my hands. "Stop." I needed more time to think.

There was a second of silence before Claudia came to sit across from me. "We're here to help, but we can't do that if you sit there staring at nothing, trying to fix everything yourself. What did your visions show you? Just tell us, and maybe we can come up with some answers."

I knew she was right, but this was on me. At least it felt like it was. I leaned back in the chair and stared up at the ceiling of the plane. "My visions were horrible. Nothing we tried worked. I died—we died. Every. Time. I saw at least thirty versions of the next two days."

"No," Adrian said as he and Chris came to sit on the couch. "You were out for a minute. It couldn't have been that many."

"I think that's why my head is pounding. Magical overload."

"If you tell us what happened, then maybe we can come up with something you didn't try," Chris said. "We each have our own perspective. Together we can figure this out."

He was right. "I just don't know where to start." It felt like I was just starting to process what I'd seen, let alone find the words to explain it all out loud. It had happened too fast, and I felt like I was getting a bird's eye view rather than living through it. The more I thought back, examining each piece of it, the more freaked out I got.

Claudia reached across the table, grabbing my hand, but I pulled away. She looked to Lucas, but he just gave her a little nod of encouragement. "Just start at the beginning," she said. "What was the first vision you had?"

I took a second, trying to picture it. "We stayed too long. I mean—we left, but we waited for Samantha to quickly gather her stuff. That minute and a half was enough for Astaroth to come through the portal. We thought we were golden, but he was there in the parking lot and..." I rubbed the back of my neck. I could almost hear the snap. "Next time we ran right away. Got on a plane. We went to the meeting with the other Alphas at St. Ailbe's, but there was too much talking. Nothing was getting accomplished." I couldn't remember anything that would've triggered Astaroth showing up. "I don't know how it happened, but suddenly Astaroth was there."

"Wait. Where?" Claudia asked.

"In the conference room at St. Ailbe's," I said.

"That's impossible," Adrian said. "He couldn't—"

I wasn't going to argue. "Is anything really impossible at this point? All I know is that he showed up and we all died."

"Fuck," Chris said. "And you lived through this?"

I nodded. "Over and over again."

"No wonder you're upset." He got up for a second and came back with a candy bar. "This might help with the headache."

"Thanks." It came out short, so I took a breath. "Thank you."

"No problem."

"So, Astaroth showed up at the meeting. What happened after that?" Claudia asked, keeping us on task.

I blinked as I tried to sort one time out from the next. It wasn't until recently that I'd been able to see the future in my visions, and before I'd lived a possible future—a single future where I'd made a mistake—and then gone back to the present. My visions were a warning so that I didn't make grave mistakes. Usually, it was just one vision—one warning—and I could easily avoid doing that one thing. But this time, I'd had so many visions, and they'd come so fast—right on top of each other...it felt like there were way too many ways this could go wrong.

My head throbbed as I tried to make sense of them. "Next time we went to the compound. We were digging around the remains of Luciana's house and..." I rubbed my temples, trying to ease the headache that was forming behind my eyes. "I don't know. He was suddenly there."

"Were we doing a spell?" Claudia asked.

"No." I tried to remember—it was all getting blurry—but I didn't remember doing any spells. "No witchcraft. Nothing. Just literally looking through half-burned books and then all of a sudden he was lifting me in the air by my neck. And then..." I swallowed the lump in my throat. "I need water." I started to get up, but Adrian passed me a bottle before I could. "Thanks."

"What happened next?" He asked.

"We went to talk to Tía Rosa. He showed up."

"And then?"

I rubbed a hand across my forehead. "We flew to Ireland. We went to meet up with Meredith, who had some friends she was going to hook us up with. That was a disaster. Innocent humans died. Like a lot of them."

"Did we go to Peru?" Lucas asked.

I laughed. That had been a massive mistake. "We died as soon as we landed. Total shit show."

"This has to be a joke," Adrian said. "If there's nowhere we can run to... How is he even getting through at all these places?"

I wished it was a joke and I really, really wished I had an answer as to what we were supposed to go or how Astaroth was managing to beat us every single time. "I don't know. And I don't know what to do anymore. I'm open to suggestions. Because running doesn't work. As far as I experienced in my visions, everyone we went to for help from here on out ended up dying. We never straight up fought him, but I think that's defi-nitely the worst idea ever."

"I agree. He's too strong, and there's too much at stake if we lose." Claudia got up and started pacing up and down the small aisle. "We're thinking about this the wrong way."

If she thought this was the wrong way, then she had to have

an idea of the *right* way. I leaned forward, on the edge of the seat. "How are we supposed to be thinking about it?" If she had an even half-way decent idea, I was down for trying it.

"Well, you tried running. What about magic?"

I wasn't sure. "I think we tried a couple of spells, but we never got far with them before he showed up. I don't think we even finished a spell."

"Okay. So, we don't run. We look for a spell."

"What about Eli?" Chris asked.

I sat for a second. "I don't know. He never showed back up."

"But he said he would if you were on the right path. Right?" Adrian asked.

"Right. You're right. So, it makes sense that all of the visions ended badly and that he never showed. I was basically shown a long ass list of what not to do." I thought back on what the archon told me. "Eli said that with the fey gone and the Seven a mess that the seal between the planes was broken. So, we have to find a way to fix the seal before he'll show up. It seemed like a tangent to our goal, so we just never focused on that. But maybe that's where we went wrong."

"I think that's exactly where we went wrong." Lucas was usually so quiet. When he spoke, my hope soared. "Think about it. This all started with Astaroth breaking free, and that's what it sounds like we were focusing on in your visions. Literally how to stop him—magic against magic. How to keep him out of our plane. But there's more to it than that. The meeting that Michael is having is about the reformation of the Seven. Who's to take the empty spots? And—"

"Yeah. I was in one of those meetings. It was a bunch of chest beating and a whole lot of wasted time. Not to mention, Astaroth somehow showed up there, too."

"The meeting doesn't matter, but what did you learn in it?"

Holy shit. Lucas was on to something. "Their bond can't be

restored for five months. They need a lunar eclipse, and we can't hold on that long. That's why it seemed like a dead-end. Eli said we had to restore the seal and that the Seven had to be fixed, but we can't hold Astaroth off for a few days, let alone five months. Plus, it was fey magic that formed the bond, and they're not going to help us."

"No. They won't," Chris said. "Even if they knew what was at stake. They're too pissed at us for messing with their lives when we were outed. They're so stubborn. So stuck in their ways. They won't think outside of what they want and their rules." He crossed his arms and sunk back into the couch. I wondered who he was talking about just then—the fey in general or Cosette.

"Yes, but the bond of the Seven is the key," Lucas said, his voice had a quiver of hope. He was on to something, but I was missing it. "Eli isn't going to show up until you find a way around all of that and restore the seal between the planes."

I crushed the plastic bottle in my hands. "That's an impossible task. Maybe more impossible than beating Astaroth in a fist fight." We were so screwed.

"I know," Lucas said. "That's why we weren't in a rush for the meeting, but something needs to happen. We're not going to defeat Astaroth until we figure out a way around the rules. We're just as stuck in our ways as the fey. So, we need to be thinking bigger."

I turned to Claudia. "Can we force a lunar eclipse magically?"

"I don't think so. I mean..." She twirled the end of her braid in her fingers as she thought. "I've never heard of such a thing, so I don't think it's possible, but I could do some digging. I wish that we'd manage to scrounge some of the books on the compound before it was burned. We didn't have a library as large as the one in St. Ailbe's or the one in Peru, but every house had books. The books on craft at the school aren't great. And without better information..." She slid past Lucas to sit in her seat and grabbed her phone. "I'll see what I can dig up online, but it might not be doable."

I got up and started pacing where Claudia had left off. "Okay. So we have to find a balance. And the Seven is broken. So..." I froze. Oh, shit. Lucas wasn't the only one with an idea. And it wasn't something I'd tried in my visions.

"You've thought of something you didn't try in your visions?" Chris asked as if he was reading my mind.

I nodded.

"We're all ears," Adrian said. "What's your idea?"

"Maybe I'd failed because we were too focused on trying to fix what was broken instead of trying something totally different." I looked at Lucas. "What if we made a new Seven that wasn't the Seven?"

Lucas frowned. "I'm not sure I'm following."

"The Seven is old news. Done. Past tense. Instead of trying to fix the bond that the Seven had, what if we made something new? Something similar but better. Stronger. Something we wouldn't need a lunar eclipse for."

"I..." Lucas was quiet as he thought. "I guess I've never thought about abandoning the Seven entirely. I just..." He pressed his lips together. "The Alphas are not going to like it at all."

I agreed, but that shouldn't stop us. "Who gives a shit what they like? We're talking about stopping the apocalypse. If the Alphas had paid attention and maybe, I don't know, *not killed Ferdinand* without a way to replace him immediately, or not let Donovan leave, then we wouldn't be in this position. They're going to have to think outside of the box with this one."

"And if they can't?" Lucas said, a little too quietly.

"Screw them." I spat it out, and I meant it. "We don't need

any of them to approve what we do or how we stop the apocalypse."

"You might grow to regret going against the Alphas." Lucas' voice was a low rumble, and I knew I'd pissed him off a little, but I didn't care.

"Maybe, but at least we'll be alive." And at the end of the day, that's all that mattered. If the Alphas had a problem with how we save the world, well then, that was on them.

CHAPTER FOURTEEN

THE MORE WE sat and talked, the more complicated everything got. Figuring out how to do a spell as big as the Seven without drawing Astaroth in and without the fey seemed insanely impossible. We were landing soon and still didn't have any idea how to make it happen.

This was beyond *no bueno*. I wanted to have our next step in place so we could start fixing this whole mess when we hit the ground, but so far, we'd yet to agree on anything.

"You're still going to need a fey," Mr. Dawson said. We'd Skyped him a while ago, but the only thing he'd done was shoot down my plan and anything anyone else came up with.

"But say we can get Cosette—" I said.

"You can't count on that." Mr. Dawson cut me off. He was being a real Negative Nancy and wasn't being shy about it.

I shot Chris a look, who shrugged. "I've messaged her, but he's right. I've said it already. You can't count on her being able to get away, and you can't hold it against her. She's in a tough spot." When I asked about finding her, Chris had pulled out his phone, saying that they'd been emailing. He wouldn't say how often, but his cheeks had turned a lovely color of spring rose. I wasn't sure how she had email in her fey realm, but I wasn't going to question it or whatever was going on between her and Chris.

From what Mr. Dawson had told us over and over and over, the fey magic amped up the bond of the Seven, which in turn sealed the plane. So, it made sense that we'd need that kind of magic, but we needed to think of something outside the box, and I refused to count on Eli for it. He hadn't shown up in any of my visions. Not even one. But at this rate, I might have to.

"We might not have the support of the fey courts, but there have to be other options. What about a djinn? They're real, right?"

"No!" Everyone on the plane and Mr. Dawson yelled in unison.

"Okaaaay." So, that was clearly a bad idea. "Not a djinn." There was one idea that I'd been scared to bring up.

Luciana's spells got us into this mess. What if she left something behind that could get us out of it?

I knew even stepping onto *la Aquelarre's* land was tricky. I'd learned that much from the visions that Samantha helped me have. I'd died there a few times. I couldn't even believe I was contemplating it, but there was magic brewing there. Strong magic. That's the only way that Astaroth could've come through so quickly in my visions. So, what if I could find it and use it?

There were two problems with this. Whatever magic lasted there was probably black magic and trying to go get it would likely trigger Astaroth's arrival. Which meant I should just shove this idea where the sun don't shine. As in it was monumentally stupid. But I kept circling back to it in my mind.

I leaned back in my chair and stared at the fasten seatbelt sign like somehow it was going to give me the answer I needed.

"Whatever you do, the bond between the new council members has to be stronger than a pack bond. I just don't know

how you're going to achieve that. Even with witchcraft."
Michael's voice came through the speakerphone. "I don't see it
working without using the existing bond of the Seven. It's
broken, but that was allowed in the space of the magic. It can be
renewed. Holding on for a while seems like the smartest option,
but I don't know how we can hold on that long. There was
another demon attack at the compound."

"What?" Claudia yelled. "First you hold out on telling Tessa
or me about what was going on while we were away. And you're
just telling us now about another demon attack after we've been
on the phone for at least an hour with you."

"Right?" I said. This was total bullshit.

"I did what I thought was best. That's my job as the Alpha
of this pack."

"You can say that for Tessa because she's in your pack, but
I'm not. That land is mine, even if I want nothing to do with it.
If there was an issue with the coven's land, you should've come
to me."

"You're right. I'm sorry, but what you keep forgetting is that
all of you are young. I'm not. It's my responsibility to take care
of the younger pack members. Not have you rushing off into
danger."

I growled, ready to jump into what a load of horse shit that
was, but Lucas stepped in for me. "But I'm older than you and
more alpha. So, you should've at least told me."

I clenched my fists to stop myself from grabbing the phone
and crushing it. Mr. Dawson was driving me insane, but at least
I wasn't alone in that feeling.

Arguing with him now about what he should or shouldn't
have told us was a waste of time. "Astaroth isn't going to wait to
attack us," I said, bringing us back to the real problem. "We have
days at most, and maybe not even that. We try to wait around
for a lunar eclipse, we'll all die. Everyone." At this point, I'd

turned into a broken record, too. "If we make something new then—"

"I'm not saying you can't make something new," Mr. Dawson cut me off. Again. "We were already going to be struggling to try and fix the bond that's broken. But starting from scratch isn't a great idea." He kept talking, but I wasn't listening anymore. I appreciated his opinion, but he was stuck in the past. I wanted something better for the future.

What I didn't get is why it had to be *just* werewolves in the new council. If we added in some witches and some fey, then maybe we'd be better off? More magic seemed better to me. And diversifying meant that the safety and well being of every soul on this plane wouldn't be the responsibly of the Weres alone anymore. The fey and witches would be forced to work together with the werewolves. That seemed like a good thing. But apparently, I was wrong.

I don't think you're wrong, Dastien said. *Michael really is on a tear.*

Right? What do you think would happen if I just hung up on him? You think we could get everyone to say it was a bad connection?

Dastien laughed. *Probably.*

"What are you guys talking about?" Claudia asked as she motioned between Dastien and me.

I rolled my eyes and pointed to the phone. Mr. Dawson was still talking, but I was still fully ignoring him. It was time to hang up. He wasn't bringing anything new to the table.

"I think I can explain why Michael is so against leaving the framework of the Seven entirely," Lucas said.

I shrugged. "Please." Because clearly, I was missing something.

"My pack has the benefit of having a few non-werewolves with us. We've looped them into our pack bond, kind of how

I've done with Claudia, but bonds between unlike supernaturals are not necessarily as strong as the ones between like."

"Between like?" I wasn't sure where he was going with this.

"Think about it this way—You're overflowing with werewolf power, and that power gets amplified by the power that Dastien has. You can borrow each other's power when needed. Right? I've seen you do it."

"Right. We can." We used that all the time in fights.

"You're also a witch, which means that you have another well of power that's filled with magic, but it's a separate power. They're two different things." I started to say that it wasn't, but he didn't give me a chance. "When you talked about the night when you were stripped of your powers, there wasn't one jar. There were two. Right?"

"Yes. That's right." I didn't like thinking about the jars, but there were two.

"That's because you've got two sides. Both powerful. That's why Astaroth wants you. You have *two* deep wells of power."

"Right. So what does this have to do with the Seven?"

"The best comparison I have is that Dastien cannot boost your witch side and—"

Nope. "That's not true. Ever since I became a Were, my magic has been growing stronger. My visions have changed so much in the last few months. Isn't that because I'm a Were? So it can't be totally separate."

"Your magic is what it was always going to be—incredibly strong—because you were meant to *lead* a coven. As you grow further into adulthood, it will keep getting stronger."

I rubbed a hand across my forehead as I tried to understand what Lucas was saying. "I guess I never thought about it that way." Being a werewolf and my visions changing seemed to go hand in hand, but maybe that was a big assumption on my part.

"Your mate bond hasn't given Dastien any magic has it?" Lucas asked when I didn't say anything else.

"No," Dastien said. "I'm just as bad at spells as always."

"See?"

Damn it. That made sense to me.

"No matter how much I wish it weren't true, the bond I have with Claudia isn't as strong as it is between you and Dastien. And—"

"It's not?" Claudia asked. Her voice wavered just the slightest bit, and I imagined she felt like a kid finding out that Santa Claus wasn't real.

Lucas really put his foot in it, huh? I said to Dastien.

Pretty much.

"No. It's different than theirs, but that's okay." Lucas held her hand. "If you want to become a werewolf, we can talk about it. But I've done what I can to make our bond as strong as I can."

"I thought—" She cut herself off and I could tell they were talking to each other by the focus that they had on each other. After a moment, Lucas pressed a soft kiss to her lips, and she took a breath. "Okay. But I don't know if I'll ever want to be a werewolf."

I wanted to encourage her, but I wasn't sure which way. It was too permanent of a choice for anyone to make for her.

"I wouldn't have brought it up if I wasn't trying to help Tessa understand why the Seven was formed with just were-wolves," Lucas said. "There was an excellent reason that particular choice was made so long ago." He looked to me now.

"I get it." Lucas was making a lot of sense and was way more helpful than Mr. Dawson. "You're saying that the bond of the Seven was made between werewolves only to ensure that their power would be exponentially stronger together. If they had three Weres, three witches, and three fey, then the bond of the nine of them together wouldn't have been as strong as just seven werewolves."

"Exactly." Lucas grinned. "You seem to be leaning towards taking this new pact across species, and I think it's probably the right move in the long run, especially with how the fey just disappeared on everyone. Something like this would ensure that they'd come back—at least to some extent—but you're going to have to find a way to make those new bonds across different supernatural lines stronger than my pack has found possible."

At least he hadn't shot my idea down entirely. "What do you think we'd need to make a stronger version? Maybe there's some magic we could use to amplify it?"

"We'd have to do more than amplify it, right?" Adrian said.

"Yes. Amplify might be too weak of a word," Lucas said. "You need something that's going to tie this whole realm together. That's what made the Seven so powerful. They are the most alpha werewolves that are alive, and they bound their power together. Each wolf's powers were magnified six fold. And then to top that off, the bond had some fey magic to make them even stronger."

Wait a second. "That didn't weaken the bond?"

"No. It just cemented what was there, rather than being the source. Does that make sense?"

"Kind of." This was way more complicated than I wanted and it was making my head hurt trying to wrap my head around it.

"You're going to need a power source to fuel the bond, and I don't have any suggestions on how you could accomplish that. But I figure if you understand the problem a little better, maybe you can find a solution that I can't."

"Thank you. I appreciate the explanation." I hated to go back to Eli, but there was a reason he'd shown up on *la Aquelarre's* land. I couldn't rule him out. Maybe this new bond was what he had in mind when he was talking about making a deal. "Eli might be able to help with the bond. He—"

"There's not much information on archons, but from what I understand, they wouldn't want to be the power source," Mr. Dawson said. "That would take too much personal power from him. And even if he would agree to it, you're not going to want to pay the price."

I refused to believe that this was impossible just because it'd never been done before. If I needed a power source, then I'd just have to find one. "How much power do you think we actually need?"

"To seal this plane from the next? You need something with the equivalent of ten magical nuclear bombs going off," Mr. Dawson said. "That's why it was done the way that it was—with a lunar eclipse and fey magic—working to unite seven of the strongest werewolves alive."

I looked around the cabin of the plane. My friends all wore grim faces, but I wasn't going to stop, especially not when we were finally getting somewhere. "This mega nuclear bomb going off will create the bond, but are we going to need more power to keep the bonds going strong? I don't want to have them break on me once I find a way to make them."

"You're making this from scratch, so you could build it however you want it." Lucas was quiet for a second, but the way his lips pressed together, I had a feeling more was coming.

"What?"

He looked at Claudia, an apology clear on his face, and I knew what he was going to say. "I hate to say it, but—"

"I'm going to have to go back through Luciana's things."

Claudia hissed. "No. She can't!"

Claudia wasn't the only one pissed at that idea. Even though Dastien was still sitting in his chair, I felt him fighting the urge to smash his fist into Lucas' face for suggesting it.

Calm down. It might be—

You said you died in your vision when you went to the compound. Multiple times. You can't go back there. That's not just dumb, it's insane, and I...

Dastien kept ranting in my head while Adrian and Chris jumped on board. Claudia was silent, but from the way she was looking at her mate, he was getting the what-for through their bond. I could almost see the steam coming out of her ears.

I took a breath before I waded into the fight. "With how quickly Astaroth got to me and the demon attacks that are popping up every night there, I have to assume there's an active circle at the compound," I said loud enough for everyone to stop talking. "I think that means that something didn't burn in Luciana's house. And if something didn't burn, then that means she might have some magic there that could help strengthen the bond. You said it yourself, that the books on magic at St. Ailbe's aren't amazing. What if Luciana has a stash somewhere? A room that didn't burn? Even a storage shed somewhere in the woods? If it's there, we need to find it."

"I don't want to use anything that she did," Claudia said. "She—"

"Luciana was evil." That was a given. I wasn't about to argue about how bad she was. "But that doesn't mean that we can't find something of hers that could help us. Magic isn't inherently bad or good. It's all about how you use it, right? That's what Tía Rosa told me."

Claudia shrugged. "Some things. But there is dark magic and—"

"I won't use anything black. Or even gray." Probably. Maybe. "But if there's power that I can use? Something that allowed Astaroth to come through? Then we have to figure out what it is. Especially if we can use it to fuel the bond." I sighed. My next statement was going to get me in even more trouble with my friends. "But we need some fey. What about the ones who didn't clear out with the courts?"

"I've been fighting those assholes for the past few weeks. No way are we asking any of them for help," Chris said as he pulled out his phone. "I'm emailing Cosette again."

"Donovan is trying to get through to the Lunar Court, but he's gotten no answer yet," Mr. Dawson said. "At this point, I think you have to count them out."

"Then what we have left is a bunch of Alpha werewolves, some witches, possibly a few rouge fey if we can find them, and one archon. We'll make it work." At least I hoped we would, but honestly, I wasn't sure it'd work.

I wasn't sure we had enough magical power—even with whatever had survived the fires at the compound.

I wasn't sure if any of this would be enough to stop Astaroth.

I wasn't really sure of anything anymore. My plan was insane and suicidal, but I had to try.

CHAPTER FIFTEEN

WHEN WE GOT BACK to Texas, we split into two groups. Dastien and Chris went with me to the compound, while everyone else went back to campus to start researching a spell to make this all work. Claudia didn't want to step even a foot onto the coven's land again, and I didn't blame her. Not even a little bit. She would be better off researching anyway. For everything I learned about spells, I felt like there were twenty things I didn't know.

We turned a corner, and the sound of the tires on the cattle guard filled the car.

We were officially on the coven's land.

My stomach twisted into a tight ball of anxiety. "God, I hate this place." Not counting my visions, I'd been here twice in the last couple of days, and that was two times more than I wanted. Even though it was daylight, this place was still way too creepy. The burned remains of the houses and the abandoned cars parked in front of them reminded me of everything that had been lost here. It felt starker in the daylight, and I wanted to get gone. Fast.

Agreed. Let's keep this quick.

Yes, please. Even if I'd had a nice time getting to know my cousins, I wouldn't say that the short time I'd lived here had been enjoyable. I'd been here against my will, and only because Luciana wanted to drain me of my power.

I shook myself free of the past and focused on what I needed today: to find whatever magic was still active here and take anything I could use to forge a bond across supernatural lines. That was the only reason I was here. To detect the magic and counter it if I could.

"In two of my visions, we were digging through the remains of Luciana's house, and that's when he came. Which means somewhere in that mess—" I pointed to what was left of Luciana's house. "There's an active circle."

"What happened the third time?" Chris asked.

"You don't want to know, but there's a reason demons keep showing up in those woods." We were lucky nothing worse had happened when we'd met Eli, but I assumed that was because the archon was there.

Dastien stopped the car in front of the burned down remains. The chimney was left, as well as a couple support beams, but the rest was ash. When the pack torched a place, they didn't leave much behind.

"How the hell is it possible for a circle to be active in there?" Chris said as we got out of the car. "There's nothing left but some tile floors and the slab foundation."

I shivered as I got out of the car. It was so much colder here than LA. I was glad I'd brought a change of clothes with me on the plane. I was still in my Uggs and leggings, but I switched my T-shirt for a cozy plaid button-down and sweater. I reached back into the car for my hoodie and zipped it all the way up.

I shoved my hands in the pockets and looked at the house in question. "I'm not saying it makes sense, but that's what happened. So, I have to assume that there's an active circle inside that mess. The craft room was over there somewhere to the left of where the front door was, but it's gone. Which means any circle left in the craft room should also be gone." This was going to suck. "Something in there is still doing its thing, and we've got to find it."

"Well, at least we know it's not safe for you to go in there," Chris said. "And to be extra cautious, I don't think Dastien should step anywhere near this house. I don't know anything about demon ties, but if you're tied to a demon and Dastien is tied to you, then I can't be certain that Astaroth doesn't have at least a weak link to Dastien. But *I* should be able to go in there without an issue. I don't have a tie to the demon and Luciana's magic never touched me. If I step into the circle accidentally, I don't think it'll have the same effect, but be ready to run."

"We'll be ready," Dastien said.

Chris started forward, but I grabbed his arm. There was a lot I wanted to say to him—most importantly that he shouldn't go in there, but someone had to and he was the best choice. It was smart, but that didn't mean I had to like it. "Be careful." It was all I could come up with, and it was all that really mattered.

He nodded and then started forward again.

Dastien got back in the car and turned it around, ready for a quick exit. *Just in case,* he sent to me through the bond as I watched Chris step into the burnt-down house.

I placed a shaking hand over my stomach and reminded myself that this was different than the two times we'd gone in there in my visions. Everyone had been with me. I'd led the charge through the compound. Just because I was here didn't mean that Astaroth was about to show up.

Chris grabbed a pipe from the ground and pushed the mess around.

He'll be fine, Dastien said as he came around the car to stand with me.

He has to be. If something happened to him because I was too scared to go first, I'd never forgive myself.

My eyes started to burn, but I couldn't look away. I was too afraid to blink. I didn't want to miss anything. If something happened, if we were wrong and Astaroth showed, we weren't going to have a second before we needed to run.

Chris dropped the pipe with a clang as he squatted down, clearing a space on the floor. "Are there basements in these houses?"

I shrugged. "I don't think so. I mean, I don't think Claudia and Raphael's house had one." At least not that I remembered. I started toward the house. "What'd you find?"

"I don't know, but I thought this solid cement was the foundation." He looked at me, and I could see a glow in his eyes. His wolf was rising, and I knew he had to be freaked out, but other than the electric blue light from his eyes, I wouldn't have known. "There's a trapdoor here." He was standing in the middle of the living room. I didn't remember that many details from Luciana's house, but I thought there was a rug in the middle of the room, which would've covered a trap door.

I grabbed my cell, dialing Claudia. "What do you know about basements on the compound?" I asked as soon as she picked up.

"We don't have any."

"Luciana's house did. Chris found a trapdoor where her living room used to be."

"I..." She was quiet for a second. "The compound was built when Luciana was a kid, but it makes sense that there would be a place for the coven leader to store information. I never thought about it, but besides the schoolhouse, we didn't really have a library or even a central place to practice together, unless we were outdoors. I just assumed nothing like that existed there, and I never questioned it."

"Why would you? You weren't alive when this place was built. Who knows what this place is hiding, even now."

"I guess. I just..." Her exhale hissed across the line. "If it runs under her craft room, I wouldn't doubt that her circle was both on top and under. Which would make sense for it to still be active. Astaroth was the demon she was dealing with, and he'd want to leave a way in and out of this plane."

I nearly dropped the phone. "Shit."

"Exactly. Be very, very careful, *prima*."

"I'll do my best." I hung up and slid the phone into my pocket. "The circle is probably under the craft room. I can't tell exactly what was where in this mess without the walls, but probably about five to seven feet to the right of where you're standing."

Chris looked around the rubble. "If it's that big, then the basement might even be as big or bigger than the footprint of the house. I bet she's got all kinds of shit down there."

I didn't want to think about what she'd been hiding, which meant one thing. "I should go down—"

"No!" Chris and Dastien yelled at the same time.

I held up my hands. "Fine." But I was going to have to check it out eventually.

"Let me see what's down there," Chris said. "If it's cool, I'll get you to come down, okay?"

"That works." I wasn't sure what qualified as "cool," but I was reasonably certain I was going to have to see what Luciana had stocked her lair with.

"Here goes nothing." He crouched, and the metal groaned as he pried the trapdoor open. "Oh man. It smells like something died down there." He made a face, and then jumped down, disappearing from sight.

Instinctively, I stepped toward the house, but Dastien held me back. "Just wait, *chérie*. We can trust him."

I trusted Chris with my life, but I didn't like the idea of him going down there alone. Not even a little bit.

Me, either. If Chris isn't back soon, I'll go down after him.

I wasn't sure what good that would do. Dastien wasn't going to disappear down that hole without me.

What felt like hours later but was probably only a minute or two, Chris popped back up. I grabbed Dastien's hand. *Thank God. Maybe he found something,* but even as I said that through the bond, I noticed that Chris wasn't carrying anything with him as he walked toward us, except for a noxious odor. The closer he got, the worse the stench got.

"The circle is there—on the ceiling and a mirror of it on the floor. Don't know what that means, but it can't be good. And the room is filled with stuff and—" Chris ran his hand over his beard. His skin looked a little green as he stopped to stare up at the sky. "I don't want you to go down there, but I don't know what to take and what to leave alone. The thing is..." He swallowed. "The thing is, I was right. It smells like something died down there because they did. There are bodies in pieces piled up against one of the walls. Must've been witches, since there haven't been any missing person reports around here that we haven't already looked into, but kind of seems like what was done to Muraco. At least from what I've heard and the quick peek that I saw. I don't know what Luciana was doing down there or if it was Astaroth or what, but whatever happened down there...it's bad."

"Son of a bitch." I closed my eyes, saying a silent prayer for whoever had been killed down there. This was so much worse than I'd imagined. "I should see if I can break the circle."

Dastien's fear pounded at me. "That sounds like a terrible idea, *chérie.*"

"I don't like it either, but I like the fact that Astaroth could come through here anytime even less."

Dastien muttered something in French, but he knew I was right. "Fine. We all go."

"Let me go first," Chris said. "I'm going to need a tarp from the car. I can't do a damned thing about the smell, but I can cover the bodies for you."

I nodded. "Thanks." That was appreciated. I didn't really want to see them.

I moved away from the SUV as Dastien opened the trunk and started rummaging through the supply bag. "You wouldn't happen to have some tote bags or anything we could use to stash whatever we want to take with us in there, would you?"

Dastien looked over his shoulder at me. "Of course I do." He gave me a wink.

I was always impressed with how much crap the Weres kept in the back of their cars. From extra clothes to protein bars to first aid supplies, and now Dastien was pulling out two folded up tarps and three black reusable shopping totes.

Jesus Christ. The bag wasn't big enough to fit all of that stuff. "Who hooks you guys up with these magical bottomless supply bags? Because I could totally use one."

"JK Rowling. Obvi," Chris said with a look of complete seriousness on his face.

It took me a second to process his words, and then I snorted I was laughing so hard.

I bent over, trying to catch my breath. "Oh, shit. That was not what I was expecting."

Chris smiled, but it wasn't his full smile. "Figured you needed a laugh. You gotta be even more exhausted and stressed out than I am, and that's saying something."

I huffed as I straightened up. "Funny enough, I'm not that tired. I don't have time for it, and the fear really helps keep the exhaustion at bay." If we got through this, I was going to take one hell of a nap, though. I might not get out of bed for days.

"The duffels are just well packed, and honed from years of use. The Cazadores know what's typically needed, but the totes are a newer addition. They're those reusable grocery sacks. They fold up smaller than my wallet and can carry up to fifty pounds of crap. Suckers come in handy."

"I've got four in here," Dastien said, handing me two of the tightly folded nylon bags. "Hopefully that's enough."

"I hope so, too."

Chris took the tarps from Dastien. "You ready?"

"No," I laughed again, but this time it was a lot more desperate. "But let's do this anyway."

The dirt and debris crunched under our feet as we made our way to the trapdoor. The smell got worse and worse the closer we got, and I tucked my nose under my shirt. It didn't do anything for the smell, but it made me feel like it helped.

I looked down into the hole. The basement wasn't tall, but it was still a six-foot drop to the floor. "How did Luciana get in and out of here?" I could make it back up here with a jump now that I was a werewolf, but before? No way. Not a chance.

"There must've been a ladder or something that she stashed here that burned." Chris shrugged. "Give me a sec." He jumped down the open door, landing with barely a sound. After a little rustling, he yelled up to us. "All set."

I took one look at Dastien to gain the strength and then jumped. The ground was cement. I'd been expecting dirt for some reason. I squinted as I looked around the darkened room. "Any lamps down here?" I asked as Dastien landed next to me.

"I tried some, but none of them work," Chris said. "We could light one of the candles—"

"No!" There was no way I'd burn any candle that Luciana had down here. A little bit of sun came through the trap door, shedding a ray of light and shadows across the closest parts of the room. The rest of it was pitch black. "I can see. Sort of." And the parts that I couldn't see I could avoid.

A massive spell was written on the ground in white chalk and something brown, which I assumed was dried blood. Black lines crisscrossed through the circle. The candles on each point of the inverted pentagram had died out a long time ago—only puddles of hard black wax remained—but that didn't mean that the spell had burnt out. I could feel it tingling along my skin.

In the center of the inverted pentagram was a short altar— only six inches off the ground and three feet long. Rotting bodies of a black chicken and a black goat lay on the stone. They were mostly gone. What flesh was left was swarming with maggots.

At least nothing on the altar was human. It was gross, but it wouldn't give me nightmares.

A few items in the circle caught my eye. A goblet. A dagger. A quart-sized jar that had a few different things in it—the biggest of which was a feather. My fingers itched to hold them, but there was no way I was going to chance crossing the circle to get them just because I was drawn to them. Astaroth hadn't shown up yet, so he didn't know we were here. But if I crossed the circle? I had no doubt that he'd be here within minutes.

But why was I drawn to them?

I forced myself to look away and take in the rest of the room. I tried not to look at the waist-high, tarp-covered pile beside me, but my gaze kept darting toward it. "We're going to have to do something about them."

"We'll get a team here and burn everything once you get what you need," Dastien said. "It's the best we can do."

I nodded. If any of those people had any attachments to Astaroth, it really was safer than burying them. They were already dead. They wouldn't care what happened to their bodies now.

As my eyes adjusted to the darkened room, I noticed that it was a little bigger than the house. A few support beams ran through the area, but besides that, it was a wide open room. I still couldn't see the back wall—it was too dark—but on two of the closer walls, there were bookshelves. They were loaded to the point where I wasn't sure how they hadn't broken yet. A black, intricately carved armoire took up the middle portion of one of the walls, and my gut told me that there was going to be some essential stuff in there.

I turned to the guys. "Grab anything on magic about stealing powers. Calling up demons. Anything that mentions Astaroth in the title or table of contents or looks like it will help us make the spell we need or close off the magic Luciana did—including spell ingredients. Any books or ingredients that looks unfamiliar—take it. Even if it's evil. We can burn it later. But this house was someone else's before it was Luciana's. Could be that not everything down here was evil before she took over. So we're taking everything we can, and I want to be out of here in the next five." I'd only been down here for a minute, but my skin was crawling.

"Let's do this," said Chris.

With that, we all got to work.

I started looking at the books. Anything that had the word demon in the title went into my bag. After the eighth book went in, I started moving faster. Nearly every title had something in it that freaked me out. *Black Magic for the Discerning Craftworker. Channeling Demons: A Survey Study. Spells of Blood and Ash.* What the hell. "Nix my last. Just take everything."

"We're going to need some boxes," Chris said.

"Any chance you have some in your bag?" I asked Dastien.

He raised a brow. "What do you think?"

"Yes?"

He walked under the trapdoor and leaped up. A few

seconds later he was back with bankers boxes. "I only have three," he said as he started making them. "It'll have to do for now. We'll get this stuff. What do you think about the circle?"

"I was hoping not to think about it."

If we can break it safely, then we have to do it. I don't think either of us will sleep tonight if it's here.

He was right. I knew he was, but that didn't mean I wanted to get any closer to it.

"Any chance you have salt or—"

Dastien shook his head. "I really only have the traditional Cazadores bag. Spare clothes, first aid, food supplies, things to cover up something supernatural..." He shrugged. "Before all this stuff started with Luciana, if there was something magical going on, we'd just call a witch. We should probably update the bags."

"For sure, but that doesn't help us right now."

"Found it!" Chris said. "Here. Sage, too."

He held out a glass jar along with a bundle of dried sage. I took the jar and glanced at the label. "It says salt, but..." The metal lid sang as I turned until it opened. I gave it a big sniff, and it smelled like salt alright. I grabbed a little pinch and tasted it. "Seems like normal salt and I'm not feeling anything magical with it." I wasn't sure I could really cleanse anything with the pile of dead bodies in the corner, but I could try to at least break the circle. Dastien was right. I wasn't going to be able to sleep knowing that it was here.

I walked around the circle, dumping salt over it while saying the *Our Father* prayer. I would've thought that was enough, but the circle was still making my skin itch, so I went around it again.

And again.

"This isn't working." But I hadn't tried the sage yet. I found a match by the edge of the circle and struck it against the cement floor. The scent of the match covered everything up for a split second, but when it was gone, the rotting bodies smelled twice as bad.

I gagged as I lit the sage. "Hopefully this will help." I walked around again, cleansing the circle, and then continued around the room. To the corners. The bookcases. I set my intentions on getting rid of the old and evil, and urged the ones who'd died in this room—human and not—to move on.

When I was done, I wanted the room to feel better, but it didn't. Instead, it felt like the walls were closing in on me. "I think I can safely say that it didn't work. I can't break the circle."

"It has to have worked." Chris paused as he filled up the last box. "You were saying the right things. Maybe you just don't feel it because of all the other crap in this room?"

I looked at Dastien for a second before shrugging. *What do you think?*

I don't feel magic like you do. I'm a fighter and a werewolf. This place feels wrong, but I don't know if what you did worked or not. It should've, but we both know that not everything works the way it should.

I glanced back at the circle. The white salt was covering up most of the black circle now. Salt typically neutralized magic, but I wasn't sure what the deal was. The circle still felt evil as fuck. *The only way to know if it worked is to cross the circle, and I don't think I have the guts for that.* "Any chance the Cazadores keep grenades in their bags?"

Chris let out a surprised laugh. "No, but now I wish they did."

"What else do you have in your car that could—" A tingle of magic started tickling the back of my neck, and I scrunched up my shoulders. The urge to look at the circle grew stronger, so I ignored it and stayed facing the guys.

This is bad.

What's wrong? Dastien took a step toward me. I could actually feel *him* getting closer to the circle.

"You're mine!" The voice sounded right in my ear, and I jumped across the room. I slammed into the wall. A couple shelves broke with the impact, scattering books and jars to the ground. But I didn't care. My body felt cold even as sweat started dripping down my forehead, but I couldn't look at the circle.

Chérie!

I might have been imagining Astaroth's voice, but I wasn't about to take the chance. Not after what I'd seen in my visions.

I grabbed one of the totes from Dastien. "We're leaving. You've got ten seconds to grab whatever and then we're out of here."

What the hell is going on? Dastien asked.

"He's coming." I forced myself to look at the circle. Nothing had changed, but I couldn't deny what I'd heard. I ran to the armoire and threw open the doors.

Jackpot. Inside were some ceremonial knives, a few hidden baggies of things I didn't want to look too closely at, and ten more books.

The circle in the floor started to glow, confirmation that the salt and sage hadn't worked. Not even a little bit.

I scanned the room once more for anything I'd missed, but I kept going back to the objects in the center of the circle.

The goblet. The dagger. And the little jar with a feather.

The circle brightened, lighting the room with a red sheen.

He was almost here.

Dastien was grabbing some books, but it was past time to go. *Come on! We have to get out of here.* I yelled through the bond.

What do you see?

Don't you see the circle? It's glowing.

No. I don't see anything.

Shit. I glanced at it one more time, but the same three objects were calling to me.

It could be a trap. I wanted to take them, but I didn't know why. But Samantha had said to keep my eyes open. That I needed something that existed on both planes to cut the tie, and there was something about that dagger...

Screw it. Astaroth was coming anyway. And if any of those three things could save me from Astaroth, then I had to grab them.

Thinking about it more was a waste of time. I jumped into the circle. The black film of magic coated my skin like slime.

Ignoring Chris and Dastien's cursing, I grabbed the things I needed, throwing them quickly in my bag. "Run!"

Chris was already jumping through the trapdoor with the Bankers boxes when I turned around.

I sprinted to the trapdoor.

"You first!" Dastien picked me up and threw me through the hole. I landed on my feet and started running without looking back. I could feel Dastien jumping through the trapdoor after me and heard the thud as he hit the ground.

I'd never moved so fast in my life. Chris had gotten there first, so he was in the driver's seat. Dastien and I jumped through the open trunk.

I reached up to pull the SUV door closed. "Go! We have to get the fuck out of here! Now!" I screamed as Chris slammed on the gas, racing down the tiny road before I'd gotten the door fully closed.

I didn't want to, but I couldn't stop myself from looking back.

A figure flew out of the basement. I couldn't see any wings, but they had to be there. I'd never seen anything move like that before—hovering for a second before swooping to the ground.

The little boy from the diner landed ten feet behind the car.

The impact shook the earth. Dust and dirt splattered against the car windows.

I froze. Watching Astaroth come toward us.

Chris was driving fast, but not fast enough.

You're mine. Astaroth was getting smaller in the distance, but I could hear his voice like he was sitting next to me.

A cold sweat broke out on my face, and I covered my ears. I didn't want to hear his voice. I didn't want to be this close to him again.

There was a roar so loud I thought the windows on the car would shatter.

One of the witch's abandoned cars flew through the air, landing right in front of us.

Chris swerved, barely missing it. "Shit. What are we going to do?"

"Go faster," I said as I climbed into the front seat. "Samantha said that he loses power the farther we get from the circle. And it's daylight. He should turn back." I hoped she was right this time. Something about that circle felt different... "Just put as much space as you can between him and us."

"Shit," Chris said. "Shit. Just fucking shit." He took a turn too fast, and the wheels of the car started to lift off the ground.

You can run, but you're still mine.

I closed my eyes. "Did you hear that?" I whispered.

"No," Chris said.

After a second, Dastien said, "I did."

I spun to face him. His eyes were wide and lit with his wolf. His normally tanned skin looked ghost white, and a glimmer of sweat beaded on his brow. "You did." It wasn't a question because I could see it on his face. I could feel the answer from the panic I felt from him.

"Through the bond." *This is bad, chérie.* His terror burned like acid.

Dastien being scared amped up my own fear. We couldn't both be terrified. Otherwise, I wasn't going to get through this. I tightened up the bond, and he growled, stopping me.

"I can't handle your fear and mine right now. Try to calm down, please." I wanted to be able to send some reassurance through the bond like he had for me so many times, but I was struggling to find any, especially with how bad Dastien was freaking out.

There was something entirely unnerving about seeing my rock turn to dust, and he couldn't do that. Not right now. I needed him to stay my rock.

I'm trying. I just, I think I know why you've been having nightmares. And the terror when you had that vision or whatever it was... Tessa. Please tell me we're going to get through this.

"Can he come on St. Ailbe's grounds?" Chris asked.

I shrugged. "Luciana didn't draw a circle there that I know of, but her magic is there. So eventually, maybe? He came through in some of my visions." My heart started to slow to a more reasonable pace. "I'm hoping he's stuck back there for now."

"Me, too," Chris said. "But I'm not slowing down."

"No. Don't you dare slow down." The smell in the car was sickly sweet, and I knew it wasn't just me and Dastien that were scared.

The terror from Astaroth was real. Tangible. It had weight, but as we raced back to campus, I realized that I had to shut the fear down. It wasn't going to help me, not even a little bit. Fear never did. Astaroth wanted me too scared to think straight, and I couldn't let that happen. He already had the upper hand. He was powerful.

I shoved my fear deep down and built a wall around it. "That was way too close, but we got away." Thinking positive would have to get me through this.

"Any ideas on how to keep from running into him again? Because I want to never be that freaked out again," Chris said.

I wished I had a good answer for him. The truth was, we'd probably see him at least one more time. "I don't know anything more than I did a few minutes ago, but at least we know for sure that the circles Luciana cast are still open. I don't know how that was possible, but the fact that I don't know isn't that surprising. I'm so new to—"

"You're not that new," Chris said. "You're learning fast, and you have a good head on your shoulders. What does your gut say?"

"Claudia might know more..." I let out a breath. "But we got some stuff from Luciana's lair, and that's not nothing." Going through it all was going to take time we didn't have, so I was counting on Claudia to help figure out what was immediately useful.

"We're going to stop Astaroth," I said it aloud to make it feel more real. "I'll make it happen."

"Good," Chris said. His grip loosened a little on the steering wheel. "Good. Thanks. I needed to hear that."

"Me, too." And so did Dastien. He was currently bowed over his knees with his head in his hands. His thoughts were choppy as he tried to come to grips with what he'd heard.

That voice. The way Astaroth could shake the earth like it was going to rip in two. The fact that he could drag us down to Hell with him.

It was one thing for me to tell Dastien about Astaroth, for him to run from a beast in LA, but it was another thing for him to hear Astaroth's voice. It was like nothing else.

I'm going to figure this out, I sent through the bond, but he was still freaking out. It was understandable. I'd freaked out the night before, so he was due, but I had to make a plan.

First up was to get back to campus and sort through this

stuff. And then I was going to have to find a way to get in touch with Eli. Because if I couldn't make a deal with him, then maybe we really were screwed.

Dastien squeezed my hand. *We'll get through this, right?*

Of course. I just prayed I wasn't lying.

CHAPTER SIXTEEN

THE SECOND we stepped into the Admin building, I could hear arguing. There were a few voices layered on top of each other, which made it so that I couldn't quite figure out what anyone was saying or what the fight was about.

I followed the sound down the hall and into the library, with Chris and Dastien trailing behind me. I'd gotten off easy, only carrying one of the totes. The guys had the rest of the haul from Luciana's lair. The dark feeling that we were on borrowed time hung over my head, and the fact that my friends were fighting didn't make me feel any more hopeful about our situation.

I braced myself as I opened the door to the library. My friends were all standing around the table. Adrian was quiet. He had a stack of papers and some books in front of him. He was the only one actively doing research in the room. The gold star went to Adrian.

The rest of them...

Lucas was red-faced and seething in one of the chairs as he watched the commotion, which—shockingly enough—was mostly caused by Claudia. My sweet, proper cousin who blushed when I cursed was currently yelling at Mr. Dawson. And Raphael? He was screaming even more.

I was glad to see Raphael was back, but whoa. This was a mess.

I'd thought they were going to help me come up with some solutions, not sit around and bicker. What had gotten into my cousins?

I dropped the bag of books on the floor with a loud clunk, but the fighting kept going. "What's going on?" When no one stopped talking, I looked at Dastien and Chris, both of whom looked just as confused as I did.

Dastien gave me one of his half-shrugs, but he knew what they were talking about. He was much better at listening to select voices at the same time.

I'm not sure, but I think Michael said something that basically blamed the witches for everything that's happening.

Yikes. *How in the hell did that come up?*

Don't know.

Fighting right now wasn't helping. "This needs to stop. We just outran Astaroth. Again. I don't think we're going to get that lucky a third time."

"I'd prefer if there were no third time," Chris muttered as he set the two boxes on the ground.

"Ditto. We need to get them working again." It was past time for me to step in. "Hey, everyone."

Nothing.

I clapped my hands. "Hey!"

Nothing.

I couldn't do the loud, fingers-in-your-mouth-whistle thing, so I did the only thing that I figured could work, even if it could be considered a bit rude. But I couldn't think of a faster way to shut everyone up. "Stop talking! Now!" I shoved a ton of power with the words through the room.

Instantly the room went quiet.

I hadn't expected it to work that well, especially on Lucas and Mr. Dawson. "Thanks. Now, can someone please tell me what you've figured out?"

Everyone started talking at once, and I held up a hand.

I scanned the faces of my friends and found Lucas' gaze. I could almost feel him pushing against the power, straining to answer. "Lucas. Please, tell me what's going on."

"I'd be happy to, but next time, less power."

"Of course." As long as they didn't all start fighting again. "I'm guessing whatever you've found out, it's bad."

"The problem is that we've found nothing. I think most of this is stress. If we all just agree to put the poorly stated words from Michael behind us, then we can get back to work."

"Poorly stated words?" The question was full of venom. Her gaze narrowed as she took another step toward Mr. Dawson. I didn't think I'd ever seen Claudia this mad before. I had to admit, my cousin was kind of scary. "He's repeatedly stepped in when it wasn't his place. He still has yet to apologize for not notifying me about the demon attacks, and now —*now*—he says that it was *my* fault." Claudia shot her mate a look, but he pulled her down on his lap. They were quiet for a second before Claudia sighed. "You're right. We'll deal with this later."

"Fine," Mr. Dawson said, even though I was pretty sure he didn't mean it was any kind of 'fine.' "I have some other things to see to. I'll be back later." With that he stormed from the room, slamming the door behind him.

The room was quiet for a second, and Claudia sighed again. "What'd you find?" she asked me.

"Not sure, but we got a lot. Her basement was massive. Maybe a little bigger than her house."

Claudia's face went white. "No. How could it be so big? I

don't know for sure, but I really don't think anyone knew about a basement. Right?" She looked to her brother.

Raphael shook his head. "It's the first I'm hearing of it."

"I wasn't sure what I should take or not, but..." I looked back at the pile of stuff the guys had placed on the floor. "Hopefully it's something more than what you've found."

"Which is a whole bunch of nothing." Adrian shoved away the book he'd been reading.

"Well, maybe we have something now." I grabbed the bag from where I dropped it and walked to one of the tables. "So, there's good news, bad news, and really fucking shitty news," I said as I started putting the objects I'd taken last minute.

Claudia hissed when she saw the knife. "What's the bad news?"

"There are a lot of dead bodies in Luciana's basement. Not sure if it was Astaroth or Luciana—"

"My guess is Astaroth. Some of the bodies were fresh," Dastien said.

How did you know that? I asked him.

I'm a trained Cazador.

Right. But I just pictured Dastien staying around St. Ailbe's and teaching martial arts all the time. I guessed there was more to my mate than I knew.

"What's the good news?" Lucas said.

"We escaped Astaroth and made it back here alive." That was pretty amazing news in my book. "Go us!"

Adrian jumped up so fast his chair toppled to the ground. "Is he coming here? Is that the really fucking bad news?"

"No. At least not right away. Eventually, probably." I was trying not to think about that, though.

I put the last of the objects on the table and folded the bag before looking at each of my friends. "But the more important thing to note is that there's an open, active circle down there that Astaroth can enter whenever he wants, and I couldn't break it." Claudia made a whispering noise, but I kept going. "Not with sage or salt or prayer. I didn't have much time before he showed, so maybe it's still possible? But I'm not going back, and I'm not sure any of us should mess with it. The only reason we're still alive is because—as of now—he's still tied to that circle, but if he gets enough power to escape it, then we're screwed."

"What are you going to do?" Raphael asked. He was visibly shaking, and I didn't blame him. He was still tied to Astaroth. Just like I was. And since I was Astaroth's endgame, Raphael was probably up next.

I sighed. "We're going to make a new bond that seals this plane."

"We need to do it soon," Claudia said. "Tonight is impossible. There's not enough time to go through the books and find the magic and prepare a spell, but tomorrow or the next night at the latest." She paused and came around the table to me. "*Por favor, prima.* Tell me you found something awesome in there that will solve all our problems." Her eyes were wide, and from the sickly sweet scent, I knew she was scared. I was too, but that was a tall order, and I didn't have a great answer for her.

"I don't know. We got a lot of stuff, but we'll need some time to figure out what's usable. But for some reason, I felt compelled to take these three objects from Luciana's basement. Any thoughts on them?" I asked her.

"Other than that I don't want to touch anything Luciana used?" Disgust was thick in her voice as she crossed her arms.

"Yeah. Besides that." I knew she wasn't going to like anything I took from the basement—she'd made that perfectly clear—but I didn't have as many qualms about using anything that would save our butts. She was going to have to be a little more open-minded.

She sighed, leaning down to take a closer look. "The dagger feels evil to me." She squinted and then gasped, nearly tripping over her feet as she stepped back from the table. "The markings on it. I thought it was just texture, but it's people. And flames." She rubbed her arms. "I... I don't think we can use that for anything good."

The dagger's blade was about three or four inches long. I hadn't noticed that it was carved—I'd been in too big of a hurry —but now that she did, I could see the flames licking up the blade. The handle was long and curved at the end. I'd noticed that it felt bumpy, but I'd been in too much of a rush to actually see why. Now I could.

The flames crawled up the first quarter inch of the handle. Beyond that were naked people crawling on top of each other, terror on their faces, trying to get away from the flames. The ones closest to the flames were screaming in pain.

I rubbed my hands on my jeans. "Shit." I regretted even touching it. "The carving is so intricate that just looking at it, I feel like I can see the people moving and screaming, trying to get away from the flames. But they're tiny, and it's metal and... Shit. That's an optical illusion, right?"

Claudia frowned at me. "I can't believe you touched it."

Twice. I'd touched it twice. Once to take it from the circle and once to put it on the table. "I can't believe it either." I didn't want to ask, but I had to know what the deal was with the other two objects. "The jar?"

Claudia shook her head. "It's a spell or a talisman or something. I don't know. It could be anything, and if it was in the circle, there's no chance it's good."

Just fantastic. "And the goblet?" I didn't even want to look at it.

"I don't know. It looks fine, but I can't say for sure. Especially when you found it in Luciana's basement."

"She took them from the circle, next to where there were dead animals on an altar," Chris said.

Claudia crossed herself while some of my other friends let out some colorful curses.

"Why would you do that?" Raphael asked.

I shrugged. "I don't know. Astaroth was coming, and I just grabbed anything that caught my eye. I didn't think."

"Clearly," Raphael snapped.

"Watch it," Dastien said. The rumbling threat clear in his voice. "We're all doing our best here, and we don't know what could help us. We can't rule anything out."

"I think it's safe to rule those out. Nothing good is going to come from them." Claudia motioned to another table. "Come on. We can look through the books and the rest of the stuff over here."

I felt a little like a dumbass for taking that stuff. In retrospect, I shouldn't have even thought about crossing into the circle, let alone taken anything from it. But even as I walked away, there was something about the dagger especially that caught my eye. I itched to take it, but I wouldn't let myself.

I shoved my hands in my pockets and went to the other table where my friends were already gathered.

Are you okay? Dastien asked.

Just a little freaked out.

He put an arm around my shoulders. *Me, too.*

Tell me honestly, is this going to work?

It will because we'll make it work.

I had to take faith in that, even if I had no answers. Yet. Chris was already pulling everything out of the boxes and bags so that we could sort through it all.

"There are books and ingredients and other odds and ends. It might not be what we need, but it's a start to figuring out what we can do. We have to stop thinking about what's wrong and how messed up everything is and how we can't possibly fix it." I said that for myself as well as for everyone else. "We're all strong. Not one of us is without some—or a lot—of magic or power. The Seven might be broken, and everything might be going to shit, but that gives us an opportunity to do something amazing. We're going to form a new bond. Something bigger. Better. Stronger."

An idea hit me, and I went with it. "We're going to need three witches, three fey, three werewolves, and one..."

"One what? Don't say djinn," Chris said. "Because I'm not about to go start looking for some damned lamps. Those assholes are tricksters."

"No, although now I'm really getting curious." Shit. I couldn't believe I was signing up for this. "And one me. Because I'm a witch and a Were and a human. Although I don't know what to call myself."

"But how are we going to link such different supernaturals and have it be as strong as the Seven was?" Claudia asked. "Did you find anything about that? Because we haven't."

I was really getting tired of her nay-saying. She wasn't even giving this a chance to work. "I haven't had time to go through this stuff, but we're going to figure that out." I took a breath, trying to gain some confidence. Everyone here was just as anxious as me. "Something here is going to help us. Chris, any word from Cosette?"

He pulled his phone from his pocket. "Yes." The word whooshed out of him quietly. A grin spread over his face as he read the message and then he laughed and started typing.

"Don't leave us hanging," Adrian said. "What's the word?"

Chris' eyes brightened a little. "She's going to try to get here. It's not certain yet, but she wouldn't say that if she wasn't going to make it happen."

I really hoped he was right. "Tell Cosette we're going to

need more than her for the spell. I'll leave it up to her to pick, but they should be strong. And I don't care if they're rogues or whatever. But we need them."

"I'll let her know."

"Alright. Good." That was huge. If we had that and we had witches and Weres, then maybe this could really work.

I took another breath to steady myself, letting it out slowly. We were going to figure this out. We had to. "Let's pull the rest of the books in this library on magic—fey, angelic, witch, whatever. Claudia and Lucas, maybe you can be in charge of that? Anything you think we can use. And we need to form a bond between the new ten members. I'm open to any suggestions of what kind, but it should amplify power. Once we form the bond, Astaroth will be on our ass. My tie to him is still there, and there will be magic involved. So it's a given that he's going to show up."

"I'll see what I can find, but I'm not expecting to find much," Claudia said.

I ignored her negativity and grabbed the closest book. "Let's also look for anything about the portals between the planes. We need those sealed tight. Especially the one on the compound. If it were an ordinary circle, the salt should've killed it. So, it's something else. I don't want any demons coming through anymore. Maybe Raphael and Adrian—could you look into that? And if anyone finds anything about breaking a demonic tie, let me know. That has to go before all of this will work."

"What else do you need?"

"I don't know. Chris—maybe look into fey magic? If we understood what they used for the Seven's bond, then maybe we could recreate it. And Dastien and I will organize what's left. We'll need some whiteboards or something for ideas—"

"On it." Dastien walked deeper into the library.

"Okay. Let's make this happen," I said. Nerves were making

my inside flutter, but we were going to do this. We'd been in tight spots before, and we always came up with a solution.

I had to stay positive. No one was going to suck me down to a place I didn't want—or deserve—to go. Not even Astaroth.

AFTER WHAT FELT like ten hours later, but was probably only three, I found something that could actually work. The book was more like a journal, bound with three brass brads. The words were handwritten, with notes scrawling up the margins. Extra pages had been added—different colors—with no rhyme or reason. I'd almost written it off just because it looked worse than something I made for a school project in third grade. The writing was a little hard to read, but once I got used to it, the words flowed. Slowly, the journal started to make more and more sense.

The cover was black cardstock with white paint on it: *M la F.* I wasn't sure what that meant, but when I got to the part that said *"...power bonds between supernaturals aren't easy to achieve, but I know there's a way. Béibhinn has an idea that we shall try in the morning, but we need..."* chills ran over my arms.

I flipped through the pages faster and faster. "This could be it." The room quieted as I scanned the next couple of pages. "This is it. You guys. I thought this looked like just a personal journal, and it is, but it's more than that. Luciana was obsessed with gaining more power, and I think this is what she used to—"

"No! Absolutely not. We cannot use a spell that Luciana cast. There's no way that—"

I sighed. Claudia had been like this since we got back. She was being so stubborn about not wanting to use any of Luciana's things that she made me want to pull my hair out or strangle her. I wasn't quite sure which, but something was going to happen if her attitude didn't change. "Would you give me a second? Try to forget the association that Luciana brings to it."

Claudia slunked down in her seat. "Fine. But if it's dark magic, I'm not doing it."

"Believe me, neither will I." I already felt like I was treading a fine line by touching Luciana's things. "But this actually looks like something that might be fey."

"What?" Lucas reached for it. "Can I take a look at it?"

"One sec. I just want to read you this passage. See if it'll apply."

Lucas gave me a nod.

"It talks a bit about the moon and the stars here. But I don't know if that's important. You can read it and let me know. But this part feels like it's exactly what we're going to do."

Béibhinn was right about some of it. Fey and coven do not bond as we had hoped. The blood tie is essential, as well as magical intent. That was enough for now, but it is not as strong of a bond as I have with my own coven sisters. Adding in the ashes of those that came before us strengthened the bond as we expected. It is indeed better than the ones that I have seen before, but we need more power if we are to stop the dark days ahead.

We failed last night, but there is hope. I will not be deterred.

Going down a dark path would be the easiest, but with what is to come, it is not wise. We need another to bind the tie. I believe it is possible to stay on the side of light.

We shall endeavor to find a wolf on the full moon. The pack runs close to these parts. They have been

> *proven to be skittish of my kind, but I shall find a way to get at least one to agree.*
>
> *Tomorrow, we shall try to call an angelic force to us. If any still live.*

"What do you think?" I asked looking up from the page. "Sounds to me like this lady and her fey friend were trying to fight something bad. They needed a Were to make it stronger. Maybe my gut was right. It's a mix of *all* of them that make this possible. And then they said something about an angel. I don't know how to get one of those, but an archon is like an angel. Right?"

"Not really," Lucas said. "But Eli is powerful."

"Did it work?" Claudia reached for the book, and I handed it across the table to her. Lucas leaned over her shoulder to read.

"It doesn't say. The author goes into a little more detail about the candles and wording for the spell, but that's the last entry." Which made me worry that maybe it didn't work. But if the dark days they were talking about was an apocalypse, then it hadn't happened.

I glanced at Adrian to see what he thought, but he just shrugged. "Sounds like confirmation of your plan. Blood and ancestors' ashes aren't hard to come by. At least for us. But the fey? I mean—can the fey even die?"

"Course they can," Lucas said. "They like us to believe it's impossible. Makes them seem more powerful." He muttered the last, eyes never wandering from the pages Claudia was reading.

"The note here in the margin?" Claudia pointed to the page.

"Yeah. I didn't read those, what's it say?"

"It's in Luciana's handwriting. She was thinking of forming a bond with a werewolf and a fey but getting Astaroth to solidify it. She wanted to modify this part here—take away the sharing of power and keep it for herself."

"At least she was consistent."

"I know." Claudia shook her head. "I think that's why she agreed to have Cosette stay with us. She had to have known—"

Chris' phone vibrated, and he shot up from the table. "Be back," he said as he walked quickly out of the room.

As I watched the door swing shut, I reached through my bond to Dastien. *What do you think?*

I don't know. I only know the basics that they teach here. You're way ahead of me magic-wise.

I'm no expert, and you've been around this stuff your whole life.

You know more than you think.

No. I'm faking it and trying hard not to screw up. I wish I had it more together. That I knew for sure what the answer was, and—

"I think this is it," Claudia said. "With a few tweaks. Unless Cosette has another idea when she gets here. It's almost too easy."

"The spell didn't seem easy to me. The ingredients alone are going to be tough to track down."

"Not that. I mean—that Luciana had it. That you took the book. It's too easy."

"I know, but we don't have a ton of time. Maybe it's divine intervention."

Claudia and Lucas shared a look, and then Claudia nodded. "Okay. I'll call it divine intervention because this spell is too perfect not to try."

"We need ashes of our ancestors. It sounds like you need direct ones, at least a few generations removed, from each person involved. Do we have that?" Worst case, I knew we could dig up some of the bodies from the compound and burn them.

"We have werewolf ashes. Some of the ancients, which tie to all of us. What about witch ashes?"

Claudia shook her head, but Adrian started digging through the box. "I saw something..." he said as glass jars clanked together. "Here." He passed it to Claudia.

Her brows scrunched as she read the label. "This is our great, great grandmother's ashes. Luciana must've dug her up and..." She placed the jar on the table with a thunk. "I hate that she did that."

I didn't want to upset her, but we were using them. "Are they tainted by anything that Luciana did?"

She yanked the rubber band off of her braid. Her fingers trembled as she quickly rebraided it. "I don't know," she said, finally. "I just don't like it."

"We can use all of our blood," Adrian said. "That's not a problem. Lepidium meyenii is maca root. We should have that. Ground celestite should also be stocked in our labs, but I don't know about the rest. You said you took some stuff from Luciana's room?"

"I don't want to use anything she used. Even in preparing it, she could have tainted it with her dark magic," Claudia said.

"We might not have a choice, especially with the ashes," I said. If it was between using something Luciana had touched one time or not doing the spell at all, I was going to try it. "Maybe we can cleanse them?"

"It doesn't work that way."

I blew out a breath. If Claudia wasn't going to give on anything, then I wasn't sure what to say. "Let's at least look to see what we have before we make any decisions." It was time to see what we grabbed from Luciana's craft room.

Dastien was already getting up, grabbing the box that held all of the ingredients we'd taken from Luciana's lair. After taking a first glance at everything, we'd quickly decided to look at the books first, and put everything else back in the boxes until we had a plan.

"It says we need a candle that has rendered fat from a fey," Adrian said, with a shudder. "I've never seen a fey with enough fat to spare, and I sure as hell don't know where we'd find one willing to part with their flesh."

I blew out a breath. That not only sounded disgusting, but impossible. "We'll just have to improvise with something else."

"You're doing a lot of improvising." Claudia's frustratingly snippy tone got under my skin.

"Seriously? What is with your attitude?" This was so not like her.

Lucas shot me a look like he'd be happy to skin me alive, but I ignored him. If we were going to make this work, then she had to be on board. The one thing I'd learned about witchcraft was that it was mostly intent and willpower. The words in the spell weren't as important as the intention and the power given to you by how much you believed them.

This whole thing was going to be held together by grit and determination, but one seed of doubt could turn the spell into a dumpster fire.

Claudia finally met my gaze. "I'm just mad."

"At me?" She had to be kidding. "What did I do?"

"Nothing." She winced. "You've done nothing wrong except being the unlucky one that's trying to problem solve. You're talking about all these crazy solutions, and the thing is—I don't want to do any of this."

"The spell? You don't like it? I thought it was divine intervention?"

"I don't like *any* of what we're talking about. I don't like using Luciana's leftovers. I don't like looking at a book that has her writing in it. The idea of it..." Tears welled, but she quickly blinked them away. "I thought all of this was over. I'd survived

217

against everything Luciana had done. And so had my brother and a few others, but the rest of the coven died. Everyone I knew and loved *died*. But for whatever reason, we lived. And I ended up with Lucas. And I was done with Luciana and her stupid blood oath and black magic. I could finally live my life. Everything was great. But it's not over, and I'm not sure it ever will be." She slouched in her chair, head bowed, silent sobs shaking her.

I hated that this was happening as much as she did. Even if it wasn't exactly Luciana messing with us from beyond the grave, it felt like it was. This all started because of her, and we were *still* dealing with the fallout.

"I get it." I really did. "I was on my honeymoon, and then everything changed. I've almost died a few times over in the last couple days. But you have to let that go, or we don't have any hope of fixing this."

"I know. I do." Claudia squeezed her eyes shut as she swiped her tears away. "I'm mad that this is happening. That Luciana is dead and she's still messing with my life. And seeing her stuff here? Reading her handwriting? Somehow it makes it worse."

I went around the table to Claudia and leaned down to where she was sitting in her chair, giving her a hug. "We're going to fix this," I told her softly. "It will be over. Say it in your head a million times, but don't you dare let a seed of doubt enter your mind." I pulled away but held onto her shoulders. I needed her to hear this part. "I can't have you in this spell if you don't truly believe it will work."

"It will work. I'm just..." She wiped under her eyes again. "I'm frustrated, and I've been taking it out on you. I'm sorry, *prima*."

"It's okay." We were all having a rough time, but this was going to pass. We were going to get through it. Not because we knew how to or had it all figured out. But because that was what we had to do.

Chris came into the room, and I straightened. "Please tell me you heard from Cosette."

"Better." He moved aside, revealing her.

A grin spread across my face, and I felt as if I was floating. I ran to Cosette and nearly tackled her to the ground. She wasn't big on hugging, and neither was I, but in that moment, I felt like my plan was coming together.

Her being here meant everything.

I had a real shot, and that's all that mattered to me.

This was so fucking happening.

CHAPTER SEVENTEEN

A LITTLE WHILE LATER, I had a pile of notes, some missing ingredients, and a pretty solid idea of what we needed to do. I had a minute to revel in the fact that my shitshow of a plan was coming together before we were put to the test.

Mr. Dawson stuck his head in the library. "It's time."

"Time?" My immediate worry was that Astaroth was here, but he was way too calm. "For what?"

"The meeting. The Alphas are waiting."

It was like someone had dumped a bucket of ice water over my head. The shock that I'd completely forgotten about the stupid meeting was that sharp.

I couldn't imagine doing anything other than what I was doing right that second—making sure that we had everything we needed to take down Astaroth. The Seven and other Alphas weren't going to like that I was about to demolish their whole system of rule. Telling them now was not only going to be a waste of my time, but also extreme drama. And that was all before factoring in the fact that in my visions, Astaroth showed up during the meeting.

To say that I was unmotivated to show up for the meeting

would've been an extreme understatement. It was the last thing I wanted to do. "Can we reschedule?"

"There's no rescheduling."

"You're joking." When he started to shake his head, I put down the pen I'd been making notes with. "Why would they care if I was there or not? I'm just some kid. A newbie Were when you think about it. They won't care if I skip. Let them sit around and argue about the Seven. I'll get this done in the next day or two, and that meeting will be moot. Tell them I'm having horrible cramps or something." I honestly didn't care what excuse he made. Going to the meeting wasn't a priority.

Mr. Dawson stepped fully into the room. "You might be new to this life, but you've already proven to be a powerful alpha, especially to the group that's gathered for this meeting. And according to the media, you're also the unofficial spokesperson for the werewolves. If I could get you out of this by saying you were having cramps, believe me, I would, but you're going to have to trust me that this is something you have to do."

Trust him after he kept critical information from me?

He meant well. He was just trying to do his job. Being Alpha.

By keeping us ignorant of a brewing problem? If he'd come to us two weeks ago, we would've had more time.

I know, but he didn't. So you have to let that go, and deal with what's in front of us.

That's what I'm trying to do, but now I have to go talk to the Alphas? I glanced around the room, but my friends were just waiting for me to decide. All except for Cosette. "If you go, I'll go, too," she said.

"Thanks." I appreciated that, but I didn't want to go at all.

"Your ultimate goal is to unify the wolves, right?" Mr. Dawson asked.

I wasn't sure my goals were that lofty. "I just want to live."

"And beyond that?"

I shrugged. "Honestly, I've been living a little day to day since I got bitten. I'm just trying to keep up with everything." It was weird how I'd gotten accustomed to living crisis to crisis.

"Well, I'd like to think that you want to keep the peace between werewolves," Mr. Dawson said.

That didn't sound like a bad thing. "Sure."

"You skip this, and you won't. Maybe I could convince the Alphas to have the meeting without you and Dastien, but when you do this spell and rework our whole system of governing? They won't forgive you. You'll be making very powerful enemies for life."

A chair squeaked behind me. "As much as I hate to admit it, Michael's right," Lucas said as he stood from his seat, pulling Claudia with him. "We're going. I won't tell you what to do, but I will say it would be stupid if you didn't at least show-up and give them a warning."

Cosette started toward the door, too.

"It seems like a massive waste of time," I mumbled to myself, but it sounded like I was alone in that thinking. *I guess we go?*

Adrian and Raphael can keep digging up the ingredients. We can always walk out, but I think we have to at least warn them. They can't stop us from what we're going to do, but we'll have to deal with the Were community eventually.

"Alright. Let's go," I said, and Mr. Dawson looked a little relieved at my words. "Adrian and Raphael? Do you mind staying to keep working on this?"

"Sure," Adrian said.

"You want me to stay here and help?" Chris asked.

"Nah. Come with us." He'd been key to getting Cosette to show up, and I figured that meant he'd earned his spot there.

His eyebrows rose. "Okay. Sure."

Before I left the room, I went over to the pile of discarded stuff and grabbed one thing. The dagger.

I didn't know why, but I needed to take it with me. Leaving it behind felt wrong. Especially if this was what Samantha had meant. If I could use it to break the tie, then I needed it with me. Only Raphael and Dastien saw me slide it into the pocket of my hoodie. Raphael shook his head at me, and I quickly looked away.

You sure that's a good idea, Dastien said.

No. It was probably a terrible idea to take something this creepy and evil in the first place, but it could be useful.

I have to trust my instincts, even if I don't have my visions right now. But even as I said that, my stomach twisted into an even bigger knot. There were so many ways the fight with Astaroth could go, most of them bad. And I had to stop everything to deal with the Alphas on top of it all?

No. I didn't want to go to this meeting. Not even a little bit. Aside from the visions I'd this morning, I'd been in the conference room with this group exactly one other time, and I'd somehow ended up the spokesperson for the Weres. Now I was going to tell them that I was reworking their whole power structure.

This was going to be loads of fun.

Drama was brewing already. The power rolling down the hall made my skin itch. My friends all stopped walking to let me and Dastien go first. I looked over at Chris, who was gritting his teeth. If I was having a little bit of trouble with the power, then he was probably barely hanging in.

The conference room was around the corner from the library. It was large enough to fit a banquet table long enough to seat twenty-four—ten rolling black leather chairs fit comfortably on either side of the table, with two more at each end. The table was a light colored wood, polished until I could see my reflection in it.

I stood in the doorway for a second, taking in the room. Along one wall was a small buffet table. Usually, it had some legal pads, pens and highlighters, some water and that was it. Today, none of that was there. Instead, there were enough donuts and pastries and sandwiches to feed an army, but it was a room of werewolves. We could probably down that between five of us. Maybe less. The scent of the food made my stomach rumble embarrassingly loud. I moved inside the room—Dastien on my heels—and grabbed a couple ham and cheese croissants before doing anything else. Now was not the time to lose control of my wolf.

I bit into the first one and noticed that Meredith and Donovan were conferenced in via a bank of flatscreen panels that hung on the far wall. "Hey!" I said around my mouthful as Meredith waved. It was the middle of the night their time, but they looked more rested and put together than I did. My hair was twisted into a messy knot, and I'd been running around in these clothes for far too long.

I could hear Chris outside the door whispering to Cosette, and I figured they needed a second. The room was going to go crazy when they saw her.

I smoothed down my sweater and shoved up the sleeves of my hoodie. I should've traded out leggings and Uggs for jeans and boots. Too late to do anything about it now and my clothes didn't really matter in the grand scheme of things. What I was wearing wasn't going to soften the blow I was about to deal to the room.

I took a chair at the head of the table opposite the TVs, not because I thought I should have that spot, but because I wanted to be able to see everyone's face. With the power being tossed around the room, I was surprised it wasn't already taken.

As I sat down, I noticed Lisette was at the other head of the table and barely contained my wince. Moving now would look like a retreat, but I didn't love that I was now sitting across from her. She might have been my least favorite of the Seven that I'd met so far. Something about how prim and proper she was and how haughty she seemed with her power rubbed me exactly the wrong way. Her lip curled as I sat across from her. Apparently, the feeling was mutual.

Lisette wore a tasteful pantsuit, her blonde hair twisted up in a perfectly coiffed French twist. Not a hair stood out of place. Her cream, silk blouse, and pearls made her seem sophisticated and done up, but I wondered how practical her outfit was. If she were to get into a fight, she'd trash her clothes, and those pearls would be scattered all over the floor, but I bet she was thinking all kinds of things about my outfit, too.

I wasn't sure what to think of Jackson, who was sitting two chairs down from Lisette. His skin was dark as night, and I wondered if his wolf was the same color. If so, I was sure he'd be a fantastic hunter. He'd seemed okay the last time I'd seen him, but that could all change as soon as I told everyone what I was up to. For now, he sat relaxed in the chair, almost looking bored, but I knew he was paying attention. He had to be.

The leader of the Cazadores, Keeney, gave me a nod without pausing from his conversation with a man I didn't recognize. He rubbed his hand over his bald head absently as he listened. His crisp black blazer over the typical black-on-black pants and shirt was a fancier version of the look the Cazadores favored, but he was in charge of all of them. That fit in my mind.

Who's Keeney talking to? I asked Dastien.

Blaze.

Oh! He was the only other member of the Seven that I hadn't met yet. I took a second to really get a read on him. His skin was a warm brown, and I wasn't sure where he was from.

But chiseled features, his black hair, deep-set dark eyes, thick eyebrows, and plump lips made him look like he slid off the cover of a magazine. He was probably the most handsome person in the room, and that was saying something.

Hey.

I'm not saying you're not handsome.

He's just more handsome?

I rolled my eyes. *Stop it. Blaze seems nice though.* He was smiling as he talked to Keeney about something that they did the last time they were together. Apparently, they were good friends. Who knew?

The Canadian, French, and Eastern European Alphas were also seated at the table. The Canadian Alpha—Albert—hated me because I had power. He wasn't happy that I was the one who spoke to the news about werewolves, and I was pretty sure that he was going to be the most upset about my new spell. Albert craved fame and power, and I was about to take away his chance at it for a second time.

Nah, Dastien's voice came through the bond. *I wouldn't worry about him as much as I would about Lisette. She'll be the most upset.*

You think?

Yes. You're bitten, so you are much less than equal in Lisette's eyes, regardless of how much power you have.

My eyes couldn't have been wider as I looked at my mate. *You've got to be kidding.*

Unfortunately, no. We'll have to be careful with Lisette. She might retaliate.

Great. Because all I'd wanted to do was save the world, and she was going to get on me because I'd been bitten? That just stank.

Sebastian gave me a little wave. He might be scary as hell with his powers, but I'd found him to be perfectly nice. It was he and Donovan who'd come to see what was going on when Dastien bit me. For a second I'd been afraid that they'd punish me for it, but turns out both of them had become pretty solid allies. I was glad he was here. I needed every ally I could get.

Claudia and Lucas had already filed in after me, all taking empty seats around the table. But when Chris and Cosette finally finished their talk and stepped through the door, it was like everyone took a breath at the same time. The room was dead silent.

She did a little finger wave. "Hello."

Meredith leaned forward so close to the camera that only her eye and part of her cheek filled the screen. "You can come out for a werewolf meeting, but you can't come to see me?"

Cosette shrugged. "This was urgent, so I was given a pittance from my mother."

"Shopping *is* urgent, too," Meredith muttered. "Not to mention my Full Moon Ceremony."

Donovan tugged Meredith back. "I think we're all accounted for. Shall we start?"

Mr. Dawson had been standing by the door waiting for Chris and Cosette to come in. He closed the door as they found seats. "We've got a big problem," he said as he walked to me. "Tessa? Want to fill them in?"

Great. Mr. Dawson was just throwing me to the wolves. "Sure. Why not." I stood up from my chair because it seemed like the thing to do. I started with Muraco's death and the pain I felt during it. Then told them as briefly as I could about my vision, what I knew about Astaroth, and what happened during our trip to LA. I finished with what happened on the compound.

I took a breath and was about to dive into my plan, but all of a sudden, everyone was talking all at once. The noise was deafening. I fought the urge to cover my ears with my hands.

Dastien leaned back in his chair. *This is going well.*

I nearly laughed. *It's about what I expected. What are they even saying?*

Eh, just some finger pointing really. Nothing that's helpful.

I sighed. *They're going to hate what I say next.*

Dastien grabbed my hand. *Stay strong. Your plan is the best one.*

It's also the only *one I have.*

That, too. Dastien gave me a wink.

I didn't want to use power to shut them up—Lucas had been polite about it, but I was pretty sure no one else in this room would be—so I did the first thing that came to mind.

I hopped up on the table with one swift jump and walked to the center of it. "If you're all going to keep yelling at once, then I'm leaving. We've got Satan's second in command coming after us, and I've got better things to do than sit here and listen to you bicker." I could feel the chatter about to rise up again, but I didn't stop. "The Seven is broken. Done." There was some pointing of fingers and yelling, but I stomped my foot on the table. "Blaming each other is a waste of time. The Seven was ruined the day Ferdinand was killed. We can't fix the bond that used to be there because to do that, we'd need an eclipse and the backing of the fey. *Both of them.* We don't have *either*." That had them all shutting up. "So, we're doing something new. I know that I've only been a werewolf for a little while, but from my perspective, it seems like everything is incredibly divided. And it's not just the werewolves that are broken and fighting amongst themselves." I sent a pointed look to the Canadian Alpha and Lisette. "The fey are gone. Each court hiding in their little holes."

"I wouldn't call them holes or little," Cosette said, and there were a few laughs.

"Whatever. But you're hiding. That can't last, you've said it yourself."

She nodded.

I took a breath and dove back in. "The covens are all a mess. The ripples of what Luciana did have hit everyone. And the more I dig, the more I think we've all been played. Astaroth found a way to get to us. How long ago did he get to Luciana? When did Ferdinand go rogue? This has been a long time coming, and no one saw it. None of you prevented it. And the fey seem to have divested themselves of everything."

I paused to catch my breath. Everyone was listening to me quietly, and I figured that was as good as it was going to get with this bunch.

"The truth is that the seal that separated our plane from the next is broken. That means that in a matter of days, we could have demons taking over the world. Everyone will die, and we won't be able to stop it. Unless we fix the seal. Even if we somehow managed to defeat Astaroth another way, there's always going to be another bad guy. There's blood in the water. And the sharks? They're coming for us. For *all* of us. It's time to make a change. So, I'm doing something new and permanent. I have no doubt that a few in this room are going to be mad. This is going to change everything. I—"

"Excuse me." Lisette's voice had my teeth grinding in frustration. "You're very bold in the way you're saying this, but everything that you're saying leads me to believe even more firmly that we must reinstate the Seven."

Of course, it was Lisette who interrupted me. "It is my understanding that you need the fey courts as well as a lunar eclipse to re-make the Seven. Is that not correct?"

"No. That's correct, but—"

"And do you have a way to get around the eclipse and also have fey queens come out from hiding for us?"

Little lines formed around her mouth and she slowly shook her head.

"You don't. No one does. It's over, and it's best if we all just let the idea of the Seven go right now. Okay?"

The room was so quiet I could only hear my own breathing.

"Great. So, now when I say I'm going to form something new, something entirely different, I hope each of you will understand why we have to do this." I walked around the table, stopping to look at each Were sitting. "We can't keep holding on to something that's broken and hope that it'll magically save the day. Because it won't. This is a new day, and that means a new chance—a new opportunity—to build something lasting. So here's what I know."

I started explaining my plan to form a bond that included Weres, fey, witches, and myself, but as soon as I mentioned that there were going to be only three spots for Alphas, they all started bickering about who would be on it.

I sat back, letting them fight it out, because when the time came, I was going to have to the final say and I had some ideas of my own.

Me.

Three fey: Cosette and whoever she could get. I couldn't be picky there.

Three witches: Claudia was in for sure. It couldn't be Raphael. He never loved the witch stuff, and that had only gotten worse. Plus, I was pretty sure that he wasn't going to stick around once all of this was done.

Three werewolves: Dastien was a given because I wasn't doing it without him. Lucas was too because I was sure Claudia was going to feel the same way about her mate being a part of this. Which left one spot, and for some reason, I really thought Chris should have it. Chris wasn't very alpha, but even if he wasn't as strong as the other werewolves in the room, I couldn't deny his link to the fey. I didn't know what the connection was exactly, but he'd gotten Cosette to show up when no one else could.

But if I picked Chris, then the rest of the Alphas in the room were going to be pissed because I'd left room for exactly zero former members of the Council of Seven.

Even knowing all of that, I still had a lot of empty slots to fill.

Cosette showed up, but she was alone. Could she even get two others to agree to my whackadoodle plan? And if she could, would the queens let two other fey out of hiding?

What other witches did we know and trust? Could I convince Shane to come back? Would that seriously piss off Adrian? Did Adrian's feelings really matter when we were talking about such high stakes?

Just about everyone I wanted in the spell straddled the line between supernaturals. Claudia was a witch, but she was mated to a Were. I was a witch and a Were, and Dastien was mated to me. Cosette had been living with the witches when we met, *and* she was a part of the Lunar court, which was tied to the Weres.

So the fact that Chris had a tie to the fey—even if I didn't know what it was? That was huge. He was in. The more I thought it through, the more right it felt.

Which meant this room was about to be filled with a bunch of pissed off werewolves.

When should I tell them? I asked Dastien.

There's no sense in waiting if you've already made your choices. And I think you have. So, might as well get it over with.

That wasn't what I wanted to hear.

Maybe not. But this isn't a time for procrastination.

Albert was currently telling the room that he should be in on the new Seven and Sebastian was shaking his head.

I agreed with Sebastian one hundred percent. Not a chance.

I hadn't been around for long, but even I knew a power-hungry Were was an extremely dangerous creature.

Say something.

I turned to my mate. *Now? They're all fighting.*

We don't have much time. The sun is setting. We have to wrap this up and be prepared for whatever might come.

I checked the time and gasped. *Jesus. This conference room is in a time warp.* I hadn't realized how late it'd gotten. Just knowing it was night again had my heart racing, but I didn't want to be the one to stop the meeting. To tell everyone exactly what they didn't want to hear.

That's what being the Alpha is. Doing the hard things to protect everyone in your pack.

I sighed. *Fine. But when this goes to shit, I get to say I told you so.*

He smiled, dimples denting his cheeks. *Deal.*

I cleared my throat. "This isn't going to work..." No one stopped talking. They kept on arguing. I turned to Dastien. *Do I get up on the table again? Because I was kind of hoping that was a one-time thing.*

Be rude.

I raised an eyebrow at him. *Really? Because Lucas hated it.* As I thought of him, I glanced his way. Apparently, he'd noticed that I was trying to get their attention because he was watching me.

I shrugged. "I'm going to do it again," I said quietly, but Lucas was paying attention. I knew he'd hear me just fine.

"I think you should," he said just as quietly. I watched his mouth move so I could be sure I was hearing him correctly. "Show them what you really are."

That was a bit deep. What was I really? Who was I? I wasn't sure yet. I was still way too young to have all the answers. Or any answers if I was being honest. But I shoved that all aside, and I let my wolf rise, feeling her tingle along my skin. Power built until I felt like I was going to burst at the seams. "Stop." I pushed power, making my voice heard over all the chatter. "Everyone shut up."

The room quieted in an instant. I sneaked a look at Albert, who was turning red but remained silent.

"About damned time," Cosette said. "I was beginning to wonder why I came all this way."

"What the hell was that?" Blaze said.

Blaze has been perfectly lovely, and I didn't take any joy in pissing him off. "We're running out of time tonight," I said as calmly as I could manage. "I don't know what we're in store for, but Astaroth is close. He nearly came through the open circle in what's left of Luciana's house a few hours ago in daylight, and I know he'll come tonight if he can. She did magic here, and I'm just not certain..." I didn't need to get into all of that. "We don't have time to do the spell to form the new ruling bond now—I don't even know if we have all the ingredients yet—which means we have to be prepared to run any minute now." I was praying that was an extreme exaggeration.

"And who made you boss?" Albert said.

I shrugged, trying to ignore his shitty tone. "Dastien bit me a few months ago, so you could blame him? Or you could say that since I was supposed to rule the Texas coven, you could blame my grandmother? Or you could really go for the big one and blame God?" Cosette laughed, and I barely held in my own snicker. "As soon as we've figured out everything we need, I'm going to have to cast a circle to do the spell. Any way I cut it, it has to happen because I'm going to be the link between the supernaturals. When I do, Astaroth is going to come through. He'll be pissed and want to stop us. I'm going to need you guys to fight while the rest of us form the bond."

"Who's fighting and who's forming the bond?" Blaze said. "Just to be clear."

I blew out a breath. "We need three of each—witch, fey, and Were. And then me, because I'm a mix. I'm thinking—"

"May I make a suggestion?" Blaze interrupted.

"Sure." I was open to suggestions, within reason.

"How about four each? That makes twelve. One more—you—makes thirteen."

"Isn't thirteen bad luck?" I asked him.

"The number thirteen is a lot of things to a lot of different cultures and religions. It can be good or bad luck, depending on the purpose, but most everyone agrees that it's a powerful number. I hope that for your purposes the added power boost would be worth the risk."

I wasn't sure I wanted any more risk than I was already taking, but if the result was more power? That was too good to pass up. "So, that changes things. For witches, I'd been thinking Claudia, Shane—if I can convince him—and I'm not sure who else. Cosette, can you get three others?"

She sighed. "I can get one for sure. I have an idea for another, but I'll do my best."

"And the queens?" Meredith said. "Will they be okay with this?"

Cosette laughed, and it sounded like bells. "My mother didn't want me coming, but she agreed to it. Three more, not a chance. But I have some leverage I'm can try to use. We can't stand by when our leaving helped cause some of this death and destruction." She sighed. "She'll agree if I can be convincing enough."

I blew out a breath. It wasn't a firm this-is-happening, but it was about as close to that as I could hope for.

Donovan leaned closer to the camera, nearly filling up the whole screen. "Who're ya thinkin' for the Weres?" His eyes glittered as he grinned. "I'm out of the running—I've enough on my hands here—but I'm curious what this lot is going to do when you tell 'em."

"How do you know it's going to piss them off?" It was. For sure. But how did Donovan know?

"Because you're friends with my mate, and I know who she'd pick."

"Who would you pick, Meredith?" Sebastian asked. His chair creaked as he leaned back in it. If I didn't know better, I'd think he was enjoying this as much as Donovan was.

Being far away gave Meredith a bit of an advantage. She could say what she thought without feeling the wrath in the room. The way she rubbed her hands together as she thought almost made me laugh. "Dastien is a must. You can't have Tessa doing something magical at all without her mate. They're stronger as a pair." Exactly. "Lucas because of Claudia, same reason. Chris for sure. He'll balance them. And that leaves one spot."

"Who're you likin' for it?" The t on his 'it' was heavy with his Irish accent. Donovan was having fun.

Meredith did an eenie-meanie-miney-mo. "Blaze."

Blaze shook his head. "No. If it's a new group, then I should be out, too. I was just as big of a problem as the rest of them."

"That's exactly why she should pick you. I've met you a few times over the years, and you're kind, generous, and *powerful*. It's a good combo," Meredith said. "Plus, you're admitting that you did something wrong. That counts for a lot. Experience makes up for the difference."

If I was not mistaken, the Alpha was blushing. "It's kind of you to say."

"And that's such a Blaze thing to say," Meredith said as she crossed her arms and leaned back in her chair.

Donovan laughed, but the rest of the room turned to me.

"How correct was she?" Sebastian asked.

"Aside from Blaze, exactly right."

"And who did you like instead of Blaze?" Lisette asked.

I shrugged. "I wasn't sure. I had that spot empty. I figured there was going to be a fight, so I was going to leave that up to you."

"Ah. I see," Sebastian said.

I waited for the outburst, but it didn't come. I wasn't sure why, until I saw Cosette rise from her chair. "Blaze is acceptable to the fey," she said, effectively ending the argument. "I'll be back soon with the others."

She was leaving? No. She couldn't. Not now. She'd just gotten here. "When are you coming back?" I shouted at her as she strode to the door, hoping I didn't sound too desperate.

"Soon." She looked over her shoulder and her gaze met mine. "I won't leave you hanging." The door closed, but I wanted to ask her who she was bringing back and what the hell soon meant exactly.

I chased after her, but as I stepped into the hallway, she was gone.

I jogged to the front entrance, but she wasn't there either. Night had fallen on St. Ailbe's, but as far as I could see, there was no one out there.

I knew she couldn't do that whole teleporting thing without Van, but I hadn't seen him. So, how did she leave?

The sound of angry voices built as I walked back to the conference room. The reaction I'd been expecting was there. It'd just been delayed.

Shit. I didn't want to go back into the conference room. The sun had already set, which meant we were running out of time. I could feel Astaroth's fingers wrapping around my neck as the time slipped away.

Come back. We'll wrap this up and leave, Dastien said through the bond.

You feel it, too? I asked him.

No. But you do, and ever since this afternoon...I don't want to fight something I can't win.

So what do we do?

We need off this land tonight.

So we run? That's what I thought we should do, but would running send Astaroth the wrong message?

He already knows we're afraid and that we're not prepared. But we will be. Part of being a leader is to know when to retreat.

We're going to have to clear out the entire campus. Surrender it completely. I wasn't about to leave people behind. Not a single kitchen hand. Not the strongest Alpha. That was a hard pass for me.

So now I was going to have to make them agree not only to my new spell that would wrench ruling power from the claws, but also run like scared little sheep?

I stepped into the conference room again. It was like war had broken out at the UN. I couldn't understand anything that was being said, and not just because it was too loud to hear myself think. Lisette was leaning over the table, shouting in French at Blaze, who was sitting there as calm as I'd ever seen anyone. Every bit of piss and vinegar she was spewing at him was blowing right past him.

Albert joined in with Lisette, clearly as pissed as she was. Sebastian and Jackson were arguing in German. Donovan and Meredith were sitting back in their chairs in Ireland, looking pleased as punch not to be here in person.

But my friends were calmly taking all of this in. At least we were being levelheaded. Fighting together a few times had really solidified our group. We trusted each other. It was the older generation that was going to have an issue.

Chris gave me a wink, and I almost felt bad that I hadn't asked him about being involved like this. *Are you mad?* I mouthed to him, gesturing in a circle in case he didn't catch what I said.

His eyes widened. *No. Honored,* he mouthed back to me.

That was a relief. I sat down in my chair, waiting for a pause in the talking, but that wasn't going to happen. I was going to have to jump in. Again. This was starting to get—

You're mine. His voice echoed in my head.

My skin went ice cold. We were too late. Astaroth was here. I grabbed Dastien's hand, squeezing it tightly. *We have to run.*

My gaze found Claudia's as she slowly stood from her chair.

Raphael burst into the room.

But no one except my friends noticed. The "adults" were still arguing.

My lungs burned, and I realized I'd stopped breathing. I exhaled and inhaled again, quickly. Too fast. "He's here," I said too quiet, but those two words silenced the room.

All eyes were on me.

"We have to run," I said it aloud this time. "Now!" I didn't look to see who followed me as I raced out the door. The ones that trusted me would come. The rest could fuck themselves because I wasn't waiting. Not one millisecond.

CHAPTER EIGHTEEN

THE FLOOR RUMBLED under my feet.

A crash sounded from the library, and I froze.

No. No. Wrong.

I was going the wrong way.

I turned and threw open the closest door—the one to Mr. Dawson's office. The doorknob broke off in my hand as I twisted it.

Not caring about anything other than getting away, I threw the knob off to the side, grabbed one of the chairs in front of his desk, and hurled it through the window. The crash was sure to draw Astaroth, but that didn't matter. He was here. The fear was making my bones shake, but I kept moving. Because he was here.

He was here, and we were so screwed.

Panic clawed its way up my spine.

I leaped through the shards. *We have to get everyone away from here,* I said to Dastien. I hit the ground outside and kept running. There were soft thuds behind me, and I knew that everyone had taken my cue. Thank God.

A siren broke through the early night. I didn't know who

had tripped the alarms, but I hoped that lit a fire under everyone's ass. Anyone who was still on this campus needed to leave. Now.

Running was our only option.

There is no running, the words seeped into my head, dripping doubt and hopelessness into every nook and cranny of my soul. I started to trip on my own feet, but Dastien caught me, lifting me into his arms without breaking his stride.

Are you okay?

Yes. You can put me back down.

You sure?

Yes. I was sure. Astaroth could make me feel terrible, but only if I let him. And I wasn't going to let him. Not again.

And I couldn't let him take me. Especially since it hadn't even been twenty-four hours since I'd gotten a dose of Samantha's blood. Her warning ran through my head, and my fear grew stronger.

I pictured a brick wall surrounding my mind as I sprinted for the parking lot, but all I could hear was his laughter. It drowned out everything else.

The sound was coming from inside my head. From inside my soul.

But no one owned my soul. No one but me. I had to keep telling myself that or I'd lose.

I built up the wall around my mind even thicker, and his laughing cut off. I wasn't sure if my mental barrier was actually working or if he'd backed off to make me more confident. It didn't matter either way. We were leaving, and he wasn't getting us. Not today.

The alarms were still going, but aside from those of us who were in the meeting, no one was doing anything. The Cazadores had come to check what was going on. They stood at the entrances to the buildings, waiting for the threat to show itself. That was the wrong move.

"Everyone get off this land!" I rolled power through campus, hoping the Weres would hear my order and get the hell out of dodge. Even together, we couldn't fight Astaroth and win. Not until we had some serious magical reinforcement ready to roll.

I stopped at the beginning of the path to the parking lot, and Dastien stopped, too, standing just in front of me as if he could stop Astaroth from getting to me.

I can at least slow him down, Dastien said.

No. He'd kill you. I grabbed his hand and pulled him beside me. *We stay together.*

He squeezed my hand as he glanced down at me. *Always. No matter what.* His eyes were glowing amber, and I could feel his wolf begging to get free.

The rest of the Alphas from the meeting stopped just behind me. Lucas was carrying Claudia on his back. Her eyes were wide as she clung to him.

Raphael trailed behind us, but he didn't stop. He kept running to the parking lot, and a few seconds later I heard tires squeal as he raced away from here. Which was good. He needed to get gone. Fast.

Mr. Dawson stopped next to me in wolf form and let out a series of howls, two short, one long, three short, one long. The last one was still echoing in the night as werewolves continued to pour from the buildings. Campus had seemed so empty when we got back from our honeymoon, but it was suddenly filled with Weres I'd never seen before. Not just Cazadores in all black, but general staff.

There are fewer people here with the school closed, but since the Cazadores are still around, they still need all the kitchen, cleaning, and some general maintenance staff.

Right. That makes sense. I wished that there weren't so

many here, though. Getting them cleared out of here was going to take some time.

I just didn't understand what happened. There were rules as to when and how Astaroth could cross over. It didn't make any sense.

I turned to Claudia, hoping that she'd have at least some answer. "How did he get here? He was still tied to the circle at the compound. Is there another circle here? And it's not full dark. The sun set maybe thirty minutes ago. How is he strong enough to break through?"

"I don't know. Luciana didn't cast a circle here, as far as I know, but her magic is here." She tucked her face in Lucas' shoulder for a second before shaking her head. "Something isn't right. Even if he could've broken free of the circle, he should've had to wait until the witching hour. That's when the veil between realms is thinnest. I don't know how he's here."

That wasn't the answer I was hoping for. If Astaroth could come here now, what was stopping him from following us? Why hadn't he kept following us when we were leaving the compound? I had to know, otherwise running wasn't going to do any good.

Shit. I wanted to run, but everyone was taking too long to get out of here. My car was right there. I glanced at Dastien's glowing amber eyes. *I'm sorry. With him here, I can't leave until everyone from the school is gone.*

We're protecting the pack. It's what Alphas do. It's why they stayed. Dastien motioned to the wolves—the Cazadores—that were guarding the way for all the school's employees. And then to all of the Alphas that were standing with us.

The door to the admin building was ripped off of its hinges and thrown into the quad. The Weres running by dodged it easily.

A figure strolled through the doorway, walking slow, even steps.

Astaroth.

Gray dots filled my vision, and I realized I was holding my breath. I wasn't alone. There were others here ready to fight by my side. "Thank you for staying," I mumbled to the Alphas.

"We're in this together," Blaze said. His tone was easy and light. I didn't know him well, but I suddenly admired him. He sounded so freaking calm when I was about to shake out of my own skin. "This is the job of Alphas. And no matter how much of a fight they put up—" He looked pointedly at Lisette and Albert. "We all want what's best for everyone. They'll come around and support it. Eventually."

He's an amazing fighter, but you wouldn't know it unless you saw him in action. Blaze isn't showy like a lot of the other powerful werewolves. He's incredibly humble and kind.

I really liked that, and having an amazing fighter with us was about to come in very handy.

I watched as Astaroth grew closer. With every step, my heart rate kicked up another degree, until I thought my chest was going to rip open. He was still in the form of the boy, but he was holding something. His too-wide, jack-o-lantern grin started to spread across his face as he held it up for me to see.

The jar from the altar.

"Oh, shit." I turned to Claudia, eyes wide. "It's my fault he got here so quickly. I don't even know why I took it." I was so stupid. I shouldn't have touched something I knew nothing about. I'd had it with me in the car, but maybe he needed night-fall or to do some spell to make it work. But that was the key. That's how he got here.

"There probably was a compulsion," Claudia said. "Don't be too hard on yourself."

I didn't know if that was possible. I wanted to cry at my own stupidity, but I couldn't. I had to fight. But I didn't know if I could ever forgive myself for being so dumb.

Astaroth stopped at the foot of the stairs, watching us.

My chest grew so tight, I could've sworn he was already strangling me. I wasn't sure what he was waiting for. But if he wanted me afraid, he'd accomplished that tenfold.

I could still hear everyone climbing into cars—doors slamming and engines starting. It was going to take a few more precious minutes before the school was cleared out.

"What's he doing?" Claudia asked.

"I don't know." I rubbed my sweating hands off on my yoga pants.

Two things happened at once. Astaroth raised his arms in the air, holding the jar up, and the ground started to rumble.

He was opening a portal. "Oh shit." This was going to get worse. A lot worse.

"Hurry!" Dastien yelled to the fleeing Weres as Astaroth turned in a circle.

"Be ready," I said to the Weres.

"We've done it before. We'll do it again," Dastien said, and I hoped that was true.

"Yeah, except I never wanted to do it the first time," Chris said. "That chapel in Santa Fe was enough for me."

"Agreed," I said. "But then, nobody asked us." I didn't have any spells prepared. No weapons, except the small dagger in my pocket. Which I *really* didn't want to use. I wasn't even sure if I should have it in my pocket, but it was too late now.

The wolf begged me to let her out, ready to attack. Fur rippled along my skin and I fought it back down. Not now. Not yet. "We're holding here. Let them come to us."

The scent of sulfur burned my nose as a ring of red light circled Astaroth.

He stepped back as the ground before him shimmered,

became almost translucent, and the first demon climbed up. Its wrinkly gray skin shimmered in the moonlight.

I'd seen a variety of demons in the chapel, but these were my least favorite. The sight of them as they crawled along the ground terrified me. They were vaguely humanoid, but their legs and arms had too many joints that could bend either way. The demons could stand on two legs, but they liked to crawl—over each other, up walls, and onto the ceilings. Their eyes were twin black pools filled with death and despair.

Where there was one, there would be more, but I still hoped that I was wrong. That only the one would come through.

I wasn't wrong. A second later, there were ten more squatting next to the first.

And then ten more.

In a few heartbeats, we were so outnumbered, it was stupid. *I* was stupid. I'd made two mistakes today. The first was taking the jar. The second was not running when I had the chance.

Damn it.

He had an army, and there were maybe twenty Cazadores, my friends and the Alphas made thirty-five, plus whoever hadn't made it out of the parking lot.

As much as I wanted to run now, it was too late. We couldn't let these demons loose, and we definitely couldn't leave a portal to Hell open.

"Hurry!" I yelled into the parking lot as the last of the school employees scurried into cars.

There were so many demons now that I couldn't see Astaroth anymore. They were all contained in the circle. Climbing on top of each other like a ball of baby spiders itching to break free of their sack.

I shouldn't have worried about not being able to see Astaroth because a second later, the demons parted and he came through.

"Teresa." His voice saying my name sent terror skittering through my body.

"Leave me alone." I wasn't his. No matter what evil magic Luciana used on me.

"You *are* mine."

He was wrong. "Never." My voice sounded confident and calm when everything in me was screaming to get the hell out of here.

I needed that jar back. It had to be the key. If Astaroth used it to get here, then if I destroyed it, he would have to go back.

It was a theory, and the best I could do. I was going to focus on that and shut out all the other noise. Especially anything Astaroth said.

I think that's a good plan, Dastien said.

There was no time to consult with Claudia. The circle grew brighter, flashing so bright that I couldn't look at it. And then it was gone.

It took me a second to be able to see, but I could hear the crunching on the grass, feel the ground rumbling under their feet, smell the sulfur getting stronger.

I didn't have a backpack with supplies loaded in it. I didn't have any words that would help me fight the demons. So, I used the one weapon I did have.

I yanked off my Uggs, threw my hoodie—dagger still in the pocket—on the ground, and then pulled my shirt over my head as the wolf rose up in me, growling. Between one second and the next, I shifted from human to wolf.

My senses were stronger as a wolf. I could hear more. Scent more. See more.

The wolf was also more confident. She wanted to take on Astaroth. If this was going to be a fight, then I was going to face it. I let the wolf take hold fully and rushed forward.

My teeth slashed into a demon, grabbed its leg, and jerked.

Black blood burned my mouth, but I kept moving. I let my claws and teeth do the damage. Dastien had been training me in both forms during our honeymoon, and I was getting better. Much, much better.

I leaped from demon to demon. Ripping off a head at the neck. Clawing through their bodies.

Closer. Foot by foot. I was making my way toward the circle. Toward Astaroth.

I leaped through the air to get to another one, but a demon bit my side. I howled as pain ripped through me.

I hit the ground and power poured into me. I rushed to push the power back to him. *No. Stop.* Dastien hadn't been hurt yet, but now his attention was divided. He was worrying about me.

Focus on the fight in front of you.

He ignored my pleas, sending more power. *Take it! Get the jar.*

Fine. I hated it. But fine. I took the power, and the searing pain dulled just enough not to be debilitating. I'd take care of it later. I had to keep moving.

I tore through another demon. And another. And another.

I'd lost sight of Astaroth, but I knew he was here somewhere. But I was getting closer to the circle. I could see the red glow. I ignored the burning in my side as I kept moving faster, faster, faster.

Howls of pain filled the night, and I knew I didn't have much time left.

One more foot and I could—

A hand wrapped around my throat and I was lifted from the ground. Astaroth had grown taller. His face darkened and shadowed under the hood of the jacket. His eyes were two glowing red orbs.

"Mine," he said. The power in his voice rattled my bones, and his smile yawned in front of me. He gave me a good shake and suddenly I was back in my human form. I was naked. All of my soft human flesh exposed. "That's better."

No. Not fucking better. This was bad. I tried to shift back, but whatever Astaroth had done, I couldn't reach my wolf. I didn't have fangs or claws to fight with. I grabbed Astaroth's hand trying to pry his fingers away from my neck, but he just laughed. His dark power slimed all over me into every pore of my body, every nook and cranny of my soul. I'd never be clean again. Never.

"Dastien!" It came out more croak than anything else, but I knew he could hear me. I wasn't sure what I needed him to do. Wasting power on me right now wasn't going to do him any good, but I was going to die if I didn't get away.

A glint caught my eye, and I looked down Astaroth's body to see the mason jar hanging loosely from his other hand. The spell was glowing inside. One smash and this would be over.

I tried to kick at it, but Astaroth shook me. His laughter pricked my skin.

Get the jar, I sent along our bond and hoped he could get it. It was our only shot.

Astaroth tightened his grip, and he grew larger. My feet dangled over the ground as I fought to get air in, but it was hopeless.

The dread of what to come swamped me. Tears ran hot down my face as I kicked out again, but it wasn't working. Nothing was working.

You're mine.

The snap was coming soon, and I did the only thing I could think of.

I closed my eyes and started praying. *God, please help me. I know I'm not perfect.* If I'd had air in my lungs, I would've sobbed, but I couldn't. *If it's my time, I accept that. But please, I don't want to go with Astaroth. Please, save my soul.*

Suddenly Astaroth hissed, and the ground slammed into me as I fell.

I opened my eyes to see the light coming straight for me.

"You called."

"God?" My voice was barely more than a croak. I blinked a few times before I could see that there was a form in front of me.

A rich, deep laugh made my skin tingle. I knew that sound. It wasn't God. It was Eli. "You're not an angel." But he looked like one, glowing in the night, somehow hovering off the ground, wearing his white V-neck T-shirt and light jeans.

"No, but I'm not a demon either."

"Teresa." Astaroth's voice beat in my head, and I curled into a ball, covering my ears. My head felt like it was ripping in two, but I tried to look around. I wanted to know if he was coming, but I couldn't see him. I couldn't see anything beyond Eli's glow.

The ground started rumbling again, and the scent of sulfur grew stronger.

Eli knelt beside me. "How is he here? It's not time." The light around him was keeping the demons away, but they were still there. Fighting the Weres. We had to fix this.

"A spell. In a jar." My throat felt like it was on fire as I spoke. Astaroth had dropped the jar when he dropped me, but it'd rolled back inside the circle. It was maybe ten or fifteen feet away from me, but there were too many demons between and the jar. "It's in the circle, but there are too many demons—"

"That's an easy fix." The power built around him—making him glow even brighter—until I thought it was going to blind me, and then Eli spread his arms wide. He held them there for a few seconds before swinging them together, clapping his hands. The sound echoed outward, and with it, the power rippled.

It suddenly felt like I was sitting under the sun on a hot

summer day, but not too hot because there was an icy breeze that followed the heat.

The demons around us screamed and turned to ash.

My mouth hung open. Jesus Christ. Why had he waited so long to kill them all if it was so easy for him? And where the hell was he six weeks ago when we were fighting for our lives in Santa Fe?

Eli grinned at me. "Because I can only act when allowed. There are rules, which I follow. Unlike some demons."

Astaroth was back in his circle. The smile wasn't there, but he was still scary. And from the way he was rising off the ground, I had a pretty solid feeling he was pretty fucking pissed.

Astaroth dove at Eli and they fought. There was a flash of light, and I wanted to watch them, but the jar. I had to get the jar.

I struggled to get to my feet. My side felt like it was getting ripped open. The demon's bite was still seeping blood, and I felt spent. But I had to get up. Somehow. I had to keep fighting.

I took a few steps and then leaped, falling on top of the jar.

Astaroth roared, and I looked up just in time to see him coming for me. I froze.

Smash it! Smash it!

It took me a second to process Dastien's words. I rolled off of the jar, grabbing it, and smashed it into the ground.

Astaroth roared and this time my eardrums burst. Blood dripped down my cheeks, and I blinked. When my eyes opened again, he was gone. Astaroth had disappeared.

Oh, thank God. I slumped to the ground, panting, not really believing that it was over. That we'd somehow lived. But Astaroth didn't reappear. He was gone. Like he and his army of demons hadn't been here a second ago. Only the sulfur and the pain in my side from the demon bite were left.

Eli was still here.

My eyelids were growing heavy as I watched him approach. I was so tired. So done. I couldn't even lift my head. And my side was on fire. I wasn't sure I could move.

He pulled the white V-neck shirt over his head and squatted next to me.

He was saying something, but my eardrums hadn't healed yet.

"What?" I asked.

He lifted me up a little to pull the shirt over my head. "Thank you," I said, not knowing what he wanted from me. I tried to stay sitting up, but it was taking too much energy. I assumed I was going to owe him for this, but I couldn't make a deal right now. Whatever he wanted, I'd pay it. But he just stayed there waiting, watching me. Something about the way he was staring at me made me nervous.

He leaned so close to me that if he were shorter, our noses would be touching. He kept his eyes on mine as he started to lift my shirt by my right side.

"Hey," I shouted, even if I couldn't hear myself. Just that one word said with a little too much force was more energy than I could spare. My vision started to thin, and I fell backward, but Eli caught my shoulder and eased me to the ground.

He knelt in front of me, pressing a hand to each of my ears. They popped again, and when he moved his hands away, I could hear. Maybe better than before. The leaves in the trees rustled. The wolves panted as they recovered. Dastien growled next to me.

I'd been so focused on Astaroth and Eli, that I hadn't even noticed my mate was so close, but I couldn't take my eyes away from the concerned look on Eli's face. He was scaring me.

"What's wrong?" I asked.

"You have a bite," Eli said. "Which is bad because you're already tied to Astaroth. And there's something else wrong with your blood. I don't know what you did to it in the last day, but this is bad. Very bad. But I can help, if you let me."

My mouth went dry as I tried to process his words. Samantha's blood. Half-demon blood. It made sense that her blood would make the bite worse.

"May I?"

I wasn't sure I trusted him fully, but he'd just saved our lives. All of us. So, I lifted up my shirt. "Okay."

In human form, the bite was just above my right hip. Eli placed his hand over it, and the skin grew hot. Too hot. "You're hurting me," my voice was all whine.

"Hold still. It's about to get worse."

It was too much. I started to scream and hit Eli, but he held strong.

"Dastien!" I screamed as I tried to pry Eli's hand off of me, but he used his other hand to pin my shoulder to the ground.

Dastien growled, but Eli looked down at him. "If you know what's good for her, you'll settle down and let me concentrate."

I didn't care anymore. His hand might have just been laying still, but it felt like Eli was ripping out my insides.

I screamed and thrashed. I kicked and hit with everything I had, but Eli never moved. My back was pressed into the ground, but I couldn't help it. I had to fight him. The pain was too much not to fight, beg, plead for it to stop.

I screamed. And screamed. Until my already battered voice was raw and broken. And then I kept screaming.

Until darkness came for me, sweeping me away.

CHAPTER NINETEEN

I WAS RUNNING in the dark. Running into nothing. My legs burned and I ran. And ran.

You're mine, Astaroth's voice echoed in my head, sending a rush of fear-fueled adrenaline through my body.

"Noooo!" I screamed as I fought through the dark, but suddenly there was light.

I blinked as air heaved in and out of my lungs.

Where was I? What was happening? I didn't remember anything after Eli tried to heal me.

I jumped up in a flurry of movements. My limbs tangled in a mountain of white sheets and I fell to the floor, knocking a lamp over on my way down.

"*Chérie.*" It was Dastien's voice, but I wasn't sure if I could trust it. He stood in the doorway. "It's fine. You're safe." He walked slowly to me, his hands held out.

I looked around the room. The bay window with the padded seat. My bookcase, which was missing a good chunk of books. My favorites were now in a box in Dastien's cabin. The bed's sheets had been freshly bleached. The faint scent burned my nose when I breathed deep, and under that, I could smell lavender. My mother's favorite perfume.

This was my parents' house. I was in my bedroom—although calling it mine was a bit of a stretch. I hadn't slept here enough for it to feel like home.

Dastien's eyes were glowing amber as he closed the distance. *You're not in the black abyss.* He ran a hand down my cheek before brushing a soft kiss against my lips. *It was just a dream. You're here with me in your parents' house.* He pressed his forehead against mine.

I breathed in his scent. Pine. Woods. And something that was just him. I had to trust that this was real. This was my Dastien. This was my parents' house.

I closed my eyes and listened. My parents were chatting downstairs, along with a lot of other people, some voices I definitely didn't recognize.

Mostly our friends, but some new arrivals, too. Dastien used our bond. He hadn't done that when I'd been in the abyss.

"What happened?" I asked as I got back in bed, pulling the tangle of covers with me.

Dastien sat on the bed beside me. "Eli healed your bite, and then we cleared out. The demons were gone, but it seemed stupid to stay on campus."

"Where's everyone else?" There had been a lot of staff and Cazadores staying there.

"Their homes. Hotels. Here and there. But the Cazadores agreed to stay close by in case there's another fight. The Alphas are all close, too."

That was good news. "Everyone made it away okay?"

"Yes. Thanks to you and Eli."

"Did he say anything about needing to pay him back? For his help with the demons or with healing me."

"No. Maybe this one is on the house?"

That seemed like a stretch, but I wouldn't totally rule it out. I hadn't asked for him to show up. I'd been praying, but for God, not Eli. But the chances that I'd end up owing him were probably pretty good.

"We'll deal with that when it comes. For now, I'm just glad we're all okay."

"True. That's a pretty big positive."

He smiled. "Your cousins are downstairs, along with a few of the others. We need to figure out how we're doing the bond and get out plane sealed off from Astaroth. I don't want him coming through again."

"Me neither." But when we did the spell, he'd come. "Is Cosette back?"

"Not yet." I could feel the seed of doubt running through Dastien's mind.

"Don't." I had to shut his doubt down. I didn't want to even entertain the idea that she was going to no-show on us. "She knows what's at stake." If I couldn't trust my friends to have my back, then we'd already lost.

I kicked myself free of the covers and slid from the bed. I was wearing a T-shirt that smelled like Dastien, so I knew he'd gotten me ready for bed. "Thanks."

"Of course. But try to not get bitten by any of Astaroth's demons again. At least not for another twenty-four hours."

"Yeah," Samantha said forty-eight hours. I glanced at the clock on my bedside table. It was just past 10 a.m. "Only eighteen hours now." Assuming that she was right about how long her blood would last in my system.

He shook his head. "Add some padding. What if she undershot it? She doesn't know how long it'll take for you to get rid of her blood."

"Right." But I was still hoping it was less than that. "I'm going to hit the showers and then meet you downstairs."

Dastien nodded. "You'll need food. Your parents have been cooking nonstop. I've been helping, so I'll get back down there. Pancakes sound good?"

"Amazing. Thanks."

He kissed me quickly, but I dragged him down for another. I was alive, and I wasn't going to let him get away with just a peck. Not with everything we had going against us. Every second should count.

When he pulled away, he had a big grin on his face. The dimples were out in full-force.

I wasn't sure what to say to him—that I loved him, needed him, couldn't do this without him—because I felt all of those things and more. But I didn't need to say anything. His dimples dented his cheeks, and I knew he understood me perfectly.

He brushed one last kiss against my lips. "Go take your shower."

I reluctantly stepped away from him and went into my bathroom to start the shower. It wasn't until I pulled off my shirt that I saw my hip.

A jagged, puffy, red scar marked my skin. "Holy shit." It took a lot to scar a werewolf, which meant I was probably more indebted to Eli than I'd thought. Which was not the plan.

But I was alive. I was going to fight again today, and I wouldn't be ready for that if it weren't for Eli.

So, I'd be thankful that he showed up. Tonight, we'd fight Astaroth. Whatever happened after that, I'd deal with later—including giving Eli whatever he wanted from me.

As I stepped under the hot spray, I thought to myself—I can do this—over and over.

I kept on the steady stream of affirmations as I got dressed. I pulled on yoga pants, a comfy T-shirt, and a fresh, cozy sweater.

As I sat down on my bed to pull on my favorite pair of Uggs, something on my bedside table caught my eye.

The evil blade from Luciana's.

All the hair on my arms stood on end as I ran a fingertip lightly over the writhing bodies that covered the hilt.

It'd been in the pocket of my hoodie when shifted, and I'd totally forgotten about it.

Before I could think too hard, I went back to my bathroom and grabbed a washcloth. I rushed back to the table, wrapped the blade, and shoved it in my boot.

I knew I'd been compelled to grab the jar, and the blade was evil. I *knew* that too, but my gut told me if I left it behind, I'd die. It hadn't helped me last night, but tonight could be different. I wasn't giving up hope that this was exactly what I'd need to cut my tie to Astaroth.

I went back to the bathroom and splashed some water on my face. My eyes were a little too bright as I stared at myself in the mirror.

You can do this, Tessa. You will do this, I said to myself in the mirror. I stayed there until I believed it. If I had any doubt in my mind, I'd fail, and I couldn't afford to fail.

By the time I got downstairs, my stomach was demanding food. Loudly.

"You're up!" Mom said as she came to give me a hug.

"Thanks for having everyone over. Again."

"Oh, it's not a problem. I'm getting better at cooking on a large scale. Plus, pancakes are a breeze." She motioned to the griddle she'd placed over two of the burners. Six medium-sized ones were cooking with little bubbles on top, almost ready to flip. "I've got a stack of them in the oven if you're—"

My stomach cut her off with a loud rumble. "I'll take whatever you've got."

"Help yourself."

The island in the center had two bowls of cut up fruit—strawberries and bananas—plus a giant platter that was disappointingly only a quarter full of sausage patties. I grabbed a plate and loaded it up with sausage before turning to my mom. She held out the platter, and I grabbed ten pancakes.

"I don't think I'll ever get used to how much you eat now." Mom's eyes were wide as I stepped away from her. "It was only a few weeks ago I had to beg you to eat more than one of those sugar-filled protein bars."

"I'd still eat them if I could, but I'd have to eat like ten bars." I stuck out my tongue and made a fake barf noise. "Too much of a good thing is just gross." Nabbing the syrup from the island, I poured a puddle on top of the mound of pancakes. Done. I leaned my head against my mom's shoulder for a second. "Thanks."

"You're welcome."

I moved past her to the dining room. The table we'd moved in with had been small, but since we'd started going to my house for late lunch on Sundays, my parents had replaced it. The new table had a bench on one side, and the chairs on the other side didn't have arms so we could squeeze more in if we had to. The chairs at the head and foot of the table still had arms, though. My dad preferred them. He was sitting in the one closest to the back door.

His hair had gone grayer over the past couple months. I don't think he'd gotten exactly what he bargained for when he took the job at St. Ailbe's. The pay had been awesome, and we'd been looking to get out of LA, but there was a good reason that St. Ailbe's was looking for a PR specialist with a law degree.

"You want to take a seat?" Dad asked.

He was right. I was hovering, staring at him. It was weird. I slid onto the bench next to Dastien, who poured me a tall glass of OJ. I took in the room. Raphael had made his way back here. Claudia and Lucas were here, as was Mr. Dawson, Chris, and Adrian. Of them, only Lucas was still eating, but the plates were still there in case anyone decided to go in for more. Mr. Dawson was busy on his phone.

He's been like that all morning. I guess we created a big stir.

I guess we did. But I was still annoyed with Mr. Dawson.

He's making up for it. I promise.

My eyes caught Shane sitting next to Adrian, and it was like ten pounds of stress was siphoned out of my body instantly. He fought with us in Santa Fe and—along with Claudia—one of the only witches I would trust with my life. "You're here," I said.

He crossed his arms, showing off his colorful tattoos. "Adrian called me, filled me in on what was going on. I figured you could use my help."

"For sure." I looked at Adrian, but he gave me a small shake of his head. I wanted them to have their happily ever after, but it wasn't my business. So, I kept it zipped. For now.

Besides Shane, there was only one other person in the room that caught me by surprise. Blaze.

"I hope it's okay that I'm here," Blaze said. Apparently, the shock on my face showed.

"Sure!" That was way too high pitched. "Sure. Of course. I just wasn't expecting to see you. Not that you aren't welcome, I just—"

Dastien put a hand on my leg. "She's glad to have you here."

Blaze smiled, and I wasn't sure if I was drooling. Holy moly.

Dastien squeezed my leg harder, and I snorted out a laugh that set off a fit of giggles.

Are you serious?

I'm sorry. He's just so pretty.

261

And what am I?

I leaned into him, breathing in his scent. *Mine.* There was no mistaking that. He was my other half. I loved him, deep in my soul, and when I looked at him, all I could think of was *mine.*

But I could still admire the human form, as it were. Blaze seemed utterly unaware of how handsome he was and that—

Oh, please. He's older than dirt. He knows exactly what he looks like and how to play that to his advantage.

I thought you said he was humble.

He's humble, not dumb.

And older than dirt? Really? I looked at Blaze. He didn't have a single wrinkle on his face. His hair was dark as night, not even a speck of gray. Even Mr. Dawson had *some* gray. And Donovan had wrinkles—tiny ones, but they were there—around his eyes. Blaze looked like he was twenty-two at *most.*

"Lucas is older than you, right?" I asked.

Lucas grumbled. "Don't draw me into this."

"No, he's not," Blaze said with a laugh.

Claudia looked at Lucas and then to Blaze. "How old are you?"

"Very." Blaze smiled, looking pretty pleased with himself.

She rolled her eyes. "You're as vague as Lucas."

"I've found that age isn't important. Knowledge is. Experience. Innate power—which you're born with—"

"It can be gained," Lucas cut in.

"No. You're born with what you've got. How it's honed is important so that it can grow, but the potential is born in a person. Unless it's gained nefariously, then you've got all the power you've got from the start. Accessing it is another story."

Lucas nodded. "That I can agree with."

"Your power needs to be honed," he said to me. "Both of yours." He said to Dastien. "True mates are one thing. Powerful ones are another beast entirely. And neither of you has the training—"

"I've trained Dastien since he was a child." Mr. Dawson's defensive tone cut off Blaze.

"But he's going to need more training. A lot more."

Mr. Dawson grumbled something unintelligible and went back to typing on his phone.

Lucas put down his fork. "This isn't a contest. We're all strong."

"Not like they could be."

I shook my head. "It doesn't matter how much training we need later. If we don't figure out a way to quickly undo the mess you guys left for us to clean up, we're all going to die."

Blaze nodded. "You're right. This situation could've been avoided, and for that, I'm sorry."

"I am, too," Mr. Dawson said as he set down his phone. "I have a bit of foresight. Not like yours, but some. I knew you were coming before your father answered the ad. Even before Dastien was born. It seemed silly to join when I knew that changes were coming." When he looked at me, I could almost feel his regret and pain. "I didn't know the ripple effect killing Ferdinand would cause. I didn't see what Luciana was going to do or Astaroth showing up. If I knew I would've—"

"It's okay," I said. We'd rehashed this over and over. He needed to let it go. Honestly, we all did. We had a bigger fight coming, and I didn't want to spend it angry with anyone in this room.

"It's really not."

The tension in the room was thick enough for me to smell. Everyone was uncomfortable, and the soured milk scent of sadness and guilt was pouring off of Mr. Dawson in waves.

Dastien said something in French that I didn't understand,

but because I was in his head, I knew that he was telling him that it was okay. That he wasn't mad.

"What he said."

Dastien turned to me, and I could feel his surprise. "Since when do you speak French?"

"I didn't understand the words, but I got the sentiment." I tapped my forehead. "Benefit of being your other half."

Dastien bumped his shoulder into mine. "Eat, *chérie*."

I took a bite of the pancake and nearly moaned. Mom had put cinnamon into the mix. She was the best.

Lucas and Blaze started chatting about some fight they had a million years ago—possibly literally—and I focused back in on Shane as I ate.

He'd been hurt by a demon in Santa Fe. After the battle, we'd left New Mexico, but Adrian stayed behind while Shane was in the hospital. I thought they'd end up together, but Shane left. I never knew why and Adrian didn't volunteer any reason. He was too hurt.

But now Shane was here, and if we were going to fight together, I needed to know he was up for it. "Are you okay being here?"

His eyes grew glassy for a second, and I instantly regretted putting him on the spot. "I'm better," he said after a bit.

"I hate to ask, but you stayed away because of the demon injury? Are you okay?"

"I'm okay. What happened to Raphael was different than me. The wound I had was infected. I'm a witch, so the injury had some human side effects. Nothing supernaturally dangerous, but it was a little scary for a while. And..." He looked around the table, and stopped on Blaze and then again on Lucas. I thought he wasn't going to keep talking, but after a second, he heaved a big sigh and continued. "For better or worse, *la Aquelarre* was home for me. I'm not broken like Beth, but what Luciana did made me question everything. The thing that scared me the most was that there could be another Luciana lurking in a different coven."

The thought had occurred to me, but I'd had too many other things to deal with before I even thought about connecting with other covens and figuring out who was good or evil. "So that's what you've been doing? Checking out the other covens?"

"Yes. I wanted assurance that there wasn't another coven out there hurting like we were. If I could stop this from happening again, then maybe everyone dying wasn't for nothing."

"And what'd you find?" Raphael asked.

"Most of them didn't want to talk to me," Shane said. "We've been blacklisted. They wouldn't give me the time of day."

"Shit," Chris said. "That's messed up. The packs aren't like that."

I took another bite of the pancake as I listened, fascinated. I didn't have any experience with any other covens. I wondered what they were like.

"I started making a record of each coven I visited—what I found, who was there, if they seemed good, and how open they were to talking to me. Adrian told me that there was a database with all the Weres and I wanted to replicate that if I could."

"Yes," Mr. Dawson said. "We keep a close watch on everyone, and if there are any major changes in a pack, one of the Seven makes a point of visiting."

I didn't know that about the packs. I knew that the Alphas met every year, but beyond that—I figured everyone kept to themselves.

"Witches don't have anything like a council," Claudia said. "We're all very isolated and there's a lot of competition between covens. No one wants to share any secrets about their magic or how a spell is done."

That lined up with my first impression of them. "I remember when you gave me your book of shadows. Raphael looked like he wanted to murder you, punch me, and keep the book for himself."

Raphael's cheeks heated a little. "It wasn't that I didn't want you to learn about our magic, but that book was ours. In my mind, you hadn't earned it yet."

"That's the fucking problem," Shane shouted as he slammed his hand down on the table, rattling the plates. "We're too secretive. That's how this shit went unnoticed. And why when Luciana went to New Mexico, the coven there was fucking clueless about how evil she was. They all *died* in that chapel, and they didn't have to. If that lady had just believed us or even given us more than two seconds to explain, then—" He stopped suddenly, as if he only just realized that he was yelling. After a second, he cleared his throat. "I want to change that," he said much quieter. "We need more discussion between covens."

"We do," Claudia said as she reached across the table to him. He met her halfway, giving her hand a squeeze. "Did you go to New York?"

New York? That was where her evil ex-fiancee lived before he died.

"Yes," Shane said, but he stayed silent as he gave Claudia's hand one more squeeze and let go.

"And?" I asked, hoping that with Matt dead they'd straightened their shit out.

"If we're not careful, that coven leader's going to be Luciana all over again."

"Fuck," I said.

"Language!" Mom chimed in.

266

"Sorry." I covered my mouth with my hand. "Fuck, fuck, fuck," I muttered. Blaze chuckled, and my face heated.

I'd been so happy in my ignorance, but now checking in on all the other covens was just one more thing to add to my massive to-do list after I finished dealing with Astaroth.

There's nothing we can do about the New York coven right now.

I guess not, but it's annoying. You know? People need to get their shit together and stop being evil.

Dastien gave me a grin that showed both of his dimples. He tapped his finger on my plate, and I rolled my eyes at him. *Fine.*

I glanced at Chris as I ate a bite of pancake. His hair was one big poofball, which meant he was stressed, but he was here. I wondered if he'd emailed Cosette again after the fight. I was really hoping she'd be coming back soon, along with three other fey. I trusted her. She'd be here in time. I hoped.

The more immediate question for me was—what other witches were we going to get? Especially if we've been black-listed. "We need two more witches for the spell. Where are we going to find them? Discuss," I said, before shoving another bite in my mouth.

"I have a friend coming," Shane said. "I wasn't always welcomed at the covens, but I found one more open-minded coven that managed to stay on the light side of things. I met a guy there that—"

Adrian dropped his fork, cutting Shane off. "Excuse me," Adrian said as he pushed his chair back to get up.

"It's not like that. He's just a friend."

Adrian crossed his arms, and I could almost see the fight he was having with himself.

Shane watched him, waiting for Adrian to say or do anything, but when Adrian stayed staring straight ahead, his shoulders crumpled. "Anyway. I was actually on my way back here. My friend—

River—convinced me that running wasn't doing any good. That I needed to reconnect with Claudia and the friends I'd made here." He looked down for a second. "I was staying at a hotel in Austin, trying to get up the nerve to come back, when Adrian called."

This caught Adrian's attention, and I grinned. Maybe there was something good coming out of all this drama.

"You were?" Adrian asked softly.

"Yes." There was a moment of quiet as the two stared at each other before a knock sounded at the door. "This should be him." Shane got up quickly, retreating from the room.

Adrian seemed calmer when he heard that Shane was already back in Texas. I didn't want to assume that it was because Shane wanted to get back together with Adrian, but I was sure it had at least partially to do with their relationship. At least that's what I was hoping.

Shane came back in with a guy trailing behind him. He had long hair, tied back in a messy bun. A few pieces had escaped it, and he tucked them behind his ear as he checked out each of us. He was short, maybe only a few inches taller than me, and he was a little too thin for me. But then again, Dastien was pretty thick with muscle.

And that's a bad thing?

No. It's an fantastic thing. Have you seen your abs?

He shook his head at me, and I went back to my assessment of the witch. His heather gray T-shirt had holes along the collar, and his jeans had a tear in them at the knee, but it looked like from actual wear and tear, not for style. Maybe it was the height and the lack of visible muscles, but something about him just didn't scream that he was ready to take on one of the Evil Trinity and his army of demons.

He shoved the sleeves of his faded black hoodie up around his elbows, revealing some crystals tied on with thin pieces of leather around his wrists. "I hear you're in need of a witch for some sort of a spell?" He asked.

"Riverdream?" Claudia said.

The guy scanned the room and grinned brighter when he saw my cousin. "Claudia de Santos, right?"

She nodded.

"I just go by River now."

Her chair screeched as she got up. "It's been forever."

"I know. That whole your-coven-is-evil thing?" He winced. "Not good. Huh?"

Claudia laughed as she gave him a big hug. "It's good to see you." She pulled back but held on to his hand. "Do you want to sit? Are you hungry? It's a long drive from Alabama."

"Nah. I'm good. Been sitting too long."

"Riverdream?" I asked as Claudia went back to her chair.

"River." His gaze found mine, and he didn't look away, which I liked. I knew witches didn't have dominance displays like werewolves did, so it had nothing to do with power. But I actually missed people looking me in the eyes.

River's green eyes were bright as he took me in. "Thanks for coming," I stood from my spot. "I hope we're not putting you in a bad spot with your coven, though."

"No worries on that. My coven is a bit more progressive than others. Our magic is subtle and nature-based, and we don't mind sharing our stuff with outsiders. Plus, you've caused quite the stir in the witch community. It's nice to meet you, Teresa McCaide." He held out his hand, and I took it.

"Tessa. Tessa *Laurent*," I said, correcting him. The sound of saying my name—my *new* name—gave me a zing of energy in my soul.

River's palm was rough, but he had a firm handshake, and his gaze never left mine, which meant he was confident in who he was. A glimmer of light caught my eye. One of the crystals on River's wrist was glowing.

"Interesting," he said.

"What are those?" My fingers itched to touch them, but I forced myself to keep my hands to myself. If they were part of his magic in some way, I didn't want to insult him. Especially when we needed him to stick around for the spell. But this was the second time crystals had come up in as many days. I wondered what I was missing out on.

"Depends on which crystal you mean."

I was getting sidetracked. I'd have to ask River about them when we didn't have one of the Evil Trinity primed to kill us all. "How much did Shane tell you?"

"About what's happened? Everything."

"And you're okay with fighting demons?" Because I wasn't sure if hippie, nature-loving witches were also pacifists. This definitely wasn't going to be a pacifist group. "It's dangerous, and I want to make sure you're aware of everything we're up against."

"I've had some experience fighting demons. I know I might not look it, especially with who's in the room, but I've got power."

He was right. The room was pretty loaded in the power department, but I was curious what that meant. What experience did he have fighting demons exactly? I figured that was his to share when he was ready, but I had another question I couldn't stop myself from asking. "What kind of power?"

"Do you need a demonstration?"

I didn't, but I was extremely curious. Aside from *la Aquelarre* and Tía Rosa, my knowledge of witchcraft was pretty limited. I hadn't had time to really explore different kinds, and River's looked pretty damned different. The crystals on his wrists kept catching my attention. "If you don't mind? I'm kind of curious." I tried to tone down my excitement.

What Shane said was right—the covens are pretty closed to outsiders. But I've heard about his coven. They sell jewelry they make out of powered crystals.

I spun to Dasiten. *Really? Do they have a website?*

Yeah. I was thinking of getting something commissioned for you.

River cleared his throat. "Everything okay?"

I spun back around. "I was just talking to my mate."

"Umm..." He looked between Dastien and me like we were crazy.

I guessed I probably looked super weird silent-talking to Dastien. "It's a werewolf mate-bond thing. And rude. Sorry. It's habit now."

"Not a problem. So you talk to each other psychically?"

"Yup. That's pretty much what it boils down to."

"Huh." He looked curious but dropped it. "You ready?"

"Sure." But for what, I didn't know.

He smiled, and I noticed that one of his teeth was a little crooked. "On three."

I narrowed my gaze. "What's on three?"

River just kept grinning. I had a second to wonder what was so funny before he started counting.

"One." He muttered something in another language, one that had too many guttural sounds and consonants. "Two." One of the crystals on his wrist started to glow, and then he touched his pointer fingertips together, then his ring fingertips, then his thumbs. For a second, I thought I could see a spark moving around his hands. "Three." He twisted his wrists at the same time in one quick gesture.

It was as if something slammed into my stomach, and I flew backward, slamming into the wall.

I gasped as I slid to the floor. The room went into chaos, everyone yelling at once. Dastien grabbed River, lifting him up off the ground like he weighed nothing. I didn't have to be inside my mate's head to know what he was about to do.

Power rose within me, and I shoved it into the room. "Everyone stop!"

The Weres in the room froze, expect for Dastien. *He hit you.*

No. I told River to prove himself, and he did. He's in.

He hit you. He's out.

"I'm fine." I sent him some calm through the bond. I couldn't let Dastien piss this witch off, especially since I'd asked for him to show me what he could do. *We need him. I don't know what kind of witch he is or what those crystals are, but he has magic. Plus, we're desperate. He's in.*

Dastien wasn't happy about it, but he let River go.

"That was amazing," I said as I brushed myself off. "Do the crystals hold magic or was it in the gesture or what you said?"

River stepped away from Dastien, smoothing his hoodie down. "All of the above. We can talk about it another time, but first, someone mind filling me in on the specifics of the spell? Shane told me that we only have until tonight."

He might have looked laid back and unassuming, but River was looking better and better. I liked that he was getting straight down to it. "Yeah. You hungry?"

"No," River said. "I ate on the way."

"Cool. Sit down." I'd said it to River, but everyone else seemed to take it as time to clean up.

Blaze went to Mom, asking for a broom so he could clean up the mess from where I'd slammed into the wall. Dad was still looking pretty pissed off—probably mostly because I'd been thrown across the room, but probably also because there was a Tessa-sized dent in the wall that now needed fixing.

Mr. Dawson's phone rang, and he stepped into the kitchen to take the call. Chris was bent down, whispering something to Shane, but Adrian's gaze stayed glued to River. I was watching him carefully, too, as River bent to pick up a chair that had fallen. He didn't have the smooth way of moving that I'd come to recognize from a fighter, but he held himself confidently. Not an easy thing in a room full of Werewolves.

I might not know River very well or even at all yet, but I had a good feeling about him. "You didn't happen to bring any friends with you?" Because if he did, they were in, too.

River set the chair down. "No. Why?"

"We need one more witch."

His eyes widened. "No good comes from that much magic being harnessed. What kind of spell are you doing exactly?"

I blew out a breath. "I guess Shane didn't tell you everything."

He shot Shane a less-than-happy look. "Apparently not."

It took a good twenty minutes to explain it all, especially since he peppered me with questions every step of the way. By the time I was done, he'd pulled out his phone. "Have you talked to anyone in Washington?" He asked Claudia.

"No. I've...I haven't reached out to anyone."

He looked up from his phone for a second before going back to his phone. "This is exactly what's wrong with witches," he muttered to himself.

"That's what Shane was saying." I now realized how big of a problem this was.

"It's true." Claudia fiddled with her braid. "I meant to do something about it, but after Luciana, I just needed a break, I guess."

"I can understand that, but I think taking a break right now is a bad idea. What happened with Luciana shows that covens have to start working together or else risk more covens going dark..." River's words made Claudia frown. Lucas leaned in to say something, but Claudia grabbed his wrist.

If I were Claudia, I wouldn't want to reach out to any witches either. Hell, I wasn't even in Luciana's coven, and I'd had my fill. It was going to take a lot to make me trust another coven implicitly, and I hadn't endured the years of abuse that Claudia, Raphael, and Shane had. I was surprised to know that Shane had been visiting other covens, but it was smart.

"I'm calling Washington and Oregon," River said. "The California coven is out. There's a few scattered elsewhere, but there are some I wouldn't trust. Someone want to call Colorado?"

Shane nodded. "I can do it."

"Wait. That's where Cosette was?" I asked.

"Right," Claudia said. "Her roommate might be the best place to start."

"Shit. I don't have Karen's number," Shane said.

"I do," Chris said. "Sending you her contact info now."

We all stopped to look at Chris. "Why do you have Cosette's roommate's number?"

He shrugged as he typed on his phone. "I just do."

Okay. Now I was curious. Chris was totally holding out on me. "How close are you and Cosette?"

He threw his cell on the table and ran a hand through his already frizzed out hair. "We're just friends, and it can't ever go beyond that. So, drop it. Please."

"Why not? I—"

"Because she's the fucking princess of the goddamned *Lunar court*, and I'm not nearly alpha enough. I'd become a slave if I ever stepped foot in there." The natural rasp in his voice was turning into a growl.

My mouth dropped open. No. That couldn't be true. If that's all that was standing in their way, then there had to be something we could do. Some kind of magic or amulet or fucking fey artifact that could protect him.

"Don't. I know what you're thinking, but just don't." His chair clattered to the ground as he stormed out the back door.

"Chris!" I yelled as I followed. I was only a step behind him onto the back porch, but he kept moving. "Chris."

He moved faster, heading for the woods that surrounded the house.

"Wait!" I backed it with a tiny touch of power. He could keep walking if he wanted to, but I didn't want him to run off upset. Not with how everything was going.

His eyes were burning bright blue as he spun to me. "I can't talk about this. I need to go, but I'll be back. Just give me an hour."

"You don't have to talk about anything, and you can absolutely leave. I only want to say I'm sorry. I'm an idiot. It's absolutely none of my business. But I don't want you to leave mad. Tonight is going to get crazy, fast. And I didn't want to miss my chance to apologize. If there's anything that I can do to help, I want you to know that I'm here for you. But I won't bring it up again. Promise."

"It's fine."

"It's not fine. You're upset, and I'm a total asshole for upsetting you. You've done nothing but be there for me since we first met. I owe you the same respect."

He closed the distance, giving me a hug. "You just hit a sensitive spot, but you're my friend. It happens."

"Is there anything I can do?"

"No. It's hopeless. We both know that there's nothing that can happen between us, but trying to convince my wolf that it's not happening is another matter." He took a breath. "I am who I am. You heard what Blaze said. You're born with whatever power you have, and I don't measure up."

"But if—"

"I just need a second to calm down." He pulled his shirt over his head and threw it on the ground. "Being a part of this is a better distraction than I could've ever hoped for. I never wanted to be a Cazador. Never settling down. Never having a home. That life wasn't for me. But my home pack is small, and being back there last month wasn't good for me. Too much has happened, and I don't fit there anymore. I've been a little lost until last night. Until you picked me. I'm going to work hard to make sure I'm worthy of my spot."

Worthy? That was a load of crap. "Shut up. You're worthy. Maybe the Alphas in that room couldn't see it, but I did. Meredith did, too. You're an amazing person, and everyone who gets to call you their friend is lucky. I love your lighthearted teasing. You're kind and always there with a smile and a laugh, even when I don't think I can laugh. And especially when I need one. I hate seeing you upset."

He gave me a grin, but it wasn't his usual smile. "It happens. Don't worry about it."

"I *am* worrying about it. If Cosette is a part of this new council thing, is that going to be bad for you?" I hated asking, but I had to.

"I don't know. Cosette... I can't be what she needs in a mate, but I'll always be her friend. I can't—I can't..." He blew out a hard breath, and his eyes grew glassy. "I don't know how to say it, but my wolf made his choice, so she's it for me. I can't be her mate, but I can be her forever friend. So, it's complicated, but it'd be that way even if she wasn't part of this."

Hearing that his wolf had chosen his mate, but that it wasn't going to work out made my own heart ache like someone was pulling it apart. "That can't be it." This was so wrong. He deserved so much better than a lonely life.

"But it is." He stared at the ground as he toed off his shoes.

"I'm disappointed that I'm not powerful enough to survive a day at court with her." His voice had grown gruff with his wolf edging closer. "But life is full of disappointments. When you get smacked in the face with one, you have to pick yourself up. So, that's what I'm doing. I have to let her go and hope she finds someone worthy. But I can't leave her. Not entirely. I just hope that it gets easier because right now, I just want to be a wolf all the time." He went to unbutton his jeans, and I spun around.

"Chris..." His furry head bumped my hand, and I squatted down, gripping his hair. Chris' wolf was a light blonde color. "Take your run," I said as I stared into his blue eyes. "But know that I'm here for you. Whatever you need." He rubbed his face against mine and then took off into the woods behind my parents' house.

Come on back, chérie.

I am, I said, but I stayed where I was, feet firmly planted as I listened to the soft sounds of wolf-Chris running farther into the woods. *I wish there were a way to help him. You think it's true? About him not having enough power to be with Cosette?*

Probably.

That breaks my heart. I rubbed my chest. *I hurt for him. Do you think we could give him some power?*

Chérie... Messing with that stuff? That's what Luciana did and how we all got into this mess.

I kicked the dirt. *It's not fair.*

I know, but our job is to be there for him. And we are. There will be someone for him.

There has to be.

There will be. Dastien was quiet for the second. *Come back. We're having trouble getting any of the covens to take our calls.*

That's just perfect.

Exactly.

I started making my way back to the house, but I made a

promise to myself. Once I was done saving the world for a second time, I was going to find a way to help Chris. He might be giving up, but I wasn't.

The more shit happened, the more I realized that nothing in life was easy. It'd taken Dastien turning me and a bit of drama before we'd found our stride. If Cosette was his mate, then there'd be a solution. He just didn't know it yet.

CHAPTER TWENTY

SHANE WAS on the phone when I got inside. "I understand."

"I mean really, Shane. What the hell do you expect?" The woman on the other line was whisper-yelling through the line.

"I know, but it wasn't us. Luciana—"

"Is dead. And now what? Shit's still going down, and you're coming to *me* for help. No way. What's left of your coven is dead to us. I shouldn't have even answered the phone. If anyone knew I was talking to you, they'd kick me out."

"Come on, Ramona. You can't hold us responsible for Luciana's actions." He was quiet. "Ramona?" He glanced at the screen. "She hung up on me."

I sat back in my chair. "I take it finding another witch is going well?"

"*Super* well," Shane said.

"Okay. So, maybe the Colorado coven?"

Claudia shook her head. "Cosette's roommate didn't answer. And Chris is the only one that's had any luck getting in touch with Cosette. Maybe if he came back..."

"No." There was no way I was asking Chris to get ahold of Cosette again. Not after what I knew. "I could try messaging her, but honestly, she's made it clear that it was going to be a stretch to get herself and three other fey here before tonight. Asking for her to bring a witch, too? That feels like asking a lot." I turned to River. "Anyone else from your coven willing to come?"

He shook his head. "Nah. The closest my coven likes to get to a fight is finding power crystals and turning them into jewelry. I'm kind of the black sheep. The rest of them think I'm abusing my crystals when I use them offensively."

Well, that was a dead end. "Anyone else? Blaze? You've been around for a long time. You're bound to have come across some witches."

"Absolutely, but the ones I've reached out to are of the mind that the Seven caused this, and it's now our job to fix it."

That was fantastic. When this was over, I was going to have a serious talk with the witches.

Which witches are you talking about? Dastien asked.

All of them. Because they seriously needed to get their shit together. "Lucas? Don't you have some witches in your coven?"

"Even if some of them were willing, I don't think any could get here in time. Unless we can wait until tomorrow for the spell?"

Even him suggesting we wait made me anxious. "No. It's gotta be tonight." I got up and started pacing. I didn't know enough witches to be of any help, but I had to come up with something. "Raphael? I hate to ask you to, but what do you think?"

He leaned back in his chair. "Technically I could do it, but I'm still tied to Astaroth."

"So am I."

"But you're stronger than me and have to be in it. I bring literally nothing to the table. I barely have magic, and right now, it's tainted. I already got one person killed trying to fix it. I'm not doing that again."

"Okay." A thought crossed my mind, and I looked at Shane. "There's someone else we're not talking about."

Shane sat taller in his chair as he looked at me. He knew exactly who I was talking about. "No. We can't. She's so broken."

Maybe she was doing better. "But you know where she is?"

"No." He shifted in his seat uncomfortably. "I was calling her, but she never answered. So, I was giving her some time. I've been planning on reaching out to her, but..."

"When was the last time you talked to her?"

"When we were at St. Ailbe's. Right before we left for New Mexico."

That was a long time ago. I hadn't even thought about checking in on her either. Honestly, I didn't know her well enough. I figured she'd gone to stay with friends or something. But now I was wondering what the hell happened to her.

"I can call her, but—" Shane crossed his arms as he stared me down. Shane was pissed at me for even bringing her up. "We cannot ask her to do this."

"I'm not a monster. I'm not going to *make* her do the spell, but she's a witch, and she's from your coven. So, we won't have all the issues that we've had with all the other covens questioning our motivations."

"That's true, but—"

"She's strong." Claudia cut in. "Her whole family died, but she's strong. That's how she walked away from Luciana when everyone else stayed. She comes from generations of witches on both sides. She might be taking a break from magic, but magic is a part of her. If we can find her, she might agree. If she's anything like me, she'll want her powers used for something good, and this is good."

Mr. Dawson stepped back into the room. "Wait. You're talking about Beth?" He'd been busy on his phone most of the morning but put the cell down as he sat at the table again.

I looked around the room. The wolves were starting to catch on, but I didn't realize we'd never said her name. "Yes. I think Beth is a great option, but Shane disagrees."

"She's broken! Leave the girl alone!"

"Who is Beth?" Blaze asked Lucas quietly, as if he didn't want to interrupt, but I heard him well enough. Answering the question might give Shane a chance to calm the fuck down.

"She was the only other member of *la Aquelarre*—besides myself, Raphael, and Shane—to live," Claudia said before I could answer. "Beth was with me and Raphael and Shane in Costa Rica. By making the oath to me, they broke their bond to Luciana just in time... But Beth's family—her sister who raised her, her brother-in-law, niece and nephew—were all living on the compound. They were murdered along with everyone else." Claudia's eyes grew glassy, and Lucas grabbed her hand. "She stayed in Texas when we went to New Mexico. Her grief over losing her family...it was all-consuming. And when we got back, she was gone. I tried scrying for her, but she had her protections up. I assumed she wanted some time alone and would reach out when she was ready."

I sighed. "So no one knows where Beth is or what happened to her when we left for Santa Fe."

"That's not entirely accurate," Mr. Dawson said. "I know where she is."

"You do?" Claudia asked slowly, as if she was misunderstanding something.

"Of course." He leaned forward, meeting the gaze of the witches. "She wasn't safe to be left alone, so I got her counseling. Beth lost her whole support system, and it was hard, but she's a fighter. She's doing a lot better than she was."

"Where is she?" Shane's tone was almost accusatory. But it wasn't like Mr. Dawson had been hiding her away. At least I didn't think he would do something like that.

"She spent a couple weeks at a very nice in-patient facility. After that, I asked her what she wanted to do. If she wanted to travel or if there was a friend that she wanted to stay with, but she didn't have anywhere in mind. She wanted a break, but she needed a friend her age that understood the supernatural world. Beth's gifts are interesting and a little uncontrolled when she's upset. So, I set her up with a half-sprite in Austin, which helps her out a bit."

Claudia laughed. "I'm sure."

I was missing something, but that wasn't unusual. I'd look up what a sprite was later.

Mr. Dawson smiled. "I was glad Nell agreed. The sprite's apartment isn't great, but I thought that was better than Beth being alone, and I got her enrolled in some classes mid-term. Just basics in case she decides that college is for her."

"She's really okay?" Shane said.

Mr. Dawson leaned back in his chair. "When I said that we'd take care of what was left of your coven after we burned down your homes, I wasn't lying. I'm the Alpha. It's part of my job. That's why I've called you every week, Shane."

Shane stared at the table before shrugging it off. "I thought you were just being nice."

"It's not about being nice. Any person that's negatively impacted by the Weres, we take care of," Blaze said. "That's how the packs work."

Mr. Dawson nodded. "Exactly. And that's what I've done. I made sure that Beth has everything she needs to live a good, healthy life, and I'm going to continue to do so until she's fully back on her feet. Right now that means an apartment in Austin, close to campus. She's got a roommate that can help her, friends, and I heard she's gone on a couple of dates." He took a breath. "She wanted a normal, non-magical life, and I told her I'd do anything I could to help with that. I'll do the same for you, even though you've refused it so far, for Raphael, who has done the same, and for Claudia, but I doubt Lucas would let me."

Lucas scooted closer to his mate. "I've got her."

"Do you think Beth would do the spell?" I asked Mr. Dawson. He was the one who knew her best now.

"I don't know." He shrugged. "So far she's wanted to distance herself from magic. I don't know if that means forever or just for right now. Only Beth can answer that question for you."

"Well, then. Let's ask her." We didn't have a ton of options, and even though I didn't really know Beth very well, I remembered her being nice.

Mr. Dawson pulled out his phone and put it on speaker as it rang.

"Hi, Michael. You're calling early?" Beth answered, and she actually sounded happy to hear from him.

"Actually, it's not just me, and we're calling to ask a really big favor."

There was some rustling. "Okay. I'm sitting down. What's wrong?"

"Hey, girly," Shane said.

She let out a breath. "Hey, Shane. How are you?"

"I'm good. How are you?"

"Getting there."

"We need your help," Claudia said.

"I don't know that I have anything left to give, Claudia."

"Hey. Tessa here," I said. She was familiar with her coven members voices, but I wasn't sure she'd know who I was. "Just hear us out before you say no. I honestly wouldn't have called you if it weren't life or death."

"Okay. I'm listening."

Claudia did all the talking. She knew Beth better than I did, and I was fine to take a back seat. Today had been nothing but drama and rehashing the same details for each new person we'd roped into this mess. Honestly, I was exhausted, but there were mountains to climb before the day was out and this was just the first of many.

Dastien rubbed my shoulders, easing away some of the tension. *We'll get through it.*

I hoped he was right.

When Claudia was done, Beth was quiet. I looked around the room. Everyone was leaning forward, waiting to hear what she'd say.

"I thought this was behind us," she said finally. "But it's not. Is it?"

"No," Claudia said. "And I think it's safe to say that I'm feeling about the same as you about that."

She laughed, but it came out almost like a half-sob. The line was a little too quiet after that, and I kept checking to see if the call had failed. But she was taking a second, and that was okay.

She was going to say yes. I just knew it. And not because she was power hungry or because she wanted revenge or because she missed magic. The longer she stayed quiet, the more right she felt.

The only reason this was going to work—and end up better than the Seven—was because we were all doing it for the right reasons. Because we *had* to. There was no other option.

With the exception of Blaze, I was reasonably sure that none of us would've signed up for a job like this. Cosette was forever trying to get away from her court. Chris liked to blend in, too. Claudia was a little timid, but with Lucas, was finding her voice. But even then, she didn't want her own coven.

This was going to work because we all were in it to make it

work. Not for ourselves but for everyone else. And the fact that every person on this new council had links across supernatural boundaries meant that it was going to unify us all.

Beth was a good choice, and even if I was on the edge of my seat waiting for her answer, I was glad she was taking a second to think it through.

"Um. I need..." Her voice sounded like she'd been crying. "I need a few minutes to think about it."

The line went dead.

"Shit," Shane said, echoing my own thought. "I told you! We shouldn't have even—"

"She's texting," Mr. Dawson said as he held out the phone. Sure enough, those three little dots were blinking.

The room went dead quiet as we waited. My heart was beating in my ears as I held my breath. We needed her. Like *needed her*-needed her. If she couldn't—wouldn't come, then we were so screwed.

If she said no, the only other option was Raphael, but he said it himself—he didn't have much magic *and* he was tied to Astaroth. I wasn't sure how much of a detriment that would be to the spell seeing as how I was, too, but it couldn't be—

"She's coming," Mr. Dawson said. His words rolled like a sigh of relief, one that I was sure everyone was feeling. "She said she needs a minute to get herself together, but she'll pack a bag and be here in the next couple of hours."

"Oh, thank God." I rested my head on the table. The rush of relief was so intense I couldn't even keep my head up.

Thank God.

Dastien ran a hand up and down my back. *It's going to work out. Step by step. We'll be free of Astaroth.*

I turned my head so I could peek up at him. *I hope so.* Now that we had all the witches, and I was taking it on faith that

Cosette would come through, that meant there was only one other element that we needed.

Eli. He had to be our nuclear bomb-sized magical power to get this whole thing rolling.

I sat up and looked around the table. "Anyone know anything about making a deal with an archon? Because that's the next thing on my to-do list and I'd rather not sell what's left of my soul down the shitter." Blaze laughed, and I couldn't help but smile even though I was filled with dread.

I knew very limited things about Eli. He wasn't a demon. He wasn't an angel. He wasn't good, but he wasn't bad either.

Everyone said that dealing with the fey was tricky, but dealing with an archon? No one knew what that was going to be like, and with the way my life had been going lately, I had a feeling it was going to be anything but easy.

CHAPTER TWENTY-ONE

MY TEETH RATTLED as the car bottomed out for the millionth time. After a bit of discussion on the best practices when making a deal with an archon—which was short given that no one had actually done that before—Dastien and I decided to take a drive to our land. I'd call for him there, and hoped he'd show up. Just because Eli had helped us twice didn't mean he'd keep saving our asses.

Blaze said that all I had to do was go to a quiet place and meditate. Then I had to ask for him to appear, and if Eli deemed it worthy, he would.

I guessed that's why I failed so many times during my vision. He didn't deem my death via a snapped neck from one of the Evil Trinity worthy enough.

So what was worthy in Eli's eyes? Why was last night different than all the other versions I'd seen in my visions? What rule had Astaroth broken that allowed Eli to take action?

My teeth rattled as we went over another pothole. "We need to get this road cleared before we drive up here again." I wasn't even sure my car could make it all the way to the clearing. The undercarriage slammed into the ground with a painful crack. "Shit!" I said as my head slammed into the window. "Thank God I'm a werewolf. Otherwise, I'm pretty sure I'd have a concussion." I blinked until my vision cleared.

"We can walk from here. But yes, we'll get it paved once things settle down."

"I don't remember it being this bad." I tightened my grip on the door handle as he slowed. "Is the road worse?"

"*Ouais.*" Dastien put the car in park and turned off the engine. "There must've been some storms while we were gone. Fall is pretty rainy here."

I got down from the car, my feet squishing in the mud. "You're not kidding." *Damn it.* My favorite Uggs were going to be toast. We definitely needed to cut a road through to the land. I liked being able to come here, even if we were years away from breaking ground.

"We're not years away. We can get started whenever you want."

He came around the car, and I linked his hand with mine. "I want. As soon as we get rid of Astaroth. I don't want to wait for anything. Every moment we have here is a gift, and I want to make the most of it."

Are you okay?

No. How could I be? There was so much on the line right now, and the pressure to somehow fix it was all-consuming. *I just want to get through tonight. And then I really want things to settle down. Do you think that there will ever be a time when some evil force isn't trying to kill us?*

I can't tell the future, but I hope so. And I think having a plan for something fun will help, so let's make a plan. What do you think—brick? Stucco? Craftsman?

I'm not sure what a craftsman house is. We should definitely watch some more home shows.

He laughed as he tugged on my hand. *Sounds like a date.*

It wasn't long before I could see the break beyond the trees. Dastien had bought a giant plot of land, including a pond. The clearing was massive and completely hidden by the surrounding woods, which is why he bought it. We could run as humans or wolves without any neighbors peeking over a fence. I was going to figure out some wards to keep any intruders away. Not the horrible feeling ones like the compound used to have, but something gentler.

It's going to be amazing once we can live here. This is pretty much the perfect spot.

Dastien grinned down at me. "I'm glad you think so. I was nervous when I first brought you here, but I guess I shouldn't have been."

"Nah. We pretty much agree on most things." We got about halfway to the pond, and then I stopped. "If this goes bad—"

"Nope," he said before I could even finish the thought. "In it together all the way."

I knew that we did everything together—especially now—but I wasn't sure what would happen if I somehow pissed off an archon. Eli seemed pretty okay, but I'd had exactly two conversations with him, and the second one was in the middle of a battle. "I just—"

"That's also a no. You don't get to sacrifice yourself for me. We're mates. Our souls are joined. Where you go, I follow."

"Right. Fine. But the same goes for you."

"Wouldn't have it any other way." Before I could ask the question, Dastien nodded. "Go ahead. I'm ready as I'll ever be."

I blew out a breath, giving myself a second to let his words settle me and give me a little boost in confidence. If I was going to make a deal with an archon, then at least I wasn't alone.

I closed my eyes and took four steady breaths in and out. When I felt calmer and at peace, I called out to him in my mind.

Eli, I'm ready to make a deal.

"That wasn't so hard, was it?"

I spun to find him standing right behind me. He was wearing a white button-down shirt, a pair of dark jeans, and no shoes. His shoulder-length white-blond hair was neatly tucked behind his ears. His blue eyes glittered with laughter. Although I couldn't imagine why he found this situation funny. Even though he wasn't hovering in the air, he was at least a foot taller than me.

And holy shit. I couldn't believe it'd worked. Eli was here. "Why didn't you come all the other times?"

"Other times? In your visions?"

"Yeah."

"Because those weren't real." He tapped a finger on my nose as if I were some cute toddler who had asked a super dumb question. "They were possibilities. I wasn't going to waste my time until you'd found the right path."

Well, at least I was on the right path. Finally. Now I just needed to ask Eli my favor. "I'm hoping that means—"

"I know what you're going to ask. The answer is yes. I will be happy to back your spell with my power and seal the realm—"

A too-enthusiastic "Thank God" slipped free before I slapped my hand over my mouth.

"*But* there'll be a price."

"There's always a price." This I was prepared for. Sort of.

"The question becomes, what are you willing to give for my help?"

Before Dastien and I left my parents' house, we'd decided that the most important thing was to find out what Eli wanted from me exactly and define clear limits. But he was putting me on the spot. I didn't know much—or anything really—about what Eli would want from me. It'd be straight up stupid to just start offering up terms. "I'm afraid you're going to have to be more specific. What do you want from me?"

"Ah. That's your father talking."

"Damned straight." I'd heard so many stories about negotiations gone wrong from him. Hollywood was notorious for shitty deals and taking advantage of dumb people.

I wasn't an idiot, and I wasn't about to start being one now. So I waited, quietly. Trying to keep my mind blank.

"I'm not going to take your first born or anything horrible like that. I think you'll find that I'm pretty reasonable."

I doubted that.

"That hurts," he said, feigning shock.

I laughed. I'd forgotten Eli could read my mind.

"See, you'll like me. I'm funny. We're going to be friends." He crossed his arms as he stared down at me.

Friends seemed like a stretch. "I'm not going to be your slave."

"That's what Astaroth wants, and I'm not him." All the joking was gone from him.

Good. This was important, and I wanted Eli to take me seriously. "You saved my life last night, and so far, you haven't asked me for anything."

"No. And I'm not going to. That jar was breaking the rules, and the portal he made with it was an abomination. Healing you was good for me, too. It insured that you would be here today."

"What are the rules?"

He shrugged. "This and that. They don't matter. Except when they do."

"That is literally the vaguest thing I've ever heard." He stayed quiet, and I guessed that was the end of that topic. "I'm not going to let you use my power without my okay or drain it from me or anything else that I'm not aware of right now." I left it open-ended. I didn't know what else was possible, but I sure as shit wasn't going to let any ignorance bite me in the ass later.

"I've got enough power on my own, thank you very much. I don't want or need yours."

I sighed. *What am I missing? What does he want?*

I don't know. Just ask him.

He was right. If I wanted Eli to be clear, then I had to ask. "What do you want?"

"A vial of your blood."

I was new to witchcraft, but I wasn't *that* new. Blood could be used in too many ways—most of them not good. "Why do you want my blood?"

"I'm going to tie you to me."

Dastien growled, but I waved him back. I didn't like the sound of that either. "Why do you want to tie us together?"

"You're going to be the focal point for the spell, which means I'll need your blood."

That didn't make sense. "If you wanted it just for the spell, then I'd give it to you. But since you're asking me for it separately, that makes me think it isn't *just* for the spell. Is it?"

"Very good." He smiled down at me like he was proud I'd caught on. "No. The bond I want with you is something beyond what's needed for your spell. It will be there forever."

I didn't like the sound of that, and neither did Dastien. He was thinking about ripping off Eli's head off. *Don't. I'm pretty sure that fight won't end well.*

I wasn't sure if I could agree to that. It all depended on what kind of tie Eli wanted. If it was going to be something as thin as the ties I had to a Were from another pack, ones that could be easily broken and reformed, then fine. But if it was more like my mate bond—strong and unbreakable—then I wasn't sure. I didn't know Eli well enough to agree to that. "What kind of bond do you want with me specifically?"

"One that will let me find you any time and check in on you when I see fit."

Check in on me? I wasn't sure I liked that, but I needed more information. "What else?"

"You'll need to be more specific," he said, throwing my word back at me.

That was more difficult, because if I failed to ask the right question, then I could get myself into a shit deal. I didn't know what all the possibilities were, which was a problem when negotiating.

Go with something simple, Dastien said.

Okay. "Will I be able to say no to you?" That was non-negotiable. Free will wasn't something I was about to give up.

"Of course."

"Will I be forced to do favors or acts of any kind?" Because I wouldn't be forced.

"No. I'll do no forcing, but I reserve the right to convince you."

"Because of the blood?" Compelling me was also a hard pass.

"No. I'll be able to convince you with words like any ordinary human. Just sound reasoning."

Which probably meant that he could deliver threats. His grin widened, and I knew I'd hit the nail on the head. He definitely wasn't an angel. "Does the blood let you hold sway over my decisions?"

"No."

That was a relief. At least I could say no and argue my point if I didn't like whatever he was asking me for. "So, what? It's just magical low jack? Tell me specifically, because I'm a little ignorant here." When he said, nothing, I started to get pissed. "Don't be an asshole. Just tell me. Why do you want to be tied to me?"

Dastien geared up for a fight the second the word "asshole" slipped from my lips, but Eli only laughed.

"Fair enough. I enjoy honesty. It's why I like you so much. So, I'll give you a dose of honesty back."

Finally, we were getting somewhere.

"I can't act without a tie. There are rules I can't break, and before you ask again—no. I can't tell you what they are. That's one of the rules. Let's just say that I'm bored and want in on the fun."

I almost laughed. "You're calling this fun?"

"I enjoy a good fight, and more fights are coming. Little ones. Big ones. And I want to play. The tie with you will not only give me that ability, but it will also allow me to get you to play in some battles you wouldn't previously have been aware of."

Now that was laughable. "You decimated a field of demons without spending much effort. What on Earth would you need my help with?"

"The tie will allow me to bend the rules, but there will still be rules for me. And I can hear the question starting again, so one more time—no. I'm not telling you the rules."

"If I knew what the rules were, I might understand what you're asking of me."

"Where's the fun in that?"

Eli had some messed up sense of what fun meant.

"The bond will be less than what you have with Dastien, but more than what you have with your fellow pack members. Let's just say it's insurance. I want to know where you are and make sure you're alive. I'm not here to harm you or hold you back. It's in my best interest to keep you alive. Because the second you die, the balance in this world is thrown off again. I don't like that. I want this world to stay settled. I helped build it, and if it gets destroyed? Well, then my life will get even more boring."

I glanced at Dastien before looking back at Eli. He was handsome and seemed likable, and he'd saved my life once already, so I wanted to trust him. But I also wanted to be clear. "If I do this, your goal is to keep me alive?"

"Yes."

I didn't have a problem with that. Having someone as powerful as Eli motivated to keep me alive was a good thing. "And the people I care about? They'll stay alive too?"

"Sometimes. I'm not God, and I cannot predict the future."

I growled in frustration. "What about Dastien? He stays alive."

His dark eyebrows rose. "You're a bit of a package deal. That goes without saying."

"So you might be asking me for a favor, or you might be saving my butt?"

"Yes. This is pretty much the best deal that I've ever offered. You should take it."

I'd bet it was. The deal sounded reasonable, but we had a common goal right now. What happened if that changed? *What do you think?*

I don't know. You're asking all the right things though.

I thought for a second. "I won't do anything that would harm good people. I won't do anything evil. I won't meddle in any kind of dark magic."

Eli shrugged. "I agree to the first two, but the last one—maybe we'll call it gray magic? I wouldn't want to limit what you can use in a fight."

"Fair enough. But I reserve to the right to have a hard pass on anything you ask, and you can't blackmail or coerce me to do it."

"Of course. I wouldn't dream of blackmailing or coercing. I'm not a demon."

What do you think? I asked Dastien. *Be honest. Should we take the deal?*

I don't know, but we're in a tight spot. We need his help, and he knows it. That's never a good position to be in.

"In case you haven't noticed, I'm the only power that's helping to stop the end from coming. This is a good deal."

"So I agree to this, and you'll be popping in my life whenever it suits you?"

He grinned. "Pretty much. You'll owe me, and I'll be able to ask you for endless favors. Which you will be able to turn down or not as you will."

"Endless?" No. Not a chance.

"Fine." He rolled his eyes dramatically. "Shall we set a number?"

"Damned straight. Five favors." That was totally reasonable.

"Fifty."

He had to be joking. "No. Ten."

"Fine. Let's call it fifteen with the potential to renegotiate when the time arises. Are we agreed?"

I can turn the favors down, but do you think he'd let me?

I wouldn't think so, but he did say no blackmail. Dastien was thinking about how this deal was a bust, but he also knew I couldn't turn him down.

At least I could say no to whatever he was asking me to do in the future, but he might make my life hell for it. But figurative hell was way better than actual hell.

I let out a breath. *This doesn't seem that bad, but I'm not loving it either.*

I don't like the idea of us being tied to him. We don't know what could happen in the future—where we'll be in life and if we'll even want to entertain his requests. This bond between you and him would be forever.

There was no way Eli was going to offer up any info up that I didn't specifically ask about. I hoped I wasn't missing something big. If I could ask Claudia—

"I'm making a deal with you, not your cousin or your mate. Since you're already bonded to Dastien, I'll let him have some say. But I draw the line there."

"Is there anything else you want from me?"

"No. Are we agreed?" He held out his hand.

Do it, Dastien said.

You sure?

No, but I think we have to.

I agree. But I couldn't believe I was doing this. "Yes." I put my hand in his. Power cracked through my body, and I jerked back. My vision was filled with dots, and I tried to blink them away.

"Good. I'll get the vial from you tonight, and then I can make the bond. Sound good?"

"Sure," I said as when I could see again.

Eli rubbed his hands together, and I could almost see his excitement bubbling out of him. "Now, where do you stand with the fey? Have you found ones willing to join in on the fun yet?"

I shrugged. "Not exactly, but I trust Cosette—"

"Trusting a fey? Are you sure that's wise?"

"Uh... Yes?" Cosette was my friend, and I knew she'd come through.

"Hmm." He crossed his arms as he stared at me, and I started to wonder what was going through his mind. "Why don't you send her a message? Remind her that we're waiting."

I looked at Dastien, who gave me one of his Gallic shrugs. "I can email her I guess, but she hasn't been answering them."

"Email her again. Mention that I'm here waiting, too. Use my full name. E-l-i-l-a-i-o-s."

"Fine." I pulled out my cell phone and typed a quick message. "Okay. Sent. But sometimes she doesn't check it for a while, and it could be that—"

The field lit up, and suddenly Cosette was standing between Eli and me, and she hadn't come alone. Van stood next to her, and at least fifteen warriors were standing around the field, all dressed like Van. Their long hair braided away from their faces.

"You!" She spat the word, poking him in the chest.

Eli grinned. "Hey, sweetheart."

I stepped back from them, not wanting to get in the middle of whatever was about to happen.

"Don't you dare *hey, sweetheart* me! I'm not your *sweetheart*. And no! For the last time, I'm *not* helping you! You nearly got me killed last time!"

Any ideas as to what the hell is going on? Dastien asked me.

How should I know? Cosette was still mostly a mystery to me. I got a little insight into her here and there, but she wasn't one to just open up and spill her history. But I had a ton of questions for her about Eli now.

"Did you plan this?" Cosette asked. "Is this whole fight with Astaroth one of your little games? One of those let's-fuck-with-the-mortals games that you love so much?"

What? It felt as if all the blood were draining from my body. Cosette had to be joking.

He laughed. "No. But I like that you think this is my plan. Even I wouldn't do something this terrible, sweetheart."

Oh, thank God.

Cosette flicked her hand, and a sword appeared in it. "How can I trust you after what you did to me?"

For the first time, Eli didn't look confident. "Come on. You can't still hold that against me."

The sword started glowing with flames, and I took a few steps back. "Of course I do," Cosette said.

Ten more fey popped into the clearing, and I started to wonder who would win if there was a fight between Eli and the fey.

I had no idea what the subtext was or how Cosette even knew Eli, but the fact was, we needed both of them to complete the spell. Game or not, I had to get rid of Astaroth. If I let them fight, then we could kiss the spell goodbye.

"Cosette?" I said. "What's going on?"

They were both quiet for a second before Cosette spun to face me. "I didn't realize *Elilaios* was the archon you were dealing with. This is going to cause complications."

With that, she was gone. Along with Van and all the other fey.

"Fuck!" My heart skipped a beat. "What the hell did you do?" I yelled at Eli.

He started at the ground before sighing and grabbing my hand.

I tried to wrench it free.

"Don't worry. I have a plan."

I turned to Dastien, reaching out, but I was too slow.

The world spun as my surroundings changed.

One second we'd been in our clearing, the next, I was with Eli in a massive white marble entryway. A chandelier as big as a house hung overhead, sending glittering rainbows all over the white floor. I couldn't see much else, because we were ringed by fey warriors. Three deep. From the fact that their spears were out and pointing at us, I figured it was safe to assume they were pissed.

I scowled up at Eli, pulling my hand away from his. How was he planning to get us out of here without getting me killed?

He raised his eyebrows at me, and I realized he wasn't planning on getting us out of it.

That was up to me.

I reached out to Dastien, but the bond was silent. Not gone, just on mute. I could tell that he was alive, but that was it.

I hated when that happened. For as often as we said we were doing everything together, I was cut off from Dastien too much. I was going to have to come up with a way to fix that.

But for now, I had to deal with a bunch of pissed off fey. "I came to talk to Cosette?" My voice squeaked, and I winced. This was terrible. I was alpha. I was going to be the head of this new council. I had to get it together. Letting a bunch of fey warriors intimidate me wasn't on the agenda. "I need to speak to Cosette. Now." I almost patted myself on the back with how firm my voice sounded.

Van appeared before me and shook his head as if he were disappointed in me. "This way."

The guards parted and I hesitated for a second.

Where were we going? Where was Cosette? And how mad was she going to be that we were here?

"Quit thinking so hard." Eli pushed me, and I nearly ate it as I stumbled forward.

One of the guards laughed and my cheeks heated.

So much for making a good first impression.

I followed Van, trusting that he at least knew me well enough to know I wasn't a threat.

He knew that, right? I mean, he didn't know me that well, but he should know at least that.

"Maybe. But the fey are particular about who they let into their underhills, and we weren't invited."

This deal with Eli was going to be a much bigger pain in my

ass than I'd thought. "What happened to the whole not forcing me to do things against my will? You didn't *ask* me to come here with you. Fix this," I muttered under my breath. I was trying to mend alliances among supernaturals, not cause a war.

"I'm not causing a *war*. Don't be so human."

I shot him my very best scathing look and kept following Van.

We had some time. It was only mid-afternoon. All I had to do was convince Cosette and the fey not to hold our unexpected visit against us and get myself, Eli, her, and three other fey back to Texas in time to do the spell.

Easy-peasy.

I started laughing, and Eli looked down at me. "You okay?"

"No. How are you making things worse?"

He gave me a sly grin. "Not worse, more interesting. It's all in perspective, Teresa."

"Tessa."

"See, we're already becoming great friends, Tessy. Can I call you, Tessy?"

"No."

He laughed, and I knew I was in for it.

I'd been played by an archon, and now I was in fey territory. I knew about as much about dealing with the fey as I did about archons. If I wasn't careful, I'd end up making another shit deal.

I was so beyond screwed.

CHAPTER TWENTY-TWO

THE FEY GUARDS led us down a series of hallways in their Underhill, each intersection more elaborate than the next. The scenes painted on the ceilings were breathing with life. I hadn't noticed them at first—I was a little concerned with the number of guards surrounding us—but one caught my eye as we were taking a turn. It had wolves running, roaming the intersection of the ceiling. The full moon was low, and the clouds rolled around the painting, moving as if they were real.

I spun to walk backward as the wolves found a deer and descended on it as if I was watching a beautifully drawn animation on TV.

Eli caught my arm. "Come on."

"Did you see that?"

He grinned at me. "And you haven't even taken a look at the floor."

I stumbled over my own feet, trying to break Eli's grip on my arm as he half-dragged me behind the parade of guards. "What's going on with the... Oh. Whoa." At first glance, I'd thought the floor in the hallway was black marble with little silver flecks, but where I walked, the floor lit up, revealing the night sky. Colorful planets danced around stars. Comets flew and stars super-novaed as I watched. I could've walked around and watched the floor forever.

"Careful," Eli said, pulling me to the side.

I glanced up just in time to dodge a statue of a man standing straight. His sword stuck in the ground. His hair was braided away from his face, and the look on his face was so fierce I stumbled again.

"Do I need to carry you?" Eli asked, and even if he wasn't laughing at me out loud, I could hear it in his voice.

"No." Being carried here, in front of all guards, would show weakness. But I needed to get myself together. I couldn't keep gawking.

The ceiling caught my attention again. This time it was a daytime scene of a party.

"You're still gawking," Eli whispered in my ear.

He was right. I felt a bit like Keira Knightly in *Pride and Prejudice* when she toured Mr. Darcy's home. I couldn't help it if my jaw was dragging on the floor as I took in all the splendor. "I don't know if I'll ever be invited back here." Especially since I hadn't exactly been invited this time. "What's the harm in looking?"

Eli didn't say anything, so I went back to my gawking.

The guards led us to a massive pair of doors. The doors must've been well over two stories tall and twice as wide and, if I weren't mistaken, they were made of solid stone. But that seemed ridiculous. Who made a door out of stone? They'd be way too heavy to open, even for me. A twin set of golden rods were attached to either door like door handles for a giant.

Van stood in front of the doors and knocked three times. A second later, the doors started opening. At first, I thought they were opening by themselves, but they were being pushed open from the inside by a group of guards.

Inside was a massive ballroom. What had to be at least thirty giant chandeliers refracted the glowing yellow light, filling the room with rainbows. The floors were the same magical night sky. The walls were white also, but not marble. I couldn't tell what they were made of except that they were glowing like a full moon. I wanted to touch them to see what would happen, but I doubted that the guards were about to let me wander off.

As we walked farther into the room, the guards parted, moving to the sides and behind us, revealing a stage on the other side of the enormous room. Golden stairs curved up the wall on either side of the stage, leading up to where Cosette stood. A few people were seated in front of her, and a few others were standing around, but Cosette was all I saw as she looked over her shoulder.

She was glowing faintly, her curls were the brightest, making her look like she was standing in a halo of light. But it wasn't the glowing part that caught my attention, it was the fact that even from at least fifty yards away, I could tell she was pissed.

I was pretty sure that it was Eli she was mad at, but if I was wrong, I had no problem throwing him under the bus. This was so not my shitshow.

"That's not very nice," Eli said.

"Neither is dragging me here or reading my mind."

"Yes, but both are wildly entertaining."

Fantastic. That was just what I wanted to be. Entertaining.

He leaned closer to me. "Just so you're aware, I dragged you here to ensure Cosette would show up with the necessary number of fey for the spell. If I'd come alone, they were more likely to put up a fight, and Cosette wasn't going to get her queen to agree to it without some proof that the shit has hit the fan. Me being here does exactly that."

Oh. That made so much more sense.

"Looks like one of your new werewolf friends has shown up." A figure behind Cosette rose from her chair, but I couldn't quite make her out. "Come here."

I felt the pull. It was stronger than anything I'd ever felt before—at least ten times stronger than the power that Mr. Dawson had. My wolf rose up and pushed the order back. I was breathing hard as I concentrated on staying where I was.

Chris was right. He could never come here. If it'd taken that much energy for me to ignore one simple order, I couldn't imagine what it would be like for him.

The woman who had sent the order came to stand next to Cosette. Her long, pin-straight hair was lighter than Cosette's, glowing a bright golden color, but they were the same height and held themselves the same way. This had to be Cosette's mom, the Queen of the Lunar Court.

"Come. Here." Cosette's mother pushed a lot more power the command. My body shook with tension as I fought against the urge to take a step closer.

I ignored the bead of sweat rolling down my forehead. "I'd love to come forward and meet you, but I won't be compelled by an order."

"Interesting. I'll make it a request then."

That was good with me. I started walking toward the queen, taking even steps. Something told me every move I made was being judged right now. Slipping or tripping was not an option. "I apologize for interrupting your meeting. I know we weren't invited but—"

"I'm sure that was Eli's doing."

"Yes, ma'am." There was some grumbling up on the stage, and I wondered if I'd done something wrong.

Cosette's mom was wearing an elegant white suit. The pants were loose, but not too loose, and the jacket was perfectly fitted to her body. She didn't have a shirt under it, and the V-neck created by the buttoned-up jacket showed just enough skin, but not too much. A simple ring of gold circled her head. The woman was an example of perfection. Sleek and classy and cool. When I grew up, I wanted to be like her, but that wouldn't happen. I was too at home in my yoga pants and messy bun.

"It's nice to meet one of Cosette's friends. You've created quite the stir," she said as she tucked her hands into her pants pockets.

I stopped at the bottom of the stage. Cosette and her mother came to stand at the edge, looking down at me. "Not on purpose, but it seems to have followed me around."

"And it seems as if the stir will continue to get worse. Cosette is requesting that I let her leave with *three* others. I shouldn't have even allowed her to leave, let alone drag along anyone with her, but she's making a persuasive case." The Queen's gaze slid to Cosette. "Or she was until she popped out of here with all her guards." She turned to Eli. "Are you coming to stay for a while?"

He grinned up at her. "I don't think you'd like that very much, cousin." He gave Cosette a wink.

"I'm not your cousin," the queen said.

"No. Then what should I call you? Cosette and I are related."

Related? I looked at Cosette, and she shrugged. I wasn't sure if she meant that as a confirmation or not, but when I got a second, I was definitely going to ask.

"Calling her a relation is a stretch at best," the queen said. "But your point is made."

If I hadn't been watching her so closely, I would've missed the way the queen's fists tightened for a fraction of a second before she relaxed them again.

"Is it true?" The queen asked.

I'd been so busy looking from Eli to Cosette to the queen

and back again, that I didn't realize everyone was waiting for me to say something. "Is what true?"

"That if I don't allow this, the veil between the worlds will break."

Oh. That. "Yes. It's absolutely true."

She squatted down on the stage in front of me, which I didn't find a very queenly gesture, but what did I know of it. Her gaze was now even with mine, and I shivered. "And do you believe that the fey queens caused this?" Cold power backed her words, demanding I answer honestly, but I wasn't about to cast blame around, even if the argument could be made that the fey queens had been at least partly to blame when they went into hiding.

But I had a pretty strong feeling that telling a queen that she'd been wrong in her own kingdom in front of her some of her people were going to go totally shitty for me.

Could the fey scent lies? I wasn't sure, which meant I had to at least tell a partial truth. After another second of thinking, I settled on something I thought would be safe enough to say. "It certainly didn't help matters." I stayed still, chin tilted up just a little, holding her gaze while I waited for her reaction. There was no way I could wipe my sweaty palms off right now, no matter how tense I was.

The queen grinned, and I felt like I'd given her the right answer. "Well maneuvered." She rose slowly, keeping my gaze the whole time.

I gave her a smile. "So, can Cosette and her friends come out to play?"

"Are all Cosette's friends so funny?"

I didn't consider myself funny, but I was glad she'd found me amusing. That was far better than considering me a threat. I wasn't sure how to answer that, so I just shrugged.

"Your request is granted. I'll be meeting with the queens to pass along the information. It might be that this period in hiding is short-lived." She turned to her throne but stopped suddenly. "Oh, and Eli?"

"Yes, Helen."

"Don't pop in unannounced again."

Eli always seemed casual. He was easy to smile and laugh, but in that instant, the mask fell. He stood tall and started to glow. It wasn't the same golden glow that Cosette and her mother had. It was silver and pure white. Over the course of a few breaths, I could see his wings. They stretched, reaching at least sixteen feet wide. The feathers were beautiful, pure white tipped with gray. As they appeared, it was as if he grew bigger. More fearsome. More beautiful.

A staff appeared in his hand as he floated a foot above the ground.

Now I knew why he didn't wear shoes.

He might not be an angel, but he was the closest thing I'd ever seen, and he scared the shit out of me.

"You best don't forget where the fey live in the hierarchy."

Cosette's mother raised her hands, palms out as if she was surrendering. "Apologies for the insult. I—"

He flashed so bright I had to close my eyes, and when I opened them again, he was gone.

"Mother fucker," I muttered before I could stop myself. "He was my ride."

My cheeks heated as Cosette's mom started laughing. "I'm sure we can get you where you need to go."

Cosette cleared her throat. "Yes. We can. I'm going to show Tessa to my room and grab the others. We'll be leaving within the hour."

"Of course. You'll keep me updated."

Cosette gave her mom an over the top smile. "Don't I always," she said, sugar dripping from her tone.

The queen grinned. "No. As a matter of fact, you don't."

They laughed together, and the Queen pressed her forehead against Cosette's. She said something I couldn't understand and then stepped back.

Cosette jumped down from the stage. "Let's go," she muttered as she walked past, and I had to jog to keep up with her.

The guards parted as we walked through the doorway, leaving only Van to follow us.

Now that we were away from the queen, I had so many questions. I tried to hold them in, I really did. But it was impossible. "Soooo, you and Eli are related?" I asked as I turned to walk forward again.

She snorted. "Not really. Archons see things so oddly."

He might have been odd, but he was also impressive. "I can see the odd, but he's freaking hot, and those wings? Where the hell did those come from?"

She sighed. "Don't get me started." She grabbed my arm, stopping for a second. "Be careful when you bargain with him."

I winced. That was going to be hard, especially when it was already done.

"You already did it, didn't you?"

"Yes."

"You don't know what you've gotten yourself into," she said.

And she was right. I didn't. But I'd been out of my element ever since I got to Texas. It was my new normal, and I'd gotten pretty damned good at winging it. "It'll be fine."

"Or it won't," she said.

"I did what I had to do." And I was standing by that choice. I wasn't sure whether I'd come to regret it or not, but right now, I was saving all of our asses the only way I knew how.

CHAPTER TWENTY-THREE

"ALMOST THERE," Cosette said as we turned a corner.

I was starting to wonder how big the Lunar court was. It was hard to tell exactly how far we'd walked in the Underhill with all the turns we'd taken, but it had to be massive. I hadn't seen an end to any of the galaxy floored hallways, and we'd been walking for a good fifteen minutes. It wasn't like we were strolling either. If Cosette had amped the pace up even the tiniest bit, I wouldn't have been able to keep up without jogging.

Cosette pushed through a pair of carved wooden doors. These were only a little larger than normal but just as impressive. The painted carvings showed a field of trees and flowers. The tree limbs were bending in the wind as I watched, and—as I passed through the doorway—I swore I could smell the roses.

"Welcome to my suite," Cosette said, motioning me forward.

The sitting area was filled with a rainbow burst of colors. A girl with red curls and freckles was on sitting on a rich, deep blue velvet couch, wringing her hands. She was wearing a pair of peach silk joggers, white tank top, and a light gray jacket.

Beside her in a deep reddish-brown leather armchair was another girl with long, straight hair that was colored like the many shades of autumn leaves. She was wearing a hooded forest green dress that hit mid-thigh, thick cream knitted socks that peeked out under her tall, brown leather lace-up boots. Both looked so well put together that I really wished I'd picked something nicer to wear, but in my defense, one of the Evil Trinity was after me. Fashion really was the last thing on my mind.

The two fey girls had been chatting but stopped as soon as we walked in.

Van walked around to the armchair on the other side of the couch, kicking his feet onto the coffee table.

The redhead rose slowly, and I watched her. "How'd it go?"

"Not as bad as it could've gone," Van said.

The redhead's eyes widened, and she glanced at me for a second before focusing back in on Cosette.

"Don't listen to Van." Cosette shot him a look. "We're good to go."

"Finally," the other girl said. "I've had enough of court. Let's be off, then."

I took in the group. Cosette and two more girls made three fey. "Where's the fourth?"

"Van," Cosette said.

"Really?" He was pretty badass, but he never seemed to like being around us. He'd shown up to help in Santa Fe, but as soon as the fighting was over, he was gone. I couldn't believe that Van was actually going to volunteer to be a part of this new spell. "You sure you're okay with this?" I asked him.

"Where Cosette goes, I go. Or at least that's how it's supposed to be."

She shrugged. "I sneak away every now and then. It's not a big deal."

"To you, maybe not. To the queen..." He rose from his chair. "I guess we should get a move on."

I nodded. "That would be great. We don't have much time."

"Less now, I'm sure," Van said.

That didn't sound ominous at all. "What do you mean less time?" We needed *all* the time we could get. To say that the spell we had to prepare was complicated was a gross under-statement.

"You don't know?" Cosette asked.

She was making me nervous. "Know what?"

"Time is slower here," Van said.

"It's almost nightfall out there," Cosette said.

"Nightfall?" This was a disaster. Astaroth could be coming any minute now, and I was here, stuck in the Underhill? "We need to go. Now."

The other fey girl stood up. I didn't know either of their names, and that seemed wrong, but I couldn't wait. We'd do introductions later. For now, we needed to get back to Texas.

Van held out his hands. Cosette grabbed one and then mine. The fey girl with multi-colored hair grabbed my other hand. The redhead closed the circle. "Don't let go," Van said to me, and then everything went dark for a second.

I blinked, and we were in the quad at St. Ailbe's. My feet were on the ground, but my head was spinning so badly it was like I'd been on a tilt-o-whirl all afternoon.

My knees gave way, and I sat on my ass. Hard. "That was super not fun." I closed my eyes and prayed that the world would stop spinning. It felt like forever since I'd had the pancakes, but I was still fighting the urge to hurl them.

"It might not be the most fun way to get around, but it's effective," one of the fey girls said. I didn't want to open my eyes to figure out which one.

Tessa! Dastien yelled through the bond.

I'm fine! Just taking a second to get my bearings. I was going to have to get up, but when I opened my eyes, the world was still wobbly. Traveling with Eli had been disorienting at most, and only because I was suddenly somewhere unknown.

I felt like my legs were going to give out as I stood. I took a second to harness my chi before brushing off my pants. "How long does the feeling last?"

"Another minute or so," Cosette said. "You get used to it after a while. Traveling barely registers for me these days."

She was out of her mind if she thought I would ever travel that way with Van ever again, let alone enough times to get used to the feeling of it. That was so not happening.

"I'm going to have a chat with my friends here, and then we'll meet you inside," Cosette said as they moved a little farther away from me.

That was fine. I was going to have to figure out where Dastien was and if we had a car here so I could meet up with him.

I opened the bond wide, seeing things from his perspective as he came closer. He was running down a set of stairs, leaping down four steps at a time.

Wait. I knew those stairs, and they weren't at my house. He was about to hit the door of the classroom building. *Why are you at St. Ailbe's?* I asked.

When you disappeared, I freaked and called Claudia. She said you'd be back in time, so we came back here for supplies. They needed more room, too, and Claudia didn't want to brew in your mom's kitchen. Something that Samantha said hit home with her. We figured Astaroth was gone, so it was safe enough to be here, at least during daylight. We've been working all after-noon on the potions. He didn't stop running as he came out of the building. In a second, his arms were around me, and he was inhaling my scent. *Disappearing wasn't cool.*

That wasn't my plan. I'd much rather have stayed with him. Even if the Lunar Court's Underhill was amazing.

I know. Dastien pulled back. *I'm really glad you're back.*

Me, too. But Cosette's house is spectacular. We have to see if we can get an invite to visit. I could've wandered around the hallways forever.

Can't wait to hear all about it later, but you're going to want to see what we've been cooking up in the lab.

Right. Astaroth. Potions. "Let's go." He gripped my hand tightly in his to be sure I wasn't going to go anywhere, and we made our way into the building. At the base of the stairs, a noxious smell hit me. "What is that?"

He winced. "You don't want to know."

"What are we going to do with it?" I asked.

"You don't want to know that either."

My stomach churned, and I was suddenly back to hoping I wasn't going to barf all over myself. "We're not going to have to drink it, are we?"

"Not the stinkiest one, no. But it's going to go on our face, hands, and feet."

Blech. That was almost as bad. By the time we reached the labs, I didn't want to go inside.

Dastien opened the door to the lab and gave me a little push. "You'll get used to it."

"Nope." Not a chance of that. It smelled like a butcher's dumpster after three days in the hot sun, topped with some dog shit, and another smell that I wasn't about to investigate too closely. I held my hand over my face as we stepped inside. The room was bustling, but I couldn't get over the smell.

Chris stepped toward me, holding something in his hand.

His nostrils were wide, shoved with cotton balls and something slimy covered his top lip.

"Don't even start." Chris' rasp was mellowed a bit by the cotton balls.

I would've laughed, except I was jealous. "I need two of those."

"What do you think I've got for you?" Chris handed me a couple and then a jar of something. I wasted no time shoving cotton balls in my nose. It helped almost not at all. "What's this?" I asked, turning the jar in my hand. There was no label, and it looked like some kind of salve.

"It'll help with the smell," Claudia said from inside the room. "Just rub a little bit under your nose. Trust me."

"Done." I twisted the lid and stuck my finger in the goopy substance. It smelled like lavender and eucalyptus and something else. Rosemary, maybe? I wasn't sure, but it did the trick. I could still smell the stench in the room faintly, but the salve overpowered most of it.

Now that I could breathe again, I took in the room. The metaphysics lab was set up just like my old chem room at my normal, human school. Tall tables with metal tops filled the room, each with two stools. Gas lines were hooked up at each table with Bunsen burners so that the werewolves could try their hand at spells, but for the most part, they were all duds. Still, the werewolves thought it was good to practice and to have knowledge about all the various kinds of supernaturals, especially because they might end up fighting any number of creatures.

Mr. Dawson and Blaze stood around one of the burners with River. Shane and Claudia were saying a spell at another table. Claudia's braid lifted in the air as they muttered the words softly. The ingredients lifted in the air and swirled in front of them.

"Whoa."

"I know," Chris said. "It's been kind of intense."

Lucas and Adrian were huddled around another pot.

That was just about everyone, except... "Where's Beth?"

"I'm here," a soft voice came from behind me. Beth was coming back from the supply closet with a jar of salt. She looked thinner—her cheeks were a little hollowed—and her once long, dirty-blonde hair was cut in a short, asymmetrical bob. Luciana destroying her coven from the inside had definitely taken its toll on her, but she smiled at me. I was taking that as an excellent sign.

"Thanks for coming."

She looked at the floor for a minute before raising her chin. "I'm sorry I couldn't help at the chapel. I..." Her eyes started to go glossy, but she blinked it back. "It's been tough, but I'm okay. And who knows?" She shrugged. "Maybe it'll be better for me if I get back into magic. Lord knows staying away isn't helping me heal."

I wasn't close with Beth at all, but she looked like she needed a hug. So, she was getting one. "I'm glad you're here," I said as I wrapped my arms around her. I could feel her shoulder blades sticking out of her back, and made sure to be extra gentle with her. She was so thin, I thought she might break.

"Me, too," she said. "Thank you."

"No. Thank you." I gave her one last, gentle squeeze and stepped back. She shuffled quickly over to Shane and Claudia, but I saw her brush away a tear.

She's so not okay, I said to Dastien.

She'll get better. It'll take time, though.

Doesn't everything? As I looked around the room, there was just one other person that was missing. "Where's Raphael?"

"He left," Shane said.

"What do you mean he left? Where did he go?" I didn't like

AILEEN ERIN

him off on his own right now. I knew he had ties to Astaroth, but that didn't mean he had to leave.

"He said he didn't want to be here when everything went down," Chris said. "He thought he might be a liability, so he went to go see Samantha."

A liability? That was so messed up. There were so many things that we had to fix once tonight was over, but that was going to the top of my list. Raphael was holding himself responsible for Muraco, and if we weren't careful, we could lose him.

I walked over to Claudia. "Are you okay?"

"I have to be I guess, and I'm glad he's going to see Samantha. I'm hoping that the spell tonight would break the tie, but I can't know that for certain. I just wish he'd answer my phone calls."

It was always something. "We'll get through tonight and then try calling him. If the attachment isn't gone, then Samantha will take care of it. Raphael will be okay." Once this was over, he could go back to his life as a coder. I knew that was what he really wanted—a life without magic and evil witches manipulating him.

Claudia leaned against me for a second. "He never liked this life. Magic was never his thing, but he stuck around for me."

"He did because he loves you, but it's not your fault. I really do think he's going to be okay." Claudia felt a lot of guilt about her brother, and I wished she could let it go. He was a big boy. He could make his own decisions. "So, what's been going on here?" I motioned to the spell bubbling in front of us.

"Just be glad you didn't have to dig up dead bodies," Chris said.

That was for sure. "I am beyond glad that I skipped that part." Even if I did have to deal with a pissed off archon and a little bit of fey drama. "So, where are we with everything?"

320

River stepped toward me with a knife. "We need your blood, and then there are a few more steps, and then we should be good to go."

Oh man. Why did everything always need blood? "Glad I made it here in time." Footsteps echoed down the hallway. Cosette was bringing the rest of the bunch up. "We're in here," I shouted toward the door.

"What is that horrible stench?" Cosette said as she stepped inside the lab.

"Do you really want to know?" Claudia asked as Cosette walked inside the room.

"No. Probably not."

Van and the others stepped into the room, and Blaze growled. "You!"

Van chuckled, and I was pretty sure that was the only time I'd ever seen him happy. "Me!" Van yelled back and then bowed. I glanced back and forth between Van and Blaze before the fey spoke again. "Come on, old man. It's been a century. You can't still be mad."

"Seventy-eight years."

Van shrugged. "Yes. And?"

"And you left me there to fight the bloodsuckers by myself."

Fight the bloodsuckers? This was a story and I wanted—no, I *needed* to hear it.

"And you lived. So, I think we can agree all is well and put it behind us." Van had a smirk on his face, and Blaze—who'd been nothing but polite up until now—looked like he was ready to snap Van's neck.

I got a little closer to Cosette. "What kind of friends do you have?"

"Apparently the same kind you bargain with." She gave me a wink.

I laughed. The Lunar queen had the same reaction to Eli. "Fair enough."

"Van is...Van." She tossed her curls over her shoulder. "As for the rest of them, Kyra, meet Tessa. She's from the Solar Court, although she'd left it and has been in hiding in the human world for a few years. And Elowen's from the Court of Leaves."

"It's really awesome that you're here." I bit my tongue on thanking them. Cosette was good about letting thank you's slide, but I couldn't assume that would apply to these two fey. "I want to get to know you, but the sun is setting and—"

"There will be time for that later," Cosette said.

"Agreed," I said. I was glad we were on the same page. I wanted to get this spell done before the moon rose. "So, what do we need to do, besides getting some of my blood?"

"Actually, we'll need some from everyone," River said, brandishing the knife. "Just a few drops for that pot over there, and then some more for this." He motioned to a cup.

"Are we going to be drinking that?" I asked. "Please say no."

"Yes," he said, but he didn't look happy about it.

"What's in it?" I wasn't sure I wanted to know, but I had to ask.

"Just blood."

I contained the gag. Barely. "Fine. So that smelly shit is going on our faces, and we have to drink the blood." Man, if I didn't want Astaroth gone for real, I would rethink this whole plan.

Claudia nodded. "That's about right, and I think we're all in agreement that this sucks. Royally. But it's the best we could come up with in a day."

"Right," I muttered a few curses. "So, who wants to go first?"

"We're all good here," Beth said, holding up her finger with a band-aid. "It's just you and the fey left."

"Alright then." Van stepped past me, took the knife from River, and pricked his finger. Three drops of his blood fell into the stinky pot and three more in the cup. He handed the knife back to Kyra, who did the same. And then Elowen.

I went last. "I can't do it myself." I handed the knife back to River. I told myself I shouldn't act like a weenie in a room filled with magically powerful people, but I couldn't help myself. "I really, *really* hate this."

River smiled at me. "I'll be quick." The meanie stuck me with the point of the blade.

"Ouch!" I tried to pull my hand away from him, but his grip was tight.

"Stop it," he said with a laugh. He pressed on my finger, squeezing it until the tip turned blue.

River's grip on my finger hurt worse than pricking it. "Be careful. I don't know if I can regenerate fingers and I like all of mine."

"*Chérie*," Dastien chided me, and yes, maybe I was being a teeny bit ridiculous, but damn it, River was totally mangling my finger.

"It hurts," I mumbled.

"You're making it worse. You Weres heal so freaking quickly," River squeezed one more drop into the cup. "Done."

I stuck my finger in my mouth. "Was that even sanitary?" We'd all just been poked by the same knife. What kind of fey germs did I just get?

"Don't worry. You can't catch anything from them," a voice said from behind me.

I growled as I spun. Eli was grinning at me, arms folded across his white V-neck T-shirt. "You!"

"Eli!" Cosette said at the same time. "You shouldn't pop in and out like that. It's rude."

He raised a brow. "Am I the only one who thinks that's rich coming from her?"

"Nope," I said and then instantly regretted it when Cosette scowled at me. "What? You do that all the time." No one laughed, except Dastien and that was only through the bond.

Oh, man. I missed Meredith so damned much. She would've thought it was funny. I was pretty sure of it.

"Are we ready now?" Nerves rose up, making my mouth dry.

"One more thing," Beth said, waving Claudia over. Shane and River joined them and held hands.

They said a few words in a language that sounded like the one River used before he magically slammed me into the wall.

The pot lifted off the table for a second before falling back to the table. Smoke wafted out, and they dropped their hands.

Beth slumped against the table, gasping for air.

Blaze walked over to her and squeezed her shoulder. "Are you okay?"

She nodded. "Yeah. It's just been a while. I'm a little rusty."

"You'll get it back," Blaze said. "You'll be okay."

Beth gave him a quick look before she stared at the table. "I don't know that you can say that."

He whispered something so softly in her ear that I couldn't make it out, but her eyes widened, and she was suddenly gasping for another reason.

What do you think he said? I asked Dastien.

Don't know. I couldn't hear him.

Weird. "Let's get this over with. Where are we doing it?"

"The Quad," Mr. Dawson said. "It's got the most room."

"Plus, it's where Astaroth came through before. It'll be a weak point," Claudia said.

"And when he comes through again?" I asked.

"We'll be ready," Lucas said.

Would we? "Are you going to fight him?" I asked Eli.

"I'll be busy sealing the bond," he said.

"And we'll be busy with the spell," I said. "Then who's going to be fighting Astaroth?" I thought the other Alphas were going to come, but campus seemed pretty empty when we got here.

"They are," Blaze said as he pointed to the window. "Right on time."

I moved around the tables, careful not to bump into any stools, and stared down. In the distance, car doors were slamming. A stream of werewolves started to pour into the quad, a few of them undressing as they moved into view. I spotted the Alphas from yesterday, thankful that they weren't so upset that they wouldn't show up tonight. The rest were all in black.

Cazadores.

Wow. I didn't know there were so many of them. There had to be hundreds. Way more than had left yesterday. "Where did they come from?"

"Everywhere. We're werewolves. When the call goes out for help, we don't say no," Mr. Dawson said. He looked fierce as he stepped closer, looking down at the gathering crowd. "That's our way. That's why we've protected humans for so long and will continue to do so. It's in our blood, and it's part of being an Alpha. There might not be a Seven anymore, but I'll always be an Alpha. And I'll always be there if help is needed."

I pressed my forehead against the cold glass, watching them for a second, before glancing at Mr. Dawson.

"Thank you." He wasn't fey so I could say it. "I really appreciate that."

He gave me a nod. "I'll be outside with the other Alphas."

When he was gone, I looked at Claudia. "What do we need to take down to the quad?"

She started handing everyone things, and we hustled down there.

As I carried a stack of candles, my stomach was in knots.

Doing this spell on the land where Astaroth appeared just twenty-four hours earlier was going to be like drop kicking a hornet's nest.

It was a terrible idea, and it was the only idea.

We'd better nail it, or we were going to lose everything.

CHAPTER TWENTY-FOUR

THE CROWD of Cazadores made room as we entered the quad. We had to form a circle with me as the center. I'd be the focal point. The one that tied it all together. I didn't want it to be that way. I wished I could've pawned it off on someone else, but no one could take my place. No one else that straddled three species like I did. If I'd had a touch of fey in my bloodline, that would've been even more of a help, but as far as I knew—I was just human, witch, and Were. As I stood in the center, setting up a mini-altar while everyone else took their places in the circle. I hoped it was enough.

There was no plan B. If the spell didn't work, I was opening a portal with no real way to close it.

So, we were going to make it work.

I shoved all doubt from my mind as I rose. I could do this. I would do this. I said it again and again in my mind as I put the stinky pot on the altar next to the cup with the secondary potion and my own candle.

Everyone stood around me—werewolf, fey, witch, werewolf, fey, witch. All mixed together.

Eli was standing on a tree limb above us. I couldn't see his wings, but now that I knew they were there, I'd always see them. Those wings weren't something I could unsee.

He was on standby to seal the bond when needed. But until that happened, we were on our own.

I took a breath and let it out slowly. My hands were shaking and sweaty. I wiped them off on my pants.

You're going to do fine.

I nodded. *I just don't feel ready. I was so busy dealing with Eli and spending too much time in Underhill that I didn't prepare anything for the spell. It all feels so rushed. What if something's not right? What if someone forgot a step? What if—*

Stop. You can't think like that. No doubts, remember? And the words don't count. You know what Tia Rosa said. It's all about the sentiment behind them and how much you believe in them.

He stepped into the circle and grabbed my shoulders. *You have to trust everyone in this group. They're the ones who helped put together the spell. Leading is about getting everyone to work together, and part of that is delegating. You can't do everything by yourself. You've always leaned on us for support. Now you'll have to lean on everyone here in this circle a little more. That means you don't have to do all of the busy work and can focus on more important things. Like making sure the next Luciana isn't hiding among the covens. This is a good thing.*

He was right. I knew it.

Claudia walked over to me. "You've got the spell?"

I pulled out the crumpled piece of paper that she'd handed me not five minutes earlier from my pocket. "Yup. Got it."

"Okay. Are you ready?"

I swallowed and looked into my mate's glowing amber eyes. "Yes."

"Then let's get started," Claudia said.

Dastien pulled me in tightly. *You're the one that can make this work. So do it. No doubt. No questions. Nothing else but you and the magic.*

My chest tightened as he stepped away from me. It was a lot of pressure. So much riding on getting this right. My breaths felt hollow, and my fingers tingled.

I had to get this right.

I couldn't doubt. I couldn't question myself. I couldn't let a single inkling of doubt slip into my head that maybe this might not work. I needed confidence. The first step of that was addressing everyone who had come to fight.

"Before we get started, I want to say thank you. You're Alphas and Cazadores. You're fighters. And you've protected everyone, fighting for good, and for those who couldn't fight for themselves, and never asking for anything in return. Knowing that humans and supernaturals alike were safe was all you needed."

I looked out into the gathered men in black. "And you're here today. We called for help, and you came. Thank you." I paused for a second to let that sink in. I wanted them to know that I meant it. "Tonight will be hard for everyone here and some of us will get hurt, but after? Everyone's safety won't be on your shoulders. Now that everyone knows we exist, it's time for something new. Something stronger and better. Tonight we're breaking down barriers between supernaturals. Together, we will rise stronger. So, when shit goes wrong—because it will—I just wanted you to know what we were fighting for. It's bigger than just Astaroth. So, thank you for being here. Your support has been and will always be invaluable."

The Cazadores stood around me, watching silently. I wasn't sure if they'd liked what I said, but I didn't feel okay about starting without acknowledging them.

With that done, I closed my eyes and pushed all the doubt

out of my mind. I was going to do this. I was going to nail it. And fucking win. Because that's what I had to do, no matter what.

I opened my eyes. With my intentions and will focused on what I was doing, I grabbed a supersized container of salt and stepped just behind Dastien. It was a lot of salt, but we needed every bit of it. The circle was about eight feet in diameter. The spout opened with a pop, and I bent down a little. There needed to be a solid ring of salt to set the circle, but I also needed it to last around the entire thing. We had a backup container, but it'd be better if I didn't have to break the process of going around in the circle. The slow stream of salt fell to the ground as I walked with a gentle, steady whoosh that reminded me of the ocean.

"I set this circle with light and love. I set this circle with light and love. I set this circle with light and love. I set..." I said over and over with each step as I walked inside the line of salt.

As I neared Dastien, I felt the pressure in the circle start to build. And when the circle was finished, there was a little pop in my ears.

The circle was strong and holding. Not even a whiff of sulfur in the air.

Good. This was good. It meant that when Astaroth showed up, he'd be outside the circle.

The next step was going to be less fun. I grabbed a blade from the altar and walked back to the beginning of the circle. "Get ready." It was going to take a ring of my blood to activate the circle and set off the start of the spell.

I scrunched my eyes shut as I swiped the blade across my left wrist. The blade was so sharp that it took a second for me to feel the sting. I stuck the blade in the ground, just inside the circle and started a crouching walk around the circle. I wasn't wasting one drop of my blood, and I had to move fast because even though I'd cut myself pretty deeply, the wound would heal in a minute or two.

The drops of my blood hit the salt, instantly turning it a pink color that spread around the entire circle.

One drop shouldn't be enough to do that, but this was magic. It blew my mind. Eventually, I'd get used to seeing it, but today wasn't that day.

"My blood seals this circle to outsiders. My blood seals this circle to outsiders. My blood—" I said it over and over. The last few steps were a little hurried as I tried to keep it from healing. Slitting my wrist twice in one night wasn't going to happen.

As my blood hit the last inch of the circle, it started to glow a pulsing red color.

Doing great, Dastien said as I moved past him. His fingertips brushed my arms, sending goosebumps tingling along my skin.

The blood should keep Astaroth from coming inside the circle, but it would draw him to me. I knew it wouldn't be long before he showed up and started trying to get inside. I had to hurry.

I grabbed out the piece of paper from my front pocket. Claudia's script looked like something out of hand lettering book. My handwriting wouldn't be that pretty no matter how hard I tried. I met her gaze across the circle, and she gave me a little nod.

The circle was good. Holding strong. Step one done.

Now, I had to create the bond. Once that was done, together we could close the portals and cancel out the evil magic that Luciana had left behind.

I moved toward the cup, and the ground started to shake.

This wasn't supposed to happen.

Evil spread across the circle, making all the hairs on my arm stand on end.

A gasp ripped from my body, and my heart started to pound.

I prayed I was wrong. I prayed the rumbling meant the battle outside the circle was starting. We knew a fight was coming. There was going to be a battle outside this circle, and I had to ignore it.

But I had to hurry. I didn't want anyone hurt. Not if moving faster could save lives.

The cup shook in my hand. I read the words Claudia had written—a modified version of the spell for the Seven.

They weren't my words, but they had power in them. I had to amplify that with my own will. My own power. As I took a breath in, I let that power rise up in me. Let the confidence grow until I was standing in the circle, ignoring the growing rumbling under my feet, as I said the words.

"Werewolf, witch, and fey. We cross the lines today. Bring us together so we might fight all the things that haunt the night. Good souls to fight the bad—"

There was shouting outside of the circle. Screaming. I blocked it all out. Focusing on the magic and the words so that we could get through this. That was the only way. I couldn't stop what was happening outside the circle until I was done with my spell.

"Planes kept seper—"

I heard Dastien shout my name just before I felt the hand close around my wrist.

I spun, trying to wrench my hand free from whatever demon had gotten through my circle but it wasn't just a demon.

It was Astaroth. He was still in the shape of the boy. I tried to wrench my wrist free, but he laughed, and the world shook.

No. This wasn't happening.

He'd gotten inside my circle.

How the hell had he gotten inside my fucking circle like it was nothing?

He was grinning at me, that big, yawning grin that took up too much of his face. *You're mine.* His mouth grew bigger as the words rolled through me.

The cup slipped from my grasp. The spell with all our blood splattered to the ground. Ruined.

I looked into his eyes, and I knew what was about to happen, and there was nothing I or anyone else could do about it.

Mine, Astaroth said again, and he threw me. I slammed against the wall of the circle, and then screaming, I fell...

And fell...

And fell...

The ground had disappeared, and the abyss lay below.

I heard Dastien screaming off in the distance, but there wasn't anything he could do.

It was too late.

I fell...

And fell...

And fell...

Into the dark abyss that was Hell.

CHAPTER TWENTY-FIVE

THE LONGER I FELL, the more scared I got until all I could smell was the sickly sweet stench of fear. My own fear. The smell turned my stomach worse than the stinky potions, and all I could do was scream…

And scream…

Until finally my screams were pulled from me.

My body slammed into the ground and bounced three times before I landed face first.

My breath sounded harsh in my ears, echoing like my brain was hollow. And it felt hollow. I couldn't think. What was I going to do now? How was I going to get the fuck out of here? Was I dead?

I sure as shit hoped not.

One step at a time. I had to move. I had to get up.

It took me a second to stand, but I eventually managed it. Everything ached from the fall, but nothing was broken. Blood dripped from down one arm, where I'd scratched against the ground. The shock would wear off soon, and I'd be healed in a few minutes.

I turned in circles, but it was the same as last time. I was in Hell. Except this time I knew my body wasn't with Dastien. I'd fallen here. The scratches proved that my body has physically come here. I was here. This wasn't a vision.

I tried to think of one thing that was positive, and the best I could come up with was that at least I had the benefit of what I'd learned the last time I'd been here.

Trying to find a way out of here wasn't going to do any good. There was no way out, so I wasn't going to tire myself by running all over the place.

He was going to mess with me. He was going to use that creepy as fuck voice so I couldn't let it freak me out.

I needed to break out of here, which meant I needed some magic. Strong magic.

Don't even try it. Astaroth popped in front of me. He wasn't in the form of the boy anymore. He was tall and made of shadows. Lines of reddish-orange peeked through the shadows in spots. His red eyes burned through me and I tried to look away but was frozen. Trapped by his gaze.

His too-large mouth grinned at me. I screamed before I could slap my hand over my mouth.

You're never breaking out of here. Good thing you saw Samantha. She gave you her blood.

Samantha said she didn't know Astaroth, but he knew her. If I ever got out of here, I was going to have to have another chat with her.

My heart skipped a beat, and my eyes burned as they widened. Forty-eight hours. Samantha had said not to get sucked into hell for forty-eight hours. Because I'd be here for real. I could exist on both planes because of her blood, but not for long. If I died here, I'd be stuck here.

Be glad I haven't dismembered you for your power. Yet. A chill ran through me. *I'll be back.* Astaroth ran a fingertip down my face, and I had to fight not to stumble back. If I thought that Luciana's magic was slimy, then I wasn't even sure what to call his.

I swallowed hard.

He left, popping back out and for a second, I was relieved.

And then it hit me where he was going. Back to the circle. To my friends. To my mate.

Dastien! I shouted through the bond, but he wasn't going to be able to help me. The bond was still present but felt dead, lifeless. So there was nothing I could do to help him either.

But I had to do something.

Think, Tessa. Fucking think. Don't let this fear get to you.

I paced around, trying to get my mind to settle, but it was hard. So hard to think straight when I was terrified.

I needed to not be me for a second. If I were Claudia, what would I do?

A protection knot and a circle. I was terrible at knots, but I could do a circle. Or I used to be able to do them. Astaroth had gotten through my circle like it didn't exist.

I tried to think back to what Samantha said about the tie. I had to break the tie first. When Samantha couldn't break it, I figured it'd break when I did the spell, but she'd said that I needed to somehow be on both planes.

I was. I was alive but on this plane. So that counted.

But I needed to be able to see the tie if I wanted to break it.

I was in a black void. In Hell. With nothing. No ingredients. Nothing to make up a potion or salt for a circle, but there was one thing I did have.

Myself. My will. My magic.

I sat down and as I crossed my legs something poked hard into my ankle. "Shit." I reached inside my Ugg and wanted to cry.

Holy shit. It was still there. After everything with the trip to the Lunar Court and then racing to finish the spell and every-thing else that came with that, I'd forgotten I'd stashed it in my boot.

Thank you, God. Thank you. Thank you.

I had myself, my will, my magic, and one fucking evil dagger.

I didn't know if Samantha saw this moment coming or what, but I owed her big time. If I hadn't taken that dagger... If I hadn't held onto it...

I couldn't think about that. I had a shot. I was taking it.

This time I didn't hesitate. I sat on the ground and slashed my wrist open. Coating my fingers in my own blood, I rose up on my knees and drew a circle around myself as wide as I could reach.

This was where I'd gone wrong last time. I'd said to lock everything out, but I was tied to Astaroth. He'd sown a thread of himself through my soul, and I'd locked him in the circle with us.

I had to sever his tie before I did anything else. Dastien might be right about delegating to others, that I had to lean on my friends, but he wasn't totally right. They couldn't do every-thing for me.

I was the Alpha. I was the witch. There were some things that I just had to do for myself.

I pictured all of the ties I had and pushed them away from the circle until they were outside of it. If any of the ties cut through the circle, then I wasn't sure what I had in mind would work. I had to be in here alone so I could sort through them.

"I activate this circle. Only I am in. Only me. Only myself." The words didn't matter. Just the will, and I was doing this damn it. "I activate this circle. Only I am inside of it. Only me. Only myself."

The circle lit up, and I heard Astaroth cry out.

The ground rumbled under me, and I knew he was on his way and angry.

I had to block him.

I closed my eyes and searched my soul for magical links. Even if I was in Hell, I was still alive. Which meant the links were still there. I just had to concentrate harder.

My breath flowed in and out as I shoved away the doubt. They were there. I knew it.

And then, I felt the first one. My bond to Dastien.

Strong. Golden. It was a rope that tied our souls together. Completed us.

I searched for something else but couldn't find anything. Nothing.

My eyes opened and sitting in front of me, but outside of the circle, was Astaroth. *You won't find it. This circle won't keep me out. You're not strong enough.*

I squeezed my eyes shut, pushing him out of my mind. He could say whatever he wanted, but he was wrong. I was strong enough. That was why he wanted me in the first place, and that's why I would win.

A boom rocked against the circle, and I knew he was trying to break in. He was trying to scare me. But if even one of my hairs crossed the circle, the protective circle I'd cast would shatter like the most delicate porcelain ball.

Pleeease, Astaroth's voice crooned in my ear. *Fight. Bring up all your power for me to drink. The more you fight, the better it is for me.*

Well, I guessed I was about to make it really, really good for him. Because I wasn't going to let him taunt me.

I focused again. I needed to see the specific spot where the tie to Astaroth was anchored in me so that I could cut it out.

"Show me the demon's tie. Show me the demon's tie. Show me the demon's tie." I said it again and again. "Show me the demon's tie. Show me the demon's tie. Show me the demon's tie." My voice wasn't more than a whisper as I begged my magic to find it.

I repeated the words. Over and over. Astaroth laughed, and I ignored it.

My throat grew raw, and tears rolled down my cheeks as he taunted me. Slamming into my circle. My circle was holding, but it was getting harder.

Sweat rolled down my forehead as I struggled to hang on to my magic.

Wait. Why was it getting so hard? Why was I draining so quickly?

I tried to hear beyond Astaroth's taunting, and then finally heard it. A drip. Then another.

I looked down at my wrist, still dripping blood.

I touched the black abyss below me, but it was wet. My blood. I was sitting in a pool of it.

You can't heal here. Hell is on the supernatural plane. Any hurt you get here is a supernatural one. And one that's made with my own blade, forged in the fires of Hell. It will kill you. And when you die, you'll be mine. My slave. And the first thing you'll do is kill your friends.

My chin slouched down into my chest. My eyelids weighed ten pounds, and I wanted to give up. I wanted to go to sleep. Each breath felt heavy in my lungs, but I couldn't give in. That was the same as dying.

Pull it together, I told myself. I could do this. I would do this.

"Show me the—" My voice cracked, and I slapped my face. Hard. Time to wake up. I was not giving in. Not now. Not ever.

"Show me the demon's tie. Show me the demon's tie. Show me the demon's tie. Show me—"

I blinked my eyes open, and I saw something glowing. The words had worked all along, I'd just been too stupid and too tired to keep my eyes open.

It looked like a tiny thread of glowing orange-red string. It weaved up and down—in and out—of me before leading out of the circle to Astaroth.

The tie. I'd found it. I'd really found it.

My grip was loose on the knife. I was losing strength. Quickly. It nearly fell from my hand as I lifted it up.

I glanced up at Astaroth, and for the first time, I smiled as I sliced through the tie. The little bits that wove through me turned to ash as they fell to the ground. Useless. Powerless. No longer tying me to the demon.

No! Astaroth slammed against my circle, and I jerked back before I could stop myself. My head spun, and I started to fall over but caught myself before I fell across the circle.

Shit. That was too close. I needed to get out of here.

When I'd been in the abyss the last time, Dastien made me drink his blood to strengthen our bond. This time he couldn't do that, but I could put my blood on our bond. Hopefully that would strengthen it.

Astaroth was screaming, hitting the circle. The dark shadows started to burn away, revealing the blackened, fire demon within.

Ignoring Astaroth's shit fit, I focused all my will—all my power—into my words. "Show me the bond. Make it real. Show me the bond. Make it real." I believed it would appear in my hands and as I screamed the words for a third time, something felt heavy in my hand.

It was a knot of golden rope. The cable, thick as my forearm.

I held it gingerly. This was our power, and I wasn't about to let it go.

I ran my fingertips in my blood that had dripped onto the ground and dripped it over the bond.

"Lead me back to my mate."

The world tilted, and I rose up onto my knees. Everything spun, and it was worse than when Van transported me back to St. Ailbe's. I was spinning and falling.

I squeezed my eyes closed and screamed as I hugged my knees into my chest. Air whipped my hair around my head.

And then my side slammed into the ground, and I screamed again.

My wrist felt like it was going to rip off. I'd cut myself too deep, and I needed a bandage soon or I was going to die.

The sound of a fight surrounded me. Growls and screams. The crunch of a broken bone.

Tessa!

I blinked my eyes open and gazed at wolf-Dastien. He was protecting what was left of the spell and the goblet from a couple demons.

I glanced around the circle.

Everyone had left it. That needed to change. And fast.

We were doing this. Now. Before Astaroth could come through again. "Back to the circle!" I yelled over the din.

I looked up at Eli, who was still perched in his tree. "Are you going to just sit there? Or can you actually get off your ass and help me?"

He gave me a salute and flew down into the battle. A second later, he rose again, dropping Elowen and Blaze into the circle. Van popped in a second later with Kyra.

Chris and Lucas ran through in wolf form. Claudia was just behind Lucas. She spun around—facing the demons chasing them—and muttered a few words. A second later, a ball of flames hit the closest demon.

Eli flew in with Cosette screaming at him in one arm and Beth in the other.

One more. We needed one more.

River ran through. The last one.

The pot with the stinky spell had been kicked to the ground. I ran for it.

My vision swam as I moved too quickly, but I shook it off. Dastien pushed a bit of power, and that was enough. More than enough. I needed to do this spell, then I could rest.

I grabbed the pot and reached inside. There wasn't much. Maybe a quarter of a cup left. I rubbed it on my forehead, backs of my hands, and on the tops of my feet.

That was all there was left. There was nothing left for the others, but I hoped since I would be tied to all of them, that it was good enough.

I glanced around the circle. But we were missing something else: blood.

Beth had a cut running down her face, dripping blood. The wolves all had mats of wet fur. More blood. Claudia had a gash on her arm. River's shirt was all but torn off, which meant he was bleeding, too. Even Van had blood on the side of his tunic. Everyone looked battered and bruised, so there was more than enough blood. We wouldn't be drinking it, but it would still be there to bind us together. I ran around the circle, touching wounds from each of them. I rubbed the blood together in my hands.

I was wrong. They might not be drinking the blood or wearing the potion, but I would be. I would start the link, and Eli would bind it.

I licked my hands, swallowing the coppery tang of my friends' blood, and said the words. "We unite. Stronger together.

Our powers seal this portal forever. We stand, side by side. Until death. Protecting our plane from the one beyond."

A line of glowing light started from me in the center of the circle, branching out to reach each of them. The lines criss-crossed until there was a line connecting everyone in the circle to each other and all of them to me.

"Together united. Together strong. From our ancestors and beyond. Our power amplifies twelve by twelve, plus one."

"Eli!" I yelled at him. I didn't see where he'd gone, but he needed to get his ass back here.

I felt the wind and looked up to see him hovering over us. He opened his mouth to speak, and it was too much. The magic felt like hot pokers in my ears. I cried out as the ground slammed into my knees. I rolled onto my back and looked up at him.

He was glowing with the purest white light I'd ever seen. His shirt was gone and his wings spread wide.

I knew he said he wasn't an angel, but as I looked up at him, I wasn't sure what else he could be.

My ears were ringing, and I couldn't hear anything, but I could see his lips moving. The bonds that connected all of us together started to grow hot.

The heat intensified. And then it felt like someone was burning me. My soul was on fire, and I writhed on the ground, screaming for it to stop. It was too much. The magic was too much. It was going to turn me to ash.

Just when I thought I couldn't take anymore, there was a cool breeze. A balm on my soul, taking away every last bit of pain.

For a second, all I could hear was my breath. My heart was beating crazy, too. I laid there, staring up at Eli. His wings flowed back and forth, and I couldn't look away.

I put my hand over my chest. My heartbeat wasn't slowing. I was going to have a heart attack if this kept up. But after a second, I realized it was too many beats. I wasn't hearing just my heart beating. It was everyone's. All thirteen of us.

I rose, and so did the others.

I thought it was over. But then Astaroth appeared in front of me.

I stumbled back a step. And another. "Why?" I looked up at Eli. We'd done the spell. We'd sealed the plane. Why was Astaroth still here? This should've worked. And I knew we couldn't win in a fight.

Eli swooped down in front of me. His light was so bright I could barely see around it. He tsked at Astaroth. "You've broken the rules again." He punched his fist into Astaroth's body, ripped something out. A glowing ball of white energy.

Eli turned to me and shoved it at me.

I gasped as all the air was gone from me. And then it was back. Everything seemed a little brighter. A little better. It was like a missing piece of my soul was back, and I didn't even know it'd been gone.

What? When... I didn't understand.

"When he took your powers, he kept a piece." My mouth dropped open, but I didn't have time to process it before Eli was moving again. "It was allowing him to stay on this side, but now it's time for you to go." A spear appeared in Eli's hands. He slammed it into the ground, and a portal opened in the ground under Astaroth's feet.

"You're mine." Astaroth's voice beat into my head. His words etched fear into my soul as he hovered over the portal.

Eli wrapped an arm around me. His wings whisked the air around us, lifting us from the ground, and the next instant, Astaroth was sucked down, falling back to Hell.

Eli lowered us and slammed the spear into the ground again. The portal slammed closed.

I looked up at Eli. I wasn't sure what he could or couldn't

do, but in that moment, he seemed all-powerful. "Is there anything you can't do?"

"There's a lot I can't do." He said. His tone was the most serious I'd heard from him. "There are some excellent reasons for the rules I live by, and I won't break them. I will *not* play God. But I will bend them because they will not destroy what we've spent a millennia building. With my tie to you, there will be more than I'm allowed to take part in." He gave me a small smile. "Let's just say the next little bit is going to be fun."

"Fun?" Why did he think all of this shit was fun? He was messed up in the head.

We did it, Dastien said.

We did? "Is that it? Is it over?" It felt like it was too easy.

"I know. It's always sad when the fight's done," Eli said.

I wasn't sure if I wanted to laugh or cry. "You're out of your mind."

He laughed and let me go.

Exhausted, I slid to the ground. Wolf-Dastien came to lay by my side, and I leaned into him.

Everything was quiet. The demons were gone. Astaroth was gone.

We'd won. I didn't care what Astaroth said about coming back. He wanted me to stay afraid, but I wasn't. Because I'd won. The portal was sealed, and Astaroth? He was stuck in Hell where he belonged.

I closed my eyes, letting the relief sink in.

It was over. It had been the longest three days of my life, but now I could rest.

Something wet touched my cheek, and I pushed Dastien away. "Gross." He nuzzled me with his nose, making sure I was okay. When he got to my stomach, I laughed and swatted him away. "Stop it." Then he saw my wrist and started licking it.

"That's unsanitary." I sat up with a groan, and Eli came to kneel in front of me.

"You did well."

"Thanks."

He nodded. "You've made a powerful enemy."

I sighed. "What are the chances Astaroth stays under there?"

One of his eyebrows quirked up.

Which meant that Astaroth had a plan B. "How do I kill him?"

"You can't. He's like me. Immortal."

That's not what I wanted to hear. Especially not right now. "Can he be contained?"

He raised an eyebrow. "Isn't he contained now?"

If I had even a thimble full of energy left, I'd have punched him. Screw the consequences. "You just said he'd be back?"

"He will."

"So he's not contained."

"Containment never lasts for long. Especially when dealing with someone with Astaroth's power and resources. But don't worry. I forged our tie, so I'll be watching if he makes another play. I wouldn't want to miss out on the fun."

I blew out a breath. "No. We wouldn't want that." But with any luck, we'd have a while before Astaroth showed up again. Cosette said time went differently in her Underhill. Maybe it did the same in Hell.

I stayed on the ground as Eli rose. The air whipped around me as he flew up in the air a few feet and then disappeared. I had no doubt I'd see Eli again soon, but I just hoped he gave me time to recover first.

My body was spent. I'd get up soon, but not yet. Dastien settled next to me, and I nuzzled my face in his fur.

"I think we're going to need another vacation." My head bounced a bit as he huffed his wolfy laughs.

Okay, so maybe that was crazy. We'd just gotten back from six weeks of vacation. But I was exhausted.

I closed my eyes. "Wake me up when it's time to move." Dastien whined. "Don't worry. I'm fine. Just resting my eyes." I let the peaceful darkness take me away. No abyss. Just dreams. Just beautiful, happy dreams.

CHAPTER TWENTY-SIX

"WE NEED a new name for whatever this Council is," Chris said. "And the Avengers is already taken. So is Guardians. Mega overplayed. So, what're we calling ourselves?"

I'd laid on the ground for a while, just breathing, but eventually, I'd gotten up.

It'd been two hours since Astaroth had been sent back to Hell. All injuries had been taken care of, clean up was in progress out on the quad where a bonfire was burning the last of the demons—and everyone else was recovering. We'd already showered, changed, and come back to the cafeteria to stuff our faces, grateful that the cooking staff had been close enough to feed us. We'd stuffed our faces in the cafeteria and were now just hanging out.

We meaning the new group. Council. Whatever.

I kicked my feet up on the table and leaned back, balancing my chair on its back legs. Chris was right. We needed a name. "I got nothing," I said. "My mind is all mushy with relief. I'm just so glad Astaroth is gone."

"Is he really though?" Claudia asked.

I shrugged. "He's in Hell, where he belongs. He might find

a way to come back, but we should be good. At least for a while."

The bonds that connected us were two inches thick, glowing braids of magic. They weren't gold like my mate bond or the pack ties. Or white like Eli's magic. But they glittered with so many colors. All the different types of magic together were beautiful.

I should've still been tired—I had a short trip to Hell after all —but I wasn't. It took about an hour for the bonds to really settle in, and with every second I felt like I had more and more and more energy, until it was all I could do to sit still.

I wasn't sure what benefits we'd get from the tie. It could be that we just all had more power, but maybe other types of powers would be shared within our group. Only time would tell.

"Is anyone else feeling like their heart is racing?" Claudia asked as she leaned into Lucas.

"You, too?" Chris said.

"It's a high from the magic," Cosette said. "We should get used to it soon. I hope." I figured Cosette would leave after the spell, but she stuck around along with her fey friends. She'd gotten Kyra and Elowen settled in the dorms and then met us here without them. I guessed they were feeling unsocial. Which was fine. We had plenty of time to get to know them.

The Alphas and the Cazadores had mostly cleared out. Mr. Dawson and Dr. Gonzales were seeing to the ones that were hurt. Raphael was still gone. I hoped that his tie was gone, but if not, Samantha would take care of it. And I was going to have to call her. I had so many questions...

Blaze was settling in with the group as was River. Beth was sitting beside River, keeping quiet as she watched the conversation flow around her. She was being more stoical than the fey, so that was a start. It might take some time, but she'd grow more comfortable with us.

Adrian and Shane were sitting with way too much room between them, but I wasn't going to meddle. Dastien and I had enough to deal with.

I wanted to laugh at the fact that I was getting used to yet another magical thing, but oddly, I was okay with it. This was my new normal, and even if it kept getting weirder, I loved it.

You're amazing, Dastien said, and I did laugh.

I'm really not. I'm just me. I—

Eli popped in, and I lost my balance. My chair slipped out from under me, but Dastien reached out, grabbing me before my ass could hit the ground.

"Jesus, Eli. Give us some warning before you do that," I said. Dastien set me on my feet, and I pulled my chair upright. This time, I kept all four legs safely on the ground.

"And ruin the surprise? Not a chance." Eli's grin was hot and wicked.

"What do you want?" Cosette's tone was laced with annoyance, and I was glad she wasn't talking to me.

"Be nice, cousin." Eli wasn't bothered by Cosette's ire, and I wondered if it was because he was powerful, stupid, or insane.

"I'm not your cousin."

"Are you not? Hmm."

My gaze darted between the two as they stared each other down. This was getting interesting, but eventually, someone had to break the tension and ask the important question. When no one said anything, I guessed that was my job. "What do you want?" I asked. "Do you need my blood?"

"Do I need to have a reason to be here?" Eli asked me with a positively evil grin, one I didn't trust at all.

Eli was an archon. By nature, archons didn't show themselves unless they had a reason. It'd only been a couple hours since we'd sealed our plane from the one beyond. Everything should've been fine and dandy, but he was here. He definitely had a fucking reason.

"Eli." I hoped he felt every ounce of annoyance I'd put in that one word.

"Fine. But you're taking all the fun out of it. We'll deal with our tie once you're recovered from today. For now, I have a situation, and I'd like some help."

I glanced at Dastien, whose eyes were glowing amber. *I don't like it either,* I said. *It's too soon. We haven't even gotten a chance to breathe. He can't make us go off on some other stupid quest.*

He might want just you.

I reached over to Dastien. *No. Not negotiable.* Where I went, Dastien was going. Being apart was for the fucking birds.

"You definitely think highly of yourself," Eli said. "I was actually thinking Christopher could help me."

Everyone at the table turned to Chris, who sat frozen in place. His eyes were wide and mouth in a shocked oh. After a second, he cleared his throat. "Me?" He pointed to himself. "You think I could help you?"

"Wait. No. The deal was with me." I wasn't about to let Chris get roped into any shenanigans with the archon.

"That's right, but I need Chris. And if he's willing, that's between him and me."

Chris opened and closed his mouth a few times, before nodding. "I don't have anything planned right now. I can help you if you need me."

"Perfect." Before anything else was said, Eli and Chris disappeared.

I had a second to process that before I jumped up from my chair. "Eli! You asshole! You can't take one of my friends! That wasn't part of our deal!" I screamed at the ceiling. There hadn't even been a negotiation. Chris had just blindly accepted. That wasn't good.

I didn't know if Eli could hear me, but I sent all of my will at him. "Get the fuck back here! Eli!" I screamed so loudly my throat burned.

"Calm down," Eli said from behind me, and I spun to face the jerk. "I'll bring him back. Eventually." And then he was gone again.

"What the Hell." I couldn't think. Worry for one of my best friends set me on edge. "Eli!" I screamed again.

Dastien grabbed my hand and squeezed, cutting me off. He looked over to Cosette. "How worried should we be?"

She shared a long look with Van. "I don't know, but let's stay calm. Eli is..." She sighed. "He's a lot of things, but evil or cruel isn't one of them. He won't let Chris die after everything he did to get this new bond established, but I don't like it. There are too many things Eli could be up to." She grabbed Van's hand. "I'll do some digging and let you know what I find. Until then, just try not to worry. I'm reasonably certain Chris is okay."

"Like how certain?" I'd love a percentage or odds or some kind of ballpark figure, so I knew how hard I should fight to get Chris back.

"I don't know," Cosette said. "Don't do anything. I'll be back as soon as I know more." She nodded to Van, and they disappeared.

I sat down hard in my chair. "Damn it. It's always something."

Blaze laughed. "That's life. There will always be fires to put out, but that doesn't mean you shouldn't enjoy the victory." He pushed a carton of ice cream at me. "You've done well. So relax."

"I..." I didn't know if I could. Not without Chris.

"He'll be okay," Adrian said. "Chris is stronger than he thinks."

I hoped so. I really, truly hoped so. "Well, I guess that's it for tonight." I grabbed a spoon and the ice cream carton from the table. If I was going to celebrate the victory, then I had something special in mind. "I have a date in bed with some ice cream and shitty home improvement shows."

Dastien grinned at me, dimples winking. "Yes. We do have a date."

"See you guys in the morning," I said.

Dastien wrapped an arm around me as we walked for the door. *He's right. You've done an amazing job. This new thing? It's everything. You're changing our world and making it better.*

I looked up at him. *You're biased. You're my mate. You have to think I'm awesome.*

You don't have to believe me. Look at them. Dastien motioned behind us with his chin.

I glanced over my shoulder. Our friends were watching us go. Blaze raised his hand in a wave. I wasn't sure if what we'd done was right or meant to be, but it'd worked. And that was all that mattered.

We'd lived. Today I'd celebrate, and tomorrow? I'd deal with whatever new fire came my way. Because Dastien was right about one thing.

Just one thing?

I elbowed him. *Shut it. But you know what I mean, right? We did good tonight. This was good.*

He pulled me to a stop. *Good? No, chérie. We did amazing. Groundbreaking. Epic. This was epic. And it wouldn't have happened if it weren't for you.*

That made me a little uncomfortable. *Or because you bit me? So, it's kind of all your doing.*

He laughed, and the sound rumbled its way through my

soul. *If you say so,* he said as he leaned down to brush his lips against mine.

I threw the ice cream on the grass and grabbed his face. *I say so.* I dove into the kiss, jumping up and wrapping my legs around his waist. *Let's go home,* I thought to him so that I didn't have to break the kiss.

Best idea ever. Dastien took off running, and I couldn't help but laugh. I tucked my face in his neck, breathing in his scent. Wood. Pine. Home. Maybe I didn't need a vacation now. After the last three days of terror, I wanted comfort. My mate. My friends. My home. Nothing could be better.

I wasn't sure what happened to Chris, but I trusted Cosette to find out what was going on. I trusted him to reach out if he needed help. I trusted our friends.

Tonight was for me. And Dastien. Because in the end, tomorrow could wait. Love was all that really mattered.

The series continues with **_Lunar Court_**,
Book Eight in the Alpha Girls Series!

Chris is the guy Cosette always wanted. Fun. Funny. Light-hearted and sweet. He always manages to find beauty and laughter, even when fighting a chapel full of demons. He's exactly what she needs. Except he's a werewolf and she's a member of the Lunar Court—the only fey court that holds sway over the werewolves. Even on his best day, Chris isn't strong enough to last a few hours in the Lunar Court without becoming a slave. No matter how much Cosette's heart wants him, she knows she has to let him go.

But when Chris goes missing, Cosette realizes how much she has to lose if the worst happens.

Cosette is everything Chris wants, but he knows he'll never be enough to survive in her world. So, when Eli—a mysterious archon—requests his help, he figures why not? He needs every distraction he can get. But when he learns that Eli's quest could help him gain enough power to go against even the strongest of fey in the Lunar Court, he can't believe his luck. Except Eli never helps anyone without a price.

When it's all over, Chris will either earn the power to have the one he loves or die trying.

Now available from *USA Today* Bestselling Author, Aileen Erin
Off Planet, Book One of the Aunare Chronicles.

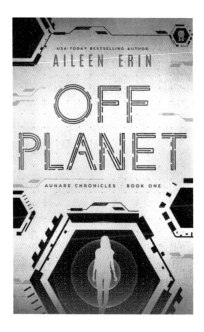

In an all-too-plausible future where corporate conglomerates have left the world's governments in shambles, anyone with means has left the polluted Earth for the promise of a better life on a SpaceTech owned colony among the stars.

Maité Martinez is the daughter of an Earther Latina and a powerful Aunare man, an alien race that SpaceTech sees as a threat to their dominion. When tensions turn violent, Maité finds herself trapped on Earth and forced into hiding.

For over ten years, Maité has stayed hidden, but

every minute Maité stays on Earth is one closer to getting caught.

She's lived on the streets. Gone hungry. And found a way to fight through it all. But one night, while waitressing in a greasy diner, a customer gets handsy with her. She reacts without thinking.

Covered in blood, Maité runs, but it's not long before SpaceTech finds her...

Arrested and forced into dangerous work detail on a volcano planet, Maité waits for SpaceTech to make their move against the Aunare. She knows that if she can't somehow find a way to stop them, there will be an interstellar war big enough to end all life in the universe.

TO MY READERS

Thank you so much for reading the Alpha Girl Series! This book was so fun to write. It defied plotting. Every time I sat down at my computer, the story took a different direction. I had a blast, and I hope you enjoyed reading.

I'm working on what's going to happen with Chris and Cosette now! When Eli's involved, you know it's going to be a crazy ride, but it'll be worth it in the end. ;)

Until next time, I'll be posting updates on my books on Instagram (@aileenerin), Facebook (@aelatcham), as well as my blog!

I absolutely love hearing from you. So, please reach out on social media or email me: aerin@inkmonster.net

xoxo

Aileen

ACKNOWLEDGMENTS

I have to say that the last few years have been totally nuts. A baby lost. A baby born. FIVE moves—out of state, out of country. Business partners coming and going. Oh boy! It's been a doozy. But this book marks me being all caught up! Huzzah! And I have a lot of people to thank for that.

Thank you to Lola Dodge for all the support and encouragement. Working with you is so fun! I can't wait to see what the next few years have in store for us! #winning

Thank you for your constant, unwavering support, Kristi! From always being the amazing grandmother to Isabella, coming in to help out while I write and take seminars, helping with moves, and copyediting my books. I'm truly thankful for the family that I married into. I count myself very blessed to have you as my mother-in-law.

To Kelly, Ana, Katie, Allison, and all the rest at INscribe, thank you for all your hard work! Your support of Ink Monster and our books is invaluable.

Thank you, Kime! You came in last minute to edit my book, and I'm so thankful for the help and support. Your comments made this book shine, and left me feeling so encouraged. Words cannot express how thankful I am that you.

To Jeremy. Thank you. I can't say it enough. Your support and positive attitude... It's everything. You're the glue that holds this family together. I wouldn't have even tried writing if it weren't for you, and I would've given up long ago if you did keep pushing me to do better and keep going. I love you so much. I'm so proud of you and everything you're doing. You're the most amazing partner, husband, and father.

Aileen Erin is half-Irish, half-Mexican, and 100% nerd—from Star Wars (prequels don't count) to Star Trek (TNG FTW), she geeks out on Tolkien's linguistics, and has a severe fascination with the supernatural. Aileen has a BS in Radio-TV-Film from the University of Texas at Austin, and an MFA in Writing Popular Fiction from Seton Hill University. She lives with her husband and daughter in Los Angeles, and spends her days doing her favorite things: reading books, creating worlds, and kicking ass.

For more information and updates about Aileen and her books, go to: http://inkmonster.net/aerin

Or check her out on:

facebook.com/aelatcham

twitter.com/aileen_erin

instagram.com/aileenerin